Helianthus
Eternal

KASSANDRA NORDBY

MILTON & HUGO L.L.C.
4407-11 Park Ave., Suite 5
Union City, NJ 07087, USA

Website: *www. miltonandhugo.com*
Hotline: *1- 888-778-0033*
Email: *info@miltonandhugo.com*

Ordering Information:
Quantity sales. Special discounts are granted to corporations, associations,
and other organizations. For more information on these discounts, please
reach out to the publisher using the contact information provided above.

Library of Congress Control Number: 2023923930
ISBN-13: 979-8-89285-000-1 [Paperback Edition]
979-8-89285-001-8 [Digital Edition]

Rev. date: 12/04/2023

Chapter

1

The Uber pulled up to what looked to be some old decrepit factory. It was an old brick building with large metal doors that had bars over the windows. The sign above the door read Moonlight Club, a rather strange name for this old building that had to have been built at least in the early prohibition era. It must have been used for metal working when it was first built judging by the crudely welded filigree design next to the name. Sarah stepped out of the car with her over enthusiastic personality barely able to contain herself. This was our last chance at finding a place to work. Or should I say my last chance. Sarah had been working as a CNA at one of the local nursing facilities but I had not yet managed to procure a job and with our onset eviction fast approaching what did I have to lose. One of her friends from work suggested that we come check out the club where she works with her brother and said that there was possibly a bartender position opening up. All I had to do was show up for an interview and the job was basically mine after she talked with her boss. I only hope this place pays better than what my first impression is getting from it.

She gave the driver his money and she walked over to me as the car drove away. She was so optimistic about me getting the job I don't even think she saw the sad state of disrepair the building was in. I hated interviews, especially ones my twin sister had to scrape up for me. I never know quite what to say or when to shut up. She smiled at me, "well, are you ready?" She said as she elbowed me in the side. Sarah can always see the good in everything. An elderly patient dying at work just means they are no longer suffering, we're about to be evicted from our crappy one bedroom apartment and about to be homeless means we might get to start a new journey someplace else. She never stops talking about the glass being half full and how when one door closes another door opens. It's disgusting really. I myself am more shy and choose to stay out of sight, out of mind. She's so caring and outgoing and I prefer to be by myself and watch from a distance.

I try to put some effort into a half smile then nod at her. We walk together towards the big metal double doors. I opened them up and we went inside. I was taken aback by how misleading this place was. The interior was nothing compared to the outside. It was enormous on the inside with a huge vaulted ceiling with exposed wood beams in the rafters with large modern looking metal chandeliers painted black hanging from them. Across from the doors was a large elevated wooden and gold stage with a grand piano sitting on it. To the left of the stage was the bar. It had to be at least thirty feet long made out of one solid piece of wood stained with golden honey varnish. There were a dozen tables or so between the bar and the right side of the building where there was another smaller stage with mirrors behind it next to the dance floor.

"See, I told you this place was gonna be worth it." Sarah squealed triumphantly. Ok, maybe she was right. This place was pretty breathtaking once you got past the rough exterior. We see a tall brunette with her hair half up talking to a broad shouldered man behind the bar. The brunette sees Sarah and begins waving frantically then runs around the side of the bar to get to us. It only took her a few seconds to bound across the empty area to get to us. "You found it!" she exclaimed. Sarah gave her a hug then looked at me. She reached out her hand to me. "My name's Lexa Vay, and that over there is my big brother Xander." I reach out my hand, "Adam Christinson." I say quietly. Her deep brown eyes just seemed to burrow deep in my skull as she looked back at me.

She let go of my hand and started talking about the architecture of the building with us. The girls linked arms and walked away leaving me next to the doorway not knowing if I should go with them or not. Lexa's brother stood at the bar wiping it off as the girls got closer. I could hear him introduce himself to Sarah. Oh great, now she's going to flirt with one of my new coworkers before I even get the job so that eventually when they do start going out and then break up my life will become unbearable to both live with her and work with him. I decided I need to go run interference to persuade my sister into not falling for the seemingly large meat head that's just going to end up breaking her heart.

Before I could make my way to the bar two more guys came out from behind the big red curtain between the stage and the edge of the bar. I started to panic. I wondered which one is going to be my new boss. The first guy to appear had jet black hair with blue eyes and wistfully placed his arm around Lexa's waist. No, couldn't be that one. Sarah would have mentioned that it was her friend's boyfriend that I'd have to be working for if that were true. What about the other guy? I was a little startled when he turned around to face me. He had a large slash like scar that ran from the top of his left eyebrow, down his eyelid and all the way to the corner of his top lip. I think he saw me wince when he looked at me but nonetheless he smiled and reached across the bar top to shake my hand. "My name is William Shepard, you and I have an appointment today right?" Shit! Well there goes this job, I hope Sarah likes sleeping in the alley because there's no way this guy is going to give me a job here after I made such a terrible face at him.

I slowly reach my hand towards his to be polite. "Yeah sorry, I'm Adam. I'm kind of shy." I nervously chuckle. "That's alright, I won't hold it against you." he says then winked out his scarred eye. I smile weakly as he points to a table in the back and motions for me to go take a seat at it. I walked over and took a seat where he pointed. As he walked over from the bar I tried to figure out what I was going to say to him. Anything but the scar. It's none of my business. You're just here to get a job so you won't be homeless. He brushed his reddish brown curls out of his face as he sat down across from me. My anxiety heightened, I hated interviews.

"So what experience do you have with bartending?" Should I lie just to get the job? I thought. No, better come clean in the beginning rather than get caught in a lie later. "None, but I used to work at a local coffee shop so I know how to deal with customers." He nodded his head at me. I watched him size me up from head to toe. "How are you in a fight? Could you de-escalate a situation?" Strange question but I guess it is a bar so fights do tend to break out once in a while. "Umm, pretty good

I guess, I suppose it would have to depend on the situation." Another truthful answer, so far so good.

He leaned in close, very serious this time. "And how are you with full frontal male nudity?" I started turning red, my eyes wide with fear. "I mean, I guess. If I absolutely have to in order to get the job I would." I blurted out. My heart was racing, what kind of a bar was this? What did Sarah get me into this time? He starts snorting which then turns into a full bodied laugh. I could see everyone else at the bar laughing too. Was this a joke? "No, no, no, I can't do this. Look at the poor guy, he's petrified. He thinks we're running some sort of gay burlesque club!" I sit there sheepishly not knowing what to do. He motions for me to stand up then puts his arm around my shoulder. "You got guts kid, I'll give you that. If someone asked me the same question I would have decked him then headed for the door, I don't care how much they pay an hour. You got the job. When can you start?" I stood there triumphant, smiling like a fool and replied, "Tonight work for you?" His laughter broke and he suddenly became serious again.

He seemed a little hesitant about giving me an answer right away as we walked back to the others at the bar. "No, I don't think she'd like that very much. She'll want to meet the pair of you before you two start. How does Friday sound?" I was confused. Two of us? I looked at Sarah as she was taking a sip of her drink. That crafty minx. She is going to work here too if not to keep an eye on me then to flirt with Lexa's brother Xander. I should have gone up with her to the bar right away in the first place so I could have stopped her. "What do you mean she? Who's SHE?" I questioned him. A hush fell over the bar. "Our boss, you know. The owner of the club. Isadora. I'm just the manager." William said. *Isadora, what an interesting name*, I thought. "She won't be in tonight?" I asked. They were all silent looking at one another for an answer. "She isn't feeling herself today, but she'll be in tomorrow though for sure." Lexa piped up. Everyone seemed to breathe easier. What was the deal with the head boss? Is she some scary haggard old lady that likes things done a certain way? "Here, have a drink. I'm Ben by the way." The tall guy with the jet black hair said as he slid me over a glass. I shook my head. "No thanks, I don't drink." They all looked at me seemingly stunned then they all started laughing at me again. "Well that's good, one of us has to be able to keep a close eye on things every night." We sat there a bit longer talking about the job and what to expect from the customers and about the entertainment when I suddenly remembered the piano sitting upon the stage. I wonder if I'd be able to play that? I haven't played since high school. Sarah must have caught me glancing at it. "Say, William. Can anyone go play the piano or only the acts that are booked for the night?" She beamed at me. "Sarah!" I snapped at her. She knew I longed to play again but I didn't want to do it in front of the others, at least not until I got a little more comfortable being around them.

"If you can play, be my guest, there's nobody here but us for the next forty-five minutes until the bar opens. And please call me Will, Izzy's the only one who ever calls me by my full name because she's known me the longest." He motioned for me towards the piano. I could feel everyone's eyes on me as my bar stool scraped against the concrete floor. My heart was beating so fast in my ears as I climbed the stairs to the top of the stage. The heat from the stage lights made me that much more anxious as they shone brightly down on the beautiful grand piano that lay before me.

I couldn't see anyone down in front of me. The shine was so bright off the sleek ebony finish. I could hear them talking amongst themselves, tidying up liquor bottles, straightening up chairs for this evening's events, trying to figure out which song I was going to play. I myself was wondering that very same question. Do I go with a more traditional piece, say *Clair De Lune* by *Debussy* or should I play more of a rock and roll song like *Don't Stop Believin* by *Journey*? There was a ringing in my ears that kept growing louder. My stomach was in knots as I sat down at the piano. Gently, I places my fingertips on the ivory keys. My right pinky fell down a little too heavy and the great beast let out a shrill plink that echoes throughout the area. The exposed beams and the brick made for such beautiful acoustics.

"Woohoo! You go Adam!" Sarah encouraged me from the floor, clapping trying to help me move past my fear. The pounding was getting louder and louder that I felt as though I would go deaf. I just closed my eyes and let my fingers move. It took me a few seconds to realize what I had started to play until I heard Sarah start singing softly. "It goes like this: the fourth, the fifth. The minor falls, the major lifts. The baffled king composing Hallelujah..." Yes, I was doing it. Somewhere deep down I had this song locked and ready in my times of fear. Our foster mother used to sing it to us when we were younger and then as I got older I learned to play it on the piano. My stomach churned thinking of the last time I'd heard this song played was at her funeral my senior year of high school when she died of breast cancer. I could hear Sarah sniffle and knew she must be thinking about it too.

We had been on our own for almost five years now struggling to survive out of the foster care system since we aged out and our caregiver had passed away. Sarah had been busting her ass to put herself through nursing school and what did I have to show for? I had been fired from every job I ever had whether it was waiting tables, washing dishes, or working a retail position. But she never gave up on me. We were twins after all and she always says from the womb to the tomb she'll be right there with me. As I came to the end of the song I saw the curtain to the left of me shift. From the corner of my eye I could see the silhouette of someone staring back at me. I let the last chords of the song ring out then lifted my head to see who it was. I gasped when our eyes met. Her eyes were the deepest shade of emerald. Her long blond hair shone so vibrant in the stage lights you would have thought it was silver. It was tied in a loose braid to one side that flowed from her shoulders all the way to her elbow where she stood with her arms crossed looking at me. She wore a sleek black satin top with dark blue denim jeans and no shoes on.

That's strange, I thought. Why be all dressed up and with no shoes on her feet? She looked annoyed with me. I wonder if she was supposed to be one of the acts tonight and I was cutting into her practice time? I stood up so fast I knocked the bench over. She remained staring at me as I quickly tried to fumble my way around to pick the bench back up. She stepped out of the shadow of the curtain and called out to the floor, "Is this one of the new bartenders?" Still looking me up and down never taking her eyes off me, she shut the lid over the keys of the piano with a loud clang.

"Izzy, we thought you weren't feeling good so we told them they can start tomorrow. Did you hear Adam play? He's almost as good as you are don't you think?" Will said as he raced up the stairs. Izzy?!? This was Isadora, my new boss? I was speechless. She was so breathtaking I couldn't say a word. I had to talk to her though. I stretched my hand out towards her. "Hi, I'm Adam Christinson." She flinched then took a step back. Did I startle her? "I'm not staying. I just came to check up on you William. And what do you mean by them? I was under the impression that only Lexa's friend would be starting today, not her boyfriend too." Had Sarah lied to me about the job or had Lexa lied to her boss about me working here? Either way I was not about to let this job go nor was about to be labeled my sister's boyfriend.

"No, Sarah's my sister. I'm not her boy." She cut me off. "Was I talking to you?" She growled at me. Her words were cold as ice like she just shot me with an arrow. I froze as she jerked her head to one side to motion to Will that she wanted to talk to him in private. He walked over to her and the two of them began whispering. What language are they using? I can't understand a word they're saying. Suddenly, the lights start dimming on the stage. Now I can make out what's happening on the floor. Xander was standing in the open doorway of the club. Naturally he would be the bouncer judging by his physique. Lexa was seating people and waitressing while Ben tended the bar while Will had a word with Izzy the owner. Now seemed as good as any for Sarah and I to get out of here. After all, we'll be back tomorrow. Maybe Isadora would be in a better mood by then.

I was starting to make my way slowly down the stairs when Will touched my shoulder. "Hey you heading out? You'll have to excuse her, she isn't always like that. She was really impressed with your playing though and thinks maybe we could use you up here instead of bartending if you wanted to, that is." My stomach dropped. Me, play every night? "I don't know about that. Let's just stick with the bartending for right now." I weakly laughed. "But she was impressed? How could you tell?" I turned back to get another glimpse at the silvery goddess. She was gone. I didn't even hear her walk away but to be fair I never heard her walk up on me either while I was playing. She was barefoot after all.

"Yeah she plays all sorts of instruments so she wouldn't have complimented you if she didn't mean it. She also said you and your sister will have a thirty day probation period for her to see if the two of you are a right fit for the job." Great, at the bare minimum I'll have thirty days to get to know her better and maybe even ask her out. I practically bounced down the stairs the rest of the way. "So is Isadora your girlfriend?" I tried to casually bring up to William as we walked back to the bar. He burst out laughing and I didnt know what I said was so funny. "No, no. She's nobody's girlfriend and she'd like to keep it that way." He had a really serious face now. "Trust me when I tell you this brother, she's bad news and she will eat up a nice guy like you in a heartbeat." He seemed very genuine and sincere in his plea to stay away from Isadora. And I would take his warning into consideration after I had made my own hypothesis.

Sarah gets off her stool once we walk to the bar. I can tell by the rosiness in her cheeks that she already had a little bit too much to drink so I decide it's time to take her home. "Adammm! What's going on? Auntie would have been so proud of you playing her song." Nope, not gonna let drunk Sarah start talking about our foster mom. That's not what she would have wanted us to do. I try to grab her arm to start leading her toward the exit. "Come on Sarah, you have class tomorrow. We'll be back tomorrow night for our first day of work." She pulls away from me then scowls angrily at me. "You're no fun, I wanna stay longerrr...We never get to do anything fun anymore." Yep, definitely time to go.

I smile at her hoping to not cause a scene now that more people have started trickling into the bar. She senses the frustration displayed on my face and sighs. "Fine!" She snaps at me then slings her purse over her shoulder. As she does this she knocks her glass off the bartop. I tried to catch it quickly but it was too late. It landed on the cement floor shattering into thousands of tiny shards. I held my breath hoping no one would notice then searched the room to see if anyone had. Luckily everyone was too busy ordering drinks or talking to their fellow bar patrons to realize what had happened.

Will came from the curtain behind the bar with a broom and dustpan trying to hurriedly sweep up the mess we had just made. "I'm so sorry. You can take that out of my first check if you need to." Sarah says with tears starting to well in her eyes. I bend down and start to help him pick up the larger pieces of glass. "It's alright. Wouldn't be the first time someone's broken a glass here." Will reassured her, sweeping up the last little bits. "I don't suppose either of you have a ride home do you? Here." He reached in his pocket and pulled out a set of keys with a fab on it. "Take my car, get her home safe, and just bring it back tomorrow. Be here around six tomorrow night." I held out my hand and looked down as he placed the keys in them on. Was he really just going to let us take his car home? He didn't know us.

"No, that's alright. We'll just Uber home." I tried to give the keys back to him but he had already turned his back to me and was heading behind the curtain with the cleaning supplies. "I guess we're taking his car home then." I said to Sarah. She nodded then waved to Lexa as we headed toward the doors. As we approached the exit Xander leaned in to say something to us. "It's the silver one parked in the back. Just use the key fab and you'll find it." *Silver car, got it.* I thought to myself. "Thanks." I say as we push past him.

I make my way through the crowd of people gathered outside. The sun had set now and the air was chilly. I zip my sweatshirt up to try to conserve some body heat. Sarah must have been freezing in her skirt and tank top. I decided to be a gentleman and ask her if she wanted to wear my sweater but as I turned to ask her about it she was nowhere to be found. "Damn it Sarah." I muttered under my breath. There she was still standing in the front of the club flirting with Xander who had produced a black suit jacket and draped it over her shoulders. Now I'll never get her to leave. He must have seen me standing there waiting for her. He leaned down, gave her a quick kiss on the cheek then sent her off my way. *How smooth*, I thought to myself. Her cheeks were flushed when she got to me and a smile never left her lips.

"Can we please go now?" I begged her. She nodded and locked arms with me. She needed me to steady her as we walked along the back of the building to try and find Williams' car. I started hitting the horn button on the fab hoping to be able to hear the car before we saw it. Suddenly, the horn went off and the headlights lit up. I gasped, "This is his car?" The car was a brand new silver Chevy Camaro. This guy had to be out of his mind letting two strangers take such a nice car home from the bar. I unlocked the doors then hesitated to get in. "You don't feel like you're going to throw up right?" I asked her hoping the answer was going to be no. She shook her head and slid in the front passenger seat.

We slowly backed out of the parking lot then headed down the street past the front of the club. Cars lined the street and people stood in a line outside the building. The neon sign that read Moonlight Club was now lit up in electric blue letters with white lights behind the filigree around the words. The place didn't look too bad with all the lights on now and all the people out front. I nodded at Xander as we drove past the entrance. Not knowing if he saw me or not through the dark tinted windows he seemed to give a little head tilt at me too.

We made it home a little past nine because I had to park the car a few blocks away from our apartment in hopes that maybe it would still be in one piece in the morning and not stolen from some local thugs. Sarah sobered up on the drive and was now complaining of a headache and that she still had loads of homework to do. She went to the bedroom and shut the door. Since we could only afford a single bedroom apartment we decided she could have it and I would sleep in the living room slash kitchen on the futon. I laid down on the bed and started thinking about the events that happened this evening. We both got jobs, I was able to play the piano again, Sarah probably got herself a new boyfriend, a new coworker lent us his car to drive home. Overall I was socially drained. How was I going to work in a place like that every night for the foreseeable future? Or at least the next thirty days.

"Isadora." I whispered her name out loud. Such a beautiful melodic name that danced off your tongue when you said it. She was so pretty but seemed so cold and distant. How did William dare talk to her ever? I hoped that I hadn't gotten anyone in trouble whilst I had been playing what I assumed to be her piano without her permission. It didn't matter. I would apologize for my behavior tomorrow if I could build up the courage to do so then maybe she'd be in a better mood too. After all, we were only human and were all bound to make mistakes.

I lay there with my eyes closed fantasizing about playing the piano again. Maybe I'd end up impressing her enough that she'd actually want to go out with me? Fat chance of that. I had had approximately three girlfriends in my short twenty-three years of life and they'd all lasted little over six months in total. There was Kelly in seventh grade who just wanted to get a good grade on our history final. Amber in tenth grade who just wanted to bet back at her boyfriend for flirting with another girl. And Beth my senior year because she didn't want to go to the prom alone. All of them ditching me as soon as they got what they wanted. At this rate I was going to die alone. Not to mention being intimate with anyone. I'd only ever kissed one of them and that was because she wanted to make her boyfriend jealous which ended up with me getting a black eye.

No, maybe I'd just heed Wills' warning about staying away from her but that didn't mean I couldn't think about her. Her silvery blond hair. Those deep emerald eyes. Her perfect pink lips. And her body, toned but still curvy in all the right places. I just wanted to wrap my arms around her and hold her. I wonder if I'll ever get the chance. Probably not. A girl like her would never go out with a loner like me. I pulled out my phone to check my notifications and saw I had a new text from an unknown number. Sarah must have filled out some sort of paperwork about the new job while we were at the bar. It read "This is Will. Xan said you found the car alright but make sure you're extra careful with it. Izzy will ring my neck if I wreck another one of her cars. Wear black dress pants and I'll give you the rest of the uniform tomorrow. See you then." Another one of Izzys cars? He gave us the keys to her car? I started freaking out. What if something happens to it while it's in my possession? I really needed this job. With Sarah going full time to nursing school she could only manage to work a few days a week at the care facility. And with our ever encroaching eviction looming over our heads I had to make this work.

Sleep wasn't going to come easy after the news about the car but I had to try. Tomorrow I was going to get up and drive the car back to the club early then just wait for my shift. That way if anything did manage to happen to the car it would still be in the Moonlight employee parking lot so I wouldn't be liable for any damages. Sarah came out of her room with a look of terror on her face. Did she receive the same text from William? She held up her phone. Yep. "Did you get a message too? You were driving extra careful on our way home right? Oh god what if something happens to it tonight while it's out on the street?" She was spiraling. I reassured her of my plan to take the car back early tomorrow and that she'd have to take an Uber or Lift to the club tomorrow after school.

It seemed to put her mind at ease. She exhaled then plopped on the futon next to my legs. "Do you think we'll ever be able to afford a bigger place?" She looked upset at my ever growing pile of dirty clothes on the floor and the stack of used dishes around the sink. I sat up and nudged her shoulder playfully with my hand. "Don't worry. I'm sure everything will work itself out. Tell you what, before I bring the car back tomorrow I'll tidy up the apartment while you're at school." She smirked at me knowing how that was going to go. She'd head to school while I'm still asleep, then I'll wake up a few hours later realizing I overslept, then rush to clean things up only to make things worse in her eyes just to have her clean it all up when we got home from the club tomorrow night. It was so predictable. Our foster mother always said the same thing, Sarah was the dependable and trustworthy one and I was the slacker with good intentions.

"Auntie Mary would be so disappointed in us. She would have made sure we had everything set up nicely. We'd both be living by ourselves instead of sharing this little shoebox apartment. I miss her." She said sadly now. I wish I could make her understand that I don't do these things on purpose, bad things just tend to happen around me. I shouldn't have played Auntie's song tonight, then maybe Sarah wouldn't be so sad. Auntie Mary was the last foster parent before we aged out of the system. She was the only one that ever gave a damn about us. All the others just seemed to see us as free labor or a paycheck.

She was a stern older woman and we tried our damnest to distance ourselves from her at first but she wouldn't let us push her away. She said she was an acquaintance of our parents long before we were born, then after our parents abandoned Sarah and I when we were four years old, she came looking for us. I had repressed most memories of our parents but Sarah was a firm believer that we'd see them again someday, more of her stupid optimistic personality shining through. Auntie always called me her little rain cloud. After all, you can't have sunshine without a little rain.

Sarah wiped away the tears from her eyes then sprung up off the futon. "No time for tears, I have a paper due tomorrow and you have a big day ahead of you tomorrow. Do you have anything to wear for your first day?" I still had a few pairs of dress pants when I worked as a bag boy at the local grocery store. I got up and crossed the room to my dresser that doubled as our tv stand. After pulling out most of its contents I found a pair of black dress pants and showed them to her. "Great, any idea on what kind of shirt you were planning on wearing?" I rolled my eyes at her and began sifting through the second drawer of my dresser. "How 'bout just a plain white t-shirt?" I questioned her. It was all wrinkled from being smushed along with the rest of my wardrobe but I figured it was better than nothing.

She furrowed her brow at my choice of clothing. "I guess that'll have to do. Didn't Will say that he was giving you the rest of the uniform tomorrow?" She was referring to the text we had both gotten earlier. "Yeah but how much of a uniform could it be? They were all wearing black pants with long sleeve white dress shirts with black suspenders. And Lexa was wearing the same thing except for wearing pants she was wearing a black skirt. I suppose that's what you'll be wearing too." The thought made me uncomfortable. Watching my sister prancing around a bar in a tight skirt handing out drinks to drunk assholes wasn't something I was looking forward to. "I wonder if I'll have to wear heels every night too. Fuck my feet are going to be killing me if that's the case." She must have had the same thought about the uniforms as she started rubbing her feet together and wiggling her toes.

"Whatever the foot situation, it'll all be worth it in the end. Lexa said we're going to make some great money working there. She said she makes close to a thousand dollars in tips a week not including what the normal hourly wage the owner pays her." Her eyes practically lit up with dollar signs when she was talking about all the money we were going to make working there. She was always so worried about our financial standings and how we were going to make it from paycheck to paycheck. It'll be nice to see some of the burden be lifted off her shoulders now that I'll be making some decent money too. I wanted so badly to do a good job and be able to help her out more with the bills.

"Hey, Sarah…" I folded my already wrinkled clothes and placed them on top of the dresser. "You know we still have to make it through the thirty day probation period right? Nothings set in stone about this job," she cut me off. "No! You're not going to do that this time. You don't get to be pessimistic about this new job without fairly giving it a try. You don't just get to decide that you're not going to put forth the effort so all the responsibility has to fall on to save your sorry butt. You're my brother and I love you but if you can't get your shit together in the next thirty days, I'm done! That's it, you're on your own. Out of a job, out of the apartment, out of my life!" She stormed to her room and slammed the door behind her.

We've had this same fight before many times over the years but this one felt different. She meant it. If I fuck this up one more time she's really going to let me fall on my ass. I needed to prove to her that I can do this, that I don't need her to hold my hand forever and clean up after my messes. I decided this was my chance to change the way people think of me. From now on starting tonight I wasn't going to be that dark rain cloud that sees everything as the glass half empty but try to see things in a different side of light. I was going to be more like Sarah and put my whole heart into everything laid out in front of me. I was going to be exceptional at my new job, make some friends, save up some money and then move out of this little shit hole. I have been alive for twenty-three years but I've never truly lived. I'm going to set aside my insecurities and do something that scares me. Starting tomorrow I am going to change my whole outlook on life and I'm not going to give up. I'm going to do my best to prove to my sister and the world that I can do anything I put my mind to.

Chapter

2

I woke up around two the next day. "Shit." I had done exactly what I thought I was going to do. Sarah was long gone, I had overslept and nothing had gotten done with the dirty apartment. I stretch then roll over on the futon. I dangle my one arm off the side of the bed reaching for my phone on the floor. I felt a piece of paper graze my finger as I grabbed my phone. Had Sarah left me a note before she left? I picked up my phone and the note. It read, "See you later. Don't worry about the mess, love you, Sarah." my heart sank. I truly didn't deserve to have such a caring generous sister like her. Anyone else would have dumped me ages ago but not her. For some reason or another, she thought I was worth saving.

Even when we were younger and were doing gymnastics she'd always be there cheering me on telling me to do my best. I loved her so much but never really knew how to let her know. I got up, made myself some eggs, then took a shower. I put my white t-shirt on a hanger and let the steam hopefully take out some of the wrinkles. It seemed to do the trick. As I got dressed, I remembered the Camaro that I needed to return today was parked on the street a few blocks from our building. I finished getting ready then headed out the door.

I made my way down the stairs trying not to make any sounds as I walked past the building managers' door. We had been avoiding him for the past few days since he taped our final warning letter to the door about the possibility of eviction. The floor creaked as I slowly made my way past. I could hear the TV blaring some sort of sports program through the door. Good, there was no way of him hearing my footsteps now. I raced down the rest of the stairs when I heard the crowd cheering. When I reached the bottom, I turned sharply to the left grabbing the railing as I rounded the corner. There, standing in the doorway was Mr. Petrov. A balding plump Russian man in a stained tank top with a gold chain around his neck. His eyes narrowed as I approached him. "You have the moneys?" He said in a thick accent. Obviously, he was not in his apartment like I originally thought. He must have heard me upstairs and decided this was his opportunity to ask about the late rent we owed.

My palms start sweating. I don't like engaging in confrontational situations. Sarah normally handles all of financial disputes with him. "No Mr. Petrov. No money yet, but I'm starting a new job this evening so we'll get the rent to you as soon as we can." He let out a sharp grunt in disbelief as tried to squeeze around him. He turned to the side to let me pass. I barely made it onto the sidewalk when he shouted after me, "No money by next Friday and you's are out!" I nodded at him sheepishly then continued on my walk down the street. I wish he hadn't yelled that at me, now everyone in the building knows we're behind on rent. Could he do that? I assume so, it was his building after all.

"Next Friday." I said quietly to myself. We had until next Friday to get him the money we owed. I wonder if Isadora was willing to front us our paychecks early if we needed her to? I'd worry about that later. We had a whole week until our final deadline, plus with the tips we were supposedly going to be making, maybe I wouldn't even have to ask. I placed my hands in my pockets and began walking faster towards the direction the car was in. First things first, I gotta return her car in mint condition before I can start asking favors.

I turned the corner at Eighth and Elm to see the beautiful Camaro just sitting where I left it. Some leaves had fallen onto the hood of the car so I walked around dusting them off. They probably would have fallen off once I started driving but I wasn't taking any chances. "No dings or scratches," I said out loud as I eyed the silver paint job making sure no harm had befallen the car throughout the night. Nope, I thought, we're golden. I took the fab out of my pocket and unlocked the doors. *Beep, bleep,* the car chipped. I opened the door and slid in. Locking the doors behind me, I started the engine.

The car rumbled to a start, purring as I slowly shifted the car into drive. My phone started vibrating and startled me. I put the car back in park. "Hello?" I answered not looking to see who was calling me. "Hey, Adam, you wouldn't wanna bring the car back a little earlier than originally planned would you? Izzy wasn't too happy with me for just letting you take it without her knowing." It was William wondering about the car. How did he know I was actually just on my way to do just as he wanted? "Umm, sure. I was actually just leaving right now to bring it back." I heard him snort then chuckle. "Yeah I know, I have an app that lets you know when your car starts anywhere on the globe." That's awesome, I thought. That makes sense though. If I had a car like this I'd wanna know where it was at all times too. "Cool!" I say out loud to him. "It'll take me around a half hour to get across town to get to the club. I hope that's alright." I didn't want to upset my new boss even further than I already had. "Yeah that'll be fine. It's just me and Izzy here right now for the next couple of hours before we open."

Yes, I rejoiced in my head. Just the three of us there until later. That would give me plenty of time to try and get to know her better and to get on her good side. "Eat me alive," I thought. Pfft. . . How does he know, maybe i'm just the type of guy she's been looking for. I mean, clearly we both have the same interests. I play the piano, she plays piano. Chicks melt for a guy that can dish out a sweet love ballad. Maybe I'd ask her if she wanted to play a duet with me, I just had to hope she wanted to play something I could remember.

"Nice. Yeah, I'll see you after a bit. Bye." Then I ended the call. My heart was fluttering with anticipation. I couldn't wait to get there. Every red light from here to the club was torture. I swear every stoplight had it out for me today. When I got to the back entrance I could see Will carrying out two black garbage bags to the dumpsters. He stopped what he was doing and waited for me to park the car. I turned the engine off, grabbed my phone and exited the car. "So long, old girl," I whispered under my breath as I shut the door behind me. It would probably be another twenty years before I ever sat in such a luxurious car again.

I crossed the alleyway to the back door where William had already thrown the trash away and was holding the door open for me. There was a dark hallway that led to two doors. One said stage with a picture of a set of stairs on it. The other one had a plaque that said dressing room to the right of it. Farther down the hall I could see light peeking out of the red velvet curtain that covered the archway. We entered next to the bar within close proximity to the stage. Even though it had only been last night since I first laid eyes on the place, I couldn't stop myself from smiling when I looked around the exquisite space.

Where was she? I thought about letting my eyes scope out the area for Isadora only to be caught off guard by William standing there holding out a shirt and a pair of suspenders for me. "What's your shoe size?" He said handing me the clothes. I looked down at my murky gray sneakers trying to remember the last time I had gotten a new pair of shoes. "I don't know, twelves I suppose?" He left through the curtain then quickly returned with a new matte black pair of dress shoes. "Try these on." he said and pointed to the far side of the bar where I had assumed the bathrooms were.

I gathered my new belongings and headed in the direction he pointed. I should have brought a small gym bag or something for my normal clothes to go into. I would remember that for tomorrow and just wear whatever was comfortable to work then change into my dress clothes once I got here. The shirt was so light and soft. It didn't even feel like I was wearing a shirt once I got it on and the shoes, they were the most comfortable pair of shoes I had ever worn in my life. I readjusted the straps on the suspenders three or four times before I got it to my liking, then carefully rolled up my sleeves to my elbows.

Stepping back to look at the full ensemble in the large mirror, I started to feel hopeful about the situation. Maybe I could pull this off. If I looked the part and acted the part, who's gonna know the difference? I ruffled my slightly wet hair trying to make myself look more presentable. I was going to need to get a haircut soon. My ashy blond hair was starting to get a little long on the top and the back needed to be faded in again. "I must say, you clean up pretty damn good." I said to myself while winking and doing finger guns in the mirror.

I folded my t-shirt on top of my sneakers then exited the restroom. I stopped just outside the door. I could hear the faint plinking of the piano in the distance. I hurried back to the bar so I could get a better view of the stage. To my surprise, no one was playing the piano. The music was coming out of the speakers of the sound system. There she was, the most beautiful woman I had ever seen. She wore a ballet costume, a strapless pink dress with a flowy tulle skirt. She twirled and jumped with such grace and poise across the stage. I was frozen again but this time at her amazing movements instead of her sharp words.

"Incredible," I whispered quietly to myself. Her hair was tied up in a tight bun on top of her head with two little wispy pieces on both sides of her face that seemed to flutter about as daintily as she did. My heart started pounding fast. I could feel the passion she was pouring out on stage as the instrumental track picked up. My stomach was in knots. I was holding my breath as I knew the song's end was drawing near. She spun faster and faster with the crescendo of the music. Then suddenly, she stopped.

The bar was silent. The only thing audible was her labored breathing upon the stage. She stood normal again for a second then sat down on the stage to stretch. I needed to go tell her I thought her performance was wonderful. She had to know I had been watching her because the second I reached to lay my old shoes and shirt down on a bar stool she spoke. "Will honey, we need to boost the treble on the left side of the stage and take the base down in the middle. Otherwise no one is going to be able to hear the band play on the floor while the singers perform." She untied her ballet slippers and continued to stretch on the stage.

William came out from behind the curtain on the stage holding a tablet. "Up the treble, turn down the bass, got it." He handed her a bottle of water. How I longed to be that bottle as she pressed her lips to it. She drank half the bottle then placed it next to her shoes. She reached up her hands and William helped her stand up. My foot slipped and I tapped the stool with my toes. They both looked at me. My face began turning red with embarrassment for disturbing their interaction. Her eyes met mine, those iridescent emeralds shimmering in the stage lights.

"Sorry." I piped up as I grabbed my belongings. William led the way down the stairs with Isadora trailing behind. As she was walking she reached up to let down her hair. It was all wavy now from being in a tight swirl on top of her head. It flowed out over one of her shoulders and down to her elbow. When they got to me William stepped aside to let Isadora take the lead. He smiled at me once she was in front of him.

What was that for? I thought. She stopped a few feet away then reached out her one hand to shake mine.

"Isadora Dragoss, pleased to meet you Adam. You may call me Izzy, Isa, or Isadora." My mind went blank when she said my name. Her accent seemed almost Italian. I hesitated for a moment then realized she was waiting for me. My hand quickly reached out to hers. "Oh sorry, yes I'm Adam." Her hand was soft, it almost mimicked the feeling of satin. But it was also cold. How could she be freezing after such a moving performance? I kept shaking her hand for a few more seconds until I noticed William stifling a laugh. I had let the hand shake go on too long now we were just holding hands. I pulled away quickly. She flashes a smile revealing her impeccably white teeth. She was dazzling to behold. I start to blush again then try to work up the courage to smile back at her.

"That was amazing what you just did up there." The words just kept falling out of my mouth. "My sister and I did a little ballet too, well, mostly her, when we were younger. I was more into gymnastics, I can still do my highschool routine from senior year if you wanted to see it sometime. Of course it will be nothing compared to what you just did. How long have you been doing ballet? Do you teach a class anywhere?" My God! What's wrong with me? Before I could keep spouting my psycho babble she placed her fingers over my mouth.

"Thank you," she said, "I have been dancing my entire life. As long as I can remember I've been doing ballet." Everything about her was so cool, calm, and collected. Even the way she shut me up was elegant. I nodded my head trying to slow down my breathing so I could calm down. She took her hand away from my lips. Well if she didn't want to date me before, I highly doubt she'd wanna date me now. She turned to face William who was starting to tear up from trying so hard not to laugh. I'm sure I looked like a complete fool to her. *What an idiot!* I thought.

She started walking back toward the curtain behind the bar then stopped to look at me again. I bashfully smiled at her when she looked at me. She smiled, her eyes twinkling, then disappeared. William walked up to me and slapped me on my back as he started cackling. "Could you be crushing on her any harder? You were practically drooling over her." His eyes were crinkled in the edges while he was laughing. The scar looked less menacing like this. "No seriously though," he put his arm around my shoulder, "just keep your distance from her. You leave her alone and she'll leave you alone."

He was really dead set on making sure I stayed away from her. Maybe he secretly liked her and didn't want to let anyone else get close to her. I did hear her call him "honey" after she was done dancing. "Why did she call you Honey just now? I thought you said there was nothing going on between you two?" He looked appalled by my question. He put his hands up defensively. "Whoa now, what Izzy and I have is strictly platonic, nothing romantic. If you want to go out with her you sure can. I just wanted to let you know ahead of time. Don't say I didn't warn you." He steps behind the bar, grabs a rag and tosses it at me. He grabs one for himself then starts walking around the club wiping down tables and chairs.

I leave my belongings on the chair and start helping him. He looked genuinely hurt by my accusations. I figured if I was going to be true to the promise I made myself last night I better keep my word and try to smooth things over with Will. "Look man, I'm sorry. I'm just not good at reading social cues and when I saw the way you two acted it kind of made me wonder, ok?" I hoped that would be enough. He stopped wiping and looked back at me. The crinkle had returned to his eyes, "She isn't normally this friendly with new people. It'll take some time for her to get used to you and be comfortable enough around you. I just don't wanna see anyone get hurt." I understood what he meant. I'd act the same way if someone was ogling Sarah. "Don't worry, I'm not going to hurt Isadora." I said, rolling my eyes. He looked down, continuing to clean, then muttered under his breath, "She's not the one I'm worried about."

Over the next few hours William trained me how to be a bartender and showed me the ropes on how things are done here. "And you don't drink at all?" He asked with disbelief. "No, I drank too much in high school and it sort of took over my life for a while so I've been sober now for a few years. I'll have an occasional drink at home with Sarah on special occasions but other than that, it doesn't interest me."

The truth of the matter was, once Auntie Mary said she was sick that's when a lot of stuff started going downhill for me. I started failing all my classes, skipping school, partying way too much. When I got my minor and lost my full ride gymnastics scholarship towards the end of my senior year, Auntie didn't even scold me. She didn't have the strength to. I could have been somebody but because of my actions I threw away my entire future. I barely even graduated high school. The weeks leading up to Auntie's death were the worst. I'd be out all night doing god knows what while Sarah stayed home to look after her. I can't even remember the funeral. All I remember is the church choir singing Hallelujah. She told us she wanted me to play it at her funeral but because of the alcohol I wouldn't have done her justice so I passed the burden on to someone else.

"That's fine, we're really not supposed to be drinking on the job anyway. Izzy isn't a big social drinker either." He snorted at that last remark. I didn't get the joke. I decided I wanted to know more about him so that maybe he can give me a few tips and tricks about asking Isadora out. I'll start someplace easy, "So where is Isa from? Did I detect an accent on her, it sounded Italian to me." He thought long and hard before answering me. "Yeah, I suppose she has an accent. Not entirely sure where she's from, somewhere European I guess." He kept straightening out the liquor bottles on the back shelf.

"Have you known her long? You must have known her for a while if your relationship is platonic, right?" He shrugged his shoulders at the question. Come on man, you gotta give me something. I wanted to get some sort of information out of him, anything, but he just wasn't going to cooperate with me. Just one more question, then I'll leave him alone. "How did all of you meet?" He took a deep sigh and turned to face me. I could tell I was really starting to get on his nerves.

"So you met everyone yesterday right?" I nodded. "Xander and Lexa are brother and sister and Ben is Lexa's boyfriend right?" He kept pausing to make sure I was absorbing all the information so he wouldn't have to repeat himself. "I met Izzy when I was really young then eventually we met the Vay siblings, then we happened to meet Ben some years later and now we all work together here under Izzy. Does that sum it up?" I felt a little foolish hearing him tell me everything. I'm not normally this inquisitive but it was just so easy to talk to him. "I'm sorry, I didn't mean to get you all riled up. Sometimes my mouth has a way of getting away from me."

He filled himself up a glass of water from the little sink that was under the bar. When he finished his drink he looked at me with the most serious expression on his face. "You of course are forgetting the most important question of all." I looked at him puzzled. "What question was that?" I wondered out loud. He leaned in really close to my face so that his scarred eye was the closest to me. "What happened to my eye?" I flinched at the question. I was curious but I wasn't going to be rude about it. He stood up straight with a smirk on his face satisfied with how uncomfortable he had just made me feel. I fiddled with a cocktail sword I found on the counter and nodded. "When I was around four years old I was outside playing when a wild dog attacked me. I nearly lost my eye because of it." I don't know what I was expecting to hear but that was not it. "It lunged at my face and started biting at me until my father heard me screaming. He came outside with his gun and shot that animal." My eyes were wide with fascination. "Did he kill it?" I asked. "No," he said, "He just scared it away when he fired the gun." I felt a chill ripple through my body.

Suddenly the bar curtain flung open to reveal Ben and Xander. The quick movement of the curtain made me jump. The three of them laughed at me. Why was I so jumpy all of a sudden? "Is he telling you about his scar?" Xander asked, "Too bad he doesn't have an excuse for the rest of his face." His laugh seemed to be as broad as he was; it filled the whole club. William jabbed Xander in the ribs when he tried to put him in a headlock. Ben stood next to me rolling his eyes and their antics. "That's enough you two, what if Izzy sees you?" He started crossing his arms. He was smaller than Xander but larger than William which made him closer to my size.

Both men stop and look at us. "She's in the back right now. If she really didn't want us to roughhouse, she'd keep this gorilla in his cage at the front door." William was referring to Xanders enormous stature compared to his own. Xander messed up Wills' hair as he walked away towards the bathrooms. "Geez, you can dish it out but you can't take it back?" William called after him. Without even turning around

Xander flipped him off and kept on walking. William chuckled then straightened out his hair then his outfit. "You'd better move your stuff before we open." He was referring to my t-shirt and shoes. Oh yeah, I had almost forgotten about them.

"Come on," Ben said, "everyone gets their own locker by the back door." He led the way back down the dark hallway. Next to the back door were half a dozen lockers with everybody's names on them. How had I missed them when I first came in? My eyes must have still been adjusting from the transition of daylight to darkness. I put my belongings in one of the lockers without a name tag on it. I wondered when Sarah would get here. It was nearly six o'clock. She should be here by now. Just as I was about to send her a text the back door swung open. In walked Sarah and Lexa giggling to themselves.

"There he is," Lexa said as she bounced through the door. She was obviously talking about Ben. She wrapped her arms around his neck and gave him a big kiss. Yep, definitely not me, I thought. Sarah looked surprised that I was standing at the back door. She was carrying a duffle bag over one shoulder, probably holding her books from school and a change of clothes for after work. "What are you doing?" She said to me. Wasn't it obvious? "I'm just putting my street clothes in a locker so they aren't sitting out at the bar." I shut my locker door and pointed to the other empty one for her. She nodded then proceeded to place her things in the empty locker. "So you made it here with the car alight I see?" Oh yeah, I still have Wills' keys in my pocket. I reached in my pocket and pulled them out. "Yeah, I still gotta return them. Or do you think I should just give them back to Isadora since it's her car after all?" Lexa plucked the keys out of my open hand. "I'll take them to her." She took her other arm off of Ben's neck. And started walking down the hall. "Come on Sarah, Izzy will have your uniform in the dressing room. It's this way." The girls walked away. Damn, I was wanting to have a talk with her myself. I looked back towards Ben. He had already started walking back to the curtain. I quickly followed behind him back to the bar.

"Lexa's back." He said to Xander and William. Xander was already waiting by the front doors when I returned. He smirked as he walked over to me. "Your sister here too then?" He asked. Great, now I gotta worry about him hitting on Sarah while I'm supposed to be working. "Yeah. She and Lexa went to get changed." I tried to make myself look busy by restocking the napkins in the dispenser at the bar. "She seeing anyone?" He asked inquisitively. I kept stuffing the napkins in attempting to brush him off. He put his hand on the dispenser so I'd have to focus on him. His eyes met mine. He had a playful smile on his face now. "She isn't, is she?" Triumphant in his assumption he let go. I shook my head at him. I didn't want Sarah to become distracted by this behemoth. She was so close to finishing her last year of nursing school to become a full registered nurse. If he got in the way of that, she'd never forgive herself. "She's really busy going to school. She doesn't have time to be distracted by going out with people." He understood the sincerity in my tone. "Hey I got a sister too and I'd do everything in my power to protect her but sometimes, you gotta just let them go. Know what I mean?" He was right. We were twenty-three. I didn't need to sabotage something before it had even started. If she wanted to go out with someone, she could. "Ok," I agreed and stuck out my hand. We shook hands then he continued past me toward the back curtain

Before he could open the curtain he bumped into something. "Oof, watch it." Sarah said as she struggled to free herself from the billowing red velvet. The frustrated look on her face changed rather quickly when she realized who was on the other side of the curtain. "Oh, sorry. I didn't see you there." She fixed her hair on her face. Her eyes fluttered up at Xander. His cheeks started to flush. "No, no. It's my bad. We usually say something out loud before we go into the back so this sort of stuff doesn't happen. You're new here so you wouldn't have known that. I should have been more careful." He backed away from her, placing his hands on his suspenders. They really accentuated his broad chest. I can see why Sarah was so into him. She twirled a piece of hair between her fingers with one hand as she playfully used the other one to lightly hit him on the chest. "You're too nice." She said leaning into him. Alright, that's enough, I thought. I pushed my way between the two of them and headed for the restroom. It's one thing to let her have a boyfriend, it was another if I had to stand by and watch her flirt.

I washed my hands then fixed my hair again. "Lookin' good." I heard a voice beside me. William must have had the same thought to go to the bathroom one last time before we opened. "Thanks" I raised my eyebrows at him jokingly. He had a red bow tie on now. I wonder if I needed one too. He reached in his pocket and pulled another one out. "Do you know how to tie it?" He asked. "Nope, not a clue." I answered honestly. He turned me towards the mirror so he was standing behind me. In one fluid motion he had the tie around my neck like a noose then gracefully presented me with the finished product.

"Damn, you gotta teach me how you do that!" I say, impressed. He turns me around to face him and finishes straightening out the bow. "You'll get the hang on it soon enough." He reassured me. We left the bathroom and headed to our positions. Sarah and Lexa would be waiting tables while Ben and Xander manned the door and Will and I tend the bar. The girls had changed into their uniforms which contained most of the same elements of the men's uniform. White long sleeve shirts with black suspenders but instead of dress pants they wore black pleated skirts with black high heel shoes. *Ha, ha.* I thought, I get to wear nice comfortable dress shoes and Sarah has to wear heels like she was afraid of. I chuckled at the thought.

I walked over to Sarah who was standing at the bar trying to tie an apron around her waist. I was just about to help her when, "let me get that for you gorgeous," Xander rushed over to her. I rolled my eyes. I couldn't tell if he was being a gentleman or just showing off to get her attention. "Thank you," she giggled then pranced away to go gush over the interaction with Lexa. I don't mind Xander as a person. I just wish I knew a little bit more about him before I let him date my sister. And it's not like she's my property or anything like that but she's the only family I have left in this world so I just wanna make sure she's safe. If he were to hurt her in any way, I don't know what I would do. Obviously, he could kick my ass if he wanted to but I'd give it all I've got. He turns around to head back to his post at the door. He stops in front of me and smiles. He knew exactly what he was doing, that slimy bastard. He continued on his way over to the doors.

"It's time," I hear Isadora call out from behind the curtain backstage. She stepped out on the stage wearing lace up gladiator heels and a tight black knee length dress with one shoulder strap and a slit up the one leg. She looked incredible. Her hair had been curled then brushed out to make it look even more glamorous. I couldn't breathe. I couldn't think. I just kept staring at her as she did the mic checks on stage when William nudged my side. "Dude, be chill." He said motioning with his eyes to the stage. I snapped back to reality. Gee, I hope she hadn't caught me gawking at her. I hurried behind the counter where Will had set up one of the bar sinks for me. I got myself a bottle of water from one of the mini fridges and placed it next to me on the bar top. As she made her descend down the stage stairs I noticed her looking at me. *Don't come over here, don't come over here...* I thought to myself. I already made a complete fool out of myself in front of her once today, I didn't need that happening again. She walked up to Will with a tablet and started talking about the band. They would be here in half an hour. I tried to make myself look busy but was still trying to eavesdrop on their conversation.

"No, I know you want me too...can't the band just play without a lead singer...fine but they better know my set list then." She was saying something about the band's lead singer being late tonight so they needed someone to open for the house band. Apparently, Isadora was going to sing in place of the lead singer until they arrived. She ruffled her hair to one side then set off towards the band's stage. "What was that about?" I asked, knowing full well what was going on. "You're in for a treat tonight. Izzy's gonna sing. Part of the band is running late and won't get here for another hour." His eyes lit up as he was telling me this like he knew something I didn't. The smart watch on his wrist started buzzing. "It's showtime!" He said enthusiastically. He flicked the light switch behind the liquor bottles to signify to Xander and Ben it was time to open the doors.

Chapter

3

Xander nodded at William and unlocked the big metal double doors. Ben went outside and was checking peoples IDs already so that when the time came people could enter the club more smoothly. A swarm of people came flooding in through the doors. My anxiety was in full panic mode. What if I forgot how to do something? What if someone ordered something I didn't know how to make? All these thoughts were racing through my head a million miles a minute that I hadn't noticed Sarah across the bar from me. "Hey, you good?" She looked very concerned. My face must be white as a ghost. I smiled weakly and nodded. She hesitated for a moment then smirked back at me. I guess she figured there wasn't much she could do to help me anyways and left me there. Ok, keep it together. Remember what Will said, service with a smile. Be friendly but not overly friendly, you don't wanna come off as creepy. I was so deep in thought I guess I didn't see Isadora make her way back to the bar.

"Adam?...Hey Adam?...Adam!" She slightly raised her voice at me. "Huh? What?" I said frazzled. She leaned over the counter and motioned with her finger to come closer. I started to sweat. My heart was racing as I took a step closer to her. "What is it?" I whispered to her. She flashed that thousand watt smile at me, I thought I was going to melt into a puddle right there. "Don't be nervous," she said, "Ben will come back to help you if Will sees you getting too overwhelmed." That's a relief, I thought. She stood back up then half turned around to survey the crowd of patrons who were making their way through the club. She was so close to me now. I could reach out and pet her hair. No you creep! I was not going to let my intrusive thoughts win. She fixed a section of hair that had fallen over her face then fluffed it again. This caused a slight breeze in my direction. Mmmm…she smells like vanilla. I breathed in deep, taking in her fragrance then sighed. She turned back to look at me. Shit, I'd been caught. Maybe she didn't notice? She winked at me then walked over to the doors where Ben and Xander were standing.

That was it. There was no turning back now. I was determined to ask her out if it killed me. That one little wink boosted my confidence so high I thought I could do anything. I stayed busy handing out beverages to customers that sat on the bar and making drink orders whenever Sarah or Lexa came to ask for one. This wasn't so bad. What was I worried about? I can totally do this. After about fifteen minutes Will turned to me and said "I gotta go introduce Izzy quick. You think you'll be alright?" His eyes were wide making sure I understood that I was going to be all alone behind the bar until he returned. "Yeah I'll be fine, I really think I'm getting the hang of this now." I boasted while handing Lexa two bloody Mary's and four shots of tequila. I made the "OK" motion with my fingers at him. "Piece of cake." He looked satisfied with my answer and made his way towards the stage. I scoped out the bar to see if I could find Isadora in the sea of people. Nope. She must already be backstage waiting to perform. I couldn't wait to listen to her sing. Her normal speaking voice was so smooth and sultry I could only imagine what she was going to sound like belting out a melody.

William made his way to the stage weaving through the tables and crowds of people in front of him. He climbed the stairs and walked over to the mic. "Hey, hey, hey! How's everybody doing tonight?" He paused, waiting for whooping and cheering to subside. "Have we got a special treat for you tonight folks. Back by popular demand, the Moonlight Club is proud to present its very own, Isadora Dragoss!!!" He motioned to the back of the stage as Isadora entered. My mouth dropped when I saw what she was wearing. She had done a full wardrobe change. No longer was she wearing that black dress that accentuated the curvature of her body but was wearing even less clothes than before.

Her hair was in a high wavy ponytail with the little wispy side pieces curled to frame her face. The shirt she was wearing, if you could even qualify it as a shirt, was metallic silver that had thin strings that tied around her neck and crossed in the back to the bottom of the shirt that was barely below her navel. She wore big silver hoop earrings as well. The skirt she was wearing was a bright cherry red leather pencil skirt that left very little to the imagination. The only thing she hadn't changed was her lace up gladiator heels. *She looks like she should be working a pole, not about to be singing for an audience!* I thought very loudly to myself.

I stood there flabbergasted about how the events of the night were about to unfold. The crowd cheered when she took the mic from Will. You could tell which sleaze balls in the audience were thinking the same thing I was by the constant catcalling coming from one table in particular. They made my blood boil. If there's one thing growing up with a twin sister has taught me, it was to respect women and treat them equally. I turned away from them hoping to distract myself with drink orders while I waited for William to return. "Thank you everyone," the crowd calmed down as she spoke. "We're gonna start with a little theater number from 1996. Maybe some of you know it," she paused as a few people hollered with excitement, "This one's called 'Out Tonight' from the rock musical Rent."

I whip my head around to the stage as the drummer starts the song, "Was she really going to sing that song?" I thought I remembered our drama director having auditions for this musical my senior year and then changing what they were going to perform because of the level of difficulty of this musical number. She started dancing around the stage in time with the music. William rejoined me now behind the bar. "Is she for real?" I whispered to him. He grinned, "Oh you have no idea." He seemed excited about the whole thing. The crowd was going wild for her. She sang that song like she was part of the original cast.

She was all over the stage, whirling and gyrating with every lyric. I couldn't look away. The air was electric. I thought I saw her look at me during one of the lines when she said "Take me out, tonight." Was she talking to me? She stared me down. She rushed down the stairs then climbed up on the bar top still singing. The bar was swarming with people trying to touch her feet. She was insane! They were going to tear her apart if she didn't get back up on the stage. She did one walk down and back on the bar before reaching her hand down to Will who had been walking alongside her from the floor. He helped her down but not before someone was able to grab her right ass cheek.

I was enraged! How dare he touch her! I started walking toward the pervert when she put her hand up to stop me. She gave me a stern look then flashed her eyes toward the doors. Xander was already on his way through the crowd to drag this asshole out of the club. She continued singing on her way back to the stage for her big finale. The cymbals crashed, signifying the song's end. She stood posed on the stage while the audience cheered. I watched as Xander drug the guy who felt her up.

Good riddance, I thought. For the next hour I tried to keep myself busy by taking orders and making drinks. Every once in a while I would catch myself staring at her then messing up what I was doing. It's like she put me in a trance or something. Nothing else seemed to matter while she was up there. She didn't come back down off the stage after that, which was disappointing. Sarah came to check on me from time to time, probably hoping I wasn't too overwhelmed by everything. I wasn't anymore. After a while, it seemed like I'd been doing this for years.

"Can I get a bottle of water, please?" She asked me. I reached into the mini fridge and pulled out a bottle for her. "Thanks," she takes a sip then continues to talk to me, I'm melting right now!" I could see the beads of sweat on her face. I suppose it's a lot more work waiting tables than just making the drinks. "Do you need some help out there? I could talk to Will and see if Ben could come back here and I'll help out you and Lexa." Her eyes widened with gratitude. "Yes! That would be amazing," she said. I leave her drinking her water and walk up to William. "Hey the girls need help on the floor, can I see if Ben wants to come back here and I'll go help them?"

He shook his head as he poured out a glass of whiskey. "No can do. The second Izzy's done up there she'll be out with the girls helping them. It shouldn't be long now, I just saw the lead singer for the band walk up to the lead guitar player." I was disappointed. I really wanted to help Sarah. He must have sensed my solemn expression. "Talk to Izzy when she's done. She probably wouldn't mind working the bar for you so you could help out your sister." That perked me up. I started beaming. He chuckled at my smile. I didn't care, I'd do anything to talk to her.

I pranced back over to Sarah who had finished her water. "Any luck?" She said eagerly. "You're gonna have to hold out a little longer. He told me I have to talk to Isa before I help you." Her shoulders slumped. "I suppose. She is the boss after all." She handed me her empty bottle then got back to work. I get to talk to Isa, I gloated in my head. I didn't want to call her Izzy. Izzy seemed too harsh of a name for such a stunning beauty like herself but her full name, Isadora, was too formal to say all the time as well. Isa was sweet and melodic just like she was.

Isa finished her set then gave a bow to the audience. She could have sang for hours and I wouldn't have complained. "Thank you everyone. You're too kind." She flashed a smile at the crowd. My heart started racing. I loved it when she did that. She handed the microphone to the lead singer of the band now that he was here. I felt sort of sorry for him having to follow her performance. Lots of people were praising her as she descended the stairs. Will stopped her from exiting through the curtain behind the bar. He whispered something to her then she looked at me. I waved at her like a love sick fool. She laughed out loud. What a moron I was. I turned away too embarrassed to face her. Suddenly I felt someone grip my shoulder lightly. I turned around. Isa was standing face to face with me. Her heels gave her quite a bit of leverage. I was over 6'2" and she was almost eye level with me. "You wanted to talk to me." She said quietly. I almost didn't hear her.

"Yeah, um, I was wondering if I could go help out Sarah and Lexa with the tables." I barely spoke above a whisper trying to match her volume. She frowned then reached out towards me. She started fixing my suspenders and straightened out my bow tie. I was stiff as a board. A lump formed in my throat. My face started to turn red. She was so close to me now. Her vanilla scent was so strong. I took a deep breath in. She pulled on my tie. "Shit I'd been caught now I was going to look like a creepy dude that likes to sniff women."

Before I could try to justify my actions she pulled on my tie bringing her lips close to my ear. "You see all these customers waiting in line at the bar?" she tilted her head to the left. "They're here because they are thirsty. Now can you please just make their damn drinks and let me worry about everything else?" She let go of my tie, making me jerk back away from her face. Her eyes were like daggers now. Had I done something wrong? I just thought they could use an extra hand, nothing too serious. She reached up to take her ponytail out then shook her hair until it was all resting on her shoulders now.

I stood there dazed, not quite sure what just happened. She walked past Will staring him down as she pushed past him and behind the curtain. He looked at me like I just got scolded by the principal. What was he looking at, he got glared at too, I wasn't the only one. He came walking up to me with a smirk on his face. "Told ya you should've stayed away from her." He seemed pretty proud of himself. He reached up and patted me on the cheek. "That'll teach you to piss her off." I was still confused, what had I done? "What did I do to piss her off exactly?" I was genuinely curious by this notion. All I'd been doing for the last hour or so was tending the bar and occasionally watching her perform.

"That thing where that guy grabbed her?" My nostrils flared just at the memory of it all. "Yeah," I said through gritted teeth. "She doesn't need anybody to save her. Izzy's pretty tough. She can handle herself." What did he mean, handle herself, all she did was wait for Xander to come and take care of it. Sensing my hostility, William continued. "You see, if someone touches her and she does something about it, then she's defending herself. If you were to do something and cause a scene the person could lash out at us saying you assaulted him. You get it?" Oh, so it wasn't that she was mad about me trying to help out the girls. Now I felt like a douchebag.

What if I lost my temper and ended up hurting the guy? He could have sued her and the club for my actions, not to mention I would have been fired for sure. I looked down in shame. "Where is she? I need to apologize." I looked past him toward the back curtain. Without saying another word I pushed past him. It took a second for my eyes to adjust to the darkness of the hall. I thought I heard William mutter something under his breath that sounded like, "Don't do it man, it's suicide." I didn't care. She deserved an apology.

I quickly made my way to the dressing room and without even thinking I turned the knob. Once inside I realized what I'd done. There she was standing in just her strapless bra and the bottom half of her black dress around her waist. I panicked and just stood there with the doorway wide open. She was in the middle of pulling up her dress when I barged in on her. She didn't even seem to notice my presence. She just kept getting dressed like nothing had happened. When she was finished, she just looked at me. I was too terrified to move. What was she going to do? What could I even say to dig myself out of this hole? "I'm sorry!" I shouted at her then turned around. It was a little late for that but it was the best I could come up with in the heat of the moment.

She walked up behind me putting her hands on my waist and her chin on my shoulder next to my ear. My ears get hot as I started to blush. What was she doing? I started breathing more rapidly now. "Next time," she said in her normal sultry voice, "maybe you'll remember to knock." She led me out of her way and into the hall again. She let her fingertips slide along my lower back as she walked back towards the bar. It sent a chill up my spine. What just happened?

It took a few minutes to compose myself before entering the bar. The band was playing something from the 80's, they didn't sound half as good as Isa had before their lead singer showed up. Sarah met me at the corner of the bar. She could tell something was up. "What's wrong?" she asked inquisitively. How was I supposed to tell her I just walked in on our boss changing because I was too dumb enough to knock first? I brushed her off, "nothing's wrong." I tried to act cool but she could see right through me. I tried to push past her to get back over to my designated bar post. "Not nothing. Lexa saw you go into the hallway then a few minutes later we saw Izzy come out of the back wearing her black dress again and then a few more minutes later you come out here looking like you've seen a ghost."

Not a ghost, but with her porcelain skin I could see the resemblance. I took a deep breath and tried to compose myself again. "Nothing happened, ok?" I insisted. She wasn't backing down, "did you just hook up with our boss?!?" My mind began spinning, how could she even think such a thing? "No!" I raised my voice at her then realized we were in a rather public space. People had begun looking in our direction at the commotion we were causing. "Fine, just tell me about it later then." She grabbed her tray off the counter then proceeded back to her section of tables.

I felt bad lying to her, but I just couldn't bring myself to say out loud what had happened. She was going to be pissed when I told her about it. I knew better than to just walk in closed doors unannounced. I found my way back behind the bar. Isadora was out waiting tables with the others now. I hoped she didn't want to fire me after what just occurred. No, she would have told me flat out if she was going to fire me. She didn't seem like the type to beat around the bush. Will noticed the distant stare in my eyes.

"So, what'd you do?" He asked. I was sure Isa had already told him. "I walked in on her changing," I muttered quickly. "Huh?" He hadn't heard me. I turned toward him and said it again, this time over enunciating my words. "I...walked...in...on...her...changing!" I growled. His eyes grew wide. He shook his head at me. "You're really on a roll tonight aren't ya?" He chuckled then continued working. Why wasn't he mad? He just brushed me off like it was no big deal. I turned back to my work station.

Ben was now behind the bar too since the amount of people at the door had died down. Xander stood in the doorway with his arms crossed surveying the crowd for any disturbances. The girls were now all three waiting tables. It seemed weird to know the owner of the club was wiping down tables and serving people drinks. Not many bosses would stoop to the level of their employees by waiting tables. But she was different. I could tell she cared about each and every one of them. Maybe not Sarah and I yet but perhaps over time she would warm up to us too.

Sarah made her way back up to the bar in front of me. She was giggling when she placed her tray down. "What's so funny?" I asked. Had Isa told her what I did? No, that couldn't be it. She wouldn't be smiling and laughing if she knew what I'd done. "Izzy told me she thinks Xander wants to give me a ride home tonight!" She was practically squealing with excitement. Phew, dodged a bullet, I thought. "That's nice. Are you gonna go ask him out or something?" Her face turned bright red as she looked up at me. "Adam!" She said embarrassed. "I can't just ask a guy like him out! What about this job? I don't want things to be awkward for us at work."

"Why not, he clearly likes you too." We both glanced at the door to see if he was looking. His eyes were focused elsewhere for the moment. She looked back at me with her soft blue eyes. "Would you be ok if I asked him out?" Her voice pleading for me to say yes. I reached out and placed my hand on top of hers, "you do whatever makes you happy and I'll try to support you, whatever your decision." Tears started welling up in her eyes as I said this. She squeezed my hand then turned around to face Xander at his post. I watched her walk away knowing what was about to transpire.

She would talk to him, he'd ask her out, she would say yes, then I would be the odd man out. The third wheel. I could see it now, Sarah and Xander, Lexa and Ben, and then there's me. All alone. Not if I could help it. I was still determined to get to know Isa better whether she wanted me to or not. It was just going to take a little convincing, that's all. Maybe if I buddied up to Will he'd give me some pointers. Probably not. He'd already warned me not to get involved with her. Still, it couldn't hurt.

There was a rowdie table of college kids sitting near the restrooms. I hadn't noticed them before. I heard Ben say something, "Not these assholes again," then he beckoned for Lexa to come over to him. "Tell Izzy to take that table." he pointed with his finger. "And tell Sarah to stay away from them as well." Sarah was still busy flirting with Xander by the door. Both of them were completely oblivious to what was going on in the rest of the club. Lexa did as Ben told her to and notified Isa in the change of table sections. "Why can't she serve that table," I asked him. He never broke his concentration on where Lexa was headed. "That table," he pointed with his eyes, "is notorious for harassing women in here." He looked so intense, ready to spring on them the first chance they messed up.

I nodded then continued on with my work, glancing around every once in a while to see how things were going. Nothing seemed to be any different. Lexa finished clearing away the empty glasses off one of her tables, Sarah and Xander were still chatting by the door, and Isa was now tending to the drunk frat boys. She leaned across the table to pick up one of the empty shot glasses and one of them started petting her leg. The hair on the back of my neck stood on end. How dare he touch her! I started to make my way behind the bar to stop him.

I hesitated when Ben reached out and placed his hand on my shoulder. "Just watch," he said. How could he just stand by and watch this happen? Again his eyes never left the table. I looked frantically towards the door to see if Xander had noticed what was going on. He had, but he wasn't moving. He just stood there and watched it happen too. I turned to William to see if maybe he was going to do anything. Both he and Ben stood on either side of me fixated on Isa and the table of college boys.

"Excuse me boys, but I don't like to be touched," I heard Isa say politely. One of the dudes laughed as his friend's hand continued to inch further and further up her leg until it rested on her butt. "What are you gonna do about it, sweetheart?" The rest of the table joined in with the laughter now. I couldn't take it, something needed to be done about these guys. I tried to push my way past Will but he wouldn't budge. He shook his head at me, never looking away from Isadora. She carefully grabbed the dude's hand and removed it from her body. "That's enough boys. I'm going to have to ask you to leave if you can't behave." She finished picking up the rest of the table then started to turn her back to them. "Hey slut, who said we were done talking to you?" He reached up and grabbed her wrist. That was it, I needed to get over there before something terrible happened.

She looked up at the bar then flung her hand around so he was no longer holding her wrist. As she did this she pulled his arm up so he had to get off his chair. After that she slammed his wrist hard on the table. You could hear the crunch of bones from across the bar. The guy screamed out in pain. "You bitch!" Another one yelled. The whole table was on their feet now. One of them lunged at her. She slid out of the way to avoid his fist. He managed to hit the guy standing right behind her. One guy grabs a beer bottle and breaks it on the table.

He stands there holding it carefully calculating his next move. Two of his friends were scuffling on the floor after one hit the other one in the nose, and the other one was wringing in agony on the floor over his broken wrist. The band stops playing. Everyone's watching to see what was going to happen next. You could hear a pin drop. Beer bottle guy jabs at her, he misses. He tries again. He misses a second time. This man is fuming now after consuming alcohol and losing a fight to a girl.

The third time he lunged forward he slashed the bottle back and forth. She ducks and grabs him by the elbow joint. In one swift motion she manages to flip him over her back and onto the next table. The table buckles from the impact and the guy rolls onto the floor. Suddenly we hear sirens outside. *Who called the cops?* I thought. "It's closing time ladies and gentlemen." Isadora says now that she's subdued her attackers. She steps over the man she just flipped over. "I suggest you close your tabs."

Everyone was in a mad dash up to the counter to pay their bills and get out before the police entered the building. Isa walked over to the bar and had a seat at one of the stools. She didn't even have a scratch on her, I thought. How did she manage to take on those four guys and come out the victor? More importantly, why didn't anyone try to help her?

She placed her head in her hand then sighed. She seemed bored of the whole affair. "So much for no incidents this week boys," she said to us glumly. The police entered the building. They looked over at the four guys on the floor then looked towards Isa. One of the officers made his way to the bar while the other two went to help up the incapacitated men on the floor. "Ms. Dragoss," he placed his hands on his hips. "What happened this time?" She explained to him that this was not their first time harassing people in her bar. Apparently, they were in a few weeks ago and we're making lewd remarks at Lexa. Tonight was the first time one of them tried anything physical so she couldn't stand for that. "So that's why you wanted them to switch tables." Ben nodded at me. The officer took down her statement then handed her one of his business cards.

"Do you want to press charges mam?" He asked. She sighed and shook her head, "no. I think they learned their lesson tonight. But they will be banned from the premises from here on out." She stood up to shake the man's hand. "Thank you officer and have a good rest of your night". The bar was almost completely empty now. The three officers managed to get the men on their feet and were escorting them out of the building. Once they had left, Xander closed and locked the doors. He was looking down as he approached the bar. "Sorry Izzy. I should have been paying better attention out there." He looked like a kicked puppy. She walked over to him then placed her hand on his cheek. "Just do better next time," she said. He nodded then carefully walked past her. "Alright everyone. Show's over, time to clean up this mess." William came out from behind the curtain and handed her the broom. She started sweeping up glass while Xander and Will picked up the broken table then carried it out through the back door. Sarah and Lexa finished clearing away the rest of the tables then began putting the chairs on top of them. I stayed behind the bar to wash glasses and wipe down the counter.

I couldn't stop imagining that guy touching her. I angrily finished my tasks then decided to go help the girls on the floor. I had to go make sure she was alright. I could tell that Sarah was visibly shaken by the whole situation. First I needed to make sure she was ok, then I could go talk to Isa. "Are you alright?" I asked her. She was trembling. She looked at me with tears in her eyes. "This is all my fault," she burst out. "If I hadn't been over there distracting Xander maybe none of this would have happened." She started to lightly sob. I wanted to give her a hug to reassure her nothing was her fault. Out of the corner of my eye, I see Isa put the broom down and start walking over to us. She stretched out her arm and embraced Sarah. She wrapped her arms around Isadora's back and continued to sob.

She stroked my sisters' hair for a while then slightly pulled away from her. "You, did nothing wrong. Those creeps have been coming here for a while now and tonight I finally decided to do something about it." Sarah leaned back in sobbing into Isadora's chest. I walked over to them and placed my hand on her shoulder. "It's alright Sarah. Nobody got hurt." I felt a sort of calm wash over me when I smelled Isa's vanilla perfume. Sarah sniffled as she looked at me then nodded. She let go of her embrace around Isa. I watched her walk back to the bar where Xander was waiting for her.

I felt something cold touch me. Isa was using my shoulder to steady herself as she undid the straps of her high heels and took them off. Her presence was so light and airy that if not for the cold feeling I felt through my shirt, I never would have noticed her hand on me. She finished taking off her shoes then stood beside me for a moment. She seemed so small now standing this close to me. Her shoes must have given her another six inches of height. Now's my chance, I could ask her out after we finished cleaning up for the night. I grabbed another set of chairs and started stacking them on the tables.

"So..." I said quietly. She looked up at me, waiting to hear what I was going to say. "Would you ever, I don't know, maybe wanna, like go out with me sometime?" My heart started beating out of my chest as the words left my mouth. I felt my cheeks start turning red. She looked surprised. Her green eyes seemed almost sad as she spoke. "Don't take it personally, but I can't go out with you." My heart sank. "Do you have a boyfriend then or maybe even a girlfriend," I said sheepishly. "No." she said dryly. "Oh, so you just don't wanna date me because I'm one of your employees?" I was hopeful with my response this time. Again she replied, "No." I didn't understand, then what was it? "It's not that I can't date you, it's just that I won't. I don't date anyone."

I was crushed. She didn't want to date anyone? How could that be? I was sure there had to be tons of suitors that were trying to claim her as their own. She started to turn away from me when I reached out and grabbed her hand. Before I knew what was happening she twirled me around, tucked my arm behind my back and had my face pressed down on one of the tables. "Get it through your head!" she hissed. "I'm not going to go out with you!" She squeezed harder on my hand making my wince in pain. "And, I don't like being touched." She let go then stormed off towards the back. Lexa and Ben took off after her.

I stood up rubbing my injured hand and rotating my shoulder to loosen it up. Everyone stared at me. She was a lot stronger than she looked, I could see now why she had such an easy time flipping over that big frat guy. "Dude," William said, "I thought I was pretty clear when I told you to leave her alone?" He looked disappointed in me. "I know, but I had to see for myself if it was worth the trouble or not." He looked at me with his scarred eyebrow raised, "and was it?" I smiled, a fire had been lit inside me now. "Definitely."

Chapter

4

Xander burst out laughing at my answer. "Fuck, do you realize she could have just broke your entire arm, or worse fired you?" Sarah shouted at me. I didn't care. She hadn't done either of those things, and I was greatful. Xander put his arm around Sarah trying to comfort her. She blushed then continued scolding me. "What were you hoping to accomplish by asking her out?" *Wasn't it obvious*? I thought. I walked up to the four of them at the bar, still smiling like an idiot.

Lexa and Ben returned from the back. "She's gone. She told us to lock up and she'd see us at home." Lexa said then grabbed herself a glass and poured herself a shot of whiskey. She took the shot then poured another one. "Man, you pissed her off big time," she chuckled, passing another glass to ben. "Cheers to you my friend." He slammed down his drink. What? They were drinking with me? I stood there puzzled. Ben read my expression. "You've got more guts than most of the guys that come in here. No one's been brave enough to ask her out in over six months. And you, well you even placed a hand on her. You really are lucky she didn't break anything though." Xander and William nodded.

"Does she turn everybody down?" They all nodded again. Well, at least she was consistent I guess. I pulled up a chair across from William at the bar. He motioned for me to take a glass too. I shook my head, politely turning down his offer. "Why doesn't she like anyone?" I asked. Will snorted as he took a drink. "Well, she likes us," he motioned to everyone else at the bar. Was it just me she didn't like? She even gave Sarah a hug and comforted her but the second I did anything she tried to dislocate my arm.

What was it about me she didn't like? I thought I was reasonably good looking, I could play the piano, I was relatively smart, what was it? I needed to get more information about her out of them. "So where is she from?" They all looked at William. He choked on his drink. Sputtering, he said, "She's from all over Europe. She's mostly from the midwest part of it though I believe." His eyes darted over at the others. "What about now, where do you guys live?" It was Xander who spoke now. "We all live together in a house twenty minutes away from here in the forest near the lake." They all live together? "All of you?" I say. "Yeah, it was a lodge before Izzy bought it and renovated it," Lexa piped up. A lodge? How could she afford that? She was around our age, where did she get enough money to buy something like that. Ben nudged Lexa in the side. "She came into some money a few years back when she had a wealthy relative pass away," she added quickly.

How very strange, all of them living together in one house. "What about you guys? Do you have any family around here?" They were all silent, looking towards one another hoping to find an answer in their expressions. "Well?" I pushed. Was anyone going to answer me? "None of us have any living family." Will said. "Xander and Lexa are the only ones who do, and that's each other." I felt guilty. Orphans. Just like Sarah and I. "I'm sorry. I didn't know." I felt like a complete asshole after pestering them with my questions. Sarah broke the tension, "OK, so let's finish up here and head home. It's getting super late and this girl's gotta get her beauty sleep." Thank you Sarah for saving my ass, I sang her praise in my head.

We dispersed from the positions we were standing in. Each person quickly finished their tasks then reconvened back by the lockers. I changed out of my dress shirt and suspenders. It felt great to take off my bow tie. I'd have to see if Will would tie it again tomorrow night. Sarah put on her scrub pants from nursing school and a sweatshirt she brought along. She and Xander were chattering in the corner by the lockers after I got back from the restroom. What were they scheming?

"What's going on?" I ask. Sarah comes prancing up to me. "Xander wants to give us a ride home. Isn't that nice." She winked at me gritting her teeth. Winking was her way of telling me she didn't want me to come along. I rolled my eyes. What did she expect me to do, walk all the way home? "I can give you a lift home if you need Adam." Will said, jingling his keys in his pocket. Yes, William for the win. "Sure," I replied, "If you don't mind." "Great, then it's settled. I'll see you at home." She was practically bursting with excitement as they walked out the door. William handed me the keys. I stood there looking at him confused. "You know which one it is. I gotta do a double check to make sure all the lights are off and the doors are locked before we go." Ben and Lexa had already left before I had returned from changing so it was just the two of us left there now.

"Ok, I'll meet you out there then." I put on my leather jacket I had brought along earlier that day. By now frost was starting to form on the grass outside. I made my way outside while William did his last few double checks. I opened the door to see the silver Camaro waiting for me in the parking lot. Hadn't Lexa given the keys back to Isa? I thought. I walked over to the car and unlocked the doors. Once inside I turned the key in the ignition to thaw out the windshield. I sat in the car a few moments warning up when my phone dinged. A text message from Sarah. It read, 'change of plans, he's taking me to his place for the night. Love you. Don't wait up. ;)

That sneaky minx. Not only was he giving her a ride but she was going to stay with him after only knowing him one whole night? "I hope she knows what she's doing," I said out loud. "Hope who knows what who's doing?" William said as he opened the driver door. It startled me and I dropped my phone on the floor. "Sarah," I said leaning down to pick up my phone, "Xander is taking her back to your guys' place for the night I guess." He didn't seem surprised at all. "Yeah that sounds like Xander. Don't worry he's a really good guy though. He'll treat you sister right." Treating her right wasn't necessarily what was on my mind. I was more concerned about her regretting her decision in the morning but she was an adult, there was nothing I could say to stop her from having a one night stand.

I text her back, 'ok. Be safe. Love you too.' I put my phone back in my pocket knowing she wasn't going to talk to me again until tomorrow. As Will was putting the car in reverse he said, "Do you like Thai food? I know a great little place not far from here." His question caught me off guard. "What? Sure. I could eat." I reached in my pants pocket and pulled out my wallet to start counting the bills to see how much I had. "It's my treat," he chimed in. Surprised, I put my wallet away. That was nice of him to offer to pay for me. Out of curiosity, I asked, "hey, so when do we get paid?" I thought Sarah had said we would get our tips at the end of each not before.

"You'll get paid next Friday with the rest of us. Izzy holds your check a week to make sure you're actually going to stick it out and then she'll give you all your tips for the first two weeks. After that you'll get paid every Friday and tips at the end of each night." It made sense. She wanted to make sure new employees were committed to the job before handing over a large sum of money. We took off down the street toward the restaurant. He drove extremely fast, it's no wonder Isa would have been upset with my wrecking her car. "So if this is Isas' car, what did she drive home?" I asked inquisitively. "She took the red one today." The red one, how many vehicles did she have? "She knew you'd be bringing this one back so we took the Corvette into town." Corvette? She had a corvette too? Wow, I guess I had seen it in the parking lot but I never imagined it would be hers too.

We pulled up to a little run down Thai restaurant next to a barber shop. The sign in the window said open but the place looked questionable to me whether or not I wanted to enter the establishment. Will turned off the car and got out. He waited on the sidewalk until I emerged from my side. He opened the door and greeted the owner of the shop who was easily in his mid to late eighties. The owner smiled then disappeared into the kitchen. William sat down at a little table and I followed.

"You come here often?" I said wearily. An older lady appeared from the back carrying two glasses of water and two sets of chopsticks. She smiled at Will as she placed them on the table revealing some missing teeth. "Yeah. All the time. It's one of the only places open this late and the food is great." He opened his chopsticks and placed them on a napkin. I did the same. Moments later the old man comes out of the back carrying four different dishes of food. Was all this for us, we didn't even look at a menu?

He placed the food in front of us then bowed at William, who respectively bowed his head back. "So you come here often enough they know your order I see." I chuckled. He rubbed his hands together excitedly, "Yeah, I've been coming here once or twice a week for the last two years. They know me pretty well here. Sometimes we all come out to eat here after work but mostly it's just Izzy and I."

Twice a week for the last two years? No wonder the owners seemed so happy to see us when we walked through the door. I wonder which dish Izzy likes most? There was pork fried rice, spicy Thai fish curry, shrimp pad Thai, and a bowl of coconut soup with chicken. Everything looked so delicious I didn't know where to start. Will started dishing himself up a portion of everything. With the space on left on one of the plates I dished myself up a little of each too. The rice was phenomenal. I can't believe I have never been here before. I tried the soup. That was the best soup I'd ever eaten in my life, I finished off the whole bowl. Will smiled at me with noodles hanging out of his mouth. "It's good ain't it?" He said with a full mouth. I nodded my head as I slurped the last few remnants out of the bowl.

"That's Izzy's favorite too. She never shares it with me either." I could understand why. I could eat nothing else but that soup forever until the day I died. We finished our meal then sat there for a while. I needed to get more information out of him about Isa. "So, you guys come here often, she lets you drive her car, you're the manager of the club, and you all live together in her house…Are you sure you're not going out with her?" I said sort of jokingly. Will cracks up laughing. "No. I can assure you, we are not going out." He takes a drink of his water. "Then what is it? Why won't she go out with anyone?" I really wanted to know the reason behind her being so distant to everyone.

"If you really wanna know so bad, why don't you just ask her instead of asking me a million questions?" He had a devilish grin now. He knew I was never going to ask her myself. I looked away, knowing I'd been caught. "But if I ask you, then I don't run the risk of pissing her off." He shrugged his shoulders. I had a point. He crossed his arms then leaned back on his chair. "She used to go out with this guy years ago who said he was going to marry her. But right before the wedding he took off." He paused for me to take it all in. "Ever since then, she's swore off dating and she plans to be alone the rest of her life." Well that was a letdown. I furrowed my brow and looked down at my empty bowl.

"That's so sad," I said. "Yeah," he continued, "she really loved him and he betrayed her like that. I don't think she'll ever forgive him or herself for that matter. She's got a lot of pent up anger about the whole thing." That made sense. If somebody stomped on my heart and left me without an explanation I'd have some animosity towards them too. Now I felt like a jerk for trying to ask her out without knowing the whole story. "Do you think she'd ever take him back?" I wasn't sure if I wanted to know the answer to this question. He shook his head, "I'd never let that happen. She's come too far to go back to the likes of him. If I were ever to see him, I'd kick his ass for her."

I was really starting to like William. He was a great guy. He took care of things at the club for her and he still cared about Isadora herself. *Why couldn't Sarah want to go out with him?* I thought. He reached in his wallet, pulled out two one hundred dollar bills and placed them on the table. My eyes grew wide. Holy smokes! Lexa wasn't joking about them getting paid really well. He saw me gawking at the money, "What?" he said putting his wallet away. "I was just wondering, Sarah and I are facing eviction if we don't pay our landlord by Friday. Do you think that maybe Isa would front us our checks before then so we didn't have to worry about it anymore?" He sucked his teeth for a second. "I don't know. It's possible but you'd have to talk with her about it tomorrow." He thought about it for a moment, "you know, scratch that. Maybe you should have Sarah talk to her since you seem so keen on upsetting her recently."

My shoulders drooped, "but I wanted to be the one to talk to her." He could tell I was disappointed in his answer and laughed. The old man and woman came back to our table to clear away our dirty dishes. She took all our plates in one hand then grabbed out empty glasses with the other. The man looked down at the bills sitting on the table and shook his head, "no no, you pay too much!" he exclaims trying to hand William back one of his hundreds. He wouldn't accept it and stood up from the table. "Thank you for the meal as always." he says and heads for the door. I followed his lead and thanked him as I exited the building.

We got back in the car. I was so full now and ready to head home for bed. "You wanna take a drive? I could show you where we live." The thought of seeing her house would satisfy my curiosity. "Sure. Let's go,"

I say. We leave what is now my new favorite restaurant in town and head off down the road. We pass lots of nice brownstone houses with white picket fences. Sarah and I could never afford to live anywhere out here. Maybe someday Sarah can after she's done with college. Hopefully we'd be out of that apartment and a little more out of debt by then.

I wonder where I'll be in ten years? I'd never really taken the time to think about it. I would one day like to be married and have a few kids but that was way in the future. Right now I just need to focus on the present. Sarah was in school and had her whole life ahead of her. Hopefully things with her and Xander would go alright so I could keep this job for a few months, maybe even a year. I really liked working with everyone but I still felt like something was off about all of them. They were so close to one another. Maybe they'd just bonded together so much now they were like a family.

We cruise along through the town making our way towards the lake. I had never been to this side of town before. I had no need to. Sarah and I used public transportation to get places. If it wasn't on the route, we wouldn't go there. The houses kept getting bigger and spaced farther apart. Finally we came to a dirt road. Was he planning on driving me all the way down the driveway? The trees were really thick at the front of the road, I couldn't even see the house. As we drove the road narrowed until we got to a large metal gate.

William slowed the car down and pressed a button that looked like a garage door opener. The hinges of the gate began creaking as they opened wide enough for us to drive through. My heart rate quickened. The first thing that popped into my head came out of my mouth, "you're not taking me on some dark twisted road to murder me are you?" I laughed weakly. I regretted it the second I said it. He laughed out loud, "maybe, it depends on how hungry Izzy is tonight if I have to kill you or not." He laughed again at his own joke, I didn't quite find it as funny.

We kept driving down the road for a few miles. My stomach was starting to feel a little iffy. I wondered if the Thai food was disagreeing with me. "How much farther is it?" I asked, gripping my door handle tight. "You feeling alright?" He said concerned. I shook my head. I was not, ok! He sped up but kept his eyes on the road. My stomach was killing me. How embarrassing. The plan was just to go for a drive by their house, not stop there so I could get a handle on my food poisoning. I sure hoped everyone else in the house was in bed when we got there, especially Isa.

The driveway curved and there was a break in the trees. You could see most of the lake now, and then up on a little hill, was the house. The house was beautiful. It didn't really look like a lodge though anymore other than the actual shape of the house. It had huge windows from floor to ceiling on the front of it with a wraparound porch going around the whole thing. You could tell the house was built into the side of the hill because there were a set of double doors below the front patio. On the right side of the house, there was a big balcony facing the water. The moonlight danced off the lake as we drove past it.

As we were nearing the house, I began to see the silhouette of someone sitting on the front steps. *Please don't be Isa*, I thought. But of course, it was. She was wearing a light gray oversized crew neck sweater and what appeared to be bike shorts. She stood up when we pulled up to the house, her long flowing hair shining in the headlights. William turned the car off and got out. I was frozen with fear. I didn't dare move for fear of doing something embarrassing in front of her.

He met her at the step and talked with her. She crossed her arms after first having them placed on her hips for the beginning of their conversation. I couldn't make out what they were saying through the windshield. She looked in my direction. I looked away trying to fight the ever growing feeling that I might explode. I looked back at them, this time Will was beckoning me forward. I released some gas while I was still in the car in hopes to make it to their nearest restroom. I closed the door and waited for the next wave of stomach cramping to pass.

"Come on in. I'll show you where the closest bathroom is." William hollered. I wish he could have been a little more discreet but it was too late for that. I'm sure he already told her that he took me out to their favorite Thai restaurant and that I obviously wasn't feeling good. I quickly followed him in the house. As I rushed past Isa she snickered at me, "couldn't handle the Thai Palace huh?" I didn't have time to talk to her, I needed to go, now!

The interior of the house was just as amazing as the outside. It was furnished to look like a medieval hunting cabin, suits of armor included.

There were large tapestries draped on the walls along with mounted animal trophies too. We passed the gorgeous open concept kitchen with white marble countertops and a large rectangular dining room table. On the other side of the kitchen was a large stone fireplace with a fire burning in the hearth. Above it was a large portrait of a lady. I didn't have time to study it properly to know who she was though.

At last we arrived at the restroom. Will opened the door and turned the lights on. "I'll be outside whenever you finish so I can bring you home," he said as I practically slammed the door in his face. "Ok," I say back to him as I lock the door and sit alone in my shamefulness.

When I finally emerged, I had to hobble because my one foot had fallen asleep. I was so embarrassed about what I had just done. I wanted to get home as quickly as possible. I quietly tiptoed my way back through the house taking in all the minute details I missed the first time. There was a rather large collection of weapons from many different eras upon the walls. There were lances and morning stars, swords and shields, there were even some old muskets on the wall that looked to be from early colonial times.

When I got to the fireplace, I stopped to get a better view of the portrait above it. It was on a large wooden framed canvas. It took up most of the wall it was on. It was a hand painted piece that must have dated back hundreds of years. The paint was fading and cracked and the wood frame looked to be starting to crumble on one side. The picture itself was that of a singular woman in a renaissance style gown. The dress was red with a black corset and lace on it. The woman had long faded yellow hair with intricate braids in it. On top of her head was a small jewel encrusted tiara. Her skin was pale with a tiny hint of rouge on her cheeks and billowing breasts.

She looked distraught staring back at me. Her face had the slightest hint of a smile on her lips like the Mona Lisa. Who was she? She looked so familiar but I couldn't quite put my finger on it. Perhaps she was some long lost relative of Isadora's. But still, I couldn't help but feel sad for the lady in the painting. Perhaps I would ask about her sometime with Isa to find out the history of the price, but not tonight.

Tonight had long since turned into tomorrow before we even arrived at the Dragoss Chateau. I hoped she wouldn't mind me calling it that from now on. I left the sitting room and made my way outside. I looked around for William but he was nowhere to be seen. Had he gone to bed and forgot about me? How long was I there? I thought about going back inside and trying to find his room but where would I even start? And with any luck I wouldn't even find his room until last. I had a fifty percent chance of walking in on either Ben and Lexa or Xander and my sister. I didn't like those odds.

Before I could make up my mind the lights flashed on the Camaro. I jumped when the light hit me. I began looking around outside to see who had pressed the button on the fab. It was Isa, sitting on the porch swing hidden in the dark of the covered awning. "Here," she said in her normal voice. She stood up off the swing and walked over to me. "Take it. It's yours until I say otherwise." I could not believe it. She was giving me permission to use her car? "But, why?" I said dumbfounded. "Why would you let me use your car? Isn't it Will's?" She shrugged her shoulders. "I don't wanna have to worry if you or Sarah will be able to get to work on time. And Sarah can use it for school too. Then you don't have to rely on others to get yourself back and forth." She held out the keys for me. I took the keys from her. "Besides," she continued, "You never know when there might be another emergency you have to take care of." I blushed and looked away. She smiled then walked back over to the swing.

Why was she still awake? Wasn't she cold sitting out here all by herself? "What are you doing?" I asked. She sprawled out across the bench and closed her eyes. "Oh, just taking in the night air." She wiggled her foot to and fro so the swing would be rocking her. "Aren't you tired?" I knew I was. "Extremely," she said. "Then why not go to bed?" I questioned. "Chronic insomnia," she said, folding her arms behind her head. "Oh, that sucks." I say leaning against one of the pillars. "Aren't you at least cold out here, I know I think it's chilly." I rubbed my hands together to indicate that I was getting cold. "It suits me just fine," she opened her eyes and looked at me.

I couldn't help but smile at her. She was so odd. Nothing about her made sense. She caught me smiling at her and winked. Instantly my face started turning red. I coughed and crossed my arms. She giggled from the swing. "Why do you do that?" I asked. She raised her eyebrows at me. "Why do you act so tough and mean one second then the next you're smiling and winking at me?" She placed one foot on the deck to stop her rocking then gracefully sat up and pulled her knees into her chest.

She looked me dead in the eyes and said, "Because I can." How infuriating! The nerve of her, 'because I can'. What bullshit. I scrunch my eyebrows in disgust. Reading my expression she stands up and slowly walks over to me. She remains making perfect eye contact with me the closer she gets. My pulse starts racing again. She stopped less than a foot away from me. I looked down at those beautiful emerald eyes. "I do it," she continued, "Simply because I know I can get a rise out of people." She inched a little closer. "If only you knew how easy it was to do." She uncrossed my arms and put them around her waist. My breathing was rapid now. What was she doing?

I couldn't look away from her, our eyes locked in a trance. She pressed her fingers on my chest and slowly moved her hands up around my neck. There was electricity in the air. I'm not sure if the hairs on my neck were standing up because of that or because her hands were cold as ice. She carefully started to stand up on the tips of her toes. I slowly started to lean my face into hers. Then she whispered in my ear, "You have no idea what I'm capable of." My heart skipped a beat as she said it.

"Adam? What are you doing here?" Sarah was standing in the open doorway of the house. Isa quickly removed her hands from my body and stepped back. I stood there for a second trying to wrap my brain around what just happened. "I...umm. Well, you see..." I stuttered trying to come up with a good excuse for what she must have just seen. Isa rescued me by saying something more intelligent. "Will wanted to show him the house but when they got here Adam wasn't feeling good but he's better now and ready to go home." I nodded in agreement. "What are you doing up?" I asked her. She looked down at her feet then spoke. "I was going to spend the whole night here but remembered I have a paper due that needs to be finished so Xander was going to bring me home so I could sleep in my own bed and finish it tomorrow before work." Xander shut the door behind them. "What's going on out here?" He said. Rather than wait for someone to fill him in on the whole story again I decided it was just time to leave.

"Come on Sarah. I'll take you home." She looked confused. "But I thought that was Will's car, wasn't it?" She was right, it was. "I told him to take it since neither of you have a vehicle and William went to bed after they got here." Thank you again Isa for rescuing me from another long conversation. Sarah said her goodbyes with Xander as I headed for the car, 'you have no idea what I'm capable of' still playing over and over in my head. Was she just teasing me, is that what she meant?

I started the car and waited for Sarah to arrive. She yawned deeply as she entered the car. "Do you remember how to get home from here?" I thought I did, but just for good measure I turned on the car's gps to help me. I tapped in the destination and it gave me a route to follow. As we were backing away from the front porch, I saw Xander start waving at us. What an idiot, I thought. He looked so stupid standing there waving with a huge smile on his face. Sarah waved at him too while grinning ear to ear.

Those two sure were smitten alright. And fast too. They'd only known each other for two days now. Isa didn't wave but she continued standing on deck next to Xander. She still had a slight smile on her face. I couldn't help but blush when I made eye contact with her again. I couldn't stop thinking about her velvety touch on the back of my head.

We sped off down the driveway. I looked back at the house in the rear view mirror. Xander had gone back in the house but she still remained outside. I looked away from her silvery outline as we rounded the curve near the lake again. A dense fog had started to settle in the forest. We slowly made our way through the labyrinth of trees out to the large metal gate.

From this side of the gate, I could see it was connected to a large fence that kept going deep in the trees out of sight from the driveway. It had to be at least twelve feet tall. I guess they don't want anyone getting onto the property. I clicked the button, opening the large metal gates. I look over at Sarah to see her resting her head on the window. She must be asleep, I thought. We continued on our drive home.

The closer to the apartment I got, the heavier my eyelids became. I gotta get home. It was almost five in the morning now. The sun would slowly be creeping up soon. We passed the brownstone houses with the white picket fences. I wish Sarah was awake to keep me company on the half hour drive back home. The street lights flashed as I passed them. I wondered if Isa would be able to get to sleep tonight or not. I wonder how often she stayed outside at night while the others slept.

She didn't seem tired at the club when she was dancing on the stage. Maybe she'd just become so used to not sleeping that she pushed through any discomfort. Personally, if left to my own devices, I would sleep all day. Maybe she did that too, after all, we didn't start work until closer to 7 o'clock at night. I suppose she got there early each day to take inventory and make sure everything was in order for the coming night though. She also apparently practiced her ballet when no one was there. I wonder what she did on her days off?

I decided not to park too far away from the apartment building tonight. We had both had a long day and was sure that neither of us wanted to walk two blocks back from where I'd parked it the night before. I pull into a parking space right out front out building. "Sarah," I shook her gently to wake her up. She opened her eyes and squinted at me. "Are we home?" She said through a yawn. I nodded then exited the car. Locking the door behind us, I helped her carry her things up the stairs. We trudged our way up the three flights of stairs, past Mr. Petrovs' door and into our own apartment. Finally, we were home.

Mr. Petrov had taped another warning letter on our door stating we had one week to pay him the money we owed him or we were out. I ripped the paper off the door as I opened it up. "Geez, I already talked to him today. Why's he gotta be an ass and make it so the whole building knows." I grumbled to myself clenching the paper in my fist. Sarah headed straight to her room without even taking her shoes off. "Goodnight." She groggily called behind her as she shut the door. I took off my street shoes and plopped down on the futon. I was so tired I was wide awake again. I plugged in my phone, it died sometime after we got to the lodge.

When the screen lit up it alerted me that I had two new notifications. I opened up my messenger app. One message was from William, 'I'm beat. Izzy said you could take my car home. See you tomorrow.' Ah, that makes sense now, I thought. And the other was from an unknown number. I opened the text to see what it said. 'I see you made it home alright. See you tomorrow, Isa.' I sat straight up on the couch. Isa took the time to follow me on her app to make sure we made it home safe. Maybe she did care about me the way I wanted to care for you? I wanted to reply to her so badly but hesitated. What if she was finally asleep? Do I do anything that would potentially wake her up?

I decided to just go ahead with a small text, a sort of a thank you for caring about our well-being message. I started replying 'thank you for worrying about me,' no that won't work. I deleted it. 'How very thoughtful of you to worry about me.' No, not that either. Delete, delete, delete. I just have started typing out my message a dozen times before I finally decided on what to write her back. Finally the perfect comeback popped into my head. What if she didn't take it the right way though? Would she be angry? I was pretty much running that risk by either texting her back or not. I wrote back, 'you have no idea what I'm capable of.' Should I add a smiley face at the end? I scrolled through the countless emojis my phone had to offer trying to settle on the perfect one to end it with. Suddenly my thumb went too fast scrolling and I hit the send button instead.

"No, no, no!" I said out loud. What had I done? What if she didn't find it funny, then what? I threw my phone on the futon and started rubbing my eyes. The fatigue was starting to set in from my lack of sleep. It was too late now. The message had already been sent and I would have to suffer the consequences later. I made my bed then turned off the kitchen light. Finally, sleep. I put my phone face up on the floor so I could hear it when my alarm went off. As my eyes were just about to close, I saw my screen light up. My stomach was in knots as I reached under my bed for the phone. It was a new message from Isa. Oh no, what was it now? I opened the message and my heart skipped a beat. I started smiling like an idiot then placed my phone back on the floor. The only thing she had replied, was a winky face emoji.

5

The next morning I awoke rather early for once. I grabbed my phone to see if there were any new messages. None. Damn, I thought, I was really hoping maybe she'd text me again. I reread our brief interaction over again. I clasp my hand over my eyes with embarrassment. How could I write that? 'You don't know what I'm capable of.' What a joke. I'm sure she could see right through me. I wasn't capable of doing anything. The best I could do was be a little musically inclined. I looked over her response of a winky face. She was teasing me again. She knew how much it drove me wild every time she winked at me. Even over text it made me smile and blush a little.

"Was she flirting with me?" I questioned aloud. I wondered if she would let me take a picture of her to use as her contact photo. Probably not. I don't think I could even muster the courage to ask her. I got up from my bed and walked over to Sarah's room. Slowly turned the knob and peaked inside. She was still sprawled out on her mattress. I quietly closed the door behind me. "I should make her breakfast." I headed towards the fridge to see what sort of ingredients we had in the house. Half a dozen eggs, butter, some milk, and a partial loaf of bread. I decided to make one of Auntie Mary's favorite things for breakfast. She called it a bird's nest. You take your slice of bread and use a glass to cut out a circle in the middle of it. Next, you butter both sides of the bread and place it in a skillet. Once the skillet is heated up you crack an egg in the open hole in the bread. Then you cook your egg and flip the whole thing over so both sides of your bread are toasted and your egg is cooked.

I made two for her and two for me. I put them on plates and tidied up the kitchen after I finished. I did the dishes and put them away. I hoped this would make Sarah happy. I let the food rest for a few minutes on the plates then carried them to her door. "Sarah," I knocked, "I made you some breakfast." I could hear her rustling around on her bed. "Come in," she called through the door. I turned the knob to see her wrapped up in her blanket sitting cross legged on her bed. Her eyes lit up when she saw what I was holding. "Are those bird's nests?" She exclaimed. I grinned and headed into her room.

We sat on her bed eating our breakfast in silence. Once finished I grabbed the plates and started to head back to the kitchen. "Aren't you going to say anything? About last night," she said. I looked at her confused. "What was there to talk about," I replied. She pulled the blanket tighter around her shoulders. "You know. About me and Xander." She couldn't look me in the eyes when she spoke. Was she that ashamed of having a one night stand with him? I thought. "It's none of my business who or what you wanna do. So long as you're happy, I'm fine with it." She smiled at my comment. "I really like him, Adam. I could really see this going somewhere." She looked me in the eyes. I could tell she meant it.

I nodded my head and continued towards the kitchen. What did she want me to say? I wasn't going to tell her no. She was an adult and capable of making her own decisions about her life. I finished cleaning up then decided to take a shower. Sarah said the night before, that she had some homework to finish so I was going to leave her alone to get it done. Maybe the hot water would clear my head. I grabbed a clean pair of clothes from my dresser and headed for the bathroom. When the water hit my face I put my arms up around the pipe holding the shower head. I leaned my head on my forearms and let the water wash all over me.

I started thinking about everything that's happened to me the last few days. I got a good job that pays well, I made some new friends, I've got this awesome car to use, and I met the most incredible woman. She was perfect, everything about her was perfect. She could sing, she could dance, she knew how to stand up for herself in a fight. She was the total package. I started fantasizing about what my life would be like if we ended up together. Her and I would run the club every night and every day I'd play for her while she practiced her ballet. I smiled thinking about this. Could that really happen though, I thought. Maybe I should start somewhere smaller like getting her flowers or something like that. That was a good idea. A beautiful girl like her would love to have beautiful flowers.

A knock on the door startled me out of my day dream. The door opened just a crack. "Aren't you finished yet? Your phone's been ringing this whole time." My phone? Who'd be calling me this early, I wondered. "Just answer if for me, will ya?" I hollered back at her. I finished washing the shampoo out of my hair. "I did. It was Isadora." My heart skipped a beat. Why was she calling me? "What did she say?" I asked her urgently. "She wanted to know if you'd come to the club early again today. She wanted to ask you something." What did she want to ask me, I pondered. "Just text her back when you're done I guess," she shut the door behind her.

I stood there again letting the water trickle down my back. "She wants me to come in early and she wants to ask me something." I thought out loud. I wondered what it could be. Did I wreck the toilet when I was there last night? God, I'd hoped not. Maybe I messed something up when I was snooping around the living room. No, that couldn't be it. I hadn't touched anything for fear of knocking something over and waking everyone up in the household.

I turned off the water and dried myself off. Were the clothes I picked out good enough for her? Probably not. She was so fancy. I had only seen her in flashy clothes when we were at the club. Even in that oversized sweater last night she looked elegant. Maybe I should stop and buy a new shirt along my way there. No. If I was going to stop and get her flowers, I couldn't afford to get a new shirt too. I put on my black t-shirt and a pair of jeans. I was going to bring my dress pants in a backpack along with a sweatshirt.

It seemed like a really nice day today. I looked at myself in the mirror. Looking at myself in the reflection I noticed the stubble growing on my face. I debated whether or not I wanted to shave. "I wonder what she thinks about guys with beards?" I quietly said. I decided against it. It didn't look too bad and if she said something about it I'd shave it off tomorrow. I spritzed a little cologne on that Sarah had gotten me last Christmas. It smelt like new leather. Hopefully Isa liked it, I thought, exiting the bathroom.

Sarah had made up the futon and was sitting there cross legged with her laptop. She looked at me then back at her screen. She looked concerned. "What?" I said walking over to her. "They found the body of a twenty-five year old male in an alley by the care facility where I work. No known cause of death yet." I could tell she was scared. I sat down beside her. This has been going on for a while now over the last few years. Once or twice a year, some random person would end up dead with no explanation to what happened to them or where they came from. There was no specific pattern to the deaths only that they were all connected.

I put my arm around her shoulders. She was shaking. "What if that had been me?" Her voice cracked. How could she think that way? I leaned over to read the date on the article. They estimated the time of death being late Thursday night, sometime between midnight and 5 am. She was right. We had our interviews at the Moonlight Club that night. If not for that, she would have taken a longer shift and not gotten home until five in the morning. She started to cry. "That poor man," she sniffled. Sarah was known to have a lot of empathy for people, especially those less fortunate than herself.

I held her close then stood up from the couch. She looked up at me confused. "Where are you going?" She asked. I grabbed the keys off my dresser. "To the club. You said Isa wanted me to go there early." She looked stunned, like how dare I leave her when she needed me the most, kind of stunned. "And what about me? How am I supposed to get there later?" She had a fair point. If I left now, how would she get to work? "Can't you text your new boyfriend and see if he can pick you up?" She frowned at me.

"Aren't you at least a little concerned for your own safety if not mine too? She crossed her arms. "The killer? Nah, he won't kill again for another few months so we should be safe until then." She rolled her eyes at me as I packed my things in my backpack. I went over a mental checklist of things I was supposed to grab; 'phone, keys, backpack, wallet.' I stopped when I got to my wallet. I think I only had ten dollars in it. I opened it up to count the ones. I looked at Sarah and gave her my best smile. She raised an eyebrow at me.

Finally she sighed, "How much do you need?" She got up and walked to the counter where she left her purse from the night before. How much were flowers these days? I had no idea. "Like forty bucks, maybe?" I questioned. She whipped her head back around at me. "What are you planning on buying for forty dollars? I could hear the suspicion in her voice. I looked down with a smirk on my face. "Flowers... For Isa." I looked back up at her to see her grinning ear to ear now. What was she so chipper about? She quickly counted out the money and handed it to me. "Get her carnations! Or roses! No, no wait, lilies!" My mind was spinning.

"I'll get her what I get her," I said, turning red. She clapped her hands with excitement. She was almost more excited than I was to get them. I placed the money in my wallet and put it in my back pocket. "See you later," I called behind me as I left the apartment. I closed the door and headed for the stairs. I pranced down steps smiling the whole way. When I got to the bottom Mr. Petrov was on his way up. He tried to say something to me but I just pushed on past him as I headed out the door. He muttered something in Russian as I did this. I didn't care. I had shit to do and places to be.

There was a small crowd around the Camaro when I got up to it. I pressed the key fab to unlock the doors. Several people jumped back when I did this. I threw my backpack in the passenger seat then walked around to the driver side. "Hey dude, this your car?" Some neighbor kid on a bike asked as I was about to climb inside. I twirled the keys on one finger, "Yep," I said. I searched my phone for the nearest flower shop. The closest one was about six miles away, perfect. I typed the address into the car's gps.

The engine purred as I put the car into drive. The leaves were really starting to fall now. It was mid-October now after all. I pulled up to the shop and shut off the car. I sat there for a minute trying to hype myself up before I entered the store. Eventually I got out of the car, locked the doors, and walked up to the door. A bell dinged as I opened it. The aroma of the shop was overwhelming. A middle aged woman came out from the back room and stood behind a counter. "Hi there, what can I do for you today?" She had a large customer service smile on her face.

I shyly walked up to the counter. "I'd like to buy some flowers," I said quietly. She came around the counter and led me to large glass door coolers with pre-arranged flowers. "Do you have a specific kind you were looking for?" I didn't know what I was looking for so I shook my head. There were tons of roses and carnations all over the place. She read the distraught expression on my face. "Is this for a special occasion? Birthday or anniversary perhaps?" No, I was just a fool crushing on a girl. "No, I'm just hopeful," I said, trying to examine the arrangements better. None of them had prices on them.

I pointed at a bouquet with roses and lilies. She slid open the glass door and picked up the vase reading the sticker on the bottom of it. "One hundred and sixty dollars. Do you want me to wrap them up?" I audibly gasped when she told me the price. Why were they so expensive? "No!" I said, raising my voice. She placed them back in the cooler quickly. I felt bad for startling her. "Is there anything I could get for around fifty?" I pleaded with her. She pursed her lips thinking about my request. "Tell you what, I'll do a dozen sunflowers and one red rose for fifty dollars, sound good?" She flashed her retail smile again.

Sunflowers? I mean, it was fall so they'd be appropriate. Maybe she'd like them. I nodded my head in agreement. "Excellent," She said. She left me standing there by the cooler. She returned shortly carrying some sunflowers and a small vase. She arrangers them in a circle overlapping the petals. Leaving the vase of flowers on the table she went back to the coolers and pulled out a singular red rose. She placed the open rose in the very center of the sunflowers. "Is the vase included in the price?" I asked quickly, after thinking about it. She frowned. "No, but it's done now so we might as well throw it in I guess." I felt bad. I didn't want her to think I was trying to take advantage of her.

I paid for the flowers and went back to the car. She had placed the vase in a tight little box so that they wouldn't tip over during the car ride. I was grateful to be out of there. The pressure of picking out flowers was harder than I thought. I let out a sigh of relief once in the car again. I typed the address of the club back into the GPS. "There," I said to myself. I had the flowers, I had my directions, everything was set.

When I pulled up to the club, only the red Corvette was sitting in the alley. Maybe it was just her there. Maybe William didn't ride with her. Doubtful, I thought to myself. He was always with her, just like Sarah and I. I grabbed my backpack and carefully grabbed my fifty dollars' worth of flowers. "I hope she likes them," I say as I walk up to the back door. I opened the door and put my stuff away in my locker. It was only 2 o'clock, I didn't need to get dressed for my shift yet. I stopped for a moment trying to listen for her. There was a weird sound coming from the bar. It wasn't the piano but it wasn't singing either. Was it a cello or violin maybe, I thought. I picked up my flowers from the floor and headed down the hall.

I was not prepared for what I saw upon entering the bar. The lights were all off except one spot light shining on the stage. She was dressed in a black ballet leopard with a light pink see through skirt and her hair was in a French braid going half way down her back. She was holding a violin, softly playing it and dancing at the same time. I stood there awestruck. She never missed a note. The way she moved with the music was so fluid and graceful. I wasn't sure what song she was playing but I didn't care. I could have stayed in this moment forever.

Now that the lights were all off and the sun was shining, I could see that at the tops of the building there were stained glass windows near the roof. The way the colors danced off her skin was breathtaking. I noticed her eyes were closed. How did she know where she was without falling off the stage? She obviously had done this before. I quietly placed the vase of flowers on the bar top making sure not to disturb her. I stood there leaning next to them waiting for her to finish the piece she was playing. She slid the bow across the violin with such ease.

The last note echoed through the building. *Do I clap?* I thought. She stood there standing with her bow held up in the air breathing heavily. She wiped the sweat from her brow then turned to face me. She stopped quickly when she saw me standing in the dark. "What are you doing?" She placed her violin back in its case that was resting on the piano. With the tablet that was next to it she turned the bar lights on. I was sad to see the prism of colors disappear from her face. She sat down on the stage and unlaced her ballet slippers.

"I'm sorry. Sarah said you called and wanted me to come in early." Had I disturbed her? Should I have waited longer before showing up? My mind started racing. "Is Will here?" I rushed to say. She shook her head as she finished taking her shoes off. She stood up again then made her descent down the stairs. "He was going to get a ride in with one of the others. It's just us here." She stopped a few feet away from me. My heart began pounding. *Just us*, I thought. She smirked. "You wanna get me a bottle of water please?" She pointed towards the mini fridge behind me.

I turned around to grab one for her. "What's this?" She said, referring to the flowers. I froze. Please don't be mad, please don't be mad, I pleaded in my head. I slowly grabbed a bottle then stood up again with my back to her. "Helianthus," she said. "What?" I had no idea what she was talking about. She had her hands around the vase now. "Helianthus," she continued, "they're sunflowers. My favorite". Her favorite. I would have jumped for joy if she hadn't been standing right there.

She leaned in to smell the rose. She sighed as she breathed out then looked at me. "Sucking up to the boss, huh?" She smiled jokingly. "I'm afraid, flattery will get you nowhere with me, my dear." She grabbed the bottle of water out of my hand and started walking back toward the stairs. My heart sank. Did she not like them? She stopped halfway up the stairs, "are you coming," she said. It surprised me. I quickly followed her up on the stage. What was she going to do? She sat down at the piano and placed her hand next to her on the bench, inviting me to sit by her. My heart quickened again. I'd never sat so close to her before.

"Can you read sheet music or do you just play by ear?" She questioned me. I thought about her question for a minute. "Both. I took lessons as a kid then eventually became good enough to hear somebody start a song then I could pick up playing where they left off." She looked impressed. "What about singing?" My anxiety was starting to take over again. Playing in front of people was one thing, singing at the same time was another. I think she could sense my fears then lifted the cover over the key and began playing. It was 'Don't Stop Believing' by Bon Jovi. The way her fingers flew over the keys was miraculous.

She began singing, "just a small town girl, living in a lonely world. She took the midnight train going anywhere..." she continued playing and nodded her head at me to join in. I took a deep breath and began playing along with her. I started to quietly sing too, "just a city boy, born and raised in south Detroit. He took the midnight train going anywhere..." We continued to play together. "Good," she said, "louder now, feel it in your core!" The next line in the song came and she harmonized with me. We were now both playing and belting out the lyrics.

My fingers were dancing as fast as they could go trying to match her every note. I was at home. There was no place I'd rather be than sitting right here beside her. We were nearing the end of the song now when she stood up but kept playing. She stopped singing first then let go of the keys. "Keep going!" She yelled encouragingly. I did as she said. I couldn't have stopped even if I wanted to. She stood behind me then placed her hands on my shoulders. A sudden wash of pride came over me. She thought I was good enough to keep playing by myself. I ended the song and sat there quivering. She leaned down pressing her soft cheek into my stubbly face. "I knew you were capable of great things," she said quietly then removed her face from mine. Now I really wished I had shaved before coming here.

She took her hands off my shoulders, sending a shiver down my spine. We gotta get this girl some gloves or something, she must have really poor circulation to be this cold all the time, I thought. She walked back around the piano and opened her violin case. She pulled out a piece of paper. "Could you play these?" I read over the long list of songs she had typed up for me. I knew most of them but they were a few I'd have to listen to a few times to get the hang of it. "Do you have a pen on you?" I said. She motioned towards her outfit stating the obvious that she had nowhere to put one.

I rushed off the stage to the bar to grab one. I put a checkmark beside every song I knew then added a few more at the bottom of the page. She slowly followed me to the bar. I handed her the list once I was finished. She looked it over. "I could work with this, you wouldn't have to sing all of them if you didn't want to. I'd just need to let the lead singer know which ones you preferred before you performed tonight."

She started to walk away from me. I stuttered, "t-tonight? What's happening tonight?" She looked back at me, "you're playing tonight. That's what I told Sarah to ask you. Didn't she tell you?" Sarah you little shit! Had I known I probably would have just flat out told her no but now, I'd already checked the list and even made suggestions.

I started hyperventilating thinking about all those people sipping on their drinks listening to me play. I couldn't do that. I can't just play for an audience every night. On the one hand, I'd love to play more, on the other the fear of not being liked was a big possibility. Isa could tell I was spiraling and walked around the counter to me. "Hey," she said softly, "I won't make you do anything you're not comfortable doing. I just thought since you were so talented maybe you'd like to use your talents for some extra money." She clasped both her hands around one of mine

Instantly I started calming down. "Extra money?" I said, intrigued. Her brilliant smile glistened across her face. "Yeah, I pay the band members two hundred and fifty dollars a night and they only play for five hours. You could tend bar part of the night and play the rest." I liked the sound of that. Was that really the only thing she was going to ask me though? Couldn't she have just sent that in a text? Either way, I was delighted with the time spent alone with her.

"I'll do it," I said, gripping my other hand around hers. She looked down at our hands then pulled hers away quickly. What was that about? I thought. She put her hands behind her back now. "Uh, why don't you start practicing the list I gave you. I'm gonna go change in the back." I nodded my head. We parted ways, she was headed to the dressing room and I was headed for the stage. As I made it up the stairs I saw the bar curtain swishing out of the corner of my eye. I looked back to see she had taken the flowers with her. I smiled then sat down at the piano to practice for my upcoming show.

For the next two hours, I practiced all the songs on the list until I felt confident enough with how they performed. This was going to be great. I was really going to make Sarah proud by taking initiative for once, even if she did have to trick me into it, which I was still upset about. Isadora returned from her dressing room wearing a low sitting pair of dark wash jeans and a black long sleeve shirt with buttons down the front. Even though she had more clothes on than before, I was catching myself staring at her midriff. I thought to myself how funny it was that the sunflower was supposedly her favorite flower but judging by her pale complexion that she herself didn't spend much time in the sun. I chuckled out loud at the thought. "Something funny?" She asked when she came back on stage to get her violin case and her ballet slippers. Uh oh, I didn't want to seem like a jerk for making fun of her fair skin but there was nothing else I could think of saying to justify my laughing.

"It's nothing," I stammered, "it's just that, you said you liked sunflowers yet you're so pale. I'm sorry that's dumb." I looked away ashamed. "You're right," she said, "It's very ironic, isn't it." She wasn't upset with me? She continued, "It's just like my name, Isadora. It means 'gift of the goddess Isis' referring to the Egyptian goddess. She was known as a powerful entity that resembled life, rebirth, and healing. She was also known for her roles as a nurturer and protector." Was she giving me a history lesson now? "But how is that ironic?" I asked her, puzzled. She shrugged her shoulders and stuck her thumbs in their pockets. I could see her hip bones when she did this. I had to look away from her. I didn't want to get myself too riled up. "It just means that I will do whatever it takes to protect those I deem close enough to be family and defend them from anything harmful. That's all."

She turned her back to me and walked off the stage. She was still barefoot. More often than not did I catch her without shoes on. I wonder if her feet hurt from doing ballet all the time or maybe from wearing heels every night? I brushed it off and continued to practice. Each song I played sounded better than the last. It was all coming back to me, my love of music. I thought I buried that part of my life with Auntie Mary. She would be so proud of me doing this. She'd have been here every night in the front row cheering me on.

Every once in a while I could hear her singing along as I played. If I stopped playing, she stopped singing which was really frustrating. I really wanted to hear her sing some more. After playing for two hours straight I decided to take a break. When I turned to get off the piano bench she was standing right behind me. She startled me and I almost fell off. "You snuck up on me," I said, had she been wearing shoes maybe I would have heard the tap of them on the floor and wouldn't have been so jumpy.

She grinned, making her eyes sparkle. I loved it when she did that. She backed away so I could resume standing up. I stood there in front of her looking her over head to toe. She wiggled her toes at me. "Hey, my eyes are up here," she says with a smile. I look her in the eyes. "How come you're always barefoot?" I ask her, pointing at her feet. She seemed surprised by my question. "You noticed that, huh?" I looked away sheepishly. "Yeah, you seem to always have your shoes off when I see you." She walked around me and onto the center of the stage. "I prefer to be barefoot. It helps me be able to feel the vibrations through the floor." She went up on her toes and spun around in a circle.

"Why don't you dance barefoot then?" I asked, intrigued. She stopped spinning and looked at me again. "Because I wouldn't be able to stand all the way up on my toes for long. You've seen me dance, why don't you try it?" She motioned for me to join her. I hesitated for a moment then went to her. I used the piano to steady myself as I took my shoes off. *Do I keep my socks on?* I thought. I decided to keep them on. She did a pose then waited for me to mimic her. She stood on her tiptoes then swung her one leg behind her almost kicking herself in the head. Did she want me to do that too? There was no way I could do that. She waited for me again to copy her. I did my best but I couldn't manage to get my leg half as far as she did.

She giggled. Now she put her hands on her hips and put one foot on her knee while the other foot remained on her tiptoes. This I could do. I did as she did. "Very good. Now how about this?" She took a few steps away and started lightly jumping, flitting her feet back and forth. She did this for a few seconds then spun around and dropped down into the splits. I'll try, I thought to myself discouragingly. My feet thumped as I jumped up and down. I did a little spin then chickened out on doing the splits at the last second. "Nope!" I said, fumbling my footing. I slipped and fell on my butt instead. "Ow," I said embarrassed. She crossed her legs, put her elbow on one knee and placed her head in her hand. "Not so easy, is it? "She said, staring at me.

I shook my head, "no, I guess not." I started stretching my legs, maybe that would help. "Ok, so I can't do ballet but I'll bet I'm better at gymnastics than you." I taunted her. She stood up now holding her right hand out to me. "Perhaps," she said as I took the help up. I stood

66

there holding her hand. I just wanted to clasp my fingers in hers. She pulled away before my thoughts could turn into actions. Dang, so close. She started to make her way across the stage. She seemed a bit flustered. Did I make her feel uncomfortable?

There was a knock on the front door. I jumped at the sound. She quickly darted across the club to reach the doors. She unlocked one then opened it. There was a young man standing at the door holding a box of pizza. She took out some cash from her pocket and handed it to him, took the box, and shut the door again, locking it behind her. She had ordered pizza? "Hungry?" She asked, sitting down at a table near the bar. I suddenly realized that breakfast was a long time ago. I put my shoes back on then went down to join her. "I got the everything pizza but it seems they forgot to keep the jalapeños off for you." Jalapeños? Why would I not want jalapeños? I looked at her confused. "Why?" I asked. She grabbed a napkin and handed me a slice. "Because of what happened last night. You couldn't handle my spicy soup." My stomach dropped.

Of course she was referring to last night. How could she not, I probably spent a half hour in the bathroom after we got to the house. That was thoughtful of her to think of me and try to prevent it from happening again though. "Oh yeah, thanks," I said weakly. "How do you know it wasn't just food poisoning?" She swallowed a bite on her pizza, "because, Will just ordered what we always get and I always ask for extra spices in my soup so they just brought you that." That made sense. I thought it was a little spicy, but it was really good.

"So you like really spicy things I guess," I said, picking off the jalapeños from my piece of pizza. She nodded then covered her mouth as she chewed. "The hotter the better," she says. We continued eating our food at the table. I was really hungry but didn't want to look like a pig in front of her so I stopped after two pieces. She raised an eyebrow at me, "you're full?" I leaned back in my seat pretending that I was. "Maybe I overestimated you. Will made it seem like you could eat more." She took another piece of pizza.

Was she going to eat the whole thing? I'd never think she could eat all that. She stared at me as she took another bite. Was she challenging me, I thought? I grabbed another piece and started eating it. We both began eating our pizza as quickly as possible. There was one piece left. She grabbed it first but before she could bring it to her lips I stood up and lunged my face towards her hands. I managed to take a bite before she did. Her eyes grew wide. What came over me? Never in my life had I ever done anything like that before.

I stood there holding the pizza between my teeth, she was still holding on to it as well. She blinked twice then released it. I didn't know what to do. She sat there, eyes locked on mine. I could feel my mouth salivating so I swallowed hard, making a gulp sound. She burst out laughing. I grabbed the pizza and placed it on my napkin. She was still laughing when she said, what was that? Did your animal instincts kick in?" She had tears in the corners of her eyes. I smiled and started laughing too. Her laugh was so infectious.

She stood up grabbing the empty box off the table and brought it over to the garbage bin behind the bar. I finished the last slice of pizza then wiped my face with a napkin. Now I was full. I couldn't eat another bite. "That was great," she said, catching her breath. "It's been a long time since someone caught me off guard like that." She wiped the moisture from her eyes. I smiled at her, "well that's good, at least I'm good for something." She looked back at me with a concerned look on her face, "who told you otherwise?" I wasn't prepared for that question. I looked down at the floor not wanting to make eye contact with her.

"Well my parents just up and left Sarah and I when we were little and then we were bounced around from place to place in foster care until we aged out. I guess I've always thought I could never do anything right." It was sad to think about. I don't usually let people see me this vulnerable but there was just something about her that made me wanna tell her everything. I was sitting on a barstool facing away from her now. She walked around to be in front of me. I looked up at her with a solemn look in my eyes. Her eyes matched my own.

"I have a similar tragic backstory. Maybe I'll tell you about it sometime." She placed one hand on my cheek petting my face with her thumb. What was she doing? My heart rate quickened as she touched me. I placed my hand on top of hers. I wanted to kiss her so badly at that moment, it seemed to last forever. "If there's anything you need, just let Will or I know," she took her hand away, "you and Sarah are part of our family now. And families look out for each other."

She started to walk back behind the bar to exit through the curtain when a lightbulb switched on in my head. "Eviction notice!" I said loudly. She turned back around waiting for me to continue. "Sarah and I are being evicted unless we pay what we owe by Friday plus this next month's rent," I paused waiting to see what she'd say but she stayed silent. "I was wondering if maybe you could pay us in advance so we didn't need to worry about it?" She crossed her arms and bit her lip, thinking long and hard about how she was going to respond.

"Tell you what, you do good the next couple of shifts and maybe we could work something out. How much do you need?" I was afraid to give her the grand total. "Let's see we're two months behind, plus next month's rent, equals $4,500." I shuddered at the amount of money I just asked for. Her eyes grew wide. "That's a lot of money, Adam. That's going to be at least two full weeks' worth of work plus tips for both of you." She was right, but what other choice did we have? "Let me think about it and get back to you on Wednesday next week since we aren't open Sunday through Tuesday. How does that sound?" She asked. That sounded great. I walked over to her with my hand out and we shook on it.

Chapter

6

Shortly after we shook on it Ben, William, and Lexa showed up for their shift. "What's going on?" Will said looking at our hands joined together. Isa pulled away first. "Nothing," she said a little flustered, "we were just making a deal." She quickly walked up to him and began ruffling his hair. I'll admit, I got really jealous of him. Why does she always do stuff like that with Will? Occasionally, I would catch her stroking the side of his face with the scar too. *Platonic my ass*, I thought. They were way too close to be like brother and sister. What did he have that I didn't? Her, that's what it was.

I pushed past their seemingly innocent interaction and made my way to my locker. I might as well get ready if our time alone was done. I grabbed my backpack and shoes then headed for the bathrooms. The four of them were whispering when I returned through the curtain. They stopped once they saw me. What were they saying about me? I continued on my way to the restroom, agitated about the whole situation. I threw my bag down and bed and began undressing. "So stupid," I grumbled to myself. If they were going to talk shit about me, the least they could do was say it to my face.

I had everything on but my bow tie now. Did I really have to wear it? I didn't want to ask William for help again. I shoved it in my pants pocket and made my way back to the bar. William was the only one standing there now. Lexa had gone to get ready and Ben was taking out the trash. Will smiled at me as I made my way to the bar. "Congratulations man," he caught me off guard. I stood there looking at him confused. "On your gig. Izzy just told us the news, that's awesome man." So it wasn't anything bad they were saying about me I guess. I nodded. His shoulders slumped, that wasn't the reaction he was hoping for. "What's the matter?" He asked. I shrugged my shoulders. It was dumb to be jealous over something that wasn't mine to begin with but I couldn't help it.

I thought we'd shared a moment up on stage and then again when I told her about my past. Was there nothing I could do to change her mind? Sensing my hostility, he changed the subject. "I saw the flowers in the dressing room. Nice move." He was grinning ear to ear now. I looked down as smirked. "How'd you manage to know what her favorite flower was?" He asked genuinely intrigued. I hadn't though. The lady had just suggested them to me and I could afford to buy them, that's all. I couldn't just tell him that though, so I came up with a good lie. "She's always so cold. I thought she could use a little warmth in her life," that was good, I'd buy that. He laughed and shook his head, "you're so full of shit," he said. I laughed too, being caught in my own lie.

"You're not wrong though," he continued, "she is cold and always seeks out the warmest things. Makes her feel more alive." What a strange thing to say. He stopped what he was doing after he said that last bit and looked at me. I nodded my head. I thought I caught him in a sigh of relief. What had he said to make him do that? I grabbed a rag and started washing down the counter with him. Next I went up to the piano and wiped it down too. I wanted it to look extra shiny for my performance tonight. I was a bit nervous. What if the people didn't like me? How was I supposed to compete with Isa after the way she performed last night?

I couldn't get her out of my head. Everything I thought about came back to her. I washed the piano, I thought of us doing a duet together. I looked at myself in the mirror behind the expensive liquor bottles, I saw her eyes staring back at me. I took down the chairs off the tables, I pictured the two of us fighting over the last piece of pizza. She was my everything and everywhere all at once.

Before long Xander and Sarah showed up. I could tell Sarah was in a good mood. She had done her hair and painted her nails, probably trying to impress Xander. What more did she need to do? She already went home with him. She was wearing her uniform minus the shoes, "what's got you in such a bad mood?" She asked, noticing my sour expression. I wasn't necessarily in a bad mood but I wasn't exactly happy either. I ignored her. She brushed off my attitude and continued talking, "I finished my paper then Xander took me out for lunch. He took me to that little diner on fifth, it was so cute…" she continued talking as I walked away. I needed to get some air.

I quickly left the club out the back door, I just needed some space from all her mushy talk. I walked over to the Camaro and leaned on its hood. I took in a few deep breaths. Why was I so angry? He already told me there was nothing going on between them but from the way they acted together I just didn't believe it. I contemplated going for a drive but didn't want to be caught in traffic this late in the day. Sarah burst through the door followed by Xander. "What the hell was that?" she shouted at me making her way over to the car. I sighed, "I needed to get some air. That's all." she wasn't buying it. "Bullshit, what's your problem? You were all happy and chipper this morning and suddenly now you're acting like a complete asshole! What happened?" I looked at her. "Isa offered me a job playing every night for a few hours." Her face showed confusion and she crossed her arms, "So, you don't want to play every night then?" she asked. "No, that's not it." She rolled her eyes at me, "then what is it? Something's bothering you and I'm not leaving until you tell me what it is!"

I placed my hands behind my head and let them rest there a while before answering her, "I'm in love with her Sar. I am completely in love with her but I'm driving myself crazy because I think William is in love with her too." They both looked stunned. Xander slowly turned around and went back into the building without saying a word. "Great, I'll bet he's going in there right now to tattle on me." Sarah made her way over to the car and sat next to me. "Are you sure you don't just have a crush on her? I mean, you've only known her for three days, Adam." I shook my head, "I can't explain it. I want to be with her all the time. I wanna do everything I can to make sure she's happy. Every time she leaves, I start to long for her to be around me again. I love Isadora Sarah, and I hate that at the end of every night, she goes home with him instead of me."

I put my arms down now sighing heavily. It felt nice to say it out loud. She linked her arm into mine and rested her head on my shoulder.

"Why didn't you just say that then?" I could tell her feelings were hurt. I didn't normally raise my voice at her. I shrugged, "you were having such a good time with Xander, I didn't want to be a burden on you. I'm sorry." I leaned my head on top of hers. "We'll figure this out," she said, squeezing my arm. I nodded my head in agreement.

The back door opened with a sudden bang. It was William looking rather upset. Oh, great, I thought. Now what? He made his way over to us. The three of us stood there in silence. "Can I please speak to your brother alone, Sarah?" She looked at me, waiting to let her leave. I nodded at her. He waited to say anything until she was fully in the club. "Do you got a problem with me?" He said flaring his nostrils. "No," I said, "it's not a problem with you, it's about you." He waited for me to finish. "It's the way she acts around you. It just makes me so mad when I see her touching you and she wants nothing to do with me." My fists were balled ready for a fight if they needed to be. "You think she has feelings for me?" he asked. I thought about it then answered, "Yes, why else would she be stroking your face and touching your hair or talking about you all the time!?" I was yelling at him now. My blood was boiling. I was really hoping he would try to take a swing at me just so I could release some pent up rage I had for him.

Will looked at the sky for a minute then placed his hands on his hips. He started slowly chucking then turned into straight hysterical laughter. I stood there, fists ready to go and he was just laughing. Did he think I was bluffing? He looked at me then took a step forward. I quickly took two steps back. He stopped and smiled at me, "obviously, she didn't tell you everything about me because I think we'd be having a little different of a conversation if she did." What was he talking about? He stretched out his arm at his sides and said, "I'm gay!"

My eyes shot open wide and I dropped my hands. "You're what?" I said dumbfounded. "Gay. And I've been gay my whole life." He put his arms down and took another step closer. I did not see that coming. I sat back on the hood of the Camaro. Gay, I thought. He joined me on the hood now. "Like I said before, anything between Izzy and I is strictly platonic." I couldn't hardly manage a sentence, "but, the face thing?" I motioned on my face what she did. "She knows how self-conscious I am about my scar and traces it all the time to let me know it doesn't bother

her." I demonstrated ruffling my hair, "And the hair?" He brushed the curls off of his forehead, "she told me I need a haircut." Had I just been assuming all this time? Was I actually fighting over the affection of a girl with someone who had absolutely zero interest in her? "Ok, what about the pet name thing?" This ought to be good I thought. "Yeah, that one is a little harder to explain," he agreed. "She calls all of us honey, sweetie, and dear. She basically took us all in so now she's assumed the motherly figure of our little band of orphans. That's all."

I couldn't believe what I was hearing. I had been so wrong about so many things. William placed his hand on my shoulder. "I'm sorry I thought you were lying to me about having feelings for her." I hung my head ashamed. "It's no big deal. You didn't know. Besides, if it makes you feel any better I'm not attracted to you at all." He slapped my back and started laughing again. I smiled, that did make me feel a little bit better, "it doesn't bother me that you're gay either. Whatever makes you happy I guess."

I felt better now after hashing it out with Will, he really was a great guy. "Are we good then?" He asked, holding out his one hand. I shook it, "Yeah, we're good." There was just one small matter left of me professing my love for Isadora in front of Xander and my sister. Hopefully neither of them would tell her until I mustered up the courage to do it myself. "What did Xander say to make you come out here?" I asked him cautiously. "He said something along the lines of 'you need to set him straight' and 'he's really riled up.'" I gave a silent sigh of relief. "Oh, and that you're madly in love with Izzy." He gave me a side eyed glace when he said this.

My pulse quickened. Oh, no. Now he knew too. Was he going to tell her? "Don't worry, I won't tell her. I'm sure she can tell all on her own." I froze. What did he mean by that? I looked at him, horror in my eyes, "is it that obvious?" I questioned him. He shrugged, "no, but you sure stare at her a lot." I started turning red. "And you do that too," he pointed to my face. Doesn't everyone blush when they see the person they're secretly attracted to, or was it just me?

We both got off of the car and made our way to the back door. I let him go in first then I followed. Everything was ready to go by the time we got back in the club. Tables were ready, the bar was stocked, lights were shining on the stage. I put my hands in my pockets remembering I still didn't have my bowtie on. William had already walked away to go see if the band needed any help setting up. I held the red fabric down at my side looking around to see if there was anyone else that could help me. I feel someone start tugging on the tie, carefully making it slip out of my fingers. I turned around to see who had done it.

Isa was standing there holding my tie between her fingers, "lose something?" she said with a smile. I felt lighter than air as I smiled back at her. "Need some help?" she asked. I nodded, feeling my cheeks starting to get warm again. She walked around the counter and sat on one of the stools, I guess it was so she could be tall enough to tie it. She carefully put the fabric behind my neck and began tying it. She leaned in close to me as she was doing so with her brows scrunched. Was she having a tough time? "There," she said, tugging the bow tight. It choked me a little but I didn't mind it. She brushed her hair behind her back letting her scent waft through the air. I closed my eyes, breathing her in. All of a sudden, she booped me on the nose.

My eyes shot open as she did this. "It's never gonna happen, sweetheart," she said, hopping down from the stool. Stunned by that comment, I followed her. "What's not gonna happen?" I said. She kept walking down the hall toward the dressing room. She looked back as she walked, "You and I," she said pointing back and forth at the two of us. "Why not?" I said. She stopped when she reached the door, looked down, and sighed. "I know you have feelings for me," she said without turning around. My heart began pounding. I was so nervous I felt like I could faint.

"I appreciate the affections you hold towards me but I cannot reciprocate them." She turned around with a sad look in her eyes. "I can only ever be a friend to you, please try to understand that." My heart sank, but I wasn't going to give up that easily. "Ok, how about, as friends, we go out sometime?" She tilted her head to the side. "Adam I," I cut her off before she could turn me down. "Just hear me out, if I can do a whole night of playing and singing, would you at least entertain the idea of going out with me?" What was I saying, a whole night? I wasn't even sure how tonight was going to go.

She thought long and hard about my offer then smirked, "fine. If you can perform one whole night, no band, just you and the piano, maybe I'll consider it. You have until Wednesday to keep your end of the bargain." I stuck out my hand for her to shake on it. She hesitated for a moment then placed her hand in mine. I wanted to pull in for a hug but decided against it after remembering her saying she doesn't like to be touched. She let go then entered the dressing room closing the door behind her. I stood there in the empty hallway silently rejoicing in my small victory.

She agreed to go out with me, well, she'd consider it. That was as good as a yes in my book. I couldn't stop smiling as I reentered the bar. Everyone looked at me as I did so. William came up to me first, "so what happened?" I decided to wait to share the good news until Sarah made her way across the room. "Is she mad? Are you fired?" Sarah's face was fraught with worry. I scowled at her but only for a moment. I shook my head, "no. She agreed to go out with me." Both of them looked surprised, especially William. "Well, technically she said she'd consider it, but that's good enough for me." I smiled again, triumphant in the situation. "All I have to do is play the piano and sing by myself by Wednesday next week."

Sarah was the first to burst my bubble, "but Adam, that means you only have today to practice in front of a live audience." I hadn't thought about that. We were closed Sunday, Monday, and Tuesday so my next day to perform would have to be Wednesday. She tricked me, I thought. She knew I wouldn't be ready by then. I started to turn around to head back towards her dressing room but Will stopped me before I could. "Let's not have a repeat of last night," he said, looking me dead in the eyes. I winced then stayed where I was. How was I supposed to practice before Wednesday? The thought had never crossed my mind, I was so preoccupied with asking her out.

William must have noticed the panic on my face and said, "You know you have a key to this place right?" I did? "What are you talking about?" I asked. "The keys for the Camaro, there's a key to the back door on it because those are my keys." I reached in my pocket and pulled out the keys. "Which one is it?" Noticing there were multiple choices, he reached out and grabbed the keys. "This one," he said, holding onto it.

I carefully took the key off the ring and positioned it closest to the car key, that way I could distinguish which one was for the door.

The lights flickered signaling to everyone that we were about to open. I made my way back behind the bar with Will. Ben and Xander stood by the doors and Sarah and Lexa stood by some tables in the middle of the room. Isa came out on stage and nodded her head at Xander letting him know it was time to open the doors. Everyone was wearing their white tops with black bottoms including Isa.

She looked stunning in anything she wore. The doors opened up and a wave of people started pouring into the bar. The realization dawned on me that I would actually have to be up on stage shortly. My anxiety began to kick in. I hoped that I'd be able to remember all my practice earlier today. I began serving drinks waiting for Isadora to call me on the stage. The place was busier tonight than it was yesterday. I started to feel uneasy about playing when Will tapped me on the shoulder, "You're gonna do fine. Just play like no one's watching." His words of encouragement seemed to help a little.

Finally when people were seated and the band was all ready for me Isa beckoned me towards the stage. "Good luck," Sarah whispered as I walked past her. Thanks, I was going to need it, I thought. I tried to loosen my bow tie that seemed to be choking me still. "Good evening ladies and gentlemen. Tonight will be the first night of our very own Adam Christinson making his debut playing the piano. Enjoy!" Isa started clapping after she introduced me. I stood there at the top of the stairs waiting for her to exit. She came over to me and loosened my tie. "Thanks," I said, taking a big breath in. "Knock 'em dead, sweetie," she whispered, walking past me on the stairs.

It made me blush when she called me sweetie, only now I knew it was just a nickname she gave everyone. I didn't care. At that moment in time, she was just talking to me. I looked out at the audience, most people weren't even looking at me but the few that were watching were watching me intensely. I suddenly began to feel dizzy and quickly sat down on the bench. Isa had retyped the list of songs I would be playing and put it on the piano for me. Thank you Isa, I praised her in my head.

I looked at the band and nodded my head. The drummer clapped his sticks together counting off the beats before we started. I placed my fingers lightly over the keys waiting for my turn to come into the song. We were playing *I Want You To Want Me* by *Cheap Trick*. An ironic choice of song I might add for this particular situation. I hummed along with the lead singer. He sounded pretty good but not nearly as good as Isadora. I kept playing then glanced out in the audience. People were singing along and dancing and just plain having a good time.

Then, I spotted her. Way in the back of the bar just inside my line of vision. She was dancing along to the beat singing the song lyrics, "I want, you, to want me," over and over again. She stopped dancing and looked me dead in the eyes and winked at me, then continued dancing. What was she trying to do, make me mess up? I had to look back at my hands to make sure I was playing the right notes. Luckily I was and finished out the song with the rest of the band. Everyone clapped and a few people whistled including Sarah who had stopped waiting tables to make sure she gave me one hundred percent of her attention.

The night continued as planned, I played every song with the band, even the ones I wasn't sure how they would play, I trudged on. After four hours my hands and wrists were starting to get tired. I knew I shouldn't have practiced so long this afternoon, I thought kicking myself. Just one more hour and I'd be done. Sarah brought me up a bottle of water between songs while we were all taking a break. "How's it sound out there?" I asked, taking a sip of water. "You're doing really great. I'm so proud of you." She gave me a hug while I was still sitting at the piano bench. "And besides," she whispered quietly in my ear, "Izzy can't keep her eyes off of you." She giggled then bounced off down the stairs.

She was watching me, this whole time? The sudden sense of stage fright emerged again. I frantically searched the crowd for her face. There in the back of the bar stood Isa just waiting for me to start playing again. Her silvery blond hair seemed to glow in the low light. I could see her mouthing the words, "Just breathe." I took a deep breath, and let it out. When the band started playing again I was a little off for the beginning but finished out strong. My nerves were shot by the time Isa yelled 'last call.' The band members congratulated me on my great first night and said they couldn't wait to play with me more in the future. That raised my self-esteem up big time.

After last call and everyone was starting to exit the building, I slowly made my way down from the stage. My neck and lower back were killing me. I was not used to playing for this long anymore. My fingers were cramping up too. I grabbed a clean rag and took a handful of ice out of the trough behind the bar. Placing the cool rag on my hands they started to feel better. I sat on a stool icing my fingers when Lexa and Ben came up behind me. Lexa gave me a quick hug, "good job up there tonight!" She said excitedly. "Izzy told us you'd be playing all by yourself next Wednesday, I can hardly wait." Ben just nodded his head and said "good job." I'd noticed he didn't say much to me or anyone for that matter. He mostly just talked to Xander and Lexa.

Sarah was next to congratulate me on my performance. "I can't believe you played all night long. That was amazing!" The compliments everyone said made me feel really good. Finally, Xander and Isa shut and locked the front doors. "You crushed it man!" Xander hollered from across the bar as he came walking closer. Isa said nothing as she slowly followed behind him. She seemed annoyed at something. What was wrong, I wondered.

She made her way past everyone and headed down the hallway. I wanted to follow her to ask her what was the matter but everyone had crowded around me now. William wrapped his arm around my neck in a playful choke hold, "I knew you could do it," he said, rocking me side to side. I reached for a rag to start washing the counter after he released me. Everyone else dispersed to do their own end of the night duties. Will and I cleaned the bar and washed glasses, Sarah and Lexa washed the tables and threw away any trash, then Ben and Xander followed behind them putting the chairs up and sweeping the floor. I bagged up the trash when they were finished and headed for the back dumpster.

When I got outside I saw a black car sitting in the alleyway close to the Camaro. I stopped to see what they were doing. They didn't move. After a while, I threw away the garbage bags and headed towards the car. I was within yards of the car when they hit the gas flinging rocks at me. I put my hands up to cover my face. They sped off down the alley and onto the next road. "What was that all about?" I said wiping the dust off my clothes. I turned around to head back inside when Isa burst through the door.

"Are you alright?" She said panting heavily. She looked worried. "Yeah, I'm fine. He just flung some rocks at me." I started walking towards her. Her eyes grew wide and I felt something hot trickle in my eye. I rubbed it thinking it was just sweat. When I looked at my hand, I saw a streak of blood. One of the rocks that hit my face must have cut me. I continued walking towards her. She looked horrified. "What's wrong?" I said, concerned. She turned her head to the side and yelled, "William!" Never taking her eyes off of me.

He came running to her side. "What's the matter?" He said, trying to evaluate the situation. She pointed at me, "he's hurt," her finger shaking as she did so. He looked at me then gasped. What was the big deal? So I got a little cut, who cares. He held up his hand motioning for me to stop. "Stop!" He yelled. I did as he said. "Lexa, we need you!" He hollered wrapping his arms around Isa. She clung to him tightly. What was going on? I thought. Lexa and Sarah quickly made their way to the back door.

"You're bleeding! What happened?" Sarah said running to meet me. Lexa hurried back inside then returned with a first aid kit. "Some assholes we're sitting in the alley then flung rocks at me with their car when I tried to approach them." I could see William whispering to Isa trying to bring her back inside. "What's wrong with her?" I asked Lexa who was now wiping my head with an alcohol wipe. I winced at the cold stinging feeling. "It's the blood, she feels faint at the sight of it." Lexa told me. William had now picked up Isa and drug her in the building out of my sight. "Is she going to be ok?" I asked concerned. "You're the one bleeding and you wanna know if she'll be ok?" Sarah scolded me.

Lexa finished cleaning me up then put a bandage on my head. It was just a small cut, nothing too serious. Ben and Xander were standing in the doorway now watching. I sure hope Isa is ok, I thought. The girls did a once over, making sure the rest of me was alright. When they were both in agreement I tried to make my way back into the club, but to my surprise neither Ben or Xander would move for me. "Excuse me." I said, trying to push through the door. The girls followed behind me, "what's going on?" Sarah asked. "Izzy's sick and wants everyone to just go home," Xander said, crossing his arms.

"I better go in and check on her," Lexa said, making her way past Xander. How come she could go in but I couldn't? This was ridiculous. I tried to push past him again. This time he held his enormous arms out across the doorframe. "What's your deal, can't I at least get my stuff?" I said frustrated. Ben left then promptly returned carrying my backpack and Sarah's duffle bag. He handed them over, "now go home, we'll see you next week." Tugged on Xanders' shirt signaling for him to shut the door.

They shut the door on Sarah and I, still standing outside not quite sure what just happened. I went up to the door and tried to open it. They had locked it. I began pounding my fist on the door, demanding that they let us back in. "Adam," Sarah called trying to soothe me, "let's just forget about it and go home." She walked over to the Camaro and waited for me to stop. After I calmed down a bit, I joined her by the car. I unlocked the doors and we got in. We sat there in silence for a few minutes before either of us spoke. "Did you happen to get the license plate number before they drove off?" she asked me in a quiet voice. No, I hadn't even thought about that, why would I? I shook my head. I was gripping the steering wheel tightly now out of frustration.

"What just happened?" I asked out loud. Sarah shrugged her shoulders and shook her head, "I have no idea." I put the car in drive and left the club. Something didn't feel right about leaving everything for them to finish up for us. I hardly did anything tonight. I tended the bar for a little while with William then I played the piano. I hoped Isa would be alright, I didn't know she would feel faint just looking at a little blood. I touched my forehead where Lexa placed the Band-Aid. It hurt a little but not a lot.

When we pulled up to the apartment I could feel my exhaustion kicking in. I had had a busy day full of stressful social interactions, I was ready for sleep. Sarah took her heels off once we got in the building and we began the three story climb up to our apartment. When we reached our floor Sarah got her keys out and unlocked our door. She headed straight for the bathroom to take her makeup off and I headed for the lumpy old futon that was calling my name. I was almost asleep when she came out of the bathroom. "Goodnight," she said as she walked past me. I waved my hand at her.

I decided I needed to take my work clothes off before going to bed. I took them off and threw them in my hamper next to the bathroom door, pulled out a clean pair of basketball shorts and put them on. Once again I laid back down on my futon, ready for sleep. I heard a buzz from the clothes basket. "Damn it." I got up again and retrieved my phone out of my pants pocket. 'One new message', it read, "What now?" I whispered, opening the text. 'First of all, I'd like to apologize for startling you with my behavior. I just don't handle blood very well. And lastly, I wanted to let you know you did a phenomenal job tonight. I can't wait to see how you perform on Wednesday.' Winky face.

I sat up after realizing it was Isa who had texted me. I responded to her, 'that's alright. How are you feeling now?' I waited with anticipation for her to message me back. Suddenly my phone buzzed again. I could hardly contain my enthusiasm. 'I'm fine now that I'm home. How about you? That seemed like a nasty little cut you got.' I turned the camera on my face and took a picture of the band aid on my head to send to her. 'I'll survive. It's nothing too serious,' send. Again I waited for her response. I could see the little bubbles at the bottom of my screen pop up indicating that she was replying. I turned my volume on so I could hear it in case I dozed off. 'Ding!' She had responded. I opened the message to see that she had sent me a picture as well. She was laying on a red comforter in a white tank top with her hair flowing all around her. She was so sexy, my heart began racing.

The message read, 'ouch, looks small enough it probably won't scar.' I wrote back, 'yeah, probably not.' I was trying to think of something clever to say back to her. 'Do you have any scars?' I sent her. I hoped she wouldn't take offense to me asking something so personal. She responded, 'only in places you can't see' ;) Was she teasing me again? I couldn't tell if she was being serious or not. 'What's that supposed to mean?' I asked her.

It took her a little time to reply to my last message, I thought maybe she fell asleep. 'Ding!' I quickly looked at it, 'it means that the only way you'd be able to see them is if I took my clothes off...' That did it. She was flirting with me and I didn't know how to flirt back. A thousand thoughts started racing through my head. I couldn't stop picturing her half naked in the dressing room at the club. I couldn't recall seeing any scars on her body, then again I didn't really take the time to get a good look at her.

Was she trying to turn me on? Because if so, it was working. 'Ding!' She had sent me another message. I opened it up warily. It was another picture, she was winking and sticking her tongue out at me. I smiled. She didn't know how hard she was making it for me to stay laying on my stomach on the futon. I shifted my weight to relieve some of the discomfort I was feeling. 'You're beautiful,' I replied to her. The bubbles didn't show up on my screen.

Oh shit, should I not have sent that? I frantically tried to come up with something else to talk about. Her family? Where she's from perhaps? I nervously waited to see what she was going to say. The bubbles reappeared. I breathed a sigh of relief, thank goodness, I thought. 'You don't mean that. If you only knew how unbeautiful I actually was.' My heart sank, she couldn't actually believe that could she? 'Yes, you are. I think everything about you is beautiful, from the way you do your hair to the way you dance and play the violin at the same time. You're beautiful to me,' send. I hoped it didn't come off as corny as I made it sound but she needed to know how deeply I cared for her.

The minutes seemed to pass by painstakingly slow and still no response. I decided I should probably go to bed. I checked the time, 3:19am. I had been waiting close to a half hour now. She must have fallen asleep. I turned the volume off and laid my phone down on the floor then covered up with my blanket. I closed my eyes hoping sleep would come easily. I heard my phone start buzzing again, this time someone was calling me. I answered the phone, "hello?" I answered quietly. "Do you wanna go for a walk?" she asked me.

"What?" I said, checking to see who I was talking to. I saw Isa's face winking back at me. I had set the last picture she sent me as her contact photo. I flung the blanket off me as I sat upright. "Where are you?" I asked her. She giggled, "Down by the car." I quickly looked out the window in the living room. There she was leaning up against the Camaro. "Why? What are you doing here?" I could see her holding her phone smiling. "I wanted to see if you wanted to go for a walk." She waved at me. I ducked down in the window so she couldn't see me. She laughed again, "but if you're already ready for bed, I could just leave and go back home…" I jumped up again, "no! No, I'll be right down."

I hung up my phone and started rummaging through my dresser. I found a clean pair of gray sweatpants and a black sweatshirt. I grabbed my sneakers and a pair of socks and headed out the door with my keys. I ran down the stairs barefooted. The floor was cold under my feet but I was so full of adrenaline I hardly felt it. I could see her through the door now, my ears started getting red remembering our conversation earlier. I opened the door and walked out to her.

She was wearing a red flannel button up and a pair of jeans. She was sitting against the side of the car. She smiled when she saw me shut the front door. I grinned at her too. Why was she here though? I walked up to her and held out my elbow for her to hold onto. She raised an eyebrow at me then took my arm. I couldn't believe she was here right now, I was on cloud nine.

We walked in silence for the first few minutes. Her hair swayed as we walked. I couldn't take it anymore, I had to ask her, "so why'd you come here so late?" She thought about it for a second, then answered me, "because I was awake and I knew you were awake too. Besides, you wouldn't want me walking alone would you?" She squeezed my arm a little tighter. It was nice being just the two of us walking together. "And what would you have done if I said, no?" She shrugged, "probably just went home again and went for a moonlight swim." A swim, this late in the year? That was insanity.

"So…is there anything in particular you wanna talk about?" I asked her trying to wrack my brain for ideas. "We don't have to talk if you don't want to," she said tilting her head up to look at me. There was so much I wanted to talk to her about but I didn't know where to start, so we just walked. "Oh! Where are you from?" I finally said. "Western Europe originally but I've been living in the U.S. for years." That was vague. "What about your family, do you have any siblings?" She loosened her grip on my arm. "That's a little bit of a touchy subject. I had a sister once, but I don't anymore."

I felt bad for asking her such a personal question. I wonder what happened to her sister? I didn't dare ask her though. "How about something simpler? Favorite flower, favorite color, favorite drink?" She pondered over the question. "I like the color black, I will drink almost anything, and you already know that my favorite flower is the sunflower." I was still stuck on the fact that it was her favorite flower. "But why?"

She stopped walking. She looked down at her feet then looked up at the sky. "Did you know that the heads of sunflowers follow the sun? They seek out the warmth and when there isn't any sunshine they look to one another to be each other's sun." She looked at me to see what my answer was. "No, I didn't know that. That's really neat." We resumed walking. "How far are we going to go?" I asked, noticing we'd already walked a few blocks. "However long you want to walk I guess.

She grabbed my arm again as we walked. I was still wondering why she was here though. I didn't want to make her mad but I just had to know. I took a chance, "so why are you really here, right now, with me?" We made it to a cross section and she started pulling me back towards the apartment so we started walking back. I saw a little bench and led her to it so we could sit down. Her hands were in her lap and she was looking down as she twirled her thumbs. She spoke softly, "I wanted to make sure you were ok after getting hurt tonight. I heard the car but wasn't quick enough to warn you to back away from it before you got hit." It wasn't her fault but she still blamed herself anyway. I wanted to put my arm around her shoulder. Do I dare? I thought.

I slowly stretched my arm out and placed it on her shoulder. She turned her head to look at me. "Is this ok?" I asked. She half grinned then leaned her head on my chest. My heart was beating so fast now I'm sure she could hear it. I leaned my head onto hers. This was nice, I could have stayed here for hours just sitting there with her. A gust of wind hit the back of my neck and I shivered quick. "Aren't you cold?" I asked her. "Not as long as I'm next to you." She said, placing her one hand on my knee. The pitter patter of my heart was beating so loudly in my ears now.

I wonder if she'd let me kiss her? I didn't dare push my luck. We sat there a few more minutes until another gust of wind blew some of her hair in my nose causing me to sneeze. She patted my knee and stood up. "Come on. Time to get you home before you catch your death of cold." She held out her hand to help me get up. I took it but didn't want to let go. Sensing this she wrapped her fingers around mine. Her velvety hands seemed to fit perfect in mine. They were so cold at first but seemed to warm up the longer I held onto them.

We walked along in silence again making our way back to my apartment building. "You know, this doesn't count as our date right?" I tried to chuckle. She pet my hand with her thumb, "I know," she said dazzling me with her eyes, they seemed to sparkle in the dim lit street lights. We finally made it back to the front doors of my apartment. Now was the time to pluck up my courage and just kiss her. "We should do this again sometime," I said smiling now. She smiled back and said, "I'd like that." She let go of my hand and turned to go back to her car that was parked behind mine. "Wait!" I said. She stopped and looked at me. Kiss her! My head was screaming at me just to do it.

I held my breath as I quickly walked over and wrapped my arms around her body. She stood there frozen for a second then I could feel her begin to relax. She lightly put her arms around my waist. I spoke barely above a whisper, "I'll be your sunshine when it's dark outside." How cheesy could I be? I continued, "I'll be your warmth when it's cold." I held her a little tighter and rested my cheek on the top of her head. The smell of vanilla was almost overpowering now. She gripped the back of my sweatshirt when I said that last bit. We stood there for what felt like an eternity but I know it was only a few seconds.

She started to pull away and I released my hold on her. I didn't want to make her uncomfortable so instead of going for her lips I settled on kissing her forehead. She must not have been expecting it because she jumped when my lips touched her. I looked down on her after I'd done this. She stared back up at me, her mouth ajar. If I had more courage I would have given her a real kiss. She let go of my shirt now and put her hands on my chest. Could she feel how fast my heart was beating? I was sure she could.

She gave me a little smile then turned around to go back to her car. She whispered, "Goodnight," before she left my side. I whispered it back. I stood there on the sidewalk, watching her get in her car and drive away. I was smiling like a fool now. What just happened? She didn't pull away from my embrace. Does that mean she has feelings for me too? I put my hands in my sweatshirt pocket to keep them warm as

I went back to my building. I made the three flight walk up very slowly, trying not to let the moment end. I couldn't believe what just happened.

When I got to the apartment it was just as I left it. Sarah was sleeping in her room and my blanket was on the floor next to my futon. I changed out of my clothes and put my shorts back on. I plopped down on the couch and took out my phone. I stared at the picture of Isa laying on her bed. Then it dawned on me, her house was at least an hour away from mine. How did she get here so fast? She must have taken this picture and immediately got in her car and drove here. That was her plan all along, to come see me. I rejoiced at my new found epiphany. She wanted to see me.

I laid my phone down on the floor and covered up again. I placed my one arm behind my head and said, "What does this mean?" Out loud. My head was spinning with all the possible scenarios that could have gone on tonight. She held my hand and she let me hold her. What if she was going to kiss me and I ruined the moment by kissing her head? I couldn't think about that now. It was too late. I just kept imagining the way her body felt next to mine. It was like we were made for each other. I was just tall enough to rest my head on hers and she was just short enough to be able to reach her arms around my waist.

Then it hit me, was I too excited when I was holding her? Was that why she jumped when I held her closer to kiss her forehead? Oh my god! How embarrassing. I hoped I hadn't scared her off with my over enthusiastic bulge in my pants. I knew I should have worn jeans. They were tighter and concealed things better. I clapped my hand over my eyes. How could I have been so stupid? No wonder she put her hands on my chest, she was trying to politely push me away from her. I was so embarrassed. How was I going to face her on Wednesday?

I grabbed my blanket and pulled it over my head. I was laying on my stomach now. The more I tried to sleep, the harder it was to get comfortable. I couldn't stop thinking about her. Finally I decided sleeping on my side would be more successful, that way nothing got pinched or bent. My phone buzzed. 'Go to sleep Adam.' ;). Oh shit, she knew. I contemplated texting her back but decided just to let it be and try to get some sleep. Eventually sleep found me and I passed out from exhaustion.

The next few days seemed to pass by slowly. I had a key to get into the club to practice but couldn't bring myself to go there. I was still too embarrassed to go there just in case she happens to be practicing herself. What would I even say to her? Sorry, I didn't mean to poke you with my boner, god, what an idiot. Sarah took the car to school and worked at the care facility everyday. By the time Wednesday rolled around my nerves were shot.

I hadn't talked to Isa since the night of our walk. Was she mad at me? Do I try to text her to find out? No, I thought. It was better just to bite the bullet later that night at the club. I dropped Sarah off at school, she said Xander would pick her up later to bring her to work. She knew something was bothering me. "What's up with you?" She said. I hadn't told her about my stroll with Isa. I didn't want her to think I was trying to sabotage my chances for staying employed there. I also hadn't mentioned the deal Isa and I made about getting the money for rent. She had enough on her plate, I wanted to take care of something for a change.

"It's nothing. I'm just nervous about tonight, that's all." She didn't seem convinced but shut the door and went into the building anyway. I drove away trying to figure out what to do with the rest of my day until I needed to show up for work. I contemplated going in to practice, but she was sure to be there waiting for me. Maybe I would just go home and try to take a nap before I had to go in. No, there's no way I'd be able to sleep either. I ended up just driving around town for a few hours to pass the time.

I circled the club checking to see if her car was there, it wasn't. Now's my chance to practice, I thought. I pulled in the alley and shut the car off. I already had my backpack with my uniform ready in the car. I grabbed it and made my way towards the door. I hesitated when I got to the knob. I gave it a turn to see if it was open or not. "Locked," I said with excitement.

I got the keys out and unlocked the door. Everything was dark when I entered the building, only the red emergency exit sign lit my way. I turned on the flashlight function of my phone, then put my stuff in my locker. Walking down the dark corridor, I began to feel uneasy. What if William had just dropped her off and she locked the door after she got here? I went back to check out her dressing room. The door was shut so I knocked on it. Nothing. Slowly I turned the handle and peaked inside. There was a large mirror at the opposite end facing the doorway. I jumped when I saw myself in the reflection. Nope, she wasn't here yet. I quickly made my way into the bar. On the counter plugged in was the tablet that controlled the lights and the sound system. I unplugged it and took it with me up the stairs of the stage. I turned the stage lights on low so there was just enough light for me to see the piano.

The sun wasn't shining today, I was sad to not see the colors dancing across the room from the stained glass windows. I sat down on the piano bench and started practicing for my upcoming night. I thought I would start off with something slow. "How about *Can't Help Falling In Love* by *Elvis*?" I said to myself. My fingers began playing the keys softly, and I started to sing, "Wise men say, only fools rush in…" I couldn't help but picture Isadora dancing while I played. I'll bet she knows this song on the violin and could accompany me playing it sometime. I kept playing until the song ended.

The last notes echoed throughout the empty space. A crack of thunder sounded, startling me. Great, now it was raining. Maybe that would mean there would be less people tonight, after all, who wanted to stand outside in the rain before entering a club? I continued practicing a few more songs then decided I should write down what I was going to play for this evening. I got up from the piano and went down to the bar. William kept the new notepads under the counter for the girls to write down drink orders.

I sat down at the bar with a pen and paper trying to rack my brain for ideas. All I could think about playing was sappy love songs. Maybe people wouldn't mind that, I thought. No, I better come up with a more diverse list than that. I threw in a few love songs but mostly stuck to the classic bar songs like *Sweet Caroline, Low Rider*, and *Bohemian Rhapsody*. I hadn't planned on singing the whole entire night. Some of the songs I would just play and let the audience listen.

Checking the time on my phone, I realized it was after four. "Where is she? She should be here by now." I said looking around the empty bar. Not long after I said it, I heard the back door open and shut. I started getting nervous again about facing her after our little interaction. I waited at the bar for her to emerge from behind the curtain. To my surprise, William and Ben came through. They were both startled to see me sitting at the bar in the dark. "What are you doing? Shouldn't you be up there practicing?" Will said motioning to the piano on stage. "I was. I just came down here to write a list of what I was going to play tonight."

He looked impressed at how serious I was taking the whole thing. I wanted to ask them where Isa was but I couldn't bring myself to do it. I gave the tablet to Will who I could see was looking for it. He turned up all the lights and started getting to work. Ben was already taking down chairs and straightening them out. "You've been here long?" He asked, taking down another chair. I nodded, "yeah at least an hour now, why?" I asked. "Maybe the next time you come here early you could help out by taking the chairs down instead of just sitting on your ass doing nothing." Jeez, what was his problem?

"Don't mind him. He's just pissy that Lexa was going to ride with Xander so he had to come in with me," William said, scowling at Ben. Ben flipped him off then proceeded taking the rest of the chairs down. "What about Isa, couldn't he have rode in with her?" I asked curiously. Will stopped polishing the glass he had in his hand and looked at me, "Izzy's not coming in tonight." What, not coming? A new fear was unlocked, was I the reason she wasn't coming in today? "Why isn't she coming?" I asked frantically. Had she told him about coming to see me? I must have made her uncomfortable enough for her to not want to come to work today.

My head was spinning, trying to come up with a logical explanation why she wasn't here. "Relax lover boy. She takes a day off once a month and lets me handle things. It's got nothing to do with you." Phew, I hoped he wasn't just telling me that and that it was actually true. "Besides, she told me to wish you luck tonight." I grinned at the thought of her wishing me luck. I just really wanted her to be here after not seeing her in four days.

I went to my locker to grab my work uniform. Sarah had done the laundry on Sunday so my outfit was all cleaned and pressed. I put it on in the bathroom and attempted to tie my own bowtie. It came out looking like a crumpled up knot. "Oh well," I said. It's not like I was trying to impress anyone tonight. I wonder what she was going to do tonight since she wasn't here. I left the bathroom with my backpack and headed back to my locker to put it away. Sarah and Lexa were in the dressing room doing their hair after being caught out in the rain. I popped my head in to talk to them. "Can someone help me?" I said pointing to my tie. They both laughed and Sarah came to my rescue. We talked as she fixed my tie, "are you nervous?" "Not particularly," I said back to her.

It was true, without Isadora being here I wasn't so nervous anymore. "I'm sorry Izzy isn't going to be here for the show tonight, I know how much you wanted her to." I shrugged my shoulders as she finished fixing my tie. "Thanks, it's fine though. One less distraction right?" I chuckled, she wasn't really a distraction but more of an encouragement really. She promised to go on a real date with me if I performed tonight. Not only that, she said she'd help us out with your financial situation if I did it. There was a lot riding on tonight. I hoped Sarah wouldn't be mad when she found out about our deal. She probably would be a little upset but she'd get over it after a while.

I left her to finish getting ready. I went back to the bar to see if the guys could use any extra help. Xander was there now too. He was standing next to the door waiting for us to open. Both Ben and Will were behind the counter of the bar now. Something didn't feel right not having Isa here too. The atmosphere just wasn't the same. I wanted to text her and ask her just to come in anyway, but something stopped me.

I didn't want to come off as clingy, and that's exactly what she would think I was if I texted her now.

My phone buzzed in my pocket. I took it out and looked at it, there was a new message. I tapped on it to see what it said. 'Sorry I won't be there tonight. Break a leg.' ;) My heart fluttered and I smiled. I wish she could be standing next to me winking at me in person. I replied, 'thanks. I will.' smiley face. Then I put my phone back in my pocket. Both girls joined us in the club now, ready for their shift.

William called Xander over to have a short meeting before we opened. "As you know, I'm in charge this evening. Xander, you'll be at the door. Lexa and Sarah, you guys will be waiting tables and taking orders. Ben and I will be stationed behind the bar and Adam will be on stage playing all night. Does anybody have any questions?" He paused for a moment waiting to see if we had anything to say. We all shook our heads or stayed silent. "Ok," he clapped his hands together, "It's show time then ladies and gentlemen." He motioned for everyone to go to their designated posts.

I stood behind the counter next to Will while the others took their positions. The thunder rumbled again. Man it was really coming down out there. William looked up at the flickering lights. "If the power goes out twice we have to send everyone home," he said to me. I hoped that wasn't going to happen. A power outage was one thing, having a room full of dunk patrons in the dark was another. I was not looking forward to that if it happened.

Xander unlocked the front doors and opened them wide. There was a rush of people trying to get inside out of the elements. I helped make drinks for the first half hour then patiently waited to be called to the stage. Eventually things slowed down and Will gave me a nod. I made my way over to the stage. My heart was pounding. You're gonna do great, everythings fine. I took a few deep breaths waiting for Will to introduce me.

"Can I have your attention please?" The crowd quieted down a little bit. "I'd like to introduce, Adam Christinson!" He clapped after saying my name. I slowly climbed the stairs and made my way to the piano. I took out my little piece of paper telling me which songs I was going to play tonight. Do I introduce the song before I start? I thought. God

I wish I'd swallowed my pride and came in to practice days sooner. I should have texted Isa asking her what I was supposed to do beforehand.

I decided not to say anything before I started to play. I began playing 'Bennie And The Jets' by Elton John. The crowd started to cheer, a good sign I guess. Now was the time to sing, I looked over at the corner of the bar where Isadora once sat and watched me play. I sang out with all my might hoping I sounded alright. It sounded good to me, and apparently to the crowd too. They started singing along with me. "B-B-B-Bennie and the jets…" The whole audience sang along with me.

It was so exciting having the audience participate with me. I kept playing and singing until the song ended. Everyone cheered for me. I decided for my next song I was just going to play an instrumental version and not sing. I hoped no one would be disappointed in me. This went on for the next few hours. When I was in the middle of playing 'Piano Man' by Billy Joel, the lights shut off momentarily. I kept on playing, never missing a beat. I glanced over at William who was signaling to all of us that that was one, if the lights did that again we'd have to shut down for the night.

I could see the lighting flash across the sky through the stained glass windows. It wasn't going to be much longer now before the power went out again. I played for another hour and the lights shut off again. I finished playing 'Anyway you want it' by Journey then stopped when Will tapped me on the shoulder. He had a microphone in his hand, "Ok folks, you know the rules. The power goes out twice and we shut down for the night." The crowd started booing him. "I know it sucks, but would everyone please close their tabs and make your way towards the exit?"

People were grumbling as they paid their bills. I went down to help at the bar. When I got there, Ben handed me a large garbage bag. "You think you can handle taking out the trash this time?" He had that same annoyed look on his face he always had. I rolled my eyes, "I think I'll be fine." I took the bag and headed down the hall. I stopped by my locker to grab my leather jacket before going outside. The rain was letting up a little but there was still a lot of lightning.

I squinted making my way to the dumpster. Out of the corner of my eye I could see that black car again. What was their deal? I ran up to the car and knocked on the window. The driver window rolled down. A waft of smoke and booze filled my nostrils. I coughed, "what are you doing here?" The driver looked familiar. He took another swig of whatever they were drinking. He belched then answered, "We're just waiting for the blond slut who owns this place." Someone from the back laughed, "Yeah, we wanna have a little fun with her."

My blood started boiling, how dare they talk about Isa that way. I opened the trash bag and threw the contents inside the open window. A large man opened the driver door followed by three others opening the other doors. "What's your deal asshole?" he slurred his words as he talked. Suddenly I remembered where I knew him from, this was the guy that felt Isa up then she broke his wrist. He was still in a cast even. "You can't talk about her like that!" I yelled. All four of them were standing in a semicircle around me now. They all laughed at my comment then the one in the cast pulled out a large knife. I tried to back away. "And who's gonna stop me?" he said, slashing the knife at me. I reached my hands out in front of me to protect myself. I felt the blade cut my palm. I clenched my fist trying to stop the bleeding.

One of the other guys beside me grabbed the back of my jacket and hurled me to the ground. I winced as the gravel hit my face. I tried to stand up but another one started kicking me in my ribs. I doubled over in pain as they took turns kicking me over and over again. They wouldn't let up. Were they going to kill me? I thought. The pain in my side was starting to go numb from the repeated kicks. The rain kept falling down on me, causing the blood on my face to go into my eyes. I tried to protect my face with my arms. It wasn't working. If I exposed my face they aimed for it, if I exposed my mid section they kicked twice as hard. This was it, they were definitely going to kill me at this rate, or at the very least I'd succumb to my injuries. I tried picturing Isadora's face one last time before I blacked out from the pain.

"Get away from him!" A woman yelled. Was it Sarah coming to check what was taking me so long? They stopped kicking me. "You're next bitch!" One of the guys yelled. I heard a low growl then screaming. I tried to open my eyes but they were swollen and caked with blood and mud. I attempted to stand but could only manage to sit up leaning next to the guy's car. I could hear a commotion of footsteps and yelling. "This bitch is crazy!" "Get away!" and "Help!" It sounded like branches being broken. The rain drowned out most of what they were saying. Suddenly someone touched my face, I flinched at the cold touch as they tried to wipe the debris off of me. I managed to open my eyes to see who it was.

"Isadora?" I said weakly. She tried to help me stand up. She was able to do it in one quick motion. Wow, she's really strong, I thought. She led me to the silver Camaro and took the keys out of my pocket. She opened the door and set me inside the passenger seat. I could see a shadowy figure coming up behind her. "Behind you!" I managed to say. She turned around and kneed him in the chest. He flew backward towards his car.

She shut my door and walked around the car. When she got it she was panting. "Put your seatbelt on," she said through gritted teeth. I did so very slowly. Everything hurt to move. She put the car in drive and left the alleyway. "Call William," she had pressed the hands free button on the steering wheel to call Will. He answered, "Hello?" She brushed the wet hair off her face, "I did something, Will." She sounded panicked now. "What happened? Where are you?" He sounded just as frantic as she did. I looked over at her. She was soaking wet wearing a black long sleeve shirt with the shoulders cut out and jeans. I could see a large gash on her right leg, "you're bleeding!" I said trying to stop the bleeding with my hands.

"Who's bleeding? Is Adam with you?" William said through the car speakers. She shook her head and squinted like she was having difficulty seeing. "Yes, Adam's with me. He got jumped by those college guys I roughed up the other night." She had to be speeding with the way she was driving. She ran every red light along the way too. "Where are we going?" I said, still trying to stop her leg from bleeding. "William, I need to get home," she paused and covered her nose. "Will he's bleeding a lot." I was bleeding a lot? She was the one with a cut down to her femoral artery.

"You can do it, just take him to the house and we'll take care of the rest." He hung up the phone. "Shouldn't we go to a hospital or call the police?" I asked her. She burst out laughing. Her laughter gave me an unsettling feeling. "That's the last thing we should be doing," She said. We made it to her long driveway. She rapidly pushed the button before we got to the iron gate. It slowly opened when we got up to it. I was starting to feel light headed like I was going to pass out. My hand slipped off her leg onto the center console.

"Don't fall asleep, Adam. You can't sleep yet. We have to get home first." She grabbed my knee and squeezed. I jumped at the pain and she let go. "Sorry," she said driving down the twisty driveway past the lake. When we got to the house I saw her red Corvette parked next to the house. How did she get to the club so fast? I wondered. She parked the car and got out. She opened my door, leaned across me and unbuckled my seatbelt. I put my arm around her shoulder and she gently helped me stand up.

When she stood me up all I suddenly started feeling nauseous. I turned to the side of her and threw up. Great job Adam, add that to the list of embarrassing things you've done in front of the girl you like. She never lost her grip on me, it didn't even seem to faze her. "Sorry," I said as we walked slowly through the rain. She brought me inside the house and set me on the sofa. She quickly tried to back away from me but I wouldn't let go of her shirt. "I have to go Adam," she said through clenched teeth. Where was she going now? I let her go. She turned away from me and held her hands to her face. Was she alright?

I tried to stand to go to her, "are you ok?" I asked reaching out for her. She took another step away shaking her head. "Stay back!" She growled. What was going on? She quickly started undressing in front of me. I was too stunned to look away. Pretty soon she was only standing in her bra and underwear, then she took off running for the front door. "Hey wait!" I yelled after her. Why was she running outside in her undergarments? I followed her to the door. Once I got to the porch, that's when I saw a giant white wolf running away from the house towards the lake.

It had stopped raining now to reveal a bright full moon in the reflection of the water. I looked all around for her, "Isa!" I shouted into the night. The wolf stopped and stared. "Isadora!" I hollered again. Nothing, no sign of her. The wolf tipped back its head and howled then ran off into the distant trees. I could see headlights coming around the driveway. That must be William, I thought. I hobbled over to the porch swing to wait. When the car pulled up, William was the first to get out.

96

A second car was pulling in behind them. That must be Xander and Sarah, she's going to be pissed when she sees my clothes, I thought with a chuckle. It hurt to laugh.

William came running up to me, "are you alright? Did she hurt you?" I looked at him funny, "What? No, she didn't hurt me. I don't even know where she is now." My voice was gravely from being kicked in the throat. He looked around outside searching for her, I assumed. Lexa and Ben came rushing up the deck, "we'll get some clean towels and the first aid bag," she said walking right past Will and I. Ben followed her in the house.

When Xander pulled up the car was barely in park before Sarah jumped out of it to run to my side. "What happened to you?" she said tears streaming down her face. I tried to give her a smile but my cheek was so swollen I doubt she could even tell. "Those guys, did you call the cops on them?" I asked her. "What guys? There was no one around, all we found was pools of blood in the mud." she grabbed my hand. "I thought someone killed you!" Where did they go? I know for a fact I saw the car still sitting there when we left. Lexa returned with a bowl of hot water and some towels. "No, let's get him in the house," Will said. Sarah and Lexa helped me to my feet and brought me back inside to the sofa. Isa's pile of clothing was still sitting on the floor.

Xander looked at it then looked at William, "we'll be back," he said and then they headed back outside. Sarah carefully helped me get my jacket off and threw it on the floor. There were cuts and scrapes along my face and my ribs were bruised. Lexa gentility washed away the dirt from my face making it easier to see. I turned my hand over to show the large mark running across it. "What happened here?" Lexa asked me. I sighed, "the one with the broken wrist pulled a knife on me and cut my hand while I was trying to protect myself." She picked all the gravel out of the wound until she pulled out a piece of blue thread. "What's this?" She asked, examining it. "That must be from Isa's jeans. He cut her leg pretty deep and I tried to stop the bleeding." She froze, her eyes wide with terror. "You used this hand to apply pressure to her wound?" She motioned to my cut hand. "Yeah, I guess I did. I didn't really have time to think about being sanitary. She was bleeding really bad." Lexa handed Sarah some more towels and stood up.

She walked over to Ben who was just standing next to the fireplace looking out the big picture window. She frantically whispered something to him then they both looked at me. What was going on? What was the big deal? "Ow!" I said as Sarah squeezed my hand to get a tiny rock out of it. "Sorry," her face was genuine. She hadn't meant to hurt me. Tears were still rolling down her face as she bandaged me up. Before too long William and Xander returned, without Isa. "Did you find her?" I asked eagerly. "Yeah but she won't be back until morning." Xander said. William looked at Ben and Lexa, "what is it?" Lexa looked at me. "We have a problem," she said, "it seems they both got slashed by the guy's knife then Adam tried to stop her bleeding with his injured hand." Williams' eyes darted towards me.

"Please tell me that isn't true?" He said getting up in my face now. I couldn't lie, it was true, and so what? I nodded my head feeling a bit woozy. I felt like I could throw up again. Xander, quickly reading my expression, grabbed me a small bucked out of the nearby broom closet. I buried my head in the bucket and began puking. Sarah rubbed my back. "He needs a doctor! He could have internal bleeding!" She said. "Good, it'd be better if he died than if he lived." Ben joined in. Lexa hit him in the stomach. How could he say that? Sarah frantically looked around the room at everyone. "Better if he dies? What's going on here!?!" She demanded to know. "I'll tell you everything," Xander finally said, taking a step forward, "but we need to take care of Adam first." William nodded, "Let's bring him to the downstairs west wing bedroom. He'll have his own bathroom then." Xander walked over to me and picked me up like a child being put to bed.

We walked past the kitchen, down a flight of stairs, and through a long dimly lit hallway. William opened the door and turned the light on. The light burned my eyes. "Turn them off," I mumbled. He did as I asked. They placed me on a large four poster bed with dark navy blue sheets. They felt expensive under my fingertips. William emptied my bucket in the attached bathroom and washed it out. I laid my head on the pillow trying to stop the room from spinning. Should they really be putting me to bed? I could have a traumatic brain injury for all they knew. "Isa..." I whispered, "I wanna see, Isa." I tried to raise my voice but couldn't find the strength. Xander left the room to go back to Sarah upstairs. "Isa is fine. She's just outside. You don't need to worry about her." William put a damp cloth on my forehead. The cool moist towel helped me focus. "Is she...alright?" I managed to say. He nodded his head at me, "yeah man. She's just worried about you. Now, get some rest and we'll talk about it in the morning." He got up off the bed and shut the door locking it behind him. Why would he lock the door? I didn't care. I was too tired to care and too weak to move. I drifted off to sleep.

As I slept I dreamt about the wolf I saw. I dreamt I chased it all around the lake. It's silvery white hair reflecting the moonlight. I chased it down to the water. When I got close to it, it laid down like it wasn't afraid of me. I slowly approached it with my left hand. It dipped its head and let me pet it. As I stroked its soft fur, I noticed something red on its fur. The cut on my hand was bleeding. Not only that but it was burning. It burned with such an intensity that it felt like the only way to be rid of the pain was to cut it off. The wolf looked at my palm and licked its lips revealing its large pointed teeth. I took a step back clenching my fist hoping to deter the wolf from my blood. It stood up and walked closer. Slowly circling me.

But I wasn't afraid. There was something familiar about this wolf. I couldn't quite put my finger on it. It came closer and I stood my ground. It sniffed my hand. I slowly opened it to reveal the bloody gash. It licked my wound and suddenly all the pain went away. I stared deep in its eyes. The eyes were like two dark colored emeralds lost in a snowstorm. "Isadora?" I spoke, reaching out with both hands this time to pet it. The wolf sat down on its haunches and tucked its head into its body. I thought my eyes were playing tricks on me. Before my very eyes, this wolf shifted from a furry white creature to a girl sitting almost completely naked on the grass. Her long silvery blond hair was covering most of her body, she was still wearing the bra and underwear set I had last seen her in before she ran away from me. She looked up at me with tear filled eyes. What was she so sad about? I tried to touch her but she turned away from me. I reached out my hand for her to grab. I stood perfectly still watching, waiting for her to take my hand. She looked back at me, her eyes cold and distant this time. She reached her hand out slowly, then the white wolf lunged at me.

Chapter

8

I sat up gasping for air. I looked around at my surroundings. Where was I? The sun was shining in from an egress window. I was still in the blue room. How long was I asleep? I tried to roll over to check if there was a clock in here but remembered my severely bruised ribs. I held my side as I made my way to the bathroom. I looked at my face in the mirror. The swelling was almost all gone on my face and my ribs were all bandaged up. I was wearing a pair of blue flannel pajama bottoms and no shirt. Who changed me? I wondered. That didn't matter. All that mattered was finding out what the hell went on last night. I grabbed the matching blue robe that was draped in the chair next to my bed and put it on. "I wonder if it's still locked," I said looking at the door. I walked over to it and jiggled the handle. It opened. Great, now I just gotta find everybody. I used the wall to keep me steady as I walked along the hallway. When I got to the stairs I groaned, "This is gonna suck," as I pulled my way up.

After I reached the top, I could hear voices coming from down the hall. I could smell bacon cooking too. Breakfast time? I thought. I slowly trudged my way to where I could remember the kitchen was. There I was William frying eggs and cooking bacon by the stove, Lexa and Ben were sitting at the dining room table, and Sarah and Xander were sitting at the island. William saw me out of the corner of his eye, "hey, look who's finally awake? You had us worried for a while there. Come on in. Pull up a chair and eat something." He motioned to the smorgasbord of food displayed on the table. Muffins, hotcakes, hash browns, sausage, eggs, bacon fruit, coffee and more.

I made my way to the table. Sarah brought me a plate and some silverware. I looked over all my choices before grabbing a muffin. They were still warm, fresh baked this morning. I put it on my plate and used my knife to cut it in half then took a dab of butter and smeared it on the pieces. Everyone was watching me. I felt like an animal at the zoo. "What are y'all staring at?" I said taking a bite. They continued what they were doing. Will brought over the pan with fresh cooked scrambled eggs and put some on my plate. "Here you go," he said as he did so.

I played around with the eggs for a second trying to let them cool down before I tried them. I picked up a chunk of egg and blew on it. It had peppers and onions in it, my favorite. I quickly ate the entire plate. Sarah snorted, "Slow down bro, there's plenty more." I couldn't help it, I was starving. I grabbed a hotcake and drowned it in syrup. I kept eating everything in sight. Next was the sausage and hash browns followed by half a plate of bacon. Nothing seemed to be filling me up. Xander took another drink of his coffee, "looks like he's got the hunger, alright." William reached across the island and snapped him with a dish towel.

What did he mean, 'I had the hunger'? Of course I was hungry, I just woke up. And where was Isadora? I hadn't seen her yet. "Did they ever catch the guys who did this to me last night?" Everyone froze. Sarah got off her chair and made her way to me. She crouched down to make herself more eye level with me. She spoke softly, "Adam, that was four days ago. You've been asleep for four days now."

My mouth hung open. Four days ago, it was Sunday now? I couldn't believe my ears. I shook my head, "there's no way I've been sleeping that long. I remembered looking in the mirror downstairs, the swelling had gone down tremendously and my cuts were starting to heal. Has it really been that long? I thought. Then a terrible thought occurred in my head.

The apartment, our rent money Isa had promised us. If I had been sleeping this long we missed our deadline and now we'd be homeless. I frantically stood up from the table, "where's Isadora, I need to talk to her!" I demanded. Sarah stood up and placed her hands on my arm, "It's alright, she's fine. Nothing to worry about." I groaned, she didn't understand. "You don't get it, Isa and I made a deal about giving us the money for rent so we wouldn't be evicted." William stepped forward, "it's all taken care of," he said putting his arms out trying to calm me down, "we got all our stuff out before Friday and paid what was owed." I was dumbfounded.

"You took all our stuff, then where are we going to live?" My head was throbbing as I was yelling at him. "We're going to live here Adam. Izzy said there are plenty of rooms for us to choose from," Sarah tried to make me sit back down. I wouldn't budge. "You can even keep the one downstairs if you like. It's got a big sliding glass door so you won't even have to come in the front door if you'd like." She wasn't helping the situation. I placed my injured hand on my face. They were both hurting now. I hunched over in pain. Ben and Lexa quickly stood up and Xander rushed to Sarah's side ushering her away from me.

Did he think I was going to hit her or something? I would never do that. "You need to calm down Adam," William said. "Calm down? You want me to calm down? Where's Isa, I need to talk to her!" I demanded. Ben came up behind me and grabbed my arms and thrust them behind my back holding me there. "She's upstairs Adam, but first I'm gonna need you to calm down." I was really starting to get pissed off. I struggled for a little bit trying to free myself from Ben's grip. He wouldn't budge.

Finally I took a few deep breaths and I was able to relax. My shoulders returned to their normal positions and Ben slowly released his grip on me. I pulled my arms away from him when he had almost fully let me go. I could hear whimpering. Sarah had her face buried in Xanders chest as he had his arms wrapped around her. Why was she crying, nothing happened? I thought. I took a step closer to her but Xander pulled her away from me. I stood there confused at what just happened.

"She's all the way up the stairs and to the right," William said, "she's waiting for you." She was waiting for me? I nodded then carefully made my way past Xander and Sarah. She wouldn't even look at me as I walked past her. I made my way through the house looking at all the same weapons and trophies I'd seen the week before. I couldn't believe I had been asleep for so long.

The staircase was rather intimidating, it went up one floor, had a landing with some more rooms then continued upwards. I made the treacherous trek up the stairs. By the time I got to the first landing, I needed to stop to catch my breath. My ribs were still sore from being kicked the other night so it made it rather difficult to breathe. I held my side as I continued up the stairs. Eventually I made it to the top. There was a long corridor with one door on the left and one on the right.

I tried the handle on the left door, locked. I made my way towards the door on the right. The handle turned. I paused for a moment to make sure my robe was tied and knocked. "Enter," I heard her say through the door. I opened it to find a large master suite. There was a loveseat and chair at one end of the room and a large vanity and bench on the other. At the far end of the room was a large canopy bed with red satin sheets on it. The drapes around the canopy part of the bed were also red satin that flowed all the way to the floor. Next to the loveseat was a set of glass French doors that were opened wide. I could barely see her standing out on the balcony through the sheer white curtains blowing in the breeze.

I shuffled in the room and shut the door. I made my way past the loveseat and headed towards the open doors. She was sitting on the railing wearing a long white sundress. It was flowing out underneath her legs and feet. I stopped to take it all in. Then it occurred to me, I'd only ever seen her in the dark or in the club. I'd never seen her in her sunshine before. Her hair shimmered in the breeze as she slid off the railing and walked over to me.

"How are you feeling?" She said, placing her right hand on my cheek. The cool touch on her hand seemed to ease me. I put my hand on hers and tilted my head. "I'm fine now," I sighed. She took my hand and led me to the couch. She sat me down then she went to the armchair sitting beside it. She crossed her legs and folded her hands in her lap. "We need to talk," she said. I could see a light colored marking on her right thigh before she adjusted her dress. She caught me looking at her leg, "Wanna see it?" She lifted her dress to the side to reveal a long line. It didn't even look like she had been cut there, it was just a scratch. I looked her in the eyes confused. She fluffed her dress covering her leg again.

"What do you remember from Wednesday?" I sat there trying to piece together what had happened. "I went to work, played until we had to shut it down because of the power flickering off, I went to take the garbage out, then those guys that were harassing you the week before were there and they attacked me after I told them not to talk bad about you." She nodded her head, "what else? Do you remember anything after they attacked you?" Her eyes were narrowed now. I couldn't remember anything, it was like the whole rest of the night was dark.

I did however, remember her taking her clothes off at one point, I looked away and started to blush. "I remember we somehow ended up here and you took your shirt and pants off then you ran off outside. Where did you go?" I asked. She leaned back in the chair and bit her lip. "I know you saw me, out by the lake. You called my name." I couldn't recall seeing her, the only thing I could think of was my dream of the white wolf down by the water. I shook my head, "no, I don't remember that. I just had a weird dream after William put me to bed." She stood up and walked a few paces away from me. "But it wasn't a dream, it was real Adam. You came looking for me after William shut the door. You must have found the patio doors and left your room. I was sitting down by the water and you found me there."

I was starting to question her sanity. I hadn't left the room, William made sure of that by locking the door. "But in my dream, all I saw was a wolf sitting by the water?" She looked away, then back at me, "Adam, that wolf was me. I was the one sitting down by the water." I couldn't believe my ears. What was she saying? "What do you mean, 'that wolf was you' that's impossible!" I raised my voice now, my head was throbbing again and the room started to spin. She took one step closer then hesitated, "Adam, I'm not what you think I am." She took another step closer, "none of us are…including you now."

I stood up and walked towards her, "what are you trying to say?" I demanded. She reached out for my injured hand and began unbandaging it. "I've been alive for a long time, and in time I grew to be lonely so I found others alone like me to make up our little family." The bandage was off now and she traced over my now healing scar. "First there was William, then we found Xander and Lexa and lastly we took in Ben. All of them with the same abilities and myself being the original." She paused and wrapped her hands around mine. "They are all werewolves, and soon you will be too." I started laughing. What else could I do? Her face was still so serious.

"And I'm a vampire Adam." I was doubled over with laughter, "you a vampire? There's no such thing." I put my other hand on top of hers and shook them. "That's great, making fun of the guy with a possible concussion." I started to walk back toward her bedroom door. In a flash she was there before me. I stopped laughing, how did she move so fast? I thought. She put her hand on the door, not letting me get to the knob. "Move please?" I asked her. She shook her head, "not until you accept that I'm telling the truth!" she shouted at me, her eyes were fierce now, growing with such intensity. I crossed my arms, ok two can play at this game, I thought. "Ok, so you're a vampire. How come you can go out in the sun then, huh?" I was taunting her and she knew it. "Because I'm not just a vampire. You think I haven't learned how to go out in the sun after a thousand years?" she stepped away from the door. "Fine, if you don't believe me why don't you go ask the others then?" she got up in my face as she said this. "Maybe I will!" I shouted back at her and reached for the door knob.

I hurriedly made my way back downstairs to try and talk to the others. They would make sense of her weird accusations. I could hear crashing and banging sounds coming from behind me. Was she destroying her own room? When I finally got to the bottom of the stairs I was met by Will. "So, I take it, she told you then?" I rolled my eyes, "not you too." I said. He looked at me puzzled. "You can't possibly believe that what she's saying is actually true? You're just trying to pull a fast one on me." I said. I began looking around for Sarah. "Sarah?" I called as I walked away from the stairs. "What do you mean, it's not true? Of course it is, why else would she have told you?" William said.

I heard a loud thump behind us. It was Isa. "Go ahead, let him go," she said. How did she get down here so fast? I didn't even hear her on the steps. I turned back to William. His look on his face was skeptical, "she's out on the porch," he pointed. I stared at Isa as I made my way toward the porch. She had her arms folded with a smirk on her face. I got to the front door, it was already open. Sarah and Xander were sitting together on the swing.

"Sarah, please tell me you're not buying into this werewolf vampire talk?" She looked at Xander then back at me. "It's true, Adam." I was stunned, they were all crazy. "They really are werewolves and Isadora is a vampire. They're telling the truth." I swiftly walked over to Sarah and grabbed her arm. "Come on Sarah, We're leaving." When I pulled on her Xander shoved me away and snarled. "What the hell man?" I yelled as I caught my footing. "She's not going anywhere!" He yelled back at me, standing defensively in front of her.

"She's my sister, get away from her!" I tried to get around him but he was quicker than me. He pushed me back again. I balled my fists, ready for a fight. "Enough!" Isa said coming between us. Lexa and Ben came out to see what all the commotion was about. "Will someone please give me a straight answer?!" William came forward, "we will," he said looking around at everyone standing there. He walked out onto the lawn, he was joined by Ben, Lexa, and Xander. All four of them stood in a line on the grass.

I stood there watching them, "is something supposed to happen?" I snidely remarked. Sarah was standing next to me and hit me in the side. I winced at the pain after she did it. I stared at them, waiting for something to happen. Instantly, one by one, they began to hunch over. Their arms began stretching and growing fur. Their faces transformed into long snouts with canine-like features. Their backs arched as tails manifested themselves on their backsides. Before I knew it, I was face to face with four wolves. The one where William was once standing had a very distinct scar across its face with reddish brown fur. Where Lexa had been standing was an ashy gray colored wolf with the one next to her being her brother, was a larger darker variation of her fur. And on the end where Ben stood, was a solid black wolf with gray undertones.

I wavered and Sarah caught me. "What the fuck?" I muttered under my breath. They all moved in a semicircle formation then either sat or laid down. I felt something touch my hand. I looked down to see Isadora trying to place her hand into mine. "How could this be?" I said to her, grabbing her hand tightly. She was telling the truth. They were all werewolves. And Isadora was supposedly a vampire. She looked at me with a somber expression. "It's a long story." she said, pulling me back towards the house.

I was a little hesitant to leave Sarah alone with them but judging by his new appearance, I was no match for Xander. The dark gray wolf sauntered up to her and placed its head upon hers. She began stroking its fur with both hands. How could she be so calm? I thought. Isa led me back downstairs to the room I had been recovering in the last four days. She closed the door behind us and directed me towards the bed. I sat down, eyes wide. My brain was still trying to wrap around what I had just witnessed. My heart was beating out of my chest.

She gently stroked my head as I stared off into the distance. If she was a vampire, and they were werewolves, why did she say that I was one of them now? She wiped my face, apparently I had a tear trickling down my cheek. She held both my hands now, they were starting to shake. "Adam, I want you to know, I never intended for any of this to happen." I looked at her face. I could see the pain in her eyes as she spoke, "I couldn't just let them kill you the other night." Another tear streamed down my face, "how?" I tried to control my erratic breathing. "How come, you said I was one of them now?" She turned my scarred hand over and moved her dress to reveal the long scratch on her thigh. "You see, I can only turn into a wolf on full moons, such as that night. And when you thought you were helping by stopping my bleeding," she placed my hand over her thigh, "You actually contaminated yourself with my blood." She spoke softly and clearly, "now on the next full moon, you will be able to transform into a wolf just like them." I started hyperventilating, I clutched my chest trying to stop it from happening but it was too late.

She stood up and quickly walked to the bathroom to get me a glass of water. When she returned I shakily drank the whole thing. I closed my eyes and tried to calm myself down. She stood back trying to let me have my moment. After a few minutes and many deep breaths, I was able to open my eyes again. She never left my side. "I'm ok," I breathed. She sat back on the bed next to me. There was still one thing I wasn't sure of though. "So, if you're a vampire, do you drink blood?"

I wasn't positive if I wanted to know the answer to my question. She looked at her feet, "yes." My heart sank, was I just food to her then? "But I never kill anyone to feed and I'm disciplined enough that I can go years without it." I suppose that was supposed to make me feel better, it kind of did. "Can you turn into a bat?" I asked her. She laughed her beautiful laugh at me and smiled, "I guess I could, but that has nothing to do with me being what I am. That's more of a spell or incantation."

Magic? She could do magic too? I sat there mulling over my new found information.

She put her hand on my knee, "you can ask me anything and I'll do my best to explain things to you without overwhelming you too much." I grabbed her hand again, it made me feel better holding her hand. She smiled. I had about a million different questions but where to start? "So magic is real?" I asked sheepishly. She smiled again, "Yes, magic is real and I'm very good at it actually." I stared at her mouth trying to examine her teeth. I wonder if she has fangs? I thought. She caught me staring and opened her mouth. I got a little closer then her upper canine teeth grew longer and more pointed. I jumped back, startled by what I saw. They shrunk back to normal size and she shut her mouth. She was a fascinating creature to behold.

I asked her another question, "do you sleep during the day then, is that why you can't sleep at night?" She smirked at my excitement. "No, I rarely sleep because I have such vivid night terrors. I only sleep once every few months or so. Otherwise I wake up screaming and don't get any rest anyways." That was awful, I felt so sorry for her. "Ok, here's another one, how old are you, really? I mean you look to be around twenty-five but how long have you been that age." I hoped I hadn't offended her with my age question. She laid down on the bed and sighed, "Now that's a tough one. Let's see, the truth is, I don't exactly know how old I am." She stood up again and began untying her dress. "What are you doing?" I asked, turning away from her.

"It's fine," she said, "don't be such a prude," she giggled. She took her dress off and put it on the bed. She was just wearing her bra and panties now. "Do you see them?" she asked, I did a quick glance. "Yep, very nice, now put your dress back on." I resumed looking at the wall. She laughed again, "not them, these." She grabbed my chin and forced me to look at her. She was standing practically naked in front of me. I looked over her body carefully. She was covered in light purple and white scars.

How had I never seen them before? I reached out towards the one around her neck but stopped myself before touching her. "What happened there?" I asked, "I was hanged for killing livestock in the dark ages." She pointed to her legs, "and this is when they burned me at the stake for witchcraft in the 1600's." The pattern on her legs resembled flames. I pointed to a mark on the left side of her chest, "and that one?" She looked down, "stake through the heart in the fourteenth century."

Were all these scars moments in time when she should have been killed? I wondered. I just stared at her now not saying anything. She placed her hands on her hips and cleared her throat, "my eyes are up here," she said. My face turned red and I looked away from her again. I felt around on the bed until I found her dress and handed it to her. "Now, don't take this the wrong way," I said after she finished getting dressed again, "but why didn't you die any of those times?" She walked around the bed and opened the big drapes on the wall revealing the patio doors that were facing the lake. She stared out the windows when she spoke, "I did. Every time I died something kept bringing me back. And it's harder to kill me each time. Death by fire, immune to fire now. Death by drowning, I swim like a fish." She looked back at me now. "How long have you known the others?" I gestured towards the door behind me. "I've known Will the longest since the late 1800's then we met Xander and Lexa in the early 1900's and Ben joined us not long after Xander and Lexa. They all have similar stories of how they came to be wolves." I wanted to know everything about them too.

"What really happened to Will's face?" I asked her. Her shoulders slumped and she looked guilty as she told me what happened. "It was a full moon one night and I haven't fed in ages, I saw a young boy playing outside, an easy kill, and I attacked." I remembered Will telling me that he was attacked by a wild dog as a child, I never could have imagined that that dog was her. She turned around and lifted up her long hair revealing a little divot on her right shoulder blade, "you see that?" I nodded, "that's where Will's father shot me with a musket."

I laid down on the bed spreading my arms out. She sat on the edge of the bed next to my feet. There was so much information floating around in my head I could hardly keep my eyes open. I wanted to ask her more questions but I didn't want to bother her. "Do you have anything else you want to ask me?" She seemed to be leaning towards one thing in particular but I didn't know what it was. I shrugged my shoulders. "Is there anything else to ask? You've pretty much given me the low down on everything so far. What else is there?" I asked. She scooted closer to me on the bed, "You, she said. "What about me?" I asked her curiously. "You are now going to become a werewolf." I sat upright. I hadn't thought of that yet.

"How does that work?" I asked with a terrified look in my eyes. "It's simple really, for the next month your senses will be heightened. Your vision will grow sharper, your muscles more defined, your sense of smell will be able to pick up the tiniest of details, and when the next full moon rises you'll transform into a wolf." My senses would be heightened? I was scared. "Will it hurt, transforming I mean?" I said I was worried. "It can be quite painful your first time but other than some mild discomfort you should be fine." She placed her hand on my forehead, now it all made sense why she was always so cold. She was a vampire after all. Her cool touch felt good on my skin.

She brought her lips up to my forehead, "What are you doing?" I barely spoke above a whisper. She pulled away from me, "I'm helping draw down your fever. My touch has healing abilities." she said. Then why didn't she just use her hand instead? I thought. I didn't want to say it out loud for fear she might not do it again. I wanted her to kiss me but I'd prefer it on the lips. She pulled at my robe strings, untying them and revealing the bandages around my abdomen. She started to undo them while I tried to keep them on. "Come on, I need to take a look at your wounds, are you going to let me help you or not?" Her voice was stern but gentle.

I sighed and stood up. Taking off the robe carefully, I suddenly realized I was just wearing a pair of pajama pants and boxers. How did I get into these? Did Sarah dress me while I was asleep? I thought. She carefully unwrapped the bandages then placed them on the bed. She then knelt down and began placing her hands all over my body. She started at my waist then slowly worked her way up to my ribs then my neck. I held my breath trying to slow my heart rate down, but it didn't work. "You know I can still hear your heart beating fast even though you're trying to make it stop right?" My heart sped up again, she smiled.

"I guess a heightened sense of hearing would be on that list of things I'm going to experience too right?" I said, smirking at her. "Yes, all the five senses will be heightened but so will your emotions, so we're going to have to keep an eye on you." She said crossing the room towards the closet. Opening the door she pulled out one of my t-shirts. When did those get here? I thought. "I took the liberty of bringing all your belongings here to this room while you were asleep, I hope that's alright?" She said, handing me the shirt. I pulled the shirt over my head, "yeah that's fine, but what about the apartment?" I was still wondering about that. "I paid what was due and then we moved you guys into here. Sarah's room is on the second floor across from Lexas'."

That was a relief, no more obnoxious Russian landlord, good riddance. "Who changed my clothes while I was sleeping and bandaged me up? Was it Sarah?" She tucked the hair behind one of her ears, "No that was me. I was the reason you got hurt so I wanted to be the one to make you better." Hold on, Isa had been the one taking care of me for the last four days? Has she seen me naked? I was mortified. She must have read my mind, "don't worry, I didn't see anything. It's not like I gave you a sponge bath or anything like that, I'm not a pervert." She giggled jokingly. I tried to chuckle too but nothing really came out.

She shut the door to the closet and walked back over to me. She was standing so close to me now, I didn't know what to do. My ears started turning red again, I could feel the blood start pooling in them. She flashed her famous smile that melted my soul. I loved it when she did that. "You'd better be careful," she warned. "That's only gonna get worse until you can get a handle on yourself." she winked at me looking me up and down.

What was she talking about? I could control my emotions, just maybe not the best around her. She took another step closer to me. I felt like my heart would burst if it were beating any faster. She put her hand over my heart feeling it flutter beneath her hand. I held my arms out to wrap around her but stopped myself. What if she was just teasing me again? She placed her head on my chest now. Her body was so cold next to mine. I tried to keep my hips back when I pulled her in. I didn't want to make the same mistake as last time. "Even after everything you know now, do you still want to go out with me?" she whispered to me. She looked up at me, her deep green eyes pulling me in. "Yes, I do." I said back to her.

She got her arms out from between us and put her arms around me. She pulled me in tight. I was embarrassed for a moment but when she didn't pull away I started to relax. "You're so warm," she said nestled in my chest. I could have stayed like that forever with her. Suddenly she lifted her head up, "Sarah's coming to check on us. She thinks I'm going to kill you." What, how could Sarah think that? Why would she save me then tell me everything just to kill me.

There was a knock on the door. Isa pushed me to the bed, sending me all the way to the pillows and then stood there waiting for Sarah to enter. I sat there catching my breath for a second before answering, "Come in," to her. Sarah opened the door, "sorry I just wanted to check and see how everything was going," she said. She looked at Isa then at me sitting on the bed. "I'll leave you two alone for a bit," Isa said. "Wait! Don't go," I wanted her to stay with me. I tried to get up off the bed but something seemed to be holding me there. Was Isa making me stay on the bed? I thought. It was possible, she said she was very good at magic and I hadn't seen her demonstrate any for me yet. Maybe that's how she changed my clothes, I wondered.

Isa left my room and shut the door behind her. As soon as the door was shut, Sarah rushed to my side. "Are you alright? She didn't hurt you, did she?" she asked frantically. "What? No, she didn't hurt me and she's not going to hurt me." I stood up from the bed with ease. Yep, it was definitely Isa keeping me on the bed. "But she's a vampire, can we trust her?" I looked at her stunned. "Oh yeah, well you're boyfriend's a werewolf, can we trust him?" I said back. "Xander said we're a bonded pair and that he'd never do anything to hurt me. He'd die before he'd ever let anything happen to me." I rolled my eyes at her. "Come on Sarah, you slept with the guy one time, he'd tell you anything to keep you around at this point."

As soon as the words left my mouth, I regretted it. She slapped me hard across the face. I deserved it. She had tears in her eyes now, "Well I believe him whether you like it or not." She stormed off back out the bedroom door slamming it as she left. "What have I done?" I groaned. I heard the sliding door open. "She's right, you know." My head whipped around to see Isa standing in the doorway. "What?" I said. "She's right about what Xander said, they're a bonded pair. In the wild wolves mate for life and Xander has chosen his mate, Sarah."

My stomach was in knots, how could I have said that to her? Had Isa heard every word I had said. "Did you hear everything?" I asked. She laid down on her side on my bed, "not if you didn't want me to," she said. What was I going to do? Sarah had never gotten mad enough to slap me before, I felt like a complete ass. "Don't worry about her, she's in good hands with Xander." I laid down at the foot of the bed by her face, "yeah, I suppose," I said.

She wiggled closer and laid her head on my chest again. I slowly began petting the hair on her head with my hand. "Was that you that kept me on the bed," I asked. I could feel her grinning through my shirt. That answered my question. I thought. "Hey, Isa?" I had another question for her. "Hmm?" she answered. "If Lexa and Ben are paired up, and now so is Xander and Sarah, does that mean you haven't found someone yet?" She sat up and looked me straight in the eyes. Oh, no. Did I offend her somehow? Her voice was cold and hard as she spoke, "I thought I had found someone once but it turned out we had different aspirations." I wanted to know more, "what happened to him, William said something about a guy leaving you at the altar or something?"

She scoffed, "he wishes. No he didn't leave me at the altar. We were together for almost three hundred years then one day after the fall of the kingdom, he left me. For dead. The townspeople burned my home and tried to kill me too. They hung me, impaled me, they even tried decapitating me, but still I wouldn't die. They finally buried me alive in a cement coffin, it took me five decades to claw my way out of there.

By then most of the people had forgotten about me until I took my revenge. I slaughtered hundreds of innocent people. When I finally found him again he wanted nothing to do with me so I cursed him to live as I live, never to die and to remain forever. I took away his thirst for blood so that he could not take out his aggression on the innocents as well. It was shortly after this that I met William again. His parents banished him to the forest I attacked him in as a child, rather than ending his life because they knew what I was."

I got a chill from hearing the whole story. How do you leave someone you love after three hundred years for dead? "Have you ever seen him again?" The storms in her eyes calmed, "not since the day I cursed him, and I hope it stays that way." Would it be clique if I told her that I would never leave her? I thought. I needed to change the subject before I said something again I would regret.

"Does it hurt to be bitten, you know, with your fangs?" I motioned with my fingers to simulate fangs. She smiled again, that was a good sign. "I've been told it's both painful and pleasurable at the same time" she said. I wonder who told her that. "Do you always go for the neck or can you bite elsewhere?" she reached out to touch my neck with her fingertips. "If I wanted to just kill you, I'd go for your jugular." Now she grabbed my wrist and turned it over. "If I wanted to have just a taste I would take it from your wrist." she kissed my wrist as she said it.

I took a deep breath and my voice cracked when I spoke, "and do you want a taste?" I looked deep in her eyes, I was suddenly taken back to my dream about her at the lake. Those same intense eyes. She quickly hopped on top of me pinning me to the bed. I couldn't move, whether out of fear or magic, I couldn't move. She leaned in close, pushing my head to the side with her cheek. My throat was exposed, she gripped my wrists tighter the closer her lips got to me. Then she whispered in my ear, "You have no idea," and began kissing my neck.

Chapter

9

My neck began tingling as she was kissing it. I tried to loosen her grip but she wouldn't let go. I was trapped there with her body on top of mine. My breathing became faster and she stopped. She closed her eyes and put her forehead on mine. She sat there for a few seconds before letting go of my wrists and getting off. What just happened? I thought. Was she really going to kill me? She stood next to the bed with her eyes still closed pinching the bridge of her nose. "I'm sorry," she finally said, still holding her eyes. "Sometimes I let my instincts get the better of me. It won't happen again, I promise." She turned her back to me and briskly walked toward the sliding glass door. She opened it but stopped before leaving, "You should probably put some jeans on and come back upstairs," she said, closing the door.

I laid there on the bed trying to calm down. She just straddled me, I thought. Why did she stop though? I looked down to see that the buttons were undone on my pajama pants. Oh great, no wonder she closed her eyes before getting off me, she was trying to be respectful and not look directly at it. God, I was such an idiot. I got up off the bed and went into my closet. She had hung up all my pants and shirts and my small dresser was in there too. I found a pair of jeans and put them on quickly. I needed to apologize to her for my unfortunate mishap.

I put on a clean pair of socks and my sneakers and headed up the stairs. As I was running up the stairs, I noticed that my ribs didn't hurt that much anymore. She really was magic. When I got upstairs I saw William walking by. "Hey, have you seen Isa?" He looked deep in thought about something. "No, but she said something about going into the club later. Maybe she already left." I rushed outside to count the cars. "Silver Camaro, red Corvette, blue Ford." Nope, they were all still here. I breathed a sigh of relief. She was still here, I thought. Something was driving me to be near her. Was this part of the wolf stuff? I wondered.

I began running through the house looking for her. She wasn't in the kitchen or living room, maybe she was upstairs in her room. I hurried as fast as I could up the stairs and burst through the door. Was she here? I looked around her room but didn't see her. I looked at the curtains blowing in the breeze and saw the lake. I go to her balcony and look out towards the water. There I could see a woman in a white dress walking near it. I ran back downstairs and out the front door nearly knocking William over in the process. The sweat was streaming down my face now as I jogged out to the lake. She was sitting under a great willow tree by the edge of the water.

When I approached her, she just kept staring at the water. I sat down next to her panting trying to catch my breath. She was sitting with her knees pulled up to her chest. "I'm really out of practice," she said. What was she talking about? "What? I said breathlessly. "I said I'm really out of practice, you know with the whole dating thing." She skipped a rock across the water. "I haven't even been on a date in over seventy-five years." She looked at me now. Wait, were we dating? I thought. I looked at her confused, "But I thought you didn't date anyone? That's what you told me before." She shrugged her shoulders, "that was before, when you were still a human. I don't date human men, they don't have a long enough life expectancy."

I raised my eyebrows, "how long is the werewolf's life expectancy then?" I said curiously. She smiled, "If you play your cards right at least two hundred years, maybe more," she said. My heart soared. But then a thought occurred, "but what about Sarah, she's still human right?" She understood my dilemma, "when Sarah is ready, and if she wants to, I can turn her into a werewolf too." I smiled. Sarah could live forever too. "I admire your love for your sister. You two are very closely bonded, that's good." She skipped another rock, "she'll forgive you for what you said, just try to think things through a little better in the future."

I nodded, but I didn't want to talk about my sister. I wanted to talk about what happened in my room. "So, what just happened between us?" I couldn't think of a better way to start the conversation. "I guess I'm just a little erotically charged, it's been a long time since I've met someone that isn't afraid of me or wasn't already spoken for." She turned her head to look at me. "Erotically charged?" I asked. Did that mean she had feelings about me too? "Yes, it means I like to tease and taunt you by making you feel aroused. Do you get it now?" She smiled as I crossed my legs together and started blushing. "You don't need to hide from me. I'm not going to hurt you. I'm just having a little fun, is all." I looked away from her and was staring at the water now. She's been nothing but honest with me. The least I could do was do the same for her. I could feel butterflies in my stomach as I began to speak, "but you see, I'm…I've never…" I could feel her staring at me. I couldn't get the words out of my mouth. "That's alright, you don't have to say it. I already know." My head whipped around. "You do? How?" Did Sarah say something to her? "That night we went for our walk, you should have kissed me for real instead of just on the head, however it was a very sweet gesture and I thank you for that." I was kind of starting to get irritated.

She knew all this time and just kept teasing and tormenting me anyways? Who does that? "Why did you keep taunting me if you already knew?" "Because, it's fun." she laughed and dropped her handful of rocks on the bank. "Oh yeah, what if I did it to you, would it be so funny then?" Her eyes shifted, they seemed more playful now. She jumped at me and we rolled down the little embankment. I managed to land on top of her this time. I held her wrists to the ground just as she had done to me. She did not resist.

Her dress was covered in dirt now and her hair was wild all around her. I knew she could over power me very easily if she wanted to but she just laid there. "What are you going to do, now that you have me here?" She asked. I contemplated kissing her but I didn't want it to seem forced. So instead I placed my forehead on top of hers for a few minutes with my eyes closed then I lightly kissed her on her head. I leaned back still holding her wrists, just staring at her. "That I was not expecting," she smiled and started lifting me off of her. I tried to keep my balance but lost it and landed face first in her chest.

She started laughing while I scrambled to get up off of her. I sat up next to her, my face red hot with embarrassment. She stopped laughing and sat up too. "What are you so embarrassed about, I'm not? You don't need to be so shy around me. I'm not silently judging you" she placed her hand on my cheek and continued, "If you're doing something I don't like I'll let you know, otherwise, just relax Adam." And she booped me on the nose.

She stood up and brushed herself off. Her dress was stained and I felt bad but she had started it. She held out her hand to help me up, I took it then wrapped my fingers around hers. She grinned at this as we walked back to the house but instead of going in the front door we stood underneath her balcony. What was she planning? She let go of my hand and walked behind me. Wrapping her arms around my torso she whispered, "Hang on." Before I could say anything she took a giant leap straight up from the ground onto her balcony and into her bedroom.

I was terrified, I didn't want to let go of her arms. "Did we just fly?" I asked out of breath like I was just the one to complete such a fantastic feat. She let go of me, "kind of but not really. We'd have to wait until dark if you wanted me to take you flying." She could actually fly? I shook my head, "no, no thank you for today. Maybe some other time. I sat down on the loveseat while she walked across the room to what I could only imagine was a bathroom slash walk-in closet. She was in there for a few minutes then returned wearing a heather gray long sleeve shirt and jeans. Was she planning on going somewhere?

Her hair was up in a ponytail now too. She put a pair of socks and shoes on then stood up, "Are you coming?" She asked. "Where are we going?" I trailed behind her. "To the club, I haven't been there in over a week so I need to take inventory." I supposed it had been that long for her hadn't it. We made our way down the stairs. The others had just sat down to eat something. It smelled good. "Wanna eat before you go?" Lexa said. "I made carne asada?" That sounded so delicious, my mouth started to water. "No thanks, we'll get something on the way," Isa said walking right past the dining room kitchen combo. "We'll be back later, don't wait up." I heard Xander start snickering in the next room and the thwack as someone hit him.

She tossed me the key when we got outside, "you think you can handle it?" she asked with a sly look on her face. I smiled, was she going to let me drive the Corvette? She got in and waited for me to join her. As the car started I could see William standing in the doorway watching us leave. He looked like he was mumbling something. "What did he say?" I asked her. "We need to make a stop at the hospital along the way," she said. Hospital? "Why?" I said. She folded her arms, "One of our friends from the other night finally woke up and I need to pay him a little visit to make sure he won't be talking."

Friends? Who did we know that was in the hospital? Then it dawned on me, what had happened to the guys who beat me up the other night? "You didn't kill anyone did you?" I said worrying out loud. She scoffed, "No, they just got in a terrible car accident after they attacked you and I made sure no one would remember a thing." It was scary the way she talked about my attackers. What kind of car accident was she talking about? She typed in the address to the hospital and we were on our way.

We sat in silence most of the ride just listening for the occasional voice of the GPS telling me which way to turn. When we got up to the hospital I parked in the back of the parking lot. She unbuckled her seat belt and got out. Was I supposed to get out too? She stood in front of the car waiting for me. I got out too and locked the doors. I held out my hand for her, she took it. My heart danced with excitement. "What are you going to do to him?" I asked. She shrugged her shoulders, "I'm going to make him forget just like I did the other guys?" "Forget?" I questioned. "Yeah, forget you, forget me, forget ever coming to the club in the first place. It'll be like we never existed."

I was fascinated at how she was going to do this. We walked up to the front doors. The automatic doors opened into a large waiting room. We walked up to the front desk. A young woman was sitting behind the counter typing on the computer. She looked up at us, "Hi, how may I help you?" She was wearing a brown turtleneck sweater and glasses. I didn't know what to say, so I looked at Isa. She calmly said, "We're here to visit a patient in room 503. He was in a car accident." The woman typed something on her computer. "Yes, he's receiving visitors now. You can go up and see him." she pointed to the right of us showing us where the elevators were.

Isa nodded her head in thanks and she pulled me towards the elevator doors. Once inside, she pressed the number five and the big metal doors closed. The doors opened on the third floor to let some people in. She made herself small in the corner, I stood in front of her blocking them from her. She grinned at me. I smiled back. When the elevator chimed that we were on the fifth floor I led her through the crowd of people and out into the hallway. "Thanks, I'm not really a fan of tight spaces." she squeezed my hand. "No problem," I said, rubbing my thumb across her hand. We walked down a long hall of hospital rooms.

When we got to room 503 she stopped abruptly in front of the door. "You don't have to come in if you don't want to. I'll be really quick, you could just wait out here." I shook my head. I wanted to face the guy that called her names and beat the shit out of me. "No, I wanna see him." She turned to face me. "Now remember, they were hurting you and it was a full moon so I didn't exactly use a lot of restraint when I was fighting them," she warned me. I tucked a strand of hair behind her ear, "I know. I just need to face him." She faintly smiled and nodded her head.

We opened the door into his room. There were a bunch of wires and tubes all over the place. He was in a full body cast from his neck down. I hesitated before entering the room fully. What had she done to him? I thought. She let go of my hand and walked around the bed checking his monitors. I slowly approached the foot of his bed. There were metal bars holding his casts in place and pillows propped up all around him. He had to be in so much pain. She took the call button away from his hand and draped it over the back of his bed.

"What are you doing?" I whispered as she was messing with one of his machines. "He needs to be fully awake when I do this otherwise it's not going to work." She whispered back continually fiddling with his IV machine. He began quietly mumbling and slowly moving in his bed. His eyes flickered then shot wide open. She covered his mouth as he frantically searched for his call button to alert the nurses. "Guard the door," she hissed and I did as she said. I stood with my foot in front of the bottom of the door and my ear to the wood, listening to make sure no one was coming to his aid. She shushed him quietly then removed her hand. He lay there immobilized, eyes darting around the room. She put her hand on his chest and began speaking into his ear. I couldn't hear what she was saying but I could see his eyes gore wider as they filled with tears. His breathing became rapid then he passed out. She removed her hand and put his call light back by his side then adjusted the machines again. I looked at her speechless. She looked at me and said, "It's time to go."

When we left his room his monitors all displayed normal readings. His oxygen levels were good, his heart rate was normal, everything seemed fine. She grabbed my hand and pulled the door open. We made our way back towards the elevator when she stopped dead in her tracks. "We need to take the stairs," she said. I followed her to the stairwell and continued our way down. Once we had walked down a flight of stairs I asked her, "Why did we need to take the stairs?" She looked back at me, "His family was coming to see him and I didn't want to be caught leaving his room. I could hear them getting off the elevator." That super hearing was no joke. I hadn't even heard the elevator chime indicating it was up on the same floor as us yet.

We made it to the third floor and got out of the stairwell. It must have been safe to use the elevator now. We got inside and rode it the rest of the way down. When we arrived at the main level, we quickly headed for the automatic doors. "Excuse me," the lady at the front desk said. We both stopped and looked at her. "I forgot to have you sign in before you went up to see your friend, do you mind?" She held out a clipboard with some papers stretched to it. My heart started racing. Oh no, we'd been caught. I thought. "Sure," Isa said and walked up to the desk.

She took the clipboard from the woman and began flipping through the pages to find an open line to sign. She finally stopped, picked up a pen and wrote something down. She then promptly handed the clipboard back to her. My heart was beating out of my chest now due to the stressful situation. Maybe she used a fake name? Could she get in trouble for that? We had committed a crime somehow, I knew it. I'm not exactly sure how they could prove anything though.

Isa returned to me grabbing my elbow and pulling me towards the door. "Have a good day," the lady called to us as we exited the building. Isa chuckled while stroking my arm, "remind me never to play cards with you. You have a terrible poker face." I breathed a sigh of relief as we got to the car. Once we were inside I sat in the driver seat trying to compose myself. "What did you do to him?" I finally said. She ran her fingers through her hair, "I made all his memories for the last few weeks disappear, I can only do that if the person is awake though so I had to wean him off some of his sedation medications." she looked at me nonchalantly.

"That's not what I meant. What did you do to make him so injured?" She sighed softly, "I may have broken most of the bones in his body and caused some internal bleeding." my mouth fell open, "How?" She lifted my chin to close my mouth, "do you really want to know?" I thought about it for a second then mumbled, "No, not really." She sat back in her seat waiting for me to start the car. "Are you hungry?" she said. I looked at her, "I'm starving," I said with a smile. She got out her phone and opened a food delivery app. "You head to the club, I'll order the food."

By now I had been driving to the club so often I practically knew the way by heart, but just in case, I turned the GPS on too. I glanced over at Isa while she was on her phone. I wonder what she's ordering? I thought. I was brought back to the last time we shared a meal and I bit her pizza before she could eat it. Then it occurred to me, if she was a vampire that drinks blood, how come she ate regular food too?

"Keep your eyes on the road Adam," she said, startling me. She giggled and put her phone down. I turned my focus on the drive. When we arrived at the club there was an old looking Subaru out front. That must be our food, I thought. My stomach growled as I pulled into the parking spots behind the building. She walked ahead of me after taking the keys out of the ignition. She unlocked the door and went inside alone. I followed a few paces behind her. She was so fast, I wonder if I'll be as fast as her soon? She was in the bar now and had unlocked one of the front doors. It opened to reveal a middle aged man carrying two bags of food.

"Hey there good lookin', you here all alone?" I could hear the man talking to her. "I could come in to keep you company," he took one step in the doorway. I couldn't stop myself, I ran to her pulling her away from him. The man jumped at my sudden appearance, "Oh, so you're not alone then? Well, you take care now." He quickly backed away and got back in his car and left. I shut and locked the door. What came over me? I thought. It was like I had the sudden urge to protect her. I stood there with my fists balled, staring at the ground.

"I see your protective instincts have started to take over then," she said, pulling two chairs off of a table. "Or was it just jealousy? It's hard to tell sometimes." Jealous of him? Never. "I just didn't like the way he was talking to you." She smiled while opening one of the bags, "yeah, some people might call that jealousy, Adam." She wrinkled her nose at me and motioned for me to sit down. I did as she wanted, grabbing one of the to-go containers in front of her.

"What did you get?" I asked as my stomach growled. "Burgers from Angelo's Cafe, they're the best." She said, opening her container. The burger was bigger than my hands when I tried to pick it up. I started devouring everything in sight. She had gotten fries, mozzarella sticks, and chicken tenders too. I ate my whole burger and moved on to the fries. Why was I so hungry? Every bite I took seemed to make me feel less full like I had a tapeworm in me or something like that. She ate her burger then sat back to watch me.

I had finished off the fries and was moving on to the chicken tenders. I glanced up to see her grinning ear to ear. "What," I said with a mouth full of chicken. She shook her head gleefully, "Oh nothing, just watching the insatiable appetite take control of you." I stopped chewing. "Is this a werewolf thing? Being hungry all the time and never feeling full?" She pushed the mozzarella sticks towards me, "Yes it is." Great, and here I thought it was just my body's way of catching up after being asleep and not eating for four days.

I ate everything on the table she had gotten. I couldn't believe it, I still felt so hungry. Isa grabbed the containers and walked them over to the garbage. I sat there feeling defeated, "Does it ever go away?" I asked her. "Yes and no," she said. "Some days you'll be able to function at a normal capacity and others you will feel so irritable and hungry that you can hardly stand it. That's how I was the day I met you. My hunger is different from yours of course." Did she mean she needed to drink blood? Could I ask her that question?

"How do you cope with it?" She looked at me funny. "The blood I mean. Isn't it hard to be around people every night?" She sat back down again, "it is hard but I've played the lonely reclusive vampire before that only comes out to feed and I never want to go back to that." She looked down at my arm and started tracing my veins. It tickled but I let her keep doing it. "How often do you, feed?" she remained looking down, "I try to do it every six months. You've caught me between feeding right now." She stopped tracing my arm. I wondered what she was thinking of. "When you feed, do you kill people?" Her head shot up, "No! Nothing like that. I don't do that anymore, I haven't done that in decades actually. No, I just go to a blood bank and take a few bags every now and again." She looked offended. "I actually fed last week when you started bleeding after that rock cut you. William had to drag me away so I didn't hurt you." That made sense now. It wasn't that she was feeling sick, it was because I made her hungry. I didn't know whether to be thrilled or terrified that she thought my blood smelled good to her.

She sat back in her chair again pouting. I placed my hand on her knee, "If there's ever a time you need it, I'm giving you permission to drink my blood." She looked skeptical, "you don't really mean that." she said. But I did mean it. I looked deep in her eyes, my heart pounding, "I trust you Isadora not to hurt me." She smiled weakly, "thank you Adam, that means a lot." She put her hand on top of mine. It was so cold. I had to ask her about it.

"How come you're always so cold?" she pulled away from me. Did I say something wrong? I thought. She stood up and started walking towards the stage. I hurried behind her. "Do you know the reason I love to dance so much?" she asked. I couldn't think of an answer, so she continued. "I love to dance because it's the only time I can get my heart to beat." She was standing next to the piano now as she slid off her shoes. "Your heart doesn't beat?" She shook her head. "Every time I leap and spin my heart beats faster with every rotation." She began doing a plie and then transitioned into a pirouette. She kept spinning around and around until she suddenly stopped with one leg raised high behind her. She was breathing heavily now.

"Come here," she beckoned me towards her. She grabbed my head and pulled me tight to her chest. I could faintly hear her heartbeat through my own ringing in my ears from being so close to her. The longer she held me there, the fainter it became. "If your heart doesn't beat, it won't circulate the blood causing someone to feel very cold." She let me go, "You on the other hand," she put her ear up to my heart now. My heart began beating faster and faster. "You have a good, strong heart and that's why you're always so warm." I froze, she wrapped her arms around my torso. I put my arms around her too. I started swaying like we were at a middle school dance. We stood there swaying for a few minutes. I seemed to be warming her up. I wonder if her heart was beating?

She squeezed me a little tighter then stopped moving, "if I don't go over the inventory now, I never will Adam." She said looking up at me. I didn't want to let her go. She belonged here in my arms. "But I don't want to let you go," I told her, stroking her head. She ducked down out of my arms. "You'll be alright," she booped me on the nose. "Why don't you practice playing while I work?" She asked, walking off the stage leaving her shoes behind. I watched her walk through the curtain by the bar and return momentarily with the tablet. She started looking over the liquor bottles and then typing things down on the tablet. I smiled watching her work.

I settled into the piano bench and began playing. I looked to see if she was watching me. She was, then continued on with her counting. It made me gleam with pride knowing she was watching me. I played another song, this time a slow melody. I could hear her singing from across the bar. She was incredible. I didn't care what she was. I was so glad she could totally be herself around me now. No more secrets, except for the feelings I harbored for her. I wonder if she'd still want to go on that date with me? Maybe even tonight.

I wonder if she can hear me whisper from here while I'm playing? I thought. "Hey Isa," I said as quietly as I could. It felt more like I was just mouthing the words instead of actually speaking. I looked over at her. She had her head down still looking over bottles at the bar. I continued talking as she squatted down behind the counter, "I was wondering if you would want to go out with me sometime, as a date?" I glanced around the room to see if she could hear me. I couldn't see her, where did she go? Maybe she went in the back and I was just whispering to myself? I thought.

I felt a sudden gust of wind and looked around me. There was a pile of clothes and a note on the seat next to me. I stopped playing to read it, 'put these on and meet me at my dressing room. -Isadora.' She brought me a new set of clothes? Why? I wondered. I grabbed the clothes and made my way to the restroom. Once inside, I changed out of my old t-shirt and jeans into a new dark gray flannel button up shirt and a pair of black dress pants. I put my shoes back on and looked at myself in the mirror. "Looks pretty good," I said out loud. I got a little water in my hands and ran my fingers through my hair trying to fluff it up a bit.

I exited the bathroom with my old clothes folded under my arm. I wonder where she went. I didn't see her around the bar anywhere. "That's weird," I said. All the lights were turned off now. I walked down the hallway towards her dressing room. When I got there, I knocked on the door. She opened the door and was wearing a stunning burgundy spaghetti strap dress with a plunging neckline revealing most of her cleavage. Her hair was down flowing all around her shoulders. She looked at me with the most mischievous smile. My mouth dropped open, she was gorgeous. She took a step closer to me, "do I look ok?" she said, turning around to reveal the low cut back of her dress.

I was too stunned to say anything. What was she doing? I stammered, "W-what's going on?" I asked her. She came up to me and adjusted the collar of my shirt then backed up to get a better look at me. "I'm getting ready," she answered. "Ready? Ready for what?" I said with my heart beating so fast I was sure she could hear it. She sat down at her dressing table and put on her matching shoes, "ready for our date," she replied grinning.

I was floored, I was sure she hadn't even heard me. Was this her plan all along? She stood up again and walked over to me. The overwhelming smell of vanilla filled my lungs and I began to calm down. "You heard me," I said, trying to compose myself. "Well, even if I hadn't heard you, I did make you a promise." She was right, we did have a deal. Was this just a pity date then? I wondered. I didn't care, she was the most beautiful woman in the world and I was the luckiest man just to be near her. She handed me my leather jacket. "Where did you get this?" I said. "You left it here Wednesday. You didn't grab it when you went to take the trash out that night." She said.

"Were you spying on me?" I asked, raising an eyebrow. She stood on her tiptoes so she was eye level with me. She put her arms around my neck, "Maybe I just wanted to see if you'd choke or not on stage without me," she said jokingly as she ran her fingers through my hair on the back of my head. It sent shivers down my spine but I liked it. She stood normal again. "So, where are we going?" she asked. I hadn't even given it any thought on where I would take her. I didn't even know what you did on a first date.

I began to panic trying to come up with something to say. She must have read my expression, "how about we just take a walk downtown. I always love looking at the trees this time of year." Thank goodness for her suggestion because I was at a total loss, it was a Sunday after all and not many places would be open. She turned the light off in the dressing room and led the way to the Corvette parked outside. As she walked in front of me, it was hard not to stare at her. That dress left little for the imagination to come up with.

I opened the car door for her. "Such a gentleman," she said before I closed the door. I took a moment to gather my thoughts together before I got in the car. You can do this, it's just a walk like last time, I thought. I got in the car and turned the key in the ignition, she was already typing in an address for me to follow. We left the parking lot and away from the club. I was feeling a bit nervous, it's not like I hadn't gone on dates before but she was immortal. I'm sure she'd been on thousands of dates with hundreds of guys. The thought of that unsettled me and I frowned. "What's wrong?" She asked sympathetically. I didn't want to tell her what I was thinking in case I offended her but I had nothing else to say to divert her. "I was just thinking about this being our first date and how I didn't know how many first dates you've been on in your lifetime," she was silent. "Please don't be mad at me," I said to her.

She smiled and looked at me, "you think I've been a tramp running around my whole life just because I'm significantly older than you?" I was appalled. "That's not what I meant!" I replied defensively. She clapped her hands together and started laughing. "I know that's not what you meant, that's just the way it sounded though." she continued to laugh at me. I was really starting to get embarrassed.

She finally stopped laughing, "I'm sorry, I didn't mean to embarrass you like that but you have no idea what you're talking about. I've never been the type of girl who goes around dating a bunch of guys, leaving a string of broken hearts. I mean you're the first person I've actually wanted to go on a date with in over seventy-five years." My ears perked up, she wanted to go on a date with me? I thought.

We were silent for a few minutes. "So, you wanted to go on a date with me?" I finally asked. She smirked, "yes Adam, I did." I was smiling now. "But that was only after my blood got contaminated with yours right?" she turned to look out her window, "no actually, it was before. There was something about you. The way you were drawn to me was so fascinating. I wanted to know you better but Will thought it would be a bad idea, which it would have been had you still been a human, but that's why I was so mean to you at first." She looked at me now. "I didn't think I would have the strength to trust myself to be around you." Her eyes showed genuine sentiment in them.

It's true, I was drawn to her like a moth to a flame. I loved her and I wanted to be with her, always. We made it to the downtown area she had typed in the GPS. There were a ton of cars everywhere. I found a place to park, way in the back of a parking lot. In the distance, I could see colorful tents and lights. "There must be some sort of fall carnival goin' on." I said to her. We got out of the car and started walking towards the festivities.

There was a dunk tank with a clown sitting on it, carnival games, cotton candy and caramel apples stands everywhere. There was even a tarot card reading booth. She reached out her hand for me to hold and I accepted it. We walked around looking at all the different stalls. Some were selling novelty items, others had handcrafted goodies. I stopped when we came to a homemade jewelry stand. There were different wild flowers cast in resin to make necklaces.

"Excuse me," I said to the stall owner, she turned around and smiled at me. "Do you have anything with a sunflower in it?" The woman began looking around her table for me. Finally she held up a triangular pendant with a tiny sunflower cut in half. "I'll take it." It was perfect, I reached in my pocket to pull out my wallet and handed her my card. I really hoped there was enough money on my card to pay for it. She handed back my card and the necklace in a little silk pouch. "Thank you," she said to me as we were walking away.

I took the necklace out of the pouch and held it up to Isadora, "may I?" I asked her. She smiled and turned around lifting her hair to the side as I put the chain around her neck. I fastened the clasp and pulled back her hair. She turned around again to show it to me. It rested about three inches above her cleavage. "How does it look?" she asked me with a smile. "Beautiful," I said, grinning back at her. We continued walking around the carnival.

We came up to the dunk tank where the clown was heckling passersby. "I'll bet you can't knock me off here, no sir. Why, especially not in front of the lovely lady," he said pointing to Isa. My heart rate accelerated, I was beginning to get irritated. "No, thank you," she said to the clown as she tried to pull me along. "Aww, what's the matter big fella, you chicken?" and he started clucking like a chicken at me. That did it, I turned around fast trying to see where it was you had to pay to knock this clown down.

"Adam, he's not worth it. He's just doing his job. You need to calm down." She was holding my wrist tighter now so I couldn't get away. I desperately searched for a way to get over to him as he was mocking me. Suddenly she grabbed my face with both her hands pulling me close to her face. "Adam," she spoke in a soft voice, "I'm right here. Just breathe." She took a deep breath in and slowly exhaled. I tried to copy her, deep breath in, slow breath out. My blood pressure began to decrease as I focused on her eyes. After a minute of breathing, I was calm again. She released my face and took my hand pulling me away from the clown. We walked all the way through to the opposite side of the carnival.

There was a small makeshift stage set up in the center of the courtyard with a magician performing. We sat down at a bench near the back of the audience. What just happened, another werewolf thing? It had to be, normally I wouldn't give two shits about some dumb clown calling me names. But he mentioned Isadora as a 'pretty lady.' I sat with my head between my knees for a while. "How do you do it?" I whispered knowing she could hear me. "How do you go about your day like everything's normal when it's not?" I looked at her and she gave me a little smile. "It just takes some getting used to. Do you think I'd be sitting here if it was my first day being what I am? No, I would have turned this place into a massacre."

She had a point, it was my first day being something I knew almost nothing about. I didn't know how to act or behave when these weird emotions took over, especially when it came to Isa. She was my anchor that either kept me calm or set me off. I needed to get a hold of myself and fast. "Hey, do you wanna just get out of here?" she asked me. I shook my head and draped my arm around her shoulders. "No, I don't want to just end our date because I keep losing control." She leaned her head against me, "I said leave here not end the date. The night's still young. We could just grab some food and head back to the lodge if you wanted. We can go for a walk around the lake." That sounded excellent to me.

I squeezed her then stood up, "that would be nice." I said. We walked around some more until we spotted a food vendor. I was starving again of course. We ordered four foot long corn dogs and a literal bucket of fries. She ate one and I ate all the rest. I felt like such a pig for eating that much but I couldn't help myself. I knew she wasn't judging me. We finished our food then made our way back around the carnival until we reached the same entrance we entered from.

I got the keys out and unlocked the doors, letting her get in first again. As we drove away I saw her playing with her new necklace. I smiled knowing that she liked it. We made our way home spending most of our time in silence. I didn't mind, I was just happy to be with her. "Do you want to go for a midnight swim when we get back?" She asked. It surprised me, "Umm…isn't it a little late in the year to be swimming?" I asked her. She shrugged her shoulders, "Maybe, but that's never stopped me before," she said. I tried to think of a logical reason for not wanting to go swimming, "but I don't have any trunks," I finally said. She leaned forward looking at me, "who said anything about wearing swimsuits?"

I gulped, was she talking about skinny dipping? My face turned white. Not only did she want to go swimming in autumn but she also wanted to do it naked? I tried to find the right words to say again. She put her hand on my knee, "Adam, I'm kidding," she said with that mischievous look in her eyes again. I breathed a sigh of relief. She left her hand on my leg for the remainder of the drive.

When we got to the big metal gates I pressed the button to open them. Nothing happened. I pressed it again. Again, nothing happened. "The battery must be dead," I said. Isa unhooked her seatbelt, "I got it," and she got out of the car. She walked up to the gates and pushed them open one at a time with minimal effort. She motioned for her to pull ahead so she could shut them again and she did. When she got back in the car she grabbed some hand sanitizer and a few napkins out of the glove box to wipe off her hands.

I looked at her stunned. "What?" she said. "How strong are you really without holding back?" I asked her. She raised her eyebrows at the question, "I don't really know," she said, "I'm not stronger than Xander but I am faster and better at outsmarting him." What did that mean? I thought. She guessed my confusion and elaborated, "I am the alpha. That means I can win in a fight against all of them. William is my second then Xander, Lexa, and Ben. William is fast but I'm stronger than him and Xander is stronger but a more predictable opponent. Lexa is sly but she isn't as fast or strong as Will or Xander. And Ben is at the bottom because he is our newest member. Well, that was before you came along."

She gave me a moment to let all that information sink in. "So that means, I'll have to fight you someday?" I asked. "Not necessarily. You'd have to fight your way up the ranks first before you could challenge me." I thought about it for a second. "So when can you challenge each other? Do they have to wait for a full moon so they can fight you in wolf form?" I was hoping my questions didn't seem too suspicious. "No," she said, "we do challengers' choice, so if you wanted to fight me now while I'm just a vampire there would be slight advantages and disadvantages for each person. I'm strongest during a full moon because I have all my abilities but it only lasts for one night so there's that."

I was fascinated by the structure and hierarchy of the group and the way she just opened up to me. "Have you ever lost?" she smiled "No, Ben's been trying to peck his way up for years but can't get past Xander." Ben has? I thought. "But what about Lexa, how come she's ranked higher if Ben can defeat her?" I asked. She rolled her eyes, "they take turns who gets to be on the bottom and for right now Lexa out ranks him."

I think I was beginning to understand everyone's dynamic in the group better now. We pulled up to the house and turned the car off. We saw that all the lights were off except the porch light. "Shall we?" she said. I opened the car door for her. She got out and immediately took on her shoes. We began walking towards the water. "Hey, I got a question. If you can only turn into a wolf on full moons, how come everyone else can do it whenever?" She smiled, "so you finally figured that out. Well, years ago I had a friend with the werewolf curse and he would go completely mad each month killing livestock, destroying villages, attacking innocent people, you get the picture. So I came up with a spell of my own to give the inflicted person the ability to regain their sanity and control the change. Ever since then I have been helping werewolves all over the world. The curse itself is almost extinct."

I was still confused, "but then, why do you still have it?" she pursed her lips, "that's the thing, along with the never actually staying dead when I die, I don't know." We made it to the big willow tree on the bank of the water. I sat down first followed by her. I looked up at the sky. It was a cool night and the stars were shining. "When you fly, do you sprout wings or ride a broom?" I said laughing. She laid her head down on my lap facing up at me. I started playing with her hair. "Both, it depends on the night." She laughed too. I couldn't tell if she was joking or telling the truth though.

She closed her eyes and sighed, "I wish I could just sleep right here," she said. I started tracing her features with my fingers. "Why can't you?" I asked. "Because, if I sleep I have night terrors of ways I've died in the past and we haven't been dating long enough for me to put you through that yet." My heart skipped a beat. Were we officially dating now?

I had to ask her, "Are we dating then?" I stopped tracing her lips. "Aren't we?" she said, opening her eyes. She sat up across from me now, her eyes shining in the moonlight. I couldn't move, my pulse was racing and my throat was drying out. I swallowed hard and licked my lips. She was still waiting for my answer. I carefully pulled a stray section of hair off her face and tucked it behind her ear. I gently caressed her face along her jawline, down her throat and around her new sunflower pendant. I'd never touched her there before. She shifted onto her knees now and crawled towards me. My back stiffened against the base of the tree. There was no escaping now. She had me cornered.

She moved forward slowly watching my reaction. Then she separated my legs slightly so she could put her one knee between mine. My head was spinning. She moved another inch closer then reached up and put her arms behind me on the tree. She leaned into my face now putting her cheek on mine. I reached up and placed my hands on her waist. Is she going to kiss me this time? I thought. She slowly started giving me little kisses on my cheek all the way to my neck. I couldn't stand it anymore. I tightened my hold on the fabric of her dress revealing more of her thighs. One of her hands came off the tree and she ran her fingers up the hair on the back of my head.

I pushed her down on the ground and I lay on top of her now. My lips found hers and we laid there holding each other. With each kiss I could feel something stirring inside of me. I wanted to devour her. The hunger was back with a vengeance. It wanted more. I pressed my face hard into hers as she lay on the ground. I loosened my grip on her dress with one hand and found the one of hers that wasn't holding my hair. I held down her wrist with all my strength. I didn't care if I hurt her.

Suddenly my eyes shot open and I realized what I was doing. I quickly got off her and stood next to the tree. My breaths were shallow and shaky. Had I hurt her? I was too ashamed to turn around to face her. I closed my eyes tight, "Are you alright? Did I hurt you?" I asked. I heard her stand up now. "Adam, I'm fine. You can open your eyes now." She said. I shook my head, "I'm sorry. I didn't mean to lose control like that. I couldn't help it." I heard her standing behind me now. I flinched when she touched my back. "Adam, you've done nothing wrong. I should be the one apologizing, I initiated it and egged you on." she tried to turn me around, I wouldn't move. We both knew that she could have made me move if she wanted to but she didn't. "Can you look at me please? See for yourself that I'm alright." She put her hand on my cheek and turned it to face her.

I slowly opened my eyes. She was fine, not a scratch on her. She had on one of her lovely smiles and her eyes were still sparkling. I pulled her in for a hug. I breathed a big sigh of relief. "Are you sure you're ok?" I said to her. She chuckled, "Yes I'm fine. I probably should have just gone in for a regular kiss instead of what actually happened. This is on me, not you. You can't control yourself yet and I should have known better." She rubbed my back while I held her, it was very soothing. She lifted her head off my chest. "Do you think we could try that again if I promise to behave this time?" I laughed at her and nodded.

This time, she put both arms around my neck and stood on her toes trying to reach me. I put my forehead on hers then leaned in to kiss her. Instantly I was back where I started two minutes ago. I picked her up so that her legs would wrap around me and turned around so her back was to the tree now. I felt myself slowly start pushing her into the tree over again. What was I doing? I thought, but I couldn't stop. She pulled my hair, yanking my lips away from hers. "Adam, you have to stop before you do something you'll regret." she whispered in my ear. I snapped out of it again and stopped pushing her against the tree.

I stood there holding her, her arms and legs wrapped around me tight. I didn't want to let her go. I couldn't let her go. She was holding on too strongly. She slowly began to loosen her grip as my heart rate decreased. Finally she was standing in front of me again. She looked up at me very sympathetically. "Adam, I'm sorry but I don't think I should kiss you until you can get a hold on this better." I knew she was right, I didn't want to admit it, but she was right.

I kicked a rock towards the water. She was holding my hand now but I let her go. I was embarrassed of my actions. I couldn't even handle one simple kiss. And what if I had taken it too far, then what? She tried to hold my hand again, I let her this time. "I just want you to be ready is all. I don't want you to feel pressured or coerced into doing anything you don't want to do." she said, petting my arm. "I know. But how do I stop this from happening again?" I looked deep in her eyes now. "With practice, we'll start out slow next time and I won't be wearing something so revealing either." I chuckled, like that really had anything to do with it. My attraction for her had nothing to do with her clothes, it was just her.

I looked her up and down, "well, maybe that would help a little." She playfully hit me and I smiled. "Come on, it's getting late." She pulled me up the bank. I didn't want our evening to end yet. Sleeping meant she would be left alone by herself for the night. I wonder if she'd stay with me in my room. "Hey, Isa?" she looked back at me, "I was wondering, since you don't sleep and I do need to sleep if maybe you could not sleep while I'm sleeping in the same room?" I wonder if she understood what I was saying? She raised her eyebrow and responded, "Are you asking me to spend the night with you?"

"Yeah," I said. She smiled and replied, "your place or mine?" I had to think about it. "Which room is the quietest?" she made a face, "mine because of the screaming night terrors there's a sound proof barrier between my floor and the rest of the house. Why?" she asked curiously. "Because I want you to try to sleep while I'm sleeping." I said. She shook her head, "I don't think that's such a good idea, maybe some other time. I'll just lay next to you." I sighed, "Could you at least try, for me?" she rolled her eyes, "OK, but don't come crying to me if I scare the everloving shit out of you later."

I stuck my tongue out, making fun of her. She quickly grabbed my face with both hands and pulled my tongue in her mouth, swirling it around with hers. It only lasted for a second then she let me go. My legs felt wobbly and I almost fell down. I looked at her with surprise. "That'll teach you to stick your tongue out at me." she said. Nothing happened. I thought. She had kissed me again and this time I didn't try to force myself on her.

She was thinking the same thing I was, "you see that, you weren't anticipating it so nothing happened." I wanted to try it again but this time I'd be ready for it. I walked up to Isa and did it again, she swirled her tongue around mine then let it go. We both rejoiced and I picked her up, spinning her around on the grass. "Maybe it was just a momentary lapse when I lost control," she didn't seem convinced. I kissed her again, longer this time. My heart began racing and I could feel the monster inside of me trying to take hold. I pushed her away, "Nope, you were right. It does have something to do with me anticipating it."

She giggled, "I don't mind it though," she said, coming closer again with a wild look in her eyes. I playfully started running away from her. She let me get a few paces ahead before the sprung up in the air. I lost sight of her when she jumped. "Where did she go?" I thought out loud. I felt a large gust of wind in front of me as I ran. I turned my head to see her levitating in front of me. She was flying! I thought. She slowly settled her feet on the ground. "How did you do that?" I said rushing up to her. "You know my last name is Dragoss right? Well in Latin 'dragos' literally translates to dragon. I have black dragon wings. The second time I was burnt at the stake, they grew and protected me from the flames."

I tried to see them in the darkness, "I don't see anything. Can I touch them?" she nodded her head. She turned around and pulled all her hair to the front and I saw scaly black dragon wings grow out of her shoulder blades. I gently stroked one of them. They felt like cold leather. They shrunk again into her backside and she turned around again. "I can make them appear like feathers or not at all if you'd prefer. They're pretty grotesque in the daylight." I wrapped my arms around her, "You are amazing just the way you are. I wouldn't change a single thing about you"

She buried her face in my chest. I couldn't tell if she was crying or not. I pulled the hair back out away from her face. She didn't want me to see her face. "What's wrong?" I asked. She looked up at me with tears in the brims of her eyes, "I've never even let Will see my wings before but when I'm with you I know that you'll never do or say anything to hurt me and I'm grateful for that." She resumed softly crying into my shirt. I just held her there.

"Oh," she said wiping her eyes, "I remembered I have something for you. I thought of it earlier today but we hadn't been home yet and now after our last few incidents, I'm sure you'll want it." I waited to hear what she was going to say next. "I have a bracelet that holds back people's abilities. I used it with William until he was able to get his pent up anger and aggression towards me out of his system." I gave her a skeptical look. "How does it work?" she looked down at the ground, "Well, it's like the magical equivalent to a shock collar. But instead of barking it stops you from losing control."

She looked at me again. "I'll try anything once so long as it means I can kiss you without trying to hurt you." She smiled at me, then continued dragging me towards the lodge. When we got to the sliding door of my bedroom I carefully opened it up. "I'll meet you up there," she said pointing at her balcony. I undressed and put a clean pair of pajama pants on. *Should I wear a shirt too?* I said to myself. I didn't normally sleep with a shirt on but I decided to wear one anyway.

I quietly and slowly made my way through the house hoping not to disturb everyone else who was sleeping. When I finally made it up to the third floor I saw that the door was ajar. I slowly opened it then shut the door behind me. "Isa?" I whispered. Not knowing if she was done changing, I decided to go stand out on the balcony to wait for her. I walked across the room to the open doors and saw her standing outside. What was she doing?

When I got closer I realized she wasn't wearing any pants. She was just in a black tank top and red panties. I turned around the moment I saw what she was wearing. "What are you doing?" she said coming up behind me. I walked away from her, headed for the loveseat, "You're not wearing any pants!" I shrieked at her. She laughed, "Yeah, so? This is how I sleep." I did everything I could to not look at her. "Here hold out your wrist if you're going to act like a child." I did as she instructed. Pretty soon I noticed she was wrapping an old leather bracelet around my wrist. When she tied it off it felt like it was somehow getting smaller like it was a snake coiling its prey.

I looked at it. It didn't appear to be anything special, just some brown leather with a silver oval on it. "And now to set the magic." she took out a pin and pricked her finger and dabbed it on the silver piece. It absorbed into the metal and was gone. "What does that do?" I asked naively. "That makes it so that only I can take it off of you again." she wiped her finger off with a tissue. "How do we know if it's working?" I said. "I know one sure fire way to check," she said with that wild look in her eyes again. I knew exactly what she was going to do. She came over and straddled me on the loveseat. My blood started pumping as she moved her hands behind my head and started running her fingers through my hair. With her one hand she lightly pulled on my chin slightly opening my mouth. She began kissing me. The whole room started spinning. I picked her up and brought her to the bed. I was on top of her again.

I could feel something in the pit of my stomach trying to break free but nothing happened. I kissed her longer and harder waiting for the monster to break free, still nothing happened. This was all me, not my animal instincts she was talking about. I pulled away slightly to look at her, she was smiling at me. "I don't think this thing works," I said, talking about the bracelet. "Trust me honey, it works. If it wasn't working you'd have ripped my shirt off already." She chuckled and my face turned red.

I rolled over and laid next to her. She curled up close with her head on my chest. I let out a big yawn. I was so tired, I didn't even care if she was only half dressed. I rubbed her shoulder with my thumb. "Hey Isa?" I whispered, she looked at me. "Do we have anything planned for tomorrow?" I asked. "No, you can sleep in as long as you want tomorrow." she said and laughed. "Good," I replied quietly. "Hey Isa?" I whispered again, I could tell she was still looking at me through my half open eyes. "You don't have to sleep if you don't want to. I just need to rest my eyes for a little bit" she giggled again and whispered back, "OK, you do that then."

"Isa?" I said one final time. "Yes Adam," she began tracing my facial features making it impossible to keep my eyes open. "What is it?" she asked. As I was drifting to sleep I whispered, "I love you..."

Chapter

11

The next morning I awoke to find myself alone. I had been covered up with the red satin comforter and the sheets were a mess. Man, I must have been tossing and turning a lot in my sleep. I thought. I sat up on the bed looking around for Isa. "Where is she?" I said. I scooted to the edge of the bed and stretched. I saw my phone sitting on the right stand on the right of the bed and grabbed it. I checked to see what time it was. "2:30!?" I said out loud. I slept most of the day away. I stood up and made a beeline for the bedroom door. Before opening it I saw there was a note taped to the wood. 'Let you sleep in. I'll be in my office next door if you need me. -Isa.' I opened the door and walked across the hall. I knocked on the door when I got to it. "Come in," she said. She was sitting on the opposite side of the door at a big black desk. It didn't match the rest of the room. There were bookshelves filled with mountains of books and different specimen jars holding various contents. Sitting on her desk was a laptop she was typing on. To the left side of the desk was a large chaise couch with decorative throw pillows. It looked like I was entering a therapist's office the way everything was set up.

She sat cross legged on her computer chair. Her long hair was braided to the side and she was wearing a cream colored sweater that slumped down her right shoulder. She looked up from her screen. "Good afternoon." She said, smiling at me. I couldn't help but smile back at her. I walked over and sat on the edge of the chaise couch. "Why didn't you wake me?" I asked. She closed her laptop, "you were so tired, I didn't want to disturb you. I knew you'd come looking for me when you woke up, that's why I left you the note." She swiveled her chair towards me. "How did you sleep?" She asked. I shrugged my shoulders. "Good I guess. I haven't actually slept on a real bed in so long I forgot what it felt like." She stood up and walked over to me. She then gently held my chin and kissed me softly. My heart was fluttering. I could feel her lips curl up when my heart started beating faster. She stopped kissing me. I leaned forward trying to keep it going. She pulled away from me. I looked at her confused. "What?" I asked her. Did I have bad breath? I suddenly became self-conscious.

She sat down next to me on the couch. "Do you remember what you said to me before you fell asleep?" She said. I thought back on last evening. My eyes grew wide, I had told her that I loved her. I looked away from her, "Yes, I remember." I wondered what she was thinking. "Are you mad?" I asked. She placed her hand on my knee. "No, I'm not mad. I just wasn't expecting it. That's all." She started drawing circles on my leg. "I don't know if I'll be able to say it back though. My last relationship left me in pieces and I promised myself I'd never fall in love again. Do you understand?" She looked at me with such sadness in her eyes. I held her hand. "I get it, and I'm sorry if I made you feel uncomfortable." She shook her head, "It didn't make me uncomfortable, I was just surprised. You can't help feeling what you feel and you can still say it to me if you'd like. I won't mind." She smiled again, softening her gaze. I smiled back at her, reaching my hand out to touch her face. She leaned into me. She was so honest with me. I couldn't believe how lucky I was to know her. "Then I'll say it again, this time fully awake. I love you Isadora." I moved in closer to her now to kiss her again.

This time she didn't back away and fully embraced my lips. I found myself putting my hand on her thigh and slowly moving it up her body. She got a little closer, slightly turning her body more towards me. I felt my hand slip under her shirt, touching her waist. She stood up, lips still touching mine and placed her knees on either side of my hips. My hand kept inching its way under her shirt until I felt the fabric of her bra. I gasped and took my hands away from her. She looked startled at my actions. "What is it?" She asked. My face started turning red. "I, umm...touched your..."and I pointed towards her chest. She laughed looking at where I was pointing.

She leaned back and took her sweater off revealing a red bra trimmed with black lace. I couldn't look away from it. "There, is that better? No more surprises." She then took both my hands and placed them on her breasts. I involuntarily smirked and she giggled. We resumed making out, my hands slowly drifting away from where she had placed them and towards her back. Was I trying to take her bra off? I thought. I could feel the animal inside me wanting more. "You don't have to take it off if you don't want to," she said. I felt my way down her back along her spine till I got to her butt. I grabbed it and pulled her closer into me. She made a sound when I did this that turned me on even more.

Abruptly, she stopped kissing me and looked at the door. She let out a big sigh, "Sarah is on her way up here looking for you." she said. Damn it, Sarah. I thought, what did she want? Isa gave me one last passionate kiss before getting off of me and put her sweater back on. She sat down in her chair and opened up her laptop. I crossed my legs to spare myself some embarrassment around my sister and waited for her to come into the room.

There was a knock on the door. "Come in," Isa and I said at the same time. Sarah opened the door and came inside. "Hi," she said shyly, "could I talk to Adam alone quick if you don't mind Izzy?" She got up from her desk, "not at all. Will wanted to talk to me about something anyway. I'll be downstairs if you need me." She walked across the room and winked at me before she shut the door. I sat there smiling like a fool because of it. "What are you doing, Adam?" Sarah asked me. I looked at her puzzled. "What do you mean?" I asked her. She gestured around the room. "This. What are you doing up here in her office by her bedroom? Did you sleep with her last night?" I was appalled at her questions. I knew what she was insinuating. "No, Sarah. We didn't sleep together. I just slept on her bed in her room with her. That's all." She crossed her arms. "What would it matter if I had slept with her? We're both adults."

She scoffed at me. What was her problem with Isa? "What's with all the questions, huh?" I asked her. She stood there silently for a while before she spoke. "I was afraid she was going to kill you. When you didn't come back until late last night and then you weren't in your room this morning I got worried that maybe she killed you and got rid of your body." Whoa, those were some wild assumptions. I was shocked.

I was starting to get agitated with her. She continued, "You know those murders that keep happening every few months or so, what if she's the one doing it?" how dare she even assume such a thing? I stood up to leave. I was too angry to talk to her. She tried to follow me, "Adam you have to believe me, she's bad news. You need to stop what you're doing with her before it's too late."

I whipped around and started shouting back at her, "how do you know? Have you even taken the time to try to get to know her? I don't believe she's the one responsible for those murders and I'm not going to just sit here and listen to you talk bad about her!" I slammed the door and stormed off down the stairs. I hated fighting with her but what if she had a point? Maybe I should ask Isa about the murders to see if she knew anything about them. But how do I ask without it sounding like I'm suspicious of her?

I marched down the stairs all the way to my room. I need a shower to clear my head, I thought. I got in my room, shut the drapes for the patio door, and locked it along with the bedroom door. I found a clean set of clothes out of my closet and threw my pajama pants on the bed. The bathroom had a huge walk in shower with frosted glass doors. I turned the water on and got in.

I let the water rain down on me. The hot water and steam felt good on my sore muscles that still hadn't healed from my beating on Wednesday night. My head was throbbing thinking about what Sarah said, 'what if she's the murderer' I kept thinking over and over again. But she said she wasn't like that anymore and I believed her. Was I too blinded by my own affections to know if she was telling the truth or not?

I shook my head and began washing my body. No, there was no way she was capable of that. I thought. Then I remembered the guys in the body cast at the hospital, if she could do that, maybe she was capable of murder. I shut the water off and grabbed a towel. I could smell her sweet vanilla fragrance on it. She must have been the one to put these in here, I thought. I walked out of the bathroom in just my towel. I jumped to see Isa laying on my bed. I gripped my towel tightly, "what are you doing here?" I said.

She rolled over so she was laying on her stomach now facing me. "Nice towel," she grinned with that playful look in her eyes. I covered myself with my hands. She laughed at me. "I came down to see if you were alright, I could hear you stomping through the house after you talked with Sarah." Did she hear our conversation upstairs, I wondered. "What did you hear," I asked her. She folded my clothes neatly on the bed in front of her. "I already told you, there's a protective sound barrier on the third floor. The conversation you had with your sister was completely private." Phew, that was a relief.

"However," she paused, "it's been brought to my attention that someone is spectating that I have been murdering people." A lump formed in my throat. Was she angry with Sarah? I hoped not. She stood up now and walked over to me. I held tight to the towel. She hooked her finger just barely in the top of my towel around my waist and pulled me closer. "You're very attractive right now, you know that?" she said, biting her bottom lip. I held my breath trying to slow down my heart rate. It didn't work, but she let go anyway, chuckling to herself.

I grabbed my clothes off the bed and went back to the bathroom to get dressed. When I was finished I returned to her. She was laying on the bed with her eyes closed. I took this opportunity to try and get back at her. I jumped at the bed trying to land on top of her. She opened her eyes just as I was about to land and put her hands up to catch me. She held me in the air like a toddler pretending to be an airplane. She threw me up in the air then rolled away. I landed on the bed with a thud. It knocked the wind out of me. "Sorry, I didn't mean to throw you that hard." I caught my breath, holding my ribs. "No, it was my fault. I shouldn't have tried to sneak up on you."

She snorted. "You, sneak up on me? I don't think so. I could smell you as well as hear you before your feet ever left the ground." I stared at her. "You could smell me? What do I smell like?" I was really curious what her answer was going to be. She smiled and sat down on the bed now. "I can't really describe it. It's more of a feeling I get when you're near me. You smell like the way sunshine feels on my skin. It makes me feel warm and safe." I understood what she meant. "I feel the same way too about you. I can always smell vanilla when you're near and it relaxes me." I held my hand out for her and she wrapped her fingers in mine.

"Being serious now, Will said that Sarah is worried about you. Xander told him that she has a theory about something. Would you care to elaborate on that?" I sighed. I guess Sarah had been talking to Xander too about Isa possibly being a murderer. "Sarah thinks you've been killing people, and she wants me to not spend so much time with you because of it." I waited for her response. She said nothing. "It's not true is it?" I asked. She stood up now letting go of my hand. "It's not what you think. They had to be killed." My heart began racing. "What do you mean, they had to be killed?" She turned to look at me, "they were other vampires Adam. Bad ones, that don't live the same type of life I lead. We hunt down the rogue ones and take care of them. I didn't want to say anything before because I didn't think it mattered." I was shocked. I couldn't believe what I was hearing. "So that guy found by Sarah's work?" I asked. "He had been preying on people in the care facility. Lexa caught him and I took care of it. Please don't think any less of me. I'm not killing just for the hell of it."

I stood up then reached down to pick her up. She put her arms around my neck and held on. I held her tight. "I don't resent you and I understand why you didn't tell me. Why didn't Xander just tell Sarah what was going on?" I asked. "Because I'm the alpha, everything has to go through me first. They were just following the chain of command." I slowly swayed while holding her. She made an almost cooing sound in my ear. It sent a shiver down my spine. "You make it so hard sometimes." She said, nestling her face in my neck. "What do I make so hard?" I asked curiously. "You make it hard for me to be good." she started kissing my neck.

I sat down on the bed still holding her. "Do you wanna bite me?" I said jokingly. She stopped what she was doing and looked me in the eyes. "Would it scare you if I said yes?" She was completely serious now. I didn't know how to answer her. It did scare me a little bit but I was also intrigued. "No," I lied. My heart was beating faster now. She opened her mouth and made her canines grow larger. I leaned my head to the right exposing my throat. My breathing became shaky and uneven. She slowly moved closer to my neck. I closed my eyes, afraid of what was about to happen. I could feel her breath upon my neck. She giggled in my ear and I opened my eyes.

I looked at her wondering what was so funny. "What?" I said. She ran her fingers through my hair. "You're such a liar. You're terrified of me." She stood up adjusting her shirt. I was not, I was genuinely curious about the whole experience, I thought. "Then why go through all that effort if you knew I was scared?" I asked her. "Because you should be afraid. I could very easily kill you by accident." She looked towards the door. She was trying to scare me on purpose. Why would she do that? "But you won't hurt me. Right?" She wouldn't look at me. She walked over to the drapes and pulled them open. I went over to her and stood behind her. "You're not going to hurt me Isa." I placed my hands on her shoulders. "How do you know?" She said. I wrapped my arms around her, holding tightly onto her body. "I'm willing to take that risk."

She nodded, still looking out the window. "We should go upstairs. I'm sure Sarah would love to hear the news about her hypothesis being correct. You should probably be the one to tell her though." She turned back around to look at me. "Can't we just have Xander explain it to her? She seems to listen to him better anyways." I pleaded with her. She smirked, "alright, but if she asks you again, you need to tell her the truth. I'll let Xander know he can tell her everything. He really likes her, Adam. I think he might have chosen her to be his mate."

What was she talking about? "His mate?" I asked her. "It's kind of like soulmates. When a wolf finds their destined mate there is an unbreakable bond that can't be ignored. You can literally go mad without them. Lexa and Ben are mated and I'm pretty sure Xander and Sarah are too." She explained to me. "So it doesn't matter that Sarah is still human?" I said. "Nope, that doesn't matter." she replied. I was interested in this new concept. Maybe that was the reason for me always wanting to be by Isa's side. I had to ask her, "Could you and I mate?" I asked.

The instant the words left my mouth I thought about what I was saying and I knew how she must have heard it too by the expression on her face. Her eyes grew wide, then she smiled. I put my hand over my face and shook my head. "No, no. That's not what I meant to say." My face was hot under my hand. I could hardly bring myself to look at her now. She was still smiling and had placed her hands on her hips. "I suppose we could," she said, giving me a devilish grin. I knew what she was talking about. I gave her a defensive look, "you know what I mean. I didn't mean to make it come out like that," I said.

"Oh well, your loss then. Some other time perhaps," she said walking towards the door. I tried to remain calm but I knew my face and sudden change in heart rate would give me away. Was she just casually talking about us sleeping together? I thought. She turned around when she got to the door and waited for me to join her. "When you say, some other time, what do you mean by that?" I asked her. She looked at me with sympathetic eyes, "I'm only joking. For now let's just stick to what we know and we can cross that specific bridge another day when you're ready. We'll ease into it eventually."

A whirlwind of thoughts raced through my mind about that day. It made me nervous to think about being with her. She obviously had plenty more years of experience than I'd ever have. What did I have to offer her? I sat back down on my bed looking down. She could tell I was in a bit of an existential crisis just by looking at my face. She slowly approached me. "Adam, I didn't mean to make you feel pressured," she said softly, "but I like you and I would really like to be with you that way." My head shot up, "You do?" I said.

She was sitting beside me now. "Yes I do. I don't just go around kissing people I don't intend to be with, I'm not that type of girl." I smiled now, she wanted to be with me, I thought. "And I want to be with you too, I just don't know how," I said. She slid closer to me, "then I'll teach you. It's really not that big of a deal," she said. I grunted, "that's easy for you to say, you've done it before" she frowned, "I'll have you know, that I haven't been with anyone in over a hundred years, so I'm just as out of practice as you are inexperienced." I'd never thought of it like that before. She had said that she hadn't been on a date in a long time. I never assumed she meant this too.

I wanted to reach out and touch her but given our current conversation it felt wrong. We sat there for a while until she finally reached out and grabbed my hand. "Do you still love me?" She said looking at the scar on my hand. "Even though I've cursed you to be a werewolf?" I pulled her hand up and kissed the top of it, "even if you'd let them kill me that night, I would still love you." She laughed lightly. I moved forward to kiss her cheek but she met me with her lips instead.

My inner demon was standing at the gates waiting for this. I put my arm around her and dipped her onto the floor. I lay on top of her kissing her all over the face and neck. She didn't struggle to get away. I have her where I want her. Suddenly with both hands I tear the neck of her sweater all the way down to the bottom revealing her chest. I start kissing her clavicle and work my way down to her sternum. "That's enough Adam," I heard her whisper but I couldn't control myself. I started to fondle her chest. She grabbed my face and brought it to hers. "Adam stop," she said, raising her voice this time. I blinked a few times trying to clear the fog from my brain. I looked around to see what had happened. I noticed her shirt first.

"What happened? Did I do that?" She nodded at me as she shimmied out from underneath me. I stayed on all fours looking at the ground. What have I done, I thought. "Are you alright, Adam?" She asked, sitting on her knees now. "No. Whenever this happens something takes over and I black out for a minute. I had no idea what I was doing. Are you sure this thing works?" I said, referring to the bracelet. "It works, it could have been a lot worse without it. We just need to train your mind how to control these urges." I sat with my back against the bed now. "How come you didn't stop me sooner?" I asked. "I wanted to see if you'd be able to snap out of it on your own first. Then I got caught up in the moment and lost my head too." She pulled her tattered sweater together trying to cover up.

"Here," I said, getting up and walking to the closet. I pulled out an old sweatshirt from high school and handed it to her. She took off what was left of her shirt and put it on. I helped her up and wrapped my arms around her. "Will this ever get easier?" I asked. "With time and practice it will." She said. "Wouldn't it be better if we just did it and got it over with?" I said crudely. "No, it's like having chicken pox, once you start to scratch the itch you can't stop." Her analogy made sense. "I'm sorry about your sweater," I said. "Don't worry about it. I'll just keep this one now." she smiled trying to lighten the mood.

We went upstairs looking for Xander and Sarah. They were sitting at the dining room table eating sandwiches. They stopped eating when we walked in the kitchen. "Xan, I need you to tell her everything after you guys are finished," Isa said to Xander. His eyes shifted back and forth between both women. "Everything?" he asked not thinking it was a good idea. "Yes, everything. If we're all going to get along she needs to know the complete truth," she said. Sarah looked at Isa suspiciously. Would she be able to handle knowing all the details about their lives? I hoped so.

"Come on, let's go talk upstairs," he said to Sarah. They took their plates of food with them as they left the kitchen. Isadora then turned to me and asked, "So what are you hungry for?" and walked over to the fridge. I was hungry but not like I'd been the day before. This was just the normal amount of hunger instead of an insatiable appetite. "You can cook?" I asked her. She seemed surprisingly offended by my assumption. "Of course I can cook, eating people isn't my only talent, you know." she said with a laugh. I loved it when she laughed, it was just as beautiful as her singing voice. "How about a Denver omelet?" I suggested. She got the eggs and other ingredients out of the fridge, then she grabbed a large skillet that was hanging above the island.

As she started whisking the eggs I noticed her humming. It made me smile. I wonder if she normally sings when she cooks too. "So what other hobbies do you have besides ballet, cooking, and anything to do with music?" I asked her, sitting down at the island counter. "Oh there's loads of stuff I like to do. Archery, fencing, horseback riding, painting… you name it, I've done it." She said. "So are all the weapons on the walls authentic then?"

She added the eggs into the hot pan, "Yes, I collect them from battles I've lived through. Some of them were actually used to try to kill me." She talked so matter of factly. I wanted to ask her about the portrait above the fireplace next. "Is the canvas in the living room a self-portrait then?" I said. She stopped putting the veggies in the skillet. "No," she said, "actually my sister painted that of me." I forgot she said she had a sister. I didn't know how touchy of a subject this could be. "Were you and your sister close?" I asked.

She continued making the omelet, "well, technically she wasn't actually my sister. She was actually a reflection of myself brought to life." I was enthralled in her story. "Go on," I said. "In the fourteenth century I hadn't developed an immunity to the sun yet so I was trapped by the lord of a castle to only venture out at night. He locked me away where no one could see me in my room. I was only allowed out for special occasions after dark to be paraded around like some show pony."

She flipped the omelet over to finish cooking. She continued, "Anyway, so I was left alone for months at a time staring at the same four walls when I was starting to go mad I happened to look at myself in the mirror. I began having conversations with my reflection for years until I one day discovered I could use sorcery to bring inanimate objects to life. She reached in the cupboard and pulled out a plate. She then carefully shifted the omelet out of the skillet onto the plate. She opened a drawer and grabbed a fork too and handed the finished plate to me. It looked amazing.

"Please continue," I said, blowing on my plate of food. "On the next full moon I had gathered all the requirements to pull my reflection out of the mirror. I waited for the moon to rise then said the necessary incantations. I reached out to touch the mirror and found that I could pass right through it. I went inside to find an exact replica of my room in reverse. I quickly returned through the mirror and smashed the glass into thousands of tiny pieces."

She motioned for me to take a bite. I cut a piece off and tried it. It was exquisite. "This is so good," I said, shoveling in another bite. She started washing the dirty pan. "And then what happened?" I said. "Well, I had just lost the only friend I thought I had so I sat down on my bed and began to cry when suddenly someone touched me on the shoulder. I looked up to see, for lack of a better word, me. She was mute at first and didn't know how to speak. I had to teach her everything. It wasn't until after the lord died and I was freed that I started to notice something was off about her. She was just like me. Looked like me, acted like me, she even knew what I was going to do before I did it but she was different. She would almost always do the opposite of what I was going to do. At some point she decided to resent me for being the original and she tried to get rid of me."

She put the now clean skillet back on its hook and took my dirty dishes to the sink to be washed. "Thank you," I said, "So where is she now?" I asked. She replied, "I did the spell again and made her look at herself in one of the broken pieces from the original mirror. It pulled her back inside but now there were thousands of her trying to get back out. It took me a long time but I eventually burned all of the pieces. It wasn't long after that my significant other of three hundred years betrayed me too and I was all alone again. The three of us had been inseparable up until I sent her back to where she came." She looked down at the floor now. "What was her name?" I asked. She looked at me, "her name was Sarrora. I gave her that name because she couldn't say my name, Isadora at first. She was my sister and my best friend for three hundred years."

"Do you ever miss her?" I said walking over to her. "Occasionally I do, yes. But I know that the world is better off without her in it." I thought about the long story she just told me and something occurred to me, "hey, is that why they say vampires don't have reflections?" She burst out laughing. I didn't know what was so funny, I was asking a serious question. She grabbed my hand, "yes, that's actually where that legend originated from."

Chapter

12

She led me through the house and out the front door. "Where are we going?" I asked her. "We're going to work on honing in your new senses and abilities." she said. We walked all the way down to the lake and stopped by the willow tree. She let go of my hand and began undressing. I looked around to see if anyone was watching. She took my sweatshirt off and began undoing the button on her jeans. "What are you doing?" I said trying to stop her from taking her pants off. "I'm going to swim out in the middle of the lake and you're going to try to get to me before William does." William? I thought.

A large reddish brown wolf came bounding out of the trees towards us. I was hesitant to get in the water. "What ability does this test?" She finished taking her pants off and folded them next to the tree. I didn't like Will seeing her like this so I tried to stand in front of her to cover her up. "It'll test your endurance. This water is super cold and you'll have to swim extra fast to try and beat Will." She started tugging on my shirt to take it off. I obliged her but kept my jeans on. "You're gonna swim in those?" she asked me. I nodded my head. "Suit yourself," she said and dove in the water. I watched from the edge waiting for her to come up again but she didn't. I started to panic. Where was she? Is she ok? I thought.

I began searching the water looking for her. William was standing next to me now wearing a pair of shorts. "You ready?" He said. I was still looking for her to come up. Finally I could see her way out in the middle of the water. I breathed a sigh of relief. "She's made it," I said, turning towards Will. "Ok, now she's going to make it look like she's drowning and you need to try and beat me to her," he said. I stood there looking at him getting ready to dive in the water. "But she's not actually going to be drowning right?" I say, taking off my shoes. He looked at me menacingly, "that all depends on you and how long it takes you to get to her." I didn't like the way he said that. I looked back at her.

I could see her bobbing in the water against the waves. What if I didn't get to her in time? I thought. We readied ourselves to jump in. "Can you hear her?" He asked me. I couldn't hear anything, just the sounds of the wind in the trees and the water hitting the shore. "No," I said, keeping my eyes locked on her. "She told me to count down from three and then we're supposed to race to her." I nodded my head. "Ready? 3...2...1...go!" I jumped in. The water was cold and made it hard for me to breathe. My body felt like it was being stuck with needles from the icy water. I began swimming in her direction. I looked over to see William slowly swimming towards her as well. Was he taking it easy on me? My chest was hurting from the cold water.

Slowly I made my way towards her. I started to faintly hear something. What is that? I thought. I stopped swimming and just bobbed in the water. William stopped too. "Do you hear that?" I asked, looking around the lake. "Yeah, it's Izzy. She's yelling and splashing around. Can you hear her now?" He said. I listened carefully. I could barely make out what she was saying, "Help!" I could hear her say. The hairs on the back of my neck stood up, she was calling for help. I rapidly started swimming in her direction. I had to get to her, she needed me. William started swimming harder too. My lungs were burning from the cold.

The closer I got to her the clearer she became. I could see her struggling to stay above the water now. My heart started racing. I swam with all my might. Will took the lead passing me in the water. I was starting to slow down. My arms and legs were getting tired but I needed to push through. I could hear her screaming now. My muscles ached as I pulled myself through the water towards her. Her head went below the water. I dove under trying to swim faster to her. I came up for air. I was almost to her now and reached out for her. I was so exhausted. She came up again, splashing about. William reached her before I did. I had lost.

I stopped swimming for her and started treading water. My legs were heavy and it made it hard to keep afloat. I could hear them talking now. My head bobbed down under the water. I began panicking trying to get back to the surface. Was I drowning now? I thought. My legs stiffened and I began sinking. "Shit!" I said as my lungs began taking in water. I coughed and sputtered, trying to come back up for air. I felt like I was being dragged down now. Everything began to go dark and I slowly sank in the water. I felt somebody grab my arm and pull me up toward the surface. A big rush of air filled my lungs. William wrapped his arm around my chest and began dragging me back to shore. He was swimming so fast now pulling me through the water.

When we reached the bank, he drug me up on shore. "You ok, man?" He said out of breath. I lay on the rocks shivering. "Yeah, I'm fine now." I said, my teeth chattering. I see Isa emerge from the water quickly behind us. She knelt down next to me, dripping water all over the place. "I was supposed to be the drowning victim, not you!" She said, trying to help me sit up. "I wasn't trying to drown," I said to her. She stood up and looked at William, "go get some towels," she said. He nodded and ran towards the house. She walked over to my shirt and brought it to me. "What about you? I said to her, "You should be freezing." She looked at herself and smiled. "Let's worry about you first," She said. I wanted to wrap my arms around her to keep her warm but she wouldn't sit back down.

Will was back now holding three towels. He gave one to Isa and one to me. I wrapped the towel around my shoulders trying to conserve my body heat. It didn't help. My jeans were soaking wet. I violently began shaking. Isa knelt down again and placed her arm around me. "Come on, you're going into hypothermic shock. We need to get you warmed up." She helped me to my feet. I was very unsteady and leaned most of my body weight on her. She caught me and held onto me as I put my arm around her shoulders. She put her towel around my waist and tucked it in my jeans. "Can you grab my clothes Will?" She asked him. He grabbed them and began following us back to the house.

My lips were blue now and my teeth were chattering. "Are you going to be ok?" I asked her. She smiled, petting my back. "Yes, I'm fine Adam." I couldn't hardly feel my feet walking across the grass. We got to the house but instead of going in the front door we stood under her balcony. She bent her knees and jumped while her arms were still around me. I felt dizzy when we landed. I let go of her, hung my head over the railing and threw up. Great, now she's seen me puke again. She opened her French doors and led me inside. We crossed her room towards the loveseat and armchair. There was a built-in electric fireplace flickering in the corner. She set me down on the floor in front of it. "Wait here, I'll be right back," she said quickly leaving the room.

I was very sleepy all of a sudden and rested my head on the couch. It slowly slid off and I laid down on the floor in front of the fireplace. When I opened my eyes again, I was laying on the loveseat with my feet hanging off the end. Isa was stroking my hair with my head in her lap. She was wearing clothes again. I sat upright, disoriented. "What happened?" I said. She stood up and walked over to a pile of clothes sitting in the chair. "I brought you these," she said. It was a dry pair of clothes and my toothbrush.

I looked at her remembering throwing up over the side of her balcony. I hung my head in shame, "Sorry," I said. She brought me my things and pointed behind her, "You can get cleaned up there." I stood up, faltering for a moment. She jerked to try and catch me. "I'm good," I said walking around the loveseat towards her bathroom. I shut the door and began taking off my wet clothes. She had brought me a pair of black sweatpants and a hooded sweatshirt. That was good, I was still freezing. I put my wet clothes in the hamper she had sitting next to the shower. I brushed my teeth next, then turned the light off exiting the bathroom. She was still wearing my old sweatshirt and a pair of short shorts now. They looked good on her

I sat back down on the loveseat with my hands in my shirt pocket. The heat given off from the fireplace felt so nice now that I was dry. She came up next to me and sat on the armrest of the couch. I took my arms out of my pocket and pulled her off the armrest so she was sitting across my lap now. She smiled but didn't say anything. What was the matter? I thought. "You OK?" I asked her. She shook her head, "You almost drowned Adam." She looked at me with sad eyes. I pulled her close, "but I didn't," I said. She shook her head again, "I shouldn't have gone out so far. I should have stayed closer to the shore." She was really tearing herself up about this. I put my hand on her head, pulling her closer so I could kiss her temple. She sighed. "You were doing really well though. You almost had him up until the end." She looked me in the eyes now. "Did you tell him to take it easy on me?" I asked her hoping to make her smile. She did, "No, William doesn't like the water but he'd rather be the one swimming against you than either Ben or Xander." She lay her head in the crook of my neck now and placed her hand over my heart.

"You really scared me, you know," she said. My heart started beating faster when she said this. "I scared you? You were the one screaming for help and bobbing underwater, I said. She chuckled, "yeah but I was never in any real danger. I just did that for a little motivation to try to see if I could get a reaction out of you." She looked devious now. "Well, it worked. I thought you were actually drowning." I kissed her again on the head. She was still so cold too. I knew holding her wasn't a very productive way for me to warm up but I didn't care. "Do you ever feel the cold?" I asked. It sounded like such a silly question after I said it. "Sometimes, if I'm out in temperatures below freezing for long periods of time." She said drawing circles on my chest. "What about the heat? I know you said you liked how warm I was."

She sat up again, "I love the heat. But I don't go out in public a lot if I'm in a sunnier climate." She lifted her sleeves, "why not?" I asked. "Because when I'm out in the sunlight, you can see my scars more clearly and it really frightens people." It was true. I couldn't tell she had any scars on her body the night she was wearing that silver shirt performing at the club. It wasn't until she actually opened the drapes in my room and she showed them that I noticed anything. I could barely see the one in her leg now. I traced over it with my fingers. Her leg jerked a little bit when I pet her. I could feel her tense up too. "Are you alright?" I asked her, concerned. "Yeah," she said, "I just like it when you do that." My face started turning red and I removed my hand from her leg.

She laughed and reached for my hand, placing it back on her thigh. "Did it hurt a lot, dying I mean?" I wanted to know more about her. She thought about it a minute before she answered, "Some more than others. Each experience was different," she said. I didn't want to push her to elaborate so I changed the subject. "Do you know if Xander told Sarah everything yet?" She nodded, "yes, she chewed me out big time for attempting to murder you today too." I looked at her surprised. "When did she talk to you?" I asked. "Oh, right after I brought you here and went down to get your clothes. She caught me while I was still in your room dripping wet. She was not happy to see me like that," she smiled. I'm sure she wasn't. If the roles had been reversed I wouldn't be happy to see Xander like that either.

"What did she say to you?" I asked. She started grinning, "she said something about not caring about your safety and that I better not take advantage of you," she said with a laugh. God damn it, Sarah, I thought. I blushed and looked away from her. She ran her fingers up the back of my head and gently pulled so that I'd face her again. "Is that what you're worried about too? Me taking advantage of you." Her face was serious now, looking deep in my eyes. "Not exactly." I said, partially telling her the truth. I didn't want her to know that I was thinking about it too. She slowly moved my hand higher up her thigh. I started to breathe more rapidly. She wouldn't look away from me and I couldn't look away from her. She kept moving my hand until I was touching the bottom of her shorts. I couldn't take it anymore. I whispered, "Stop," to her. She let my hand go and I put on the armrest of the couch.

She scooted away from me so that now only her legs were sitting on my lap. She sighed as she laid down. "I'm sorry," I said to her, "you don't have to move away from me." She folded her arms. "Yes I do. Because she's right. I might try to take advantage of you." I looked surprised at her. She would? I thought. "What?" I said to her. She remained with her arms crossed and closed her eyes, "when I look at you, a strong desire takes hold of me to be with you. So then I try to get you riled up in hopes that you will initiate something. I am taking advantage of you Adam." She opened her eyes, ashamed. I needed to process what she just said.

We sat there for a while not saying a word. "So earlier today in my room, you did that on purpose, showing up when I was done in the shower?" I asked her. "Well, I figured you wouldn't let me join you in there, so I just waited on the bed." she said. I snorted, thinking about her coming in the shower with me. "Yeah, that probably wouldn't have gone well. Would you really have come in there?" I wanted to know her answer. "Yes," she said with a smile. I crossed my legs with her feet on them still. "Why didn't you then?" I asked, giving her a playful look.

She uncrossed her arms and sat up now swinging her legs off my lap. She leaned into me and said, "I wasn't sure if you could handle it," and kissed my nose. Her lips were cold when she kissed me and it tickled my nose.

I wanted to kiss her back but I was starting to get a little flustered from our conversation. She lay her head on my lap now looking up at me. She held up her hand for me to hold and I obliged her. She then placed our hands over her heart. "I really want to kiss you," I whispered to her. She smiled and sat up again, "then kiss me." I pulled her close to me, holding her in my arms. I moved her onto my lap so we would be easier to hold. I found myself putting my hands under her shirt again and slowly making my way up her back. She leaned back, releasing my lips. "If you plan on ripping my shirt off again can I just take this off first?" She asked me. I was alarmed at her question. "I didn't mean to do that before. I don't know if I'll do it again though," I said honestly. She stood up, "then I'll just take it off," she said, taking off the sweatshirt.

My eyes grew wide. She climbed back in my lap again and put her arms around my neck. "Is this OK?" She asked. I swallowed hard, "yeah, that's fine." She began kissing me intensely. I put my hands on her waist. I wonder if she'd mind if I carried her to the bed? I thought. I stood up holding onto her and she wrapped her legs tightly around my torso. I carefully walked over to the bed and laid her down. She had her hands underneath my sweatshirt now trying to get me to take it off too. I did, then pressed my body up against hers. Her skin was so cool and soft underneath me. We laid there for a few minutes just staring into each other's eyes. I loved her so much, she had no idea.

She reached up and put her hand on my face, "what are you thinking about?" She said. "I was just thinking how much I love you." She smirked at me. "Why do you love me?" She said. I didn't really know how to answer her. It was everything about her. The way she looked, the way she acted, even her long history. "It's not just one reason. I can't quite explain it," I said sitting up on my knees. I wondered about the whole mate discussion we had earlier and whether or not that was the reason for my loving her. "Can a normal human experience the bond with a werewolf or vampire?" I said. She looked at me confused.

"I'm not quite sure I know what you mean," she replied. "You know, the whole mate situation?" I said. She pursed her lips and then spoke, "I suppose they can but I've only ever known it to happen in people with the werewolf gene. For example, Lexa and Xander were born with the werewolf gene and didn't need to be bitten or cut to be able to transform. William was scratched by me and Ben was bitten by another werewolf."

She didn't really answer my question. "No, like could I have been mated to you before we transferred blood?" I said, hoping to get my point across better. She furrowed her brow, "possibly. If you already had the werewolf gene in your blood then I suppose it's possible. What about your parents?" she asked. "What about my parents? They weren't werewolves." I said. "Maybe they were though. What happened to them? You said they just got up and left you and Sarah when you were younger, right?" She sat up on the bed now. "Yeah, we never heard from them again. That's why we were always in foster care until Auntie Mary took us in." What was she getting at? I thought. She had a wild look in her eye as she was speaking.

"Maybe they were werewolves or at least one of your parents was and they had to leave you because of hunters." What was she talking about? "Hunters?" I asked. She grabbed my hand and led me across the hall to her office. She started looking through her books on her bookshelves until she found the one she was looking for. "There are still families of werewolf hunters throughout the world but I haven't heard of any hunter related deaths in over twenty years." She flipped through the book until she found the page she was looking for. "Sometimes, packs break up to start their own families. Maybe your aunt was actually part of their original pack and came looking for you after she lost touch with your parents."

My head was spinning with all the information she was giving me. Auntie Mary, a werewolf too? I thought that was crazy. "Look here," she pointed to a page with a family genealogy written on it. "What was your aunt's last name?" "Anderson," I said, looking at the page. There written in black ink was my foster mothers name and a few spaces over was my father's name with my mom's name in parenthesis. I couldn't believe my eyes. She was right. They had been part of the same pack. "Where did you get this?" I asked her, stunned. "When you've been alive as long as me, you tend to start making lists of things to remember. I've been collecting data about different packs for centuries now. I never even thought to look in here to see if your family was in it." She said, closing the book.

"What did the brackets around my mom's name mean?" I asked. "It means that she was human and that your father was the one who was a werewolf." She replied. I needed to sit down. I lay down on her couch with my hands over my head. "My dad was a werewolf," I said, "so that means Sarah has the gene too right?" She nodded her head, sitting down at her desk. "What happened twenty years ago that was a hunter-related death?" I asked. "There was a house fire and everyone, including the two children, died. But now I believe that this was all a big cover up to throw the hunters off their trail. I think that your parents caused the fire and left you and your sister to protect you. They may very well still be alive to this day." She seemed excited now.

"But if they were still alive, why didn't they come find us again?" I asked. She shrugged her shoulders, "I don't know. Maybe they're still in hiding?" I couldn't believe Auntie Mary never told us the truth. I was heartbroken. Why go through all the trouble of raising your former pack members' kids if you weren't going to tell them anything about their parents? I was angry now. I felt the rage form deep inside me starting to boil out to the surface. I sat up with my hands on my knees looking down at the floor.

I balled my fists and began breathing heavily. How could they do this to us? I thought. Their own children, tossed away like they meant nothing to them. I began to growl. "Adam?" Isa walked over and started rubbing my back. I didn't want her to touch me. I was too enraged right now for her sympathy. "Adam, you need to calm down, everything's fine," she said, trying to hold my hand.

I snapped. I threw off her hand and hurled her to the floor. I sat on my knees on top of her and began choking her with both hands, squeezing as hard as I could. I was seeing red. There was nothing I could do. Her eyes were wide as I continued to choke her. She had her hands around mine trying to get me to release her but I couldn't. She was gasping for air and I was starting to hear the faint crunch of bones as I was crushing her throat.

I looked her in the eyes and saw a tear fall from one of them. I stopped squeezing. She ripped my hands off her neck and began coughing. She rolled over underneath me trying to catch her breath. What had I done? I thought. I jumped up and ran for the door. "Wait!" she yelled hoarsely as I opened the door. I couldn't look at her. I had to get away from her so I didn't do anything to hurt her again. I ran down the stairs and into the living room. Xander and Sarah were sitting there talking with Lexa, Ben, and William. I ran past them towards the front door.

"What's going on?" Will said, standing up chasing after me. He caught me on the porch. "Adam, what's wrong?" he said frantically. I paced back and forth debating whether or not I should actually tell him. I decided it was better to just tell the truth. "I just tried to kill Isa!" I yelled. Xander, Sarah, Ben, and Lexa were standing on the deck now too. "You did what?" Sarah said, stepping forward.

"Yeah, and guess what? Dad was a werewolf and so was Auntie Mary." She looked at me shocked. "But that's impossible, how do you know that?" She asked. "Isa has records of all werewolf packs dating back centuries and they were on the list!" She stood there just listening to me scream. "Oh, and get this. Not only did mom and dad abandon us because dad was being hunted but they're probably still alive somewhere!"

I took off running towards the lake, I needed to go for a run to clear my head. I ran past the willow tree and around the lake until I reached the trees. I ran so fast my legs felt like they were going to break. How could she ever forgive me after what I'd done? I shook my head, trying to get the image of her suffocating out of it. She looked so scared. I ran up to a big oak tree to catch my breath.

I stood there holding onto the tree, panting. How could I do that? I thought. I hit the tree once. The rough exterior of the tree hurt my hand but I hit it again. I hit it continuously until my knuckles were bloodied. I turned around and slid down the tree sitting on the ground now. My hands were shaky from the pain I had just inflicted on them. I hung my head trying to calm down now. How was I ever going to face her again? There's no way she'd still want to be my girlfriend after this.

I stayed in the forest for over an hour just trying to relax. I heard a branch snap and looked up. It was William and Xander. "What do you want?" I said almost growling. "We thought you could use some company and this." Xander said, handing me a bag carrying my shirt, a bottle of water and some bandages. "How did you know I was hurt?" I asked him. "Izzy said she could smell you bleeding out here so she sent us to check on you." William said, kneeling down on the ground to look at my hands. I showed them to him. "Man, you really did a number on yourself." he said, opening up the water for me. I took a drink then poured some out on my fingers.

He took the bandages and started wrapping up my fingers. "How is she?" I finally said looking up at Will. "Izzy? She's fine, you just startled her is all. Trust me, when I turned the first time I tried to kill her too." I shot him a dirty look letting him know I did not want to hear about that. "And what about Sarah? Is she worried about me?" I asked. "Sarah's fine, Izzy was explaining everything to her before we left. She was a bit shocked at the whole situation but she'll be alright," Xander replied

I finished my bottle of water and put my shirt on. "Are you coming back with us then?" William asked. I shook my head, "not yet. I'm too ashamed to face her right now." William placed a hand on my shoulder, "don't beat yourself up about it too much. You stopped what you were doing and that takes a lot of willpower to fight back once you've started, believe me, I know."

He was right, I did stop. Looking into her eyes made me stop and realize what I was doing. Maybe she would forgive me, I thought. "Just come back to the house whenever you're ready," Will said as they were walking away. I sat there for another half hour or so until the sun started going down. I figured it would be better to walk back while it was still light out. I made my way back through the trees and followed the lake. My legs were stiff from sitting on the ground for so long after my run.

When I made it to the willow tree I stopped to look at the house. The lights were on inside and I could see someone standing on the porch. Was it Isa? I thought. A larger person joined them on the porch. "Must be Sarah and Xander," I said out loud. I continued my walk back slowly dragging my feet trying to figure out what I was going to say to Isadora. 'I'm sorry', didn't seem to be enough for this type of situation.

Sarah and Xander had already gone back inside by the time I got to the porch. I was afraid to open the door so I decided to just sit on the porch swing for a little while. The sun went down and the porch light came on. I figured I'd sulked long enough and it was time to bite the bullet. I opened the door and walked inside. I could hear everyone talking in the dining room so I tried to sneak past them. "Adam, you're back," Sarah said before I could make my escape. I hung my head. She came up to me and gave me a hug. "It's gonna be alright. Why don't you eat with us first before you go see her?" I nodded my head at her.

I followed her into the kitchen where everyone but Isa was gathered. They were having lasagna, my favorite. Sarah dished me up a plate and I began eating. I stayed silent through the whole meal as the rest of them conversed. When we were finished I helped wash the dishes, anything to prolong the inevitable. I slowly made my ascent up the stairs towards the third floor. I reached the top to see that her door was already waiting open for me.

I took in a big breath then exhaled not knowing what I would be walking into. She was sitting in the armchair reading when I walked in and shut the door. She put her book down but remained sitting. I walked over to the bed and sat down taking my shoes off. I couldn't bring myself to look at her. "Are you alright, Adam?" she said quietly, making me jump. I answered back, "yes," then waited to see if she had anything more to say.

She stood up from her chair and walked toward the bathroom. She was in there momentarily then opened the door. She was wearing her tank top and panties again, this time they were black matching her shirt. She walked over to the bed and just stood there in front of me. I stared at her feet. "You have to talk to me Adam, I don't know what's going on in your head if you don't say something." She tried to touch my face but I turned away.

"Fine, don't talk to me then," she said storming off to the balcony. I knew she was going to be mad, I thought. She stood on the balcony with her arms crossed looking out at the water. She sighed, turning around and reentering the bedroom. "I'm not mad at you for what happened, I'm upset because you left. You could have really hurt yourself Adam. I was worried about you." She was worried about me? I looked up to face her now. She had purple bruising around her throat. I looked away again.

How could I ever do something so terrible to the woman I was in love with? My eyes began to well with tears. She came over and stood in front of me again this time pulling my head tight to her body. I tried not to let her see me cry so I buried my face in her chest. She stroked my head and shushed me like I was a child. "I'm so sorry," I said, finally looking up at her. She pulled me onto the bed and just let me lay with my head on her chest for a while. "It wasn't your fault. I shouldn't have bombarded you with information like that after I saw how you were reacting to it. Now we know how to stop any aggressive outburst in the future though." I lifted my head off of her to look at her directly. "What do you mean?" I said.

"It means that I'm your anchor. Everytime your emotions get away from you all you need to do is look me in the eyes and it calms you just like every time we're making out, if you sense that it's going too far you look into my eyes and snap out of it." It all made sense now, she was right. Whenever we were fooling around and I wanted to take it further she always brings me back to reality.

She smiled and wiped my eyes. "So you're not mad at me?" I asked. "Mad at you, no. How could I be mad at you? I'm a little sore but I'll be fine by tomorrow. I'm a fast healer," she said with a smile. I smiled back at her. "I love you," I said to her. She picked up my hand gently and kissed each finger. "We should take care of those," she said, leading me towards the bathroom. "But what about the blood?" I asked. "It's not bleeding anymore so you should be fine. Besides, if I was going to bite you it would be on your wrist anyway," she chuckled, "It doesn't flow as fast so I could savor every minute of it."

I couldn't tell if she was being serious or not about biting my wrist but if she wanted to I would let her after what I'd done to her. She turned the water on and took my bandages off. The water stung and I flinched. She got out new bandages and wound them around my knuckles. When she was fished she held out my hands so she could look at them. "There, good as new. Those should heal up nicely before work Wednesday night." she said.

We went back to the bed now. I laid on my side staring out the balcony doors. She laid down on her stomach facing me now. "So since you're my anchor and we've already established my love for you, does that mean we're mates?" She bit her lip before answering, "I suppose we are, she answered. My heart began soaring. I was overcome with joy

163

and I couldn't stop smiling. "You're so cute," she said to me, "your heart gives away your every emotion." I needed to know more.

"How so?" I said. She sat upright now while I was still laying on my side. She began to explain, "You see when I do this," she lightly kissed my lips, "your heart starts beating fast." She was right every time she kissed me it felt like my heart would burst. "But when I do this," she pushed me on to my back and slowly started moving both hands up my knees working her way towards my thighs, "your heart starts beating even faster. And if I continue up," she grabbed my hands and put them above my head while sitting on top of me, "your heart beats so fast that I want to do things to you that I'm not allowed to do yet."

My body stiffened and my heart began beating the fastest it's ever beaten before. She started kissing me, first at my lips and working her way down my neck and chest. I couldn't move. I didn't want her to stop. She kissed me all the way down to my navel, then brought herself right back up to my face. She lightly touched her lips to mine then pulled away again. I wanted more. "You're a bad influence," I said to her, smiling. She let go of my wrists and laid down on top of me. "I know, but doesn't that make it more fun?" she laughed.

I tried to move her slightly without her noticing. "Something the matter?" she said with a devilish grin. I started blushing, "you're getting me too excited," I said embarrassed. She shifted her weight over so I could be more comfortable. "Is that better?" she giggled. No, I thought, but answered, "yes." I still wanted more from her. "You know you don't have to hide that from me right? It's nothing to be embarrassed about." I couldn't believe we were having this conversation. "But it's embarrassing for me," I replied.

"What about it is so embarrassing? It's only natural, you're attracted to me and I'm attracted to you." She said, sitting upright on me now. I didn't know how to answer her. "It's embarrassing because you always know when I have one. I can't control my heart rate, I can't control my emotions, I'm completely powerless against you." I tried to roll over but she held me down with her thighs. "Do you wanna know something embarrassing about me? I planned to kill you the night I met you." I looked at her confused, "Why?" I asked. "Why? Because I was hungry and needed to quench my thirst. You smelled so appetizing to me that I

164

followed you home to kill you. But when I saw you laying on the futon saying my name something stopped me. You stopped me. I think you were right about us being mated before the incident because I want to spend every waking second with you. It hurts me to be away from you for long periods of time and it kills me that you can say that you love me but I can't say it back!"

She was trembling now out of frustration. I tried to wrap my brain around all she was saying before I spoke. "You love me too, don't you?" I said to her, "you love me and that scares you for some reason." She looked away from me, confirming my statement. "Why can't you say it back to me?" I asked brushing the hair behind her ear. "Because he ruined me. I loved him with my entire being and all he ever did was tear me down. I'm afraid that if I say it, you'll one day change your mind too." She replied. It all made sense now. She's been pushing her boundaries with me by trying to see if I'd still want to be with her. And then today when I lost my temper and I ran away from her that only validated her suspicions.

"I love you Isadora and nothing is going to change that. I don't care if you can't say it back yet because now I know you love me too." I said. A tear fell on my chest from her face. "But what if I can never say it back?" she asked. I wiped the tears off her cheeks. "Then I will tell you twice as often until you feel comfortable enough to say it." I said. She gave me a little smile, leaning down to kiss my lips. "Can you please try to say it at least once, just for me, nobody else? After all, you do have that sound protection barrier," I said.

She rolled me over on top of her, "are you gonna put out?" she asked deviously. I laughed, "Not tonight," I said. She laughed at my answer and began kissing me again. Her kisses were gentle as we lay there trying to sleep. She played with my hair, making me fall asleep faster. Before I fell asleep I felt her lips touch my ear. Barely above a whisper I heard her say, "I love you Adam" and kiss my cheek.

Chapter

13

The next morning I awoke to find her still laying in bed with me. She had covered me up and then snuggled back up to me so my arm was draped over her. Did she actually tell me she loved me last night or was it all just a dream? I thought. I didn't want to disturb her if she was sleeping so I waited for her to move before saying anything. "Good morning Adam," she said, rolling over to face me. "Were you awake again all night?" I asked. She giggled, "yeah, sorry. I still don't know if I dare fall asleep around you. My dreams can get pretty vivid and I don't want to hurt you."

I kissed her forehead, "you need to sleep too. You don't want to exhaust yourself. When was the last time you slept?" I asked. She had to think about it for a minute then said, "three maybe four months ago I think?" My jaw dropped, how could she go so long without sleep? She scooted closer and put her tongue in my mouth. It took my breath away when she was done. "Don't tell me what to do," she said, winking trying to get out from under the covers. "Now hold on," I said, dragging her back by the waist. She made a squawking sound when I filled her back. "Are you ticklish?" I asked. Her head whipped around to look at me. "No…" she replied, wrinkling her nose. I began to tickle her all over her body. She squealed and laughed as I did it. "Stop, stop, stop!" She screamed.

She laid there panting when I was finished. She grabbed my hand and wrapped her fingers in mine. "Don't do that again," she demanded, laughing, "or else," she said. "Or else, what?" I said playfully. "Or else I'll make you even more excitable than you usually are." I had to know where this was going. "Yeah right, like you could do that." I said tauntingly. She got off the bed and stood with her back to me. She then proceeded to take her tank top off. I had no idea all this time she wasn't wearing a bra underneath. She covered herself with her hands and turned around. She jumped at the bed but I tossed the blanket at her before I could see anything. While she was trying to get the blanket off her head I pinned her to the bed with the blanket still over her chest.

"Ok, you win. I give up," I said. "Good, now that that's settled you can let me go," she tried to get up but I wouldn't let her. She frowned. "Can you please put your shirt back on first?" I asked her nicely. She smiled then rolled her eyes. "I suppose I can, but you're going to have to look at them sooner or later." She joked. "I can tell they're very nice through your shirt, thank you." I said teasing her. She scoffed, "pervert." I grabbed her shirt and held it out for her. I closed my eyes and waited for her to take it. Instead she pressed herself up against me standing there. My eyes shot open and looked at her. "Fooled ya," she said with a twinkle in her eye. She stood on her tippy toes to kiss my cheek. I didn't move. "Relax sweetie, they're not going to bite you." She said. She had never called me that before. I carefully placed my hands on her back and she put hers on mine.

We stood there looking into each other's eyes. "I love you," I said. She smiled, "I know." I closed my eyes again and she backed up to put her tank top on. "I'm good," she said after she was finished. I didn't believe her so I reached my hand out to see if I could feel the fabric of her shirt against her skin. "Hey now!" She said and I opened my eyes to see I was actually cupping one of her breasts. "I'm sorry!" I said quickly, removing my hand right away. Smooth move, man. I thought to myself. She shook her head and reached out for both my hands, placing them on her chest. "There, let's just get this over with", she said. I stood there in awe. How could she be so calm? I tried pulling my hands away but she wouldn't let me. "Just relax," she said. That was easy for her to say, she didn't have anything to lose by me touching her.

She squeezed my hands around them. They were so soft and billowy. She slowly let go of my hands until she was no longer touching me. I stood there with my hands out gripping her. "See, that's not so bad is it?" She said. I grinned sheepishly, "No it's really nice actually." I said.

She laughed and they jiggled in my hands. "You can let go now if you'd like," she said. I ran my hands down her body until I got to her waist. I put my hands on her hips like I was going to pick her up. Instead of me picking her up she just jumped in my arms. I caught her and fell back on the bed. She stopped herself from crashing down on my lap which I appreciated. She kissed me passionately then slowly sat down on my lap. I knew she was trying to be careful not to hurt me.

Suddenly I heard a buzzing sound. It was her phone in the nightstand. She reached for it and answered the call. "Hello?...yep... OK, we'll be right down," she ended the call. "Who was that?" I asked. "That was Will, he asked if you were up and wanted breakfast. I told him we'd be right down." She kissed me one more time then got up to go get dressed. I lie there on the bed reminiscing on what just happened. When she returned she was wearing ripped jeans and a striped white and black long sleeve shirt. I wish she didn't have to cover up most of her beautiful skin but it was a sunny day outside so I understood. She kept her hair down at least which I loved even more because I love the way it swayed as she walked.

"Come on," she said, holding out her hand for me. I got off the bed and happily took it. We walked down the stairs only to find Will sitting at the counter eating his breakfast. "I'm gonna go into the club today and polish the floors, wanna join me?" He asked. I looked at Isa, "not really," I said, "where's everybody else?" "The girls are at school and Ben and Xander went with them to drop them off. They'll probably just wait around until they're done for the day." He said. So that meant Isa and I would have the whole house to ourselves today. That was great. Maybe we could continue what was going on upstairs today, I thought. My heart started racing and Isa squeezed my hand. She had to be thinking the same thing as me. "I made pancakes. There's plenty more, help yourselves," William said, getting up from the island. "I'll be back later. Just call if you need anything." He said walking to the front door. I listened to hear the car drive away.

She hopped up on the counter facing me. Isa looked at me with mischievous eyes and beckoned me over with one finger. Yes, today was the day I'd made up my mind. Today I wasn't going to be shy anymore. I walked up to her. She was sitting at the perfect height now. I placed my hands on her thighs. I started shivering with anticipation for what was about to happen. "Are you ok?" She asked, noticing this. I looked deep in her eyes and whispered, "I want you," to her. She smiled and pulled me closer. Her kisses seemed more intense this time. Like she'd been holding back until now. She started pulling on my shirt and I took it off. I did the same for her.

I started kissing her neck when she let out a quiet moan. Before I knew it I was pawing at her jeans trying to take them off. I managed to get the button undone and was in the process of peeling them off her when she whispered, "we should probably go upstairs in case someone comes home." She was right. We grabbed our shirts and headed back up the stairs. Once in the room I locked the door. She laid down on the bed now waiting for me. I was ready. I took her pants off to reveal that she was wearing a black lace thong. I had never seen her in so little clothing.

She tried pulling down my pants but I wasn't quite ready for that yet. She threw me on the bed and climbed on top. I reached around her to take her bra off when she giggled. "What's so funny?" I said breathlessly. She motioned to the front of her bra, "this one opens from the front. You just pinch here and it'll pop right open." She was being a good sport, helping me out knowing it was my first time ever unhooking one of these. I did as she said and it was off. I buried my face in between them. There was no going back now. I shimmied down my pants and waited for what came next. "Say something if I hurt you," she said, sweetly in my ear before sitting down. The beast inside me was rattling his cage. He needed more. She slowly began moving her hips. She was incredible.

I rolled over on top of her now pinning her down. She moaned again, making me want to go faster. She reached up and started clawing my back, it hurt but in a good way. She pulled me down closer to her and she bit my neck. I couldn't tell if she was play biting or if she actually sank her teeth in. I didn't care. I kept on going until she moaned louder. Was I hurting her? I thought for a brief second. No, she was enjoying this as much as I was. I kept on going until my time was up. I held myself up over her panting and trembling. I leaned down one last time to give her the best kiss I could. She wrapped her arms around me and held on tightly. At last, I thought.

She gasped and covered her mouth. I leaned up off of her again. She looked horrified. What was wrong? I thought. "I bit you!" She shrieked. Now that things weren't moving so fast I could see little drops of blood all over her. She pushed me away and ran to the bathroom. I touched my neck and then looked at my hand. It was covered in blood. I put pressure on the wound in hopes that I wouldn't bleed out. She returned wearing a towel and brought a wet washcloth for me. "I am so sorry. I didn't even notice I bit you until the end," she said. She placed the cloth on my neck and began wiping up the blood. She kept scrunching her eyes shut and shaking her head as she did it just like the ride home from the club after the fight. Was she having a difficult time resisting now?

"Are you ok?" I asked her. She cleared her throat, "not really. I've had a taste, now I want more." She said backing away. "What do you need me to do?" I asked, pulling my pants up with one hand and holding pressure on my neck with the other. "Go in the bathroom and take a look in the mirror to see if it's serious," she demanded backing away from me as I got off the bed. I did as she said, I went in the bathroom and finished cleaning up the blood. There was a perfect pair of dots on my neck. It wasn't very deep and mostly just pinched the skin. The bleeding had stopped and I got a new dry cloth out to hold on my neck. "It's not that bad," I said, opening the door.

She was standing right there when it opened and startled me. "See, you barely broke the skin," I turned my head to show her. She looked guilty, "you were supposed to tell me if I hurt you though," she said. How could I make her understand? I thought. "But it didn't hurt me, I thought you were just play biting me," I said pulling her in for a hug. I stroked her head and coddled her. "Was I ok?" I asked, looking at her now, "did I hurt you at all?" She smiled, "you did great, I'd say you could have probably been a little more aggressive with me. Don't worry, I can take it. You showed great control too. I'm very impressed," she replied. Could have been more aggressive with her, what did that mean? I thought. "What do you mean, more aggressive?" I asked. She simulated her clawing my back again, "you can scratch me, pull my hair, or pin my arms down. You know, more domineering I guess." I smiled at her. "But it was good for you too and not just me?" I asked her. She grabbed my face with both hands," yes, it was all very enjoyable for me too. I'm surprised I can still walk." She joked.

She headed into the bathroom now taking off her towel, "are you coming?" She asked. I quickly stripped and followed her in there. She turned the water on and we got in. We let the water fall over us as we made out. I wonder if she'd want to have a go at it again in here? I thought. I picked her up and held her against the wall. The slipperiness of the wall made everything that much easier. This time didn't last as long as the first one but it was still exciting. We finished washing ourselves and got out. She dried off and then went into her closet to pick out a clean set of clothes. All my clothes were still downstairs so I had to put on my dirty ones in order to go get them.

She came out wearing a pink strapless dress. "Do you want me just to go get you some clothes?" She asked. I couldn't hear her. All I wanted to do was take her again. I walked over to her and started kissing her, slowly easing her dress up with one hand until I could feel her panties. She pulled away, "Adam, not again. I told you once we started it would be hard to stop and now you wanna go for the third time in less than two hours?" I laughed wickedly gripping her panties tighter. "Yeah, I do" I said. She loosened my fingers from the fabric and put her dress down. "Maybe later," she said, kissing me.

We walked downstairs and checked if anyone had come home. The house was empty beside us. I went down to my room to change into some clean clothes while Isa warmed up the pancakes that William had made for us. I was thinking that something seemed awfully suspicious about everyone being gone at the same time so that it was just here. Then it occurred to me, did she tell everyone to leave for the day just so we could do it? It made me a little mad thinking about it. She'd said she would let me take my time with everything. Was that just a lie to get me into bed? I raced back up the stairs. She was sitting at the table eating her food while scrolling through her phone. She looked up at me with a smile. I frowned at her. She was taken aback by my expression. "What?" She said. I needed to know the truth. "Did you send everyone away today just so I would sleep with you?"

She put her phone down, appalled at my accusation. "No Adam, I didn't. I told you I wasn't going to force myself on you and I meant it," she said, crossing her arms. I still wasn't sure I believed her. I reached in my pocket to grab my phone. "What are you doing?" She asked. "I'm calling Sarah, she'll tell me the truth why Ben and Xander aren't here. I put the phone on speaker phone dialing her number. It started ringing, "hello?" Sarah answered. "Hey Sarah. Quick question, where are Ben and Xander right now?" I asked. "Umm, they should be at the club. Xander said something about helping Will wax the floors or something like that." I knew it, Isa must have told them to go help Will to make it seem like a valid excuse to get them out of the house. "So if I were to call William, he would be able to confirm that they were there, right?" I said. "Yeah. They should be there." Sarah sounded annoyed. "Xander said the guy with the polishing machine was scheduled to be there around noon today so they should all be there." She continued. "What do you mean scheduled to be there around noon? Didn't they already have the machine there?" I asked befuddled. "Yeah, schedule. They made an appointment to use the machine last week but couldn't because of double booking so they rescheduled it for today." She said. Last week, I thought.

My heart dropped into my stomach. Isa had been telling me the truth. She didn't plan for us to be together today, that's just how it happened. I looked at Isa with apologetic eyes. "Ok, Sarah. Thanks. Bye." And I hung up the phone. I hung my head and slowly walked over to Isa. She looked hurt. I tried to bend down to give her a hug but she put her hand up to stop me. "Don't," she said looking away from me. "Don't touch me." I tried again to at least hold her hand but she pulled it away too quickly. She stood up fast, knocking her chair over and stormed off heading up to her room. I followed her as quickly as I could, running up the stairs. She slammed the door shut behind her. I made my way to the top and tried to open the door. Luckily it was still unlocked. I went inside, shutting the door behind me. "I am so sorry, Isa. You have to believe me." She was sitting at the end of her bed staring off into the distance. "Why? You didn't believe me." She said. She had a point, I was so quick to judge her and for what? Because I was paranoid? "Can you forgive me please?" I asked.

She focused her eyes on me now. I could see the rage in them. "Forgive you?" She said staring deep into my soul. I started to feel an immense amount of pressure on my shoulders. Was she doing this? I thought. She stood up and took a step closer. With each step I began sinking closer to the ground. I couldn't fight whatever she was doing to me. I was on my knees now struggling to keep my head up. She stood in front of me now, staring down at me as I tried to remain upright on all fours. "I will forgive, but for right now you're going to listen." She spoke in a low growl. "I am your alpha and when I tell you something you have to trust me, regardless of our relationship status. This isn't going to work if you don't." She closed her eyes, breaking her concentration. The pressure was lifted off of me now. I stayed there on all fours cowering beneath her. She opened her eyes again and squatted down to be closer to me. "And besides," she spoke softly now, "it hurts me that you think I would ever do such a thing." She reached out and touched my cheek. I was up on my knees now. "What was that?" I asked. She helped me stand up now. "The true power of an alpha. You see, if I really wanted you to do something against your will, I could have just used that."

I put my arms around her waist and she put her arms around my neck. "I truly am sorry Isadora. I'll never question you again." I said, leaning my head on hers. She smiled. "Yes you will, but that's ok. Sometimes it's good to challenge me. I can be really stubborn sometimes and need to be put in my place," she said. I picked her up, "oh, I'll put you in your place alright," and I carried her over to the bed. She laughed as we started making out. I tried bringing my hands up her thighs but she stopped me. "I don't know if you deserve that," she said with a smile. I whined, my body ached to be with her again. She was right about that too, once I'd started now I just wanted more. "Please?" I begged her. She kissed me passionately one last time then got up. I groaned knowing she was right and that I didn't deserve it yet.

We went back downstairs so I could eat something. While I was eating I asked her, "So what DID you have planned for us today?" She smirked, "I was planning on trying to test your senses again. How do you feel about hide and seek?" She said. I gave her a suspicious look, "hide and seek?" I asked. She nodded her head, "yeah. We'll go out in the woods then I'll hide and you have to come find me." That seemed simple enough, I thought. After I finished eating I went down to my room to grab my shoes. This is dumb, I thought. Why was I still coming down here to get my stuff? Why hadn't I just asked her to move all my stuff up in her room? Maybe I'll bring it up to her later.

The thought of completely moving in with her kind of scared me. I wonder what she thought of it? I heard a tapping on the sliding glass door. I looked to see Isa standing outside. She had changed out of her dress and was wearing a sports bra and some leggings now. God she looked good, I thought. I opened the door for her. She came in and sat down on the floor, stretching out her legs. "You better warm up, we're gonna be doing lots of running today," she said. I sat down on the floor and stretched too. It had been a long time since I'd done this. "This takes me back," I said putting my right leg back behind my hip. She looked at me puzzled. "What does?" she asked. "I used to do gymnastics in high school and I was pretty good at it," I said. She smiled, "I'd like to see that sometime," she replied.

She stood up and reached her hand down to me. I took it and helped myself up. We exited through the sliding door and walked towards the trees. I decided I was going to show off in front of her and jogged ahead and did a double round off in the grass. I stuck the landing and stood there waiting for her to catch up to me. "Very impressive," she grinned. She walked a little faster then turned around in front of me as she did a backflip.

I was surprised when she did this. "Where'd you learn to do that? I thought you only knew ballet?" I asked. She resumed walking normally again, "you should see me on the beam," she laughed. We continued walking until we came to the edge of the woods. "Now, you're going to count to ten and then you need to use your senses to try and find me," she said. I looked at her funny, "only to ten? You're not going to make it very far then." I said. She chuckled. "Let's just see about that." she said, taunting me.

She walked in the woods a little bit and waited for me to turn around to start counting. I did so and began, "1..2...3...4...5...6...7...8...9...10!" I turned around to see her nowhere to be found. Whoa, she was really fast, I thought. I began jogging around the area looking for her. How was I supposed to use my senses to find her? I thought. I wandered around for about twenty minutes and couldn't find her. I decided to give up, "ok Isa you win. You can come out now." I shouted. Silence.

I tried yelling again, "I give up Isa, you can come back now." again, silence. I was starting to panic because she wasn't responding. My adrenaline started pumping and I began sprinting through the forest looking for her. I ran in circles trying to find any trace of her. My anxiety was in full swing. What if I wasn't able to find her? I thought. I couldn't let that happen, I needed to get to her. I stopped running to catch my breath. "Use my senses, she said. What does that even mean?" I said. I tried thinking about what the five senses were. Touch, sight, smell, sound, and taste.

I couldn't touch or see her right now, so those two didn't matter. I thought about her scent. She smelled like vanilla all the time. I closed my eyes and inhaled deeply. I wasn't sure if I could actually smell her or if it was just her scent lingering on my clothes from being around her. I steadied my breathing and tried to listen for her. I could hear the wind blowing through the leaves all around me. I could hear the creaking of the trees as they shifted. Suddenly I heard a branch snap to my left. I took off running in that direction. I could smell vanilla now. I stopped and brought my face close to one of the trees. She touched this one as she ran by, I thought. I heard another sound in the wind and followed it. I was gaining on her now.

I came to a clearing next to the lake's edge and waited. I closed my eyes again, breathing in the sweet scent of vanilla. I heard a leaf fall next to me and looked up. I saw her perched on a large limb fifty feet off the ground. My jaw dropped looking up at her. Suddenly she leapt from the branch, falling right for me. I held out my arms to catch her. She landed her arms on my shoulders, knocking me to the ground. It knocked the wind out of me when she landed on my chest. "You found me!" she said excitedly.

She kissed my mouth pushing me further into the dirt. I gasped for air. "Sorry," she said, scrambling off of me. I sat up now rubbing my chest. She was standing next to the tree she'd just fallen from with her hands on her hips. "How'd you get up there?" I asked. She then demonstrated how she climbed up the tree using her super strength. There were marks all along the tree up to where she was perched from her gripping the bark so hard. "Will I be able to do that too?" I asked. She smiled, "maybe someday. It takes practice though. There's a lot of core strength that goes into climbing a tree with your bare hands," she said.

I stood up again and brushed the foliage off of my clothes. "Did I hurt you?" she asked worriedly. I shook my head, "nope, I just wasn't expecting you to do that," I said. She relaxed now, taking a few steps closer to me. I reached out to hold her and started kissing her neck. The bruising was almost gone now but I could still see where my fingers had gripped her throat. I stopped kissing her. "What's the matter?" she asked. I still felt so guilty about what had happened the other day. "I just feel so bad about hurting you yesterday," I said, tracing the marks on her neck. She reached up and poked my neck where she had bitten me earlier. "I'm pretty sure I got you back for it, Adam," she said with a smile. I guess she was right about that.

I kissed her again on her neck. She squealed when I got to her ear. "You are so ticklish," I said, nibbling on her earlobe. She tried to get away from me but I wouldn't let her go. She started trying to tickle me now. "Jokes on you, I'm not ticklish." I laughed. "Oh yeah, I'll bet I can make you squirm too." she said tauntingly. She reached down and began stroking me. A jolt of pleasure shot through my body that brought me to my knees. I stayed there on the ground in front of her quivering before I looked up. She was beaming with pride at making good on her threat.

I carefully stood up again. She had one of her eyebrows raised playfully. I didn't know what to say. I leaned in to rest my head on hers. She wrapped her arms around me and held me close. "I love you, Isa," I said to her. I wanted to hear her say it back. We stayed there holding each other for a while. She turned away from me towards the tree she had been climbing and started pressing down hard on the bark. She crushed our initials in the tree and drew a heart around it.

"How's that?" she said to me once she was finished. It wasn't the same as saying it, but I knew she felt it. Our love was strong for one another and she didn't need to tell me out loud for me to know it was true. After she had marked our tree we began the long journey back to the house. My legs were tired from all the running I did, maybe I should have stretched more like she said, I thought.

We emerged through the forest close to the water where the willow tree was located. The house was in sight, now was my chance to ask her about moving my stuff in. "So, it's kinda inconvenient for me to sleep in your room but have all my stuff on the bottom level," I started the conversation. "I was wondering if maybe I could just move my things up there with you." Her eyes fluttered. "Oh?" she said, biting her lip. Did she not want to? I thought. "Yeah, it would just be easier if you did that. We can do that once we get back to the house." She didn't look as enthused as I'd hoped she would be.

"Is something on your mind?" I asked her. She stopped walking and looked towards the house. "Listen," she said. I listened to try to hear what she was hearing. I could faintly hear people talking. "Everyone is home now," I said. She looked at me now, "yes but what are they saying?" she asked. I closed my eyes and tried again to listen to what they were saying.

"Izzy should know better. She shouldn't be so reckless. By keeping them here and adding to the pack, it's bound to attract hunters." It was Ben talking to William. "Izzy knows what she's doing. She'd never let anything happen to us." William said. "You mean she wouldn't let anything happen to Adam. That's all she cares about now is her new toy." The last sentence Ben said started to make me angry and I clenched my fists. "What are they talking about, attracting hunters?" I asked her. I needed to distract myself from the conversation that was happening in the house.

"He means the bigger the pack the more obvious we become. There haven't been any hunters around here in twenty years but Ben has had his run in with them before and is trying to get everyone else riled up," she said. She put her hand on my fist causing me to relax. "I believe Ben will try to fight me on the next full moon to try and become the alpha. He thinks I'm weak now that I've taken a mate. He might even try to fight me before then, knowing you can't transform yet." She said. "Why would that matter if I could transform or not?" I asked curiously. She looked at me now.

"Because, he knows that if he's going to succeed the best way to take me out is through you. You not being able to transform is a huge advantage for him. If he were to attack you and something happened, I'd be more likely to surrender in order to save you." Would she really surrender to save my life? I thought "Come on, they're done talking now so we can head back to the house." she said, pulling on my hand.

Something was bothering me, I thought. "Is Ben always like that?" I asked her. She nodded, "yes." She said. "How come you let him be a part of the pack then?" I said. She sighed, "Because he's with Lexa and if he were to leave so would she and then Xander would be caught between a rock and a hard place trying to decide whether to go with them or stay. Trust me, I've been struggling with this whole debacle for decades. Now it would be even harder for Xander to choose because of Sarah." she said.

We made it to the house but went in my sliding patio door. Isa started grabbing all my clothes and put them in my dresser. Was she just going to carry it up all by herself? I thought. She placed her arms around the dresser and hauled it out the patio door. "I guess we're going that way, huh?" I said to her. She leapt onto her balcony holding my dresser with ease then looked down at me. Did she think I could do that? She smiled and jumped back down. "We can go through the house if you'd like. I know your stomach doesn't seem to like the jump up there." I blushed remembering throwing up over the side of the railing.

I nodded at her. I did a once over in my old room to make sure we had grabbed everything before shutting the door. We went up stairs into the rest of the house. Nobody was on the main floor now, it was just us. I grabbed a bottle of water out of the fridge. "Lexa and Ben are talking about us and Will is in his room watching TV." she said. "What about Sarah and Xander?" She listened some more. Lexa just said that they went out on a date." She said. Her hearing was incredible. "Can everyone else hear as well as you can?" I asked. She took my bottle and took a sip. "No, I'm surprised you could hear what they were saying all the way from the willow." she replied.

I followed her up the stairs to our room. She locked the door once we got in. My dresser was still sitting out on the balcony so she picked it up again and placed it in her walk in closet. She hung the clothes up for me in the section above my dresser. My wardrobe was significantly smaller than hers so it didn't take up too much of her space. She then proceeded to undress and put her tank top on for bed. She didn't even bother trying to be modest for me anymore. I still looked away when she changed though.

I took my pants and shirt off and was just wearing my boxers now. It was so warm in her room with the fireplace going but I knew I'd cool down soon enough when she curled up next to me. "It's so hot in here," I said laying down on the bed. The satin sheets felt nice on my back. "Well if you're too warm," she came and lay her body on top of mine, "I'll just have to cool you down. She reached down underneath her and stuck her hand in my boxers. My heart began racing. Her green eyes were wild with excitement. I didn't want to move, I couldn't move, I was at her mercy now.

She began slowly moving her hand. I tensed up as she started kissing my chest. I tried to pull her hand away but it made her hold on tighter. I arched my back causing her to slide further down my torso. What was she going to do next? She wouldn't dare, I thought. She kissed me all the way down my abdomen and stopped just below my belly button. I started to tremble. Any lower and I don't think I could take it, I thought. She released me then licked me all the way up to my mouth.

I quickly rolled out from under her and was now standing behind her. I pulled her close slamming her back into my chest. I wrapped my one arm around the front of her to squeeze her breast and with my other hand I gripped her panties. I needed her. I bent her over and proceeded. She made a noise and made me want to grab her hair and pull when I remembered her telling me earlier that it was ok to be a little more aggressive. I grabbed a fistful of her beautiful silvery blond hair and yanked on it. I heard her moan when I did this. She wanted me to do that, I thought as a shot of adrenaline shot through me one last time.

I stood there now just holding on to her. While she was still on her knees she tried to pull away but I couldn't let her go. She placed her hands over my one gripping the lace fabric indicating it was time for me to relax. Slowly I released the fabric and her hair. She turned around to face me. I was enchanted by her beauty. She softly kissed my lips. I melted into her. We fell back on the bed and just lay there together. "You weren't gonna actually, ya know, were you?" I was referring to when she was kissing her way down my body. She chuckled, "I thought about it but I didn't think you'd be able to handle it," she said. She was probably right, I thought.

I kissed her again before pulling up the covers for us to go to bed. "We have work tomorrow so you better try and sleep," I said to her. She laughed. "For you, tonight I'll actually try to sleep. But you've been given plenty of warning in case I should have bad dreams," she said. I began petting her head hoping to soothe her to sleep. I could feel her twitching. Was she already asleep? I wondered. I carefully got up to get a better look. Her eyes were closed and her mouth was slightly ajar. She was asleep. I laid back down next to her and closed my eyes.

In the middle of the night, I awoke to the sounds of her whimpering. I tried to remain calm because I didn't know how she would react if I happened to wake her up by accident. Her eyes were scrunched and her breathing was rapid. It looked like she was maybe trying to run away from something in her dream. I brushed the hair out of her face and began stroking her head. She jumped a few times, startling me. She felt really warm for once like maybe she had a fever. Could she maybe just be warm from sharing the bed with me? I thought. I got up to go get her a cool damp washcloth. Maybe that would help her.

Whilst I was in the bathroom she suddenly began screaming. The way it sounded made my blood run cold. I rushed back out to see that the bed was on fire. In a panic I ran over to her to see if I could get her out of the flames. To my surprise the bed remained perfectly fine, only Isadora seemed to be on fire. I needed to wake her up. I reached in the inferno and pulled her out. We landed on the floor with a thud. I looked around frantically to make sure she wasn't on fire anymore. I held her head up with my hands, "Isadora wake up!" I said. Her eyes fluttered open with a terrified look in them.

"What happened?" she said looking around. I pulled her closer to me, "It's alright, you just had a bad dream." I said. My heart was still pounding from the horrifying scene I just witnessed. She looked at the burn marks around her feet and ankles. She was being burned alive, I thought. "What was with that crazy fire?" I asked. She rubbed her foot, "It's not real fire, it's just my dreams manifesting in real life. Don't worry everything is flame retardant in here just in case something were to actually happen."

We stood up and got back into bed. I couldn't take my eyes off of her. I was afraid she was going to burst into flames again. She wouldn't close her eyes. "Aren't you going to try to sleep again?" I asked her. She shook her head, "no. I don't want to be a bother to you." She scooted away and curled herself up in a ball. I reached out and pulled her body right up close to mine, draping my arm over her. "There, now you're safe." I said to her. I lay there a little while waiting to see if she was going to pass out. She started twitching again in her sleep. I rolled her over so that her head could lay across my heart. Maybe it would calm her down, I thought. I kissed her forehead and whispered, "I love you," to her.

The next morning she was still sleeping on my chest when I woke up. Had she slept the entire night after that one night terror? I wondered. "Isa," I said to her quietly. She opened her eyes and looked up at me. She furrowed her brow then sat upright. "What's wrong?" I said, startled. She reached for her phone. "It's 9:30." She said. I was confused. "Yeah?" I replied to her. "No you don't get it. It's 9:30 in the morning!" She said. I still didn't understand. "What's the significance of 9:30?" I asked. She set her phone down and positioned herself the way we were sleeping. "Did we sleep like this all night?" She asked. I nodded my head. She sat up again. "Don't you realize what this means? I slept through the night last night. I haven't been able to do that in hundreds of years!" She was so excited now. "I think listening to your heart beat kept me grounded all night long. It's just like I'm your anchor for your emotions and you do the same for me." She said with a smile.

Chapter

14

I couldn't believe it, I was right. Having her right next to me calmed her down enough so that she could actually sleep without any disturbance. I brushed back her hair from her face, "how do you feel?" I asked her. She laid her head back down again, "wonderful," she said with a sigh. We cuddled there for a little while longer before she sat up again. "No, we'd better get up. Otherwise I might fall back asleep again," she said. She scooted off the bed and walked towards her closet. I got up to go use the restroom. I looked in the mirror. I needed to shave, badly. I looked around to see if she had any razors. Under the sink was my toiletry bag from when I lived in the apartment. When did they get here? I thought. I began cleaning up my face. After I was finished I took one last look in the mirror. The small marks on my neck were completely closed up and healed now. That's good, I thought, wouldn't want people to start getting suspicious

I left the bathroom clean shaven now. Isa was sitting in the chair waiting for me. She was wearing a white cropped sweater that exposed her midriff and black skinny jeans. She got up and began petting my smooth jawline. "Ah, I was starting to get attached to the idea of you growing a beard," she said. I grinned, "Why didn't you say something? I wouldn't have shaved then." I replied. She giggled and kissed my cheek. I enjoyed being able to feel her soft lips on my skin once again. She was wearing the sunflower necklace I got her at the carnival now. My heart swelled with pride knowing she liked it. I embraced her, hoisting her up off the ground. I wanted to be with her again. I started feeling up her shirt as I held her.

She held me closer so my hand couldn't reach her chest. "I know you wanna do it again. But we need to slow down a little bit. You're going to wear yourself out," she said, releasing her legs. I pouted. I felt great, each morning felt better than the last. I stuck out my lip, trying to induce a sympathetic reaction out of her. She leaned forward to kiss me but instead, chose to gently bite my bottom lip. I picked her up again, carrying her to the bed. She playfully tried to get away but didn't use her full strength to escape me. "Come on now, everybody's gone already. The only one left in the house is Will." I said. She looked at me surprised. "How do you know he's the only one left?" She asked. I stopped to think about my answer. How did I know? I thought. I closed my eyes to listen around the house. I could hear William sitting at the table scraping his fork across his plate but I couldn't hear anyone else. William spoke in his normal tone, "I don't know if you're listening Izzy, but you should send Adam down to eat something." He said. I couldn't believe it. My hearing was beginning to become even clearer now. "Did you hear him?" I asked. She rolled her eyes, "of course I could hear him. And he's right, you need to eat something." She tried to push me off but I wouldn't move. She gave me a dirty look when I kissed her nose. "I don't want to have to use my full strength against you Adam. I will win." She threatened. I gave her another kiss then got off of her.

She stood beside me now holding my hand. "Do we have to go to work tonight?" I asked. She smirked at me, "yes we have to go to work tonight. I haven't been there in over a week now." She answered. I couldn't believe it had already been a week since I had been attacked. My wounds had all healed now and my ribs didn't hurt either. I looked at my hand that had been cut with the knife. I had a large scar running across the palm of my hand now. It didn't hurt but the memory of the incident still affected me.

So many things had changed recently. I had gotten a new job, Sarah and I moved out of our crappy apartment, I was in love with an incredible woman who just happened to be a vampire, and now I was a werewolf living in a house with other werewolves. What more could I ask for? We made our way down to the kitchen where William was washing his dishes. He looked up as we entered, "good morning, you two," he said with a smile.

Isa walked up to him and tousled his hair. I instantly became jealous. William, noticing my hostility said, "Relax Adam. She's been petting my head every morning since before you were even born." That didn't make me any less jealous. I knew he wasn't a threat but I couldn't shake this feeling. I got in between the two of them to make my presence known while they were talking. He glanced my way again. I was staring at him now, not taking my eyes off of him. He motioned at me, "are you sure he can handle himself tonight?" he said. She looked at me too as I stared intensely at Will.

"Only one way to find out," she said, grabbing my hand. I broke my concentration. What were they worried about? I thought. "I don't know Izzy, the way he was looking at me makes me worried. What if he snaps again?" Will asked her. "Then I'll just take him home. It's going to be fine," she replied. "Izzy, he was just going to fight me because you touched my hair. How's he going to react if some drunk asshole tries something with you?" I felt a low growl leave my throat. William took a step back.

Isa inserted herself between us, placing her hand on my chest to hold me there. "He's going to be calm if that happens and he's not going to cause a scene, right?" she said to me. I looked her in the eyes, she had complete faith in me. I nodded at her. She slowly walked away and went to the fridge. William leaned against the counter now talking to me. "Boy, you got it bad," he said. "What do I have?" I asked him. "You've claimed her as your mate now you see everyone as a potential threat to her," he said.

That made sense, I thought. It reminded me of when Xander pushed me away from Sarah after Isa first told me about vampires and werewolves. He couldn't help it, he was in love with Sarah and just wanted to protect her, and now I was acting the same way. "Is there any way to stop me from doing that again?" I asked. "Discipline," Isa said, grabbing a bowl of fruit out of the fridge. "You'll learn to control yourself in time but staying home alone isn't going to solve anything. We have to get you out with people so you can adapt to being around them again," she said sitting down at the table.

That worried me. "But what if I can't control myself? What will happen then?" I asked, looking at them. They stared at each other for a moment before either of them spoke. "If that happens you would be putting us at risk of exposure and possible hunter involvement," Will finally said. My heart began pounding. The last thing I wanted was to somehow put everyone around me, especially Isa in danger. "That doesn't necessarily mean you're going to expose us or anything like that. It just means you'll need to think carefully about your actions before you do anything rash at the club," Isa said, "for instance, I don't think you should touch me while we're at work." I looked at her with wide confused eyes.

"Why not?" I asked. "Because it'll just make you that much more agitated if someone else were to touch her," Will said, "it's a bar man, shit happens." I felt like I was being ganged up on. They were right though, even the thought of someone else touching her made me want to hurt somebody. "Wouldn't people be more inclined to leave her alone if they knew we were together though?" I asked. He shook his head, "no, that would be worse. If they know you two are going out then guys would be more likely to do something knowing you couldn't cause a scene in front of customers," Will said.

Damn it, there was nothing I could do. I'd just have to sit back and watch if something were to happen. "Could you just stay home then and I'll go to work?" I asked her. "No, that's not going to solve anything. You can't keep me hidden here forever," she said looking at me sadly. I needed to get away from this conversation. My head was spinning and my temper was flaring. I stormed out of the kitchen into the living room and sat down on the couch.

I sat there breathing heavily trying to calm down. I wanted to be near Isa but I was afraid that the way things were headed I was going to end up hurting her again. They left me alone so I could compose myself. After a few minutes I rejoined them. Isa was done with her fruit and Will was sitting at the table next to her. I tried not to let it bother me that they were sitting so close. "Ok. I'm good now." I said reaching for the fridge handle.

"Izzy was just telling me you experienced one of her night terrors last night. Pretty wicked stuff isn't it?" he asked. I grabbed something to eat and sat across from them at the table. "Yeah, I thought she was actually on fire," I said. I felt Isa put her foot on top of mine. She was still trying to comfort me. "If you want, I could just work behind the bar tonight while you play. That way I won't be waiting on customers out on the floor and away from peoples grasp." I shook my head at her, "no, you guys are right. I need to learn to control myself. Even if that means I can't touch you at work," I said, "I'll be on my best behavior tonight." She smiled at me now.

Will didn't seem convinced but nodded. I ate my food then cleaned up after Isa and myself then sat back across from them. "What time are we planning on heading there?" I said. Isa looked at the clock on the wall, it was around 11:30 now. "I'd say we leave here closer to one. I want you to practice for a few hours before anyone gets there," she said. Sounded good to me, I thought. "Umm…did you want to go for a walk, Isa?" I asked her. William stood up from the table, "Well I can tell when I'm not wanted," he laughed, "if you two wanna go for another roll in the hay, I'll just head out then." I gulped, what did he just say?

I looked over at Isa, had she told him about us? I thought. She didn't seem to be phased by it. Will left the kitchen and headed for the front door. I heard the Camaro start up and drive away. "Did you tell him about us?" I asked her. She smiled and shook her head, "no, but he can hear just fine. He probably heard us fooling around in the woods yesterday." She said it matter of factly, like it was no big deal.

"How can you be so calm about it? Doesn't it bother you that he knows?" I asked. She stood up and started crawling across the table towards me. "Let him know, I don't care," she said. I sat back in my chair waiting for her to reach me. She leaned her head against mine. "Does it bother you?" she began kissing me on my face. I lost my train of thought. I couldn't remember what we had been talking about. I kissed her back, "no," I said breathlessly.

I guess it didn't really matter, we were all adults. She slid her legs around the table and sat on the edge facing me. I pulled her close. She knew exactly how to get my attention. "Did you still want to go for a walk or did you want to do something else?" she whispered. I was squirming in my chair now. The animal inside me was trying to escape.

I began pawing at her. She chuckled at me as I fumbled to undo her jeans. She stopped me before I ripped them off. I looked at her longingly. "Settle down," she said to me. "I can't," I said, shaking. Did she really think I could handle being at work tonight? I thought. She brought my head into her chest and held me. I wrapped my arms around her too. "What if something happens? I don't know if I'd be able to stop myself," I said. She stroked my head. "I'll be right down in the audience the whole time. Just keep playing and I'll watch over you." she whispered in my ear.

I held her tightly, not wanting to ever let her go. She fixed her pants and got off the table. I followed her outside onto the porch. "If you want, we can go in early so you can practice longer," she said. "No thanks. Let's just stay here and do nothing for a while," I said, sitting down on the swing. She joined me and laid down so her head was in my lap. I rocked us back and forth for a few minutes. Her head slowly started to lean to one side until I looked down to see that she had fallen asleep.

I scooped her up and carried her inside again. She didn't even wake up when I set her on the couch and covered her up. I stood above her, watching her sleep. She looked so peaceful but I knew if I left her side she might have another nightmare. I went to sit in one of the chairs across from the sofa next to the lit fireplace. Did they ever put it out? I wondered. Come to think of it, it didn't even look like the logs were even burning. I reached out my hand towards it. Yep, that's real fire. I thought, pulling my hand away swiftly. I wonder if she put some kind of enchantment or something on it. Anything was possible at this point.

Watching the fire dance began to make me feel drowsy. I'll just close my eyes for a second, I thought. I drifted off to sleep and dreamt about my night to come. Would I be able to hold it together if someone bothered her? Would she be angry with me if I couldn't? These questions floated around in my head causing me to stir. I didn't want anyone but me to touch her. She was mine.

I opened my eyes to see if she was still sleeping. She had rolled over now and was twitching again. Uh oh, I thought. I quickly went over to her and tried to wake her up. "Isadora, you're having a nightmare," I said to her. She didn't respond. I tried gently nudging her. Nothing. "Isa, come back to me," I said louder this time. Her eyes shot open and she sat upright so fast that she hit her head on my face.

I jerked back at the pain as I held my nose. I could feel the rush of blood flow in my hand. "Adam!" she said, leaping up off the couch. She covered her mouth and nose with her hands. I could see the hunger in her eyes. "Stay back!" I said as I tilted my head back trying to stop the bleeding. She watched me intensely as I made my way toward the bathroom. I positioned myself over the sink so the blood would flow down the drain. She followed at an arm's length away and stood in the doorway as I tried to clean myself up.

"I am so sorry Adam," she said muffled through her hand, "you startled me. You should have just let me wake up on my own." My eyes were watering from getting my nose smashed. I wiped them before I looked at her. She had taken her hands off her face now. Not good, I thought. I didn't know how she would react to all the blood. She took a step closer, biting her lip. I grabbed the hand towel and pressed it to my face. "Isa, stop!" I commanded holding my hand out to keep her away.

Her eyes met mine then followed my arm as I held it out. She lunged forward grabbing my wrist. I felt a sharp pain as she bit down on it. I could feel her begin to extract my blood. The sensation was oddly satisfying the way she held on with her teeth. I tried to pull away but she bit down harder. Was she going to kill me? I thought. "Isadora, you have to let go!" I shouted. And still she kept on. My arm was starting to grow numb now.

I had to get her to let go, I thought. I spoke quietly trying not to agitate her any further, "It's OK, Isa. Take as much as you need. I trust you." I began feeling lightheaded like I was going to faint. I slowly pulled her down with me as I sat on the floor. Just before I was going to pass out she released me. I pulled back my arm to check the damage. All that was there were two small holes and some bruising where she had held onto me. The bleeding stopped rather quickly and I reached into the drawer looking for some bandages.

I wrapped my wrist up then carefully stood up to finish wiping the blood off my face. She sat there on the floor looking away from me. She didn't move. When I finished I reached down and placed my hand on her shoulder. She jumped at my touch. She slowly turned her head up to look at me. There were tears in her eyes and blood around the corners of her mouth. I grabbed a clean washcloth and began to wipe the blood from her lips.

Her lips quivered as I wiped them off. "There. All better," I said once I was done. Tears spilled from her eyes, streaking her face. I tried picking her up but her body was too heavy for me to lift. Was she purposely making it so I couldn't hold her? I thought. I tried again this time hoisting her up with ease. I sat her on the bathroom counter. "You did not mean to do that," I enunciated, wiping the tears from her face. I kissed her lips. There was still the faint metallic taste of my blood in her mouth.

"I know you didn't mean to do it, it was my fault. I shouldn't have scared you causing you to sit up fast then giving me a bloody nose. It's alright, Isa. I'm fine," I said to her. Closing her eyes, she said, "but I'm not. I want more. That's the problem. I'm a monster." She opened her eyes again. I kissed her again, this time with more passion, "I love you no matter what you are, but you are not a monster."

She moved her hands underneath my shirt, "you should go change," she said referring to the red streaks across my chest. "Will you come with me?" I asked. She nodded and got off the counter. We went up the stairs, she was walking behind me now. I opened the door, ushering her in. She laid down on the bed while I sifted through my dresser. "Next time you bite me, can you give me a little warning beforehand?" I said jokingly. "You're lucky you got to keep the arm," she said dryly. She didn't seem too amused at my attempt at a joke. I put a clean shirt on. "What were you dreaming about anyway?" I was curious. "The guillotine and my decapitation. Did you know that if there were multiple executions scheduled for one day it was better to be first than last because the blade would dull the more people it had to cut through?"

I got a shiver thinking about how she could possibly know that. "Were you first or last?" I asked. "Sadly I was last and they had to keep releasing the blade until I died." I was fascinated. "So when you died each time, were you buried?" I asked. "Sometimes. It depended on the manor of my death or if someone wanted to take the time to dig me a grave. Most of the time I was left on display to be made an example of," she replied.

"What about coming back to life? How does that work?" I said. She thought about it then answered, "You know how when you're dreaming that you're falling you always wake up before you hit the ground? That's kind of what it's like. I'd die then suddenly I'd just wake up." "But you'd always wake up again unscathed, right? How long after each death did you wake up?" I asked inquisitively. She laughed, "Yes I would be unscathed just with a new mark. As far as how long it took me to wake up each time, it varies. Sometimes it would be days, others years. It took me thirty years after my decapitation to come back again."

She seemed to be in a better mood now. I reached down and tugged on the waist of her jeans. She smiled, "is there something you want?" she said. I knelt down on the bed above her and undid my pants. She giggled and did the same. I pulled them down around her ankles. I began kissing her starting at her stomach then worked my way up to her mouth. She made a sound that got my blood pumping. She already knew what I wanted before I did. She kicked off her pants the rest of the way and took her cropped sweater off. I rolled over onto my back so she was on top of me this time. She pinned my arms above my head and began moving her hips. I arched my back with each movement.

She eventually let one of my hands go, folding her fingers into mine. I then used my free hand to hold on to her thigh. Her moaning became louder and her movements became stronger. I couldn't hold out much longer. I lay there watching her sway when she screamed out then hunched herself over me, "I love you," she said, pressing her mouth hard onto mine. Did I just hear her right? I thought. Did she just tell me she loved me?

She sat there with her legs quivering, out of breath. I couldn't move. Still hunching over me she said it again, "I said I love you Adam." She did say it, I thought. I began to smile, "I love you too," I said, kissing her again. She loved me, I thought. She carefully got off me then laid beside me on the bed, our fingers still interlocked.

"The last few days, you have made me feel more alive than I have in over two hundred years, and I'm so sorry I didn't say it to you sooner," she said, rolling over to look at me. She continued, "I will cherish every moment with you in my eternity, my warm, caring, loving, helianthus." Helianthus, as in sunflowers? I thought. "Why helianthus?" I asked. She smiled, "because they have a deep love meaning. One who loves with sincerity, never forgets and loves until the end. That's what they stand for."

All this time, I thought she just liked the flowers but when I gave them to her they meant something completely different in her mind. She loved me from the very beginning and now she had completely given herself over to me. I ran my fingers through her hair and kissed her softly. "I never wanna let you go," I whispered to her.

Chapter

15

We got dressed again and headed down to the car. It was time for us to head in to work now. We got in the car and drove to the club holding hands the whole way there. When we arrived, I started to get nervous seeing the alley behind the building again remembering where I almost died. We got out and walked inside. She carried her things into the dressing room then went out to the bar. William was standing at the bar polishing glasses. "Why don't you go practice for a little while, I need to go over the payroll and distributor invoices with Will," she said. I gave her one more kiss then continued on my way to the piano.

Hello old friend, I thought as I lifted the cover off the keys. I began playing 'Fur Elise' by Beethoven. I listened to see what they were saying as I played. They were standing at the bar together. "You bit him? Is he ok?" I could hear William say to her. "He's fine now. It won't happen again," she said. "But what if it does? Izzy, you're slipping. I think you may need to distance yourself from him a bit." Distance herself? What did he mean? "I know but I don't know if I can. I love him, William." I heard a glass shatter as she said this. I looked up to see what happened. William had dropped a glass, Isa was now sweeping it up. I continued to listen and play. "You're treading in very dangerous waters Iz. He's too young to know what that all entails. He doesn't understand the consequences of his actions. And I say this now because I know he's listening," he paused. "Be careful you two. You're not the only ones who have something to lose. We could all be in danger if something were to happen to him." I glanced over in their direction. William was looking directly at me now.

I turned my focus back to the piano, finishing out the song. I tried to ignore them now by playing another composition. I didn't want anyone to be in danger because of our relationship, especially Isa. What would Sarah have done if she came home to Isa standing over my dead body? She would have been livid. She might have even tried to kill Isa herself. Then I thought about how Xander would react. Would he defend Isa or be on Sarah's side? If he defended Isa he would risk losing Sarah but if he was on Sarah's side he'd have to take the chance of being kicked out of the pack I would assume.

I hit a wrong note and stopped playing. I needed to shake it off and act like everything was fine. Isa had faith in me and I had a job to do. I resumed playing again. "Just breathe Adam," I heard her say. She was standing behind me with her hands on my shoulders now. I didn't look at her while I was playing so I didn't lose my concentration. She wrapped her arms around me then gave me a kiss on the cheek. I rubbed my head on hers. It made me feel better knowing she was watching over me.

She left me alone on the stage to practice some more. I played for two hours until everyone else showed up. Sarah came up to me when I had finished. "How are you?" she said, handing me a bottle of water. I took it from her. "What happened there?" she asked, frantically grabbing at my wrist. I didn't even think about it when I reached up for the water. I pulled my arm away from her. "It's nothing," I said, trying to get up from the bench. She moved in front of me. "That's not nothing," she ripped the bandage off, "that's a bite mark! Did she bite you?" she shouted. I glanced around the room. Lexa and Ben stopped talking and William and Xander stopped taking down the chairs.

They were all looking at me now. My heart rate accelerated. I looked around for Isa but couldn't see her. "Isa..." I whispered under my breath, hoping she would hear me. "Well, what do you have to say?" Sarah demanded. I had to just tell her the truth. "It was an accident," I said, pushing her out of my way. "An accident?" she repeated angrily. "Yeah, an accident. I had a bloody nose and I was too close to her. She didn't mean to do it." The others had gathered around the bottom of the stage now.

"How'd you end up getting a bloody nose in front of her?" Xander asked. I looked at him, "I startled her while she was sleeping and she hit me in the nose with her head," I said quietly. "So not only did she bite you, but she was the one to make your nose bleed in the first place?" Sarah was furious now. I tried to walk off the stage to end the conversation. She followed me down the stairs onto the barroom floor.

"Don't you walk away from me Adam! Do you realize how dangerous this actually is?" She yelled. I was starting to get irritated with her. "Just drop it Sarah. I'm fine," I said heading towards the back room to find Isa. "I'm sure she didn't mean it Sar, she normally has really great control over her hunger," Xander said, defending her. Thank you Xander, I thought. "I don't care if she normally has control over it, she still bit him. What happens if she does it again? Adam, she's going to kill you if you don't be careful," Sarah said. I stopped at the counter, the hairs on the back of my neck stood up now. "And what are you gonna do about it, try and save me from her?" I growled. I turned to face her again.

My blood was boiling as I yelled at her. "I love Isa and I trust her with my life. Screaming and yelling at me isn't going to stop that Sarah!" The room went silent. "Adam," she spoke softer now, "I know that you love her and I'm happy for you, truly I am. But you have to admit that you're being reckless." Reckless, wasn't she being a bit hypocritical? "You call me reckless but you're going out with Xander who's also a werewolf. After experiencing what it feels like to be one and all the different emotions that take over, I don't know if I think YOU'RE being safe by being with him!" I took a step closer to her to get in her face. I heard Xander growl behind her.

William quickly got in between us and slightly pushed Sarah back behind him. "That's enough Adam." He stared at me as I backed away from her. What was I doing? I was about to attack my own sister. Sarah looked at me in disbelief. "He's right. We're both flirting with death. The difference is, mine only wants to keep me safe while yours has to fight the urge to maim you every five seconds!" Sarah said. I lunged forward knocking William to the ground. Xander grabbed Sarah and used his body as a shield.

Will quickly pushed back, sending me crashing into a barstool. I turned around and was just about to rush him again when I started feeling a familiar pressure dragging me towards the ground. Everyone but Sarah was on their knees now. I frantically looked around, trying to find the source. Isa was standing on the stage now in front of the piano. She leapt down and landed silently on the floor between William and I.

I tried to resist her gaze but she pushed back harder against me. "Everyone needs to calm down right now," she said in a demanding tone looking directly at me. "What's going on? What are you doing to them?" Sarah asked her in a panic. She didn't answer her. Sarah then walked up to Isadora and slapped her hard across the face. The pressure was lifted, I was able to control my breathing now. I sat there on my knees watching Sarah hyperventilating, her hand ready to strike again. She aimed another blow when Xander caught her wrist before it could connect to Isa's face. Isa just stood there, unfazed by the incident. She looked at Sarah, "do you feel better now?" she said. Sarah balled her fist in Xander's grasp, "no! What you did is inexcusable!" she shouted. Xander wrapped his arms around her trying to calm her down, "Sarah stop it. It's done now," he whispered to her.

William, Lexa, and Ben were all standing again while I remained on the floor. "Take her home Xander. She's not going to be able to handle work tonight," Isa said gently, "I will discuss my actions with her in the near future. Go home." Xander ushered Sarah out of the bar with little resistance. "The rest of you, get ready. Ben, you'll take Xander's spot tonight and Lexa and I will be on the floor. Can you handle the bar yourself tonight, Will?" Isa asked. William responded, "Yeah, I'll be fine. Just have Adam play for half the night so I'm not swamped at closing time." She turned to me, "think you can manage that?" she said. I nodded then stood up. "Dismissed," she said loudly.

"You," she pointed to me, "come here." Everyone cleared out and got ready for the evening. I walked over to her with my head hung like a scorned child. She took my hand and led me to her dressing room. Once inside, she shut the door and sat down at her vanity. She sighed heavily, "well that could have gone better," she said. I felt ashamed. If I hadn't let Sarah get under my skin like that maybe none of this would have ever happened. I walked up to her to touch her face. There was a faint handprint on her left cheek.

195

"I'm so sorry. I never thought she was going to hit you," I said, stroking her face. She gave me a slight smile, "you think that hurt me?" she asked. Didn't it? I thought, it sure looked like it did. I sat in the chair across from her. "She's right though. I am a danger to you more than Xander is to her and I need to apologize for what I've done," she said to me. I looked at her confused. "What do you need to apologize for? She's the one who hit you," I questioned her. She shook her head, "no, she feels threatened that I might take you away from her and I need to make it perfectly clear that that's not going to happen." She continued, "She didn't just hit me because she was mad about the bite, she hit me because she was scared for you. She loves you and just wants to make sure you're taken care of, and quite frankly, with almost drowning you and now drinking your blood, I'm not doing so great at my job."

I finally understood, Sarah wasn't mad at me, she was just being an annoying overprotective sister. Isa placed a hand on my knee, "I'll talk to her when we get home tonight. I'm sure she's pretty shaken up about the whole thing. It's not everyday your werewolf brother gets his blood sucked by his vampire girlfriend," she chuckled. I smiled at her. "Do you think she's ever going to be ok with us being together?" I asked. She sighed again sitting back in her chair, "probably. But just in case, we should be extra careful not to provoke her," she said.

She began changing into her outfit for this evening, button up, long sleeve, white shirt and a black pleated skirt. I wanted so badly to rip open her shirt the second she finished buttoning it. I could faintly see her nude colored bra through the fabric. "This is gonna be hard to stay focused tonight," I said, adjusting my pants. She laughed, "you'll be fine. Just worry about the music and everything should be fine." She handed me a bag with a new set of clothes for me. I assumed they couldn't get all the blood stains out of my last shirt after I was assaulted.

I was about to leave when she tugged on my pants, "where do you think you're going?" she smiled playfully. My heart began racing, "to the bathroom to change," I replied. She began undoing my belt, "why don't you just change in here though?" she said. I took off my shirt and let her finish taking off my pants. She pushed me back down in my chair and sat on my lap. "We shouldn't do this right before work. You're going to get me too riled up," I whispered to her. She kissed my neck, "we're not going to, I just wanted to give you a little motivation to have a good night," she said softly.

We sat there a while just making out when she pulled away and said, "That's enough for now. We'll be opening soon so you need to finish getting ready." I wanted more. I tried to kiss her again but she stood up and walked towards the door. "I'll see you out there," she said and winked at me, leaving me alone in the dressing room. I quickly got dressed and went out to find her again. She was standing at the bar talking with Lexa. she smiled at me when I found her.

Ben scoffed loudly as he walked past me. What's his problem? I thought. I'd noticed he was looking remarkably annoyed this evening as he went to go stand by the doors. We all went to our designated posts and waited for Isa to give the signal. "Steer clear of Ben for a while," Will whispered to me, "he's pissed about being brought to his knees earlier." I nodded, silently thanking him for the heads up. Isa walked around the counter and gave me a kiss. "You ready?" She asked. I relaxed after she kissed me. "Yeah. I'm better now," I sighed. I heard Lexa giggle, "You guys are so cute," she said walking out to the middle of the floor.

Isa flickered the light indicating it was time to open. Ben unlocked the doors and opened them wide. People started entering the building after their ids were checked. I started to feel a bit nervous without Isadora by my side. I saw her glance my way, giving me a slight smile. She could hear my heart rate accelerating. I took a deep breath and started to tend the bar with William. Everything was going great, people were friendly and on their best behavior. After an hour Will turned to me, "go on, I got this," he said, jerking his head towards the piano. I made my way to the stage looking back to survey the crowd.

There weren't that many people sitting in the audience for a Wednesday night. I was glad for that. The less people the better, I thought. I got to the piano and sat down. "Just relax," I said to myself as I began playing. The melodies flowed off my fingers and I didn't look up for over an hour. When I did finally sneak a peek, everything was going fine. Isa and Lexa were waiting tables and no one was bothering her. I kept on playing again, trying not to think about it. She was fine, people knew not to touch her. I finished playing my set and went back down to the bar with William. "Great job," he said as I reached for a bottle of water.

"Thanks," I replied, taking a drink. The hard part was over, now I just needed to focus on the customers. I started handing out drinks. There were more people sitting out at the tables now. "Hands off, buddy. We don't do that here," I heard Isa say. I glanced up, looking around for her. There was an older gentleman with his hand on her lower back. My blood began to boil. Get your hand off of her! I shouted in my head. Isa removed his hand from her back nicely and said, "I think it's best if you leave Harold, you've had enough for tonight." She turned around to walk away from him when suddenly he smacked her ass. I stiffened, waiting to see what she'd do. I wanted to tear that guy to shreds. I started to make my way over to her when William grabbed my arm, "don't do it. She's got it under control," he whispered, gripping me tightly.

I looked out at her again, this time she was escorting the man to the doors. What happened? I thought. Why hadn't Ben done anything. He still stood in the doorway with his arms crossed. I needed to go talk to him. I pulled my arm away from Will making my way across the bar. Lexa jumped out in front of me, "not now," she said, "there's too many witnesses." I looked around at the crowds of people. She was right, I would have to talk to him after we closed. I headed to the bathroom to clear my mind. I stood there in front of the sink breathing heavily. "Get a hold of yourself," I said looking at my reflection in the mirror. The door swung open and two guys walked in, laughing. "Man that blond has a sweet ass on her doesn't she?" the one said to the other. I gripped the side of the counter. Let it go Adam, they're drunk, I thought. I splashed some water on my face. "Yeah, tell ya what, I'd like to bend her over one of the tables and make her squeal," the other joked. I growled now, turning around to face them. They seemed startled. "Geez, what's your problem?" He asked me. I got up in his face, "don't talk about her like that," I said. I started to walk towards the door when I heard him say under his breath, "damn. You'd think he was banging that bitch, the way he acted." That was it, I turned around and decked him. He stumbled back against the wall. "What the hell?" The other one said.

My heart rate was elevated again. I looked at them before backing out the door. I had to get out of there before I hit him again. I quickly made my way through the people, searching for Isa's face. She was standing at the bar getting more drinks. She turned around and locked eyes with me. "I'm sorry," I whispered. I took another step towards the bar when I felt someone grip my shoulder. I turned my head around and was promptly met with a fist. The guy I'd just hit was now landing blows one after another on my face. I wrestled him to the ground. We rolled around on the floor for a moment, each of us trying to get the upper hand. I managed to pin him down and began landing blows.

William hopped over the counter and rushed over to me. He grabbed my shoulders and drug me off the man. "Calm down Adam," he hissed in my ear pulling me back so the guy could stand up. His friend helped him up now. "What's going on?" Isa said standing between the four of us now, acting like she didn't already know what was happening. The guy stood up with his lip bleeding, "this guy assaulted me for no reason!" He shouted. Everyone in the club was looking at us now. Oh no, I thought watching the blood drop off his chin. I looked at Isa, hoping she was going to be ok. "Everybody out. We're shutting down for the night!" William shouted, releasing me. Isa put her arm around the man I'd hit and ushered him to the bar to get some ice for his face. "I am so sorry about him," she said, glancing back to look at me.

Now I've done it, I thought. I couldn't even handle one night without causing a scene. William stayed with me as Ben and Lexa went to close out peoples tabs. I sat on a chair nearby. "Do you think she's mad?" I asked Will. He sat down next to me, "Naw, she'll be fine. She might just be a little disappointed in you is all." I hung my head when he said that. Disappointed in me? I was already disappointed in myself. She had so much faith in me that I wasn't going to screw it up but I did anyway. I could hear Isa and the guy arguing about pressing charges. She was arguing on my behalf that I was going through a rough time and that I was just having an off night. She finished by saying the next time they came in, they could have free drinks on the house for the whole night if they didn't press charges. They agreed and left.

The bar quickly emptied out and we were the only ones left there. Ben locked the doors, "are you stupid?" he said, turning around to face me now. "Starting a fight like that has to be one of the dumbest things you could've done. What did he do, look at you funny?" He asked angrily. I scowled at him, "he was making lewd comments about Isa," I said to him. He rolled his eyes, "it's a bar dude! There's bound to be drunk assholes saying stupid shit here! You can't take it to heart!" He shouted. He was starting to piss me off. I stood up from my chair. "You know what?" I said taking a few steps closer, "how would you react if they said something about Lexa? Do you think you could handle it?"

He stepped sideways away from me, trying to anticipate my next move. "I wouldn't have even paid attention to them. I'm not insecure in my relationship like someone," he said, referring to me. He was trying to pick a fight with me, I thought, and I was gonna give it to him. I launched myself at him. He dodged out of my way at the last second, with a smile on his face. My adrenaline was pumping now. I got back up and tried again, this time catching his arm. I pulled his arm until I heard it come out of the socket. He yowled in pain. Lexa rushed over to him, ripping my hand from his arm. "Adam?! What's your problem?" She said, trying to access Bens' injury. I looked down at my hands. What came over me? I thought. I just played right into his hand.

Isa stood next to Will now, her eyes fixed on them. "Have you two finished trying to assert your dominance between yourselves? Or do I need to remind everyone who the real alpha is?" She snarled. She was mad, I could see the fire blazing in her eyes. I flinched when she flashed her gaze over to me. "No," I said feebly. Ben groaned as Lexa put his shoulder back into place, "No master, we're all good here," he said in an arrogant tone. They stood up and continued cleaning tables and stacking chairs. I grabbed the broom and began sweeping. I made sure to stay as far away from Ben as possible and he did the same. When we were all finished Ben and Lexa got in their car and left. William stood outside with Isa and I now.

"So...I guess I'm riding with you guys then?" he asked. I tried to hold Isa's hand but she pulled it away from me. "You two take the car back. I'll find my own way home. I need to think for a while," she said, folding her arms. I looked down at the ground, she must have been really mad at me, I thought. She then gave Will the keys and walked away towards the front of the building. William got in the car and waited for me. I wanted to run to her and apologize for how I'd acted tonight but I thought it would be pointless to try and talk to her right now, so I got in the car too. As we pulled past her I saw her look in my direction, she then continued on her walk. As we drove through the city we stayed silent.

"You need to keep your cool around Ben, he's very manipulative when it comes to picking fights. You let him get to you like that again and you're done for. He'll try to push you out of the pack," Will finally said. "Push me out? How?" I asked, curiously. "He'll try to justify why Isadora shouldn't be the alpha anymore by challenging you and when Izzy comes to your rescue, it will just prove that she doesn't have the pack's best interest at heart if she's picking favorites. Alphas have to be neutral otherwise there'd be chaos," he said, turning onto the gravel road. I thought about what he said. "But why would that push me out of the pack?" I asked. He sighed, "Because she'd have to step down as alpha in order to keep you by her side. And if she isn't the alpha there'd be no pack for you to be a part of."

"But couldn't you take over as alpha if she stepped down? Aren't you like her second or something like that?" I asked. He nodded his head, "I am her second but I don't want to be the alpha. First it would go down the line of succession. If no one wants to be alpha it falls on the next person until it reaches someone in the ranks who wants it bad enough. Xander won't want it because he's got your sister and Lexa won't want it because Ben will have already told her that he wanted to be the alpha and she would gladly back him."

My head was throbbing trying to make sense of everything. "Isn't there another way for me to stay in the pack and still keep Isa as the alpha?" I asked as we reached the iron gate. He stopped the car and turned to me, "look, the only way that's ever going to happen is if you challenge everyone and beat them up the ranks. You'd have to beat Lexa, then Ben, then Xander, and then me. Hell, just to prove a point you might even want to challenge Izzy while you're at it." I didn't want to fight anyone, especially Isa.

"But if I do this, that would mean Isa's position as alpha wouldn't be threatened, right?" I said. "If anything, you beat Lexa and Ben then you'll secure yourself a spot in the pack forever," he said with a smile, "relax. These are all just hypothetical scenarios that you need to be aware of in case something like tonight happens again." I frowned thinking about how easily I let Ben get under my skin. "If Ben is so much to handle, why hasn't he just left the group and started his own pack with Lexa?" I questioned him. He put the car in drive, "Isa thinks it's better to just put up with him than to try to kick him out. Who knows if Xander would leave now, especially now that he's with Sarah. Lexa would obviously follow Ben but I would stay with Izzy and that pisses him off."

We pulled up to the front of the house and just sat in the car. "How's she going to get home?" I said, staring up at her balcony. The lights were still off in there. He shrugged, "she'll either run or fly. Either way no one's going to see her, she's too fast." I thought about her walking all the way home by herself and my stomach churned. I let out a whine. "She'll be fine, she'll come home when she's ready. You can survive a couple hours away from her," he chuckled, getting out of the car. I got out too and slowly walked to the house. Once inside I went upstairs to take a shower.

I kept thinking about what William had said about Ben trying to take over as alpha. Why would anyone want such a huge responsibility of maintaining order and keeping everyone safe? I know I wouldn't. I suppose she'd been doing it for so long it just comes naturally to her now. I laid on the bed waiting for her to come home. I played on my phone for over an hour but she didn't show. Should I go out looking for her? I thought. Would I even be able to find her? I figured it was better just to listen to Will and let her come home on her own. I set an alarm on my phone to wake me up in an hour to see if she had come home. I closed my eyes and drifted to sleep.

The alarm went off at 3 a.m. indicating it was time for me to start looking for her. I noticed I was covered up and her shoes were on the floor by the bathroom. Had she come home and left again? Panicked, I put on a pair of jeans and hoodie to go looking for her. I made my way down the stairs as quickly as I could. I stood in the hallway by the kitchen and closed my eyes, listening to hear her voice. I could faintly make out two female voices talking upstairs on the second floor. Is Isa talking to Sarah? I thought. "I really do care about your brother Sarah and it was just a mistake. I would never try to hurt him on purpose," Isa said. She was talking about biting me. "How can I be so sure that it won't happen again?" Sarsh asked. Isa continued by saying, "I have a spell that whomever the recipient is, their blood turns to bile in your mouth making them unappetizing to vampires and makes them very I'll if they were to actually consume their blood. I've performed it on everyone else in the house but you and Adam. It's the perfect way to deter me. What do you think?" There was a long pause before Sarah spoke, "I'll agree to it but only if you swear you're never going to bite him again." Her voice sounded serious.

A spell to make my blood less appealing to her? Why hadn't she said that before? I thought. I heard them finish up their conversation and open the door. I headed out the front door towards the willow. I wanted to be near her but I also just wanted to be alone. Would she find me less attractive after doing the spell? What if it changed our relationship? I had already offered her my blood and I wasn't about to take back my word but at the same time I didn't want Sarah to hold a grudge against her either. They were both very important people in my life and I wanted them to get along but no one had consulted with me about what I wanted to do. Isa said that if she were to bite me after the spell she would be ill. How sick are we talking? Could it kill her? No, I couldn't take that chance. I wasn't going to go through with it. I sat next to the tree brooding about their conversation about me.

I heard the rustle of the branches and looked around. Standing behind me in the shadows was Isadora. "What are you doing?" she said softly, walking up behind me and sitting down. She put her legs out on either side of mine and pulled me back so I was leaning up against her. "Nothing, just thinking," I replied. She didn't seem convinced that was all I was doing. She wrapped her arms around my torso and put her hand in my pocket. I could feel how cold she was through my sweatshirt. She put her chin next to my face on my shoulder. "I know you heard us talking," she said. It gave me goosebumps when she whispered in my ear. I didn't respond.

"It's no big deal, I just extract some of your blood in a syringe, do the spell over it, and put it back in you. It's simple," she said, nuzzling my neck. I pulled away from her and stood up. "I'm not doing it. Sarah can, but I'm not," I said looking at her now. She stood up as well, "yes you are," she demanded, "I already promised your sister I'd do it to keep you safe." I was starting to get annoyed. "But you didn't even ask me what I wanted to do," I fired back. She can up and put her hands on my face, "why don't you want to do it?" She asked gently. I let her touch me but I looked away from her gaze, "I don't want to do anything that could possibly end up hurting you." She looked confused at my statement. "Hurt me?" She said, "It's like an allergic reaction or a bad case of food poisoning. It just makes me vomit black bile for about a day. Then I'm perfectly fine again." She stroked my cheek with her thumb, I looked at her now. "Why would you think it was going to hurt me?" She asked. I took her hands off my face and sighed, "Because, you said it would make you sick and I didn't know if it would make you sick enough for you to die and I didn't want to put you through that." She looked at me sympathetically. "Oh, Adam. No, I won't die from it, it'll just seem like that's what's happening," she said, squeezing my hands.

"Then I won't go through with it. I don't want to cause you any more pain." She smiled at my argument. "I'd be in more pain if I ended up killing you than I would be if I were sick for a few hours. You're important to me and I plan on keeping you around as long as I can," she said. I smiled now, "ok, I'll do it then," I said pulling her close, "when though?" I asked. She reached in her back pocket and pulled out a small syringe and needle. "Right now," she said. I hesitated but held out my arm for her. She found a vein and quickly extracted some of my blood. I could see her eyes light up when the red viscous fluid started filling the vile. She handed me a cotton ball out of her other pocket to hold where the needle was inserted.

She drew some symbols on the ground around the vile and said something in Latin I presume. She then pricked herself with the same needle and drew a tiny amount of her own blood. "What's that do," I asked cautiously. She said another phrase and then inserted the needle back into her arm, "it mixes our blood, bonding the spell to it. I won't do this exact method for Sarah since she hasn't been exposed to my blood." I breathed a sigh of relief. That's what I was worried about, I thought. She drained half the vile in her own arm then carefully placed the needle back in my vein again. "Now, you're going to feel really cold for a few minutes but just know that's my blood coursing through your veins," she said. I braced myself for it.

When she began to slowly press on the plunger, I could feel the cold sensation she was talking about. My whole arm felt like it was burning, it was so cold. I involuntarily jerked back trying to escape the pain. She held my elbow firm so I could not get away. I could feel the icy blood traveling up my arm and throughout my body. The pain was excruciating. She pulled out the needle and let me go. I doubled over, holding my stomach. Please don't throw up, I thought. I sat there on my knees hunched over. My whole body felt like it was being electrocuted as her blood slowly passed through my circular system. She stood over me waiting for it to pass. "It hurts!" I yelled looking up at her. She knelt down beside me and started rubbing my back, "just a few more minutes and it'll all be over," she said reassuring me. I closed my eyes and gritted my teeth, trying to push through the pain.

After a few minutes or so I started to feel like I was warming up again. I relaxed my shoulders and tried to stand up. I was a bit wobbly and she caught me. "Feeling better?" She asked. I nodded my head, "yeah, sort of. You didn't tell me it was going to hurt though," I said chuckling. She rolled her eyes at me, "it's different with everyone. Sometimes it hurts others it doesn't. You're just lucky I guess," she laughed. Lucky? I thought, yeah right. "How do we know if it worked?" I asked. "It'll be in full effect tomorrow. The blood needs to course through your body for at least twenty-four hours for the spell to completely sink in," she said. She took my hand and started leading me towards the house. "Come on," she said, "it's late and you need to get some sleep." I wasn't tired anymore after my nap and now this, but I let her lead the way back to the house.

We stood underneath her window. "Ready?" she said. My stomach dropped. I backed away from her. "No, that's ok. I'll just take the long way up," I said wearily. She cocked her head to one side, "are you afraid of flying?" She said with a smile, "I don't have to jump, it's just faster if I do." I walked closer to her again, "could you do it slower this time?" I pleaded with her. She walked behind me and wrapped her arms around my chest. "Hold on," she whispered to me. I held on to her arms. Slowly we began to hover off the ground then glide up to her balcony. I closed my eyes so I wouldn't get dizzy. I could hear the soft rustle of feathers behind me. I slightly turned my head to sneak a peek. They were massive. They reminded me of pigeon feathers the way the color shifted from gray to purple depending on the light. With one more flap, we had made it up. I turned around quickly to face her. She looked like an angel. I reached out to pet one of the wings. She flinched then moved her shoulder closer so I could get a better angle. I gently stroked the soft gray feathers, they were so beautiful.

She spread her wings out wide now so I could see them better. I took a few steps back to take it all in. "You're incredible," I said breathlessly. She smiled, "thanks, I don't normally like to use them because they aren't as fast and they're more noticeable in the dark, unlike my dragon ones." She folded them down now and they absorbed into her back. I ran to her and twirled her around. She giggled when I picked her up. "I love you Isadora," I said, kissing her lips. I stopped spinning and stood there holding her. She shimmied down me and pulled me into the bedroom. I followed closely behind, tugging on her shirt. She took it off and threw it on the floor. "I'm not sure you deserve this after the night you had," she teased me. She was right, I had one job to do, not cause a scene and that's exactly what I did. I went over to the bed and laid down on my stomach. She climbed on the bed and began massaging my back. "I'm sorry. I didn't mean to lose it tonight. He just made me so mad." I said. She continued to rub my shoulders and back. "I know you didn't, I could hear them before they went into the restroom. You made the right choice to go in there after Harold smacked me though. I was proud of you for that." She worked her way down to my lower back. I didn't even know my body was sore until she started working the muscles. "When they come back again tomorrow, you need to remain calm and just ignore them. If you want, I could play a few songs tomorrow with you. That way I wouldn't be on the floor as much." Us play together? I thought. That could work. I tilted my head up towards her, "yeah, they would be great," I said trying to get up off the bed.

She got off my back and walked over to the bathroom hamper. She had picked up the shirt she had thrown on the floor and took off her pants. I also took my clothes off and put my pajama pants on. I sat into the edge of the bed now waiting for her to come lay down. "Did you have a good ride home with Will?" she asked, putting her tank top on. "Yeah, he sort of put things into perspective for me," I said. She looked at me curiously, "oh yeah? What did you guys talk about?" She walked over to the bed and sat down next to me. "We talked about how Ben wants to be the alpha and that if I let him get me riled up again it could be bad for the pack," I said nonchalantly. She looked at me with a serious look on her face, "that's true. You haven't transitioned yet so he's trying to provoke you. He's hoping that you'll pick a fight with him before you transition so I'll save you, disrupting the balance between alpha and girlfriend. We can't let that happen," she said.

I held her hand, "would you really have to save me? I think I could take him." I said flexing my muscles. She shook her head, "if he stayed in human form maybe but if he goes wolf, he could seriously hurt you. He should calm down once your first moon phase passes. Then he'll just challenge you like any other member of the pack. If he wins against you though, he's never going to let you live it down," she said. That was a lot to put on my shoulders. What if he challenges me and I lost? I thought. "What happens if I lose? Could I get kicked out of the pack?" I asked. She looked at me surprised, "no, the alpha is the only one who can suggest banishment, and I'll never do that to you." That was a relief, I thought.

She laid down next to me now while I remained sitting up. "You seem worried," she said. I was but I didn't want to tell her why. "A little. Does it hurt to transform?" I asked, looking at her. She reached up to stroke my face, "I'm not gonna lie, it can be quite unpleasant the first time but after you do it a few times it becomes easier." I turned over to lay on her top half now. "What color do you think I'll be?" She laughed at my question. "I don't know. I guess if we knew what your father looked like transformed, we could tell." I stiffened at the mention of my dad. She read my face, "sorry, I didn't mean to bring him up. It's just easier to tell the genetics if you know what the parents looked like," she said. I rest my chin on her sternum. "It's fine. It's still weird to think that my dad was a werewolf too though," I said.

She ruffled my hair, "we don't have to talk about him if you don't want to," she said. I kissed her chest, "thank you," I said. We laid there for a while before she pulled me more on top of her body. "What were your parents like?" I asked finally. She sighed, "I don't know any more. It's been so long now. I remember there being a light shining around a woman but I can never picture her face and a darkness engulfing a male figure. I don't think I ever even knew their names, I just sort of came into existence, you know" she said looking up at the ceiling. How sad, I thought. I at least had some memories of my parents before they abandoned me. "If everything about your existence is true, maybe a god created you," I said. She smiled, "I've thought about that before. That explains the light but not the darkness. No, I'll probably never know exactly where I came from or who put me here. I'll just keep on living until the end of time."

I lifted myself off of her, "how long do you think I'll live?" I asked. "I don't wanna talk about that," she said, pushing me gently off of her. She stood up and walked over to the chair. What's wrong? I thought. I walked over to her. "Why?" I said. She wouldn't look at me. I tried to get her to turn around. "Why don't you want to talk about it?" I said again. She turned around, "because, I just want to keep you here and now. I don't want to think about the future just yet," she said quietly. "I don't want to live in a world without you but I don't know if I want to take away your chance at a semi-normal life by cursing you to live forever like me." I could see the sadness in her eyes as she spoke. She'd been alone for so long she didn't want me to suffer the same way she has, I thought. I wrapped my arms around her. "I will be with you, forever. As long as you'll have me. I love you and I don't want to live without you," I said, pressing my lips to her temple. She stood on her tiptoes to kiss me and I kissed her back. "You're not allowed to die, you hear me?" She said half-jokingly. I smiled at her, "don't worry, I know you won't let me," I said, kissing her once more.

Chapter

16

The next day we woke up later than usual. I was still tired from the night before but I wanted to talk to Isa more about my transition coming up in a few weeks. She lay there peacefully sleeping in my arms. I was glad she was able to sleep now. I brushed the hair off her face and kissed her awake. "Good morning," I said as she slowly opened her eyes. She wrinkled her nose and buried her face deeper into me. "No, it's too early. Let me sleep another hour," she said muffled by my arm. I started to tickle her under her arms then moved on to her ribs. She wriggled and squealed as my fingers danced across her body. "Stop it Adam!" she laughed as she quickly got out of bed out of my reach.

She stood there out of breath looking at me. "There. You happy now? I'm up," she said, fixing her shirt. "Yes," I said proudly as I got out of bed too. I stood next to her just looking at her staring back at me. "What did you want?" she said putting her hair up in a loose ponytail. "Nothing in particular, I just wanted to talk some more about me transitioning into a werewolf." She rolled her eyes and got back in bed, covering herself with the blanket. She was avoiding the conversation. I sat on top of her and pulled the blanket off of her head. "What are you doing?" I asked. "I'm laying back down. I can answer your questions just fine from here." she said sticking out her tongue. I leaned down and pulled it into my mouth, she giggled at my tongue chasing hers around.

When I was finished, I sat next to her on the bed. She sat up too, "ok, what do you want to know?" she said. I locked my fingers in hers, "everything I guess. You said it's probably going to be painful to transition the first time right? Well what about turning back to normal?

How will I know how to do that?" I asked. She pondered my questions carefully before answering. "Changing forms is based on your emotions, the calmer you are the more likely you are to turn back. It'll take some practice, but I'm sure Will can give you a few pointers," she said. "Why can't you just help me with it?" I pushed. She played with our fingers, "because I can only turn into a wolf on full moons, remember? William can do it whenever he wants, making him the utmost authority on the matter," she replied.

That made sense, I thought, I just wish she could be the one to teach me. "What about when Ben challenges me, how am I supposed to fight him if I've never fought as a wolf before?" I said now. She shrugged her shoulders, "your instincts will kick in at that point. I won't be able to come to your aid until it's done though." I didn't like the way she said that. "Has anyone ever died from being challenged?" That was my main concern. I didn't know if Ben was going to fight dirty in order to get Isa to rescue me or not. "People have died in the past but William and Xander would never let Ben take it that far. They know to step in if that were the case," she said.

How come Will and Xander were allowed to step in and she wasn't? Was it because she was the alpha and needed to remain neutral? I thought. "What does Xander think about Ben trying to take over as alpha?" I had so many questions that I needed the answers to. She tilted her head as she spoke, "well, he's not too fond of the idea. He more of less just keeps Ben pacified for Lexas' sake. He doesn't like the idea of him becoming the leader though. He knows that the safest place to be for him and his sister is under my care. There's no telling how things would go for him with Ben in charge."

Here comes the hard question, I thought. "What would you do if I lost against Ben and you had to step in? Would you leave?" My heart started pounding as soon as I asked the question. Her face was serious now, "probably. I'd most likely go settle somewhere far away from here and start fresh. I've been thinking a lot about Paris lately," she said. Paris? She'd really move to a whole other country if I lost? I held tightly to her hand. "Would you take me with you?" She looked surprised at my question. "Of course I would. I couldn't just leave you to fend for yourself. How would I ever get to sleep without you?" she joked. I chuckled dryly.

"What about Sarah? Do you think she'd come too?" I said. She picked up my hand and kissed the top of it. "She could come, but only if she wanted to. She's mated with Xander now so who knows. They may even want to go their separate way for everyone else and start their own pack," she said. I couldn't imagine not being able to see Sarah every day. We'd never been apart a day in our lives before. And to think of her leaving with Xander without me was unthinkable. "When you say start their own pack, do you mean like have a family of their own?" I needed to know what she was thinking. She nodded her head, "it could mean that or it could just mean they ventured off together and found some new members to join them." Her face looked slightly worried as she spoke.

"Do you want to have a family?" I asked. She looked at me apologetically, "Adam I can't. I would if I could but it's just not possible for me," she said. I didn't understand. "What do you mean?" I asked. She stood up now. "I mean that it's impossible for me to have children. You need to have a beating heart and constant blood supply to carry a child and that's something I'm incapable of." She looked away from me as she spoke. I'd never thought about it that way. I suppose she was right, she lacked the basic necessities to have a baby. I felt sorry for her. I stood next to her and held her in my arms. She hugged me back, "I'm sorry if that's something you wanted for our future but there's some things even I can't do," she said.

I kissed her forehead, "so we won't have any kids, so what? What are your thoughts on adoption then?" I said. She laughed, "I'd say that might be a little selfish to bring a child into our kind of world. If they were in the same scenario you and your sister were in and already had the gene I'd say yes in a heartbeat though. That's sort of how William and I came to be. I slashed him then his parents left him for dead as a child in the woods because they couldn't handle his transition. I took him in and raised him as my own, that's why we have such a special bond."

I loved hearing her talk about raising a child together. She seemed to light up talking about taking care of William when he was younger, now it made sense the way she acted with him. He wasn't just her second, she was his mother. "Is that how you see all of them, like your children?" she smiled shyly. "Is that bad?" she said. I smiled again at her, "no, I think it makes me love you even more," I said. She pulled on my shirt to bring me down to her level to kiss. I picked her up and started kissing her back. Her legs wrapped tight around my waist as I held her.

"Do you see me as one of your children too?" I joked with her. She rolled her eyes and got down. "No, just the others. They all used to call me Ma when they were younger but I made them stop when they reached a certain age. People tend to look at you funny when you have a group of adults calling you Me and you look to be the same age as them," she said. I put my hand over her heart. "I'll bet they would have been beautiful like you," I said. She gave me a little smile, "maybe, with my luck they would have turned out looking just like you, which would have been fine with me."

She had such a wonderful personality and a way of coping with things out of her control. I admired her for that. We laid back down on the bed together. "How many would you have wanted?" she asked. I had to think about that for a minute before I could answer her. "Two," I said, "a boy and a girl." "What would their names be?" she asked now. I just pulled the two most random names out of my head, "John and Susan?" I said. She made a face in disgust, "Ew, no. Too bland," she said, "how about Elizabeth and AJ?" I thought about it, "I like Elizabeth but what's AJ stand for?" I asked. She giggled, "Adam Junior."

I smiled thinking about our imaginary children. AJ and Elizabeth, I thought. They sounded perfect. "How come Lexa and Ben haven't left to start their own pack slash family before?" I asked. She sighed, "Because Ben is too much of a controlling prick that he won't let that happen. Lexa has wanted a family for years but he keeps giving her excuses why it's not a good idea. Personally, I just think he doesn't want to have to share her attention with children." I'm sure she was right. I couldn't see him being a loving boyfriend let alone a doting father figure.

"What about marriage? Are they married?" I had never thought to ask before. "Same song, different tune. Too many reasons why they shouldn't," she said. My heart began racing again, "would you ever consider getting married?" I asked, glancing at her. Her eyes stayed focused on the ceiling but I could see a faint twinkle in her eye as she spoke, "I may, if the right guy came along." I knew she was joking and referring to me. My heart soared when she answered. Yes, she'd marry me, I thought, now all I had to do was ask her, but when?

I lay there thinking of all the ways I could do it, down by the lake, out on the porch, at the club, right here and now. The possibilities were endless. She nudged my arm and I looked at her. "You know I was engaged once before, right?" Her face looked troubled now. "He left me for dead and I haven't seen him since. You wouldn't do that to me too would you?" she said. I was almost offended that she would even think I could ever do such a thing to her. "Isa, I will never, ever do that to you. I love you too much to ever live with myself if I'd done that to you. That guy will never know what he is missing out on because I will make sure you are safe and happy all the time."

Her eyes lit up again. I wanted to know more about the jerk who left her but I didn't want to bring up old wounds. "What was his name?" I asked. She furrowed her brow looking back at the ceiling, "Jake," she finally said, "Jake Rylan." She closed her eyes now, probably thinking about him. I instantly got jealous. "Do you think about him often?" I asked. She snorted, "Sometimes. Only to compare the two of you though. He never would have just sat and talked things out with me. He would have just tried to do things on his own without any help." she smiled now. I didn't like that.

"So Jake, when did the two of you first meet?" I needed to get the full story on him if I was going to turn out different from him. "Remember how I said I was locked away by a lord and was only allowed to go out on certain nights?" she asked. "Yeah," I replied. "Well, he was one of my victims. I tried to run away and only made it as far at his family's cottage just west of the town. The sun was coming up so I thought I would hunker down there until the sun set again. Once inside, I found him lying in a pool of his own blood. His father had gotten drunk and beat the hell out of him." She rolled over on her side to face me now.

"I couldn't control myself, I started draining him the moment I shut the door. He was barely alive when he asked me to spare him and kill his father. Instead of granting his request I decided to turn him into a vampire so that he could have the pleasure of killing his father himself."

I looked at her confused, "how do you turn someone into a vampire?" I asked. "You drain all their blood then make them drink your own," she said. I nodded, "so then he was a vampire now too?" I said.

"Not right away," she continued, "it usually takes until the next sunrise to kick in. So I waited there with his body until the sun went down. His father never came home that day, good riddance too. Had he come home and opened the door I would have probably burst into flames. When the sun went down I carried his lifeless body back to my chambers and waited for him to reanimate. The following morning he awoke feeling stronger and hungrier than ever. After that day we spent the next three hundred years together, until he decided he wanted more. When he left and before I was killed again, I cursed him not to be able to take the life force from another living person ever again."

"Life force?" I said to her, "Blood dear, he was a vampire that couldn't drink blood. I took away his right to die as well, making him an immortal trapped forever in an endless cycle of life just like me." There were still a few things I didn't understand. "Why did he leave you though?" I asked. She shrugged, "I'm not entirely certain. He left right around the time I killed Sarrora. The two of them had been plotting something sinister that I wanted nothing to do with," she said. "What were they plotting?" I said. She looked at me very seriously now, "they wanted to start creating more vampires to enslave the nation, and I wouldn't have it. Not all humans are bad, most of them are quite good, it's just those select few that are really radical that will literally cut your head off," she finished with a laugh.

I couldn't believe it. She had stopped them from creating their own army to try to wipe out humans. "If he was so bad, why didn't you end things with him instead?" I asked. "Because I was in love, or at least I thought I was. Our relationship was kind of like Ben and Lexas'. When it's good, it's great. When it's bad, it's terrible. I never saw how awful he was to me up until quite recently. That's why I haven't kicked Ben out of the pack, for fear of what he might do to Lexa. I think he's been holding back all these years so that when it comes time for him to show his true colors he can blow us all away."

That put an unsettling thought in my head, if Ben was holding back, could he possibly take on the others and win? How was I supposed to compete with him now? I thought. She placed her hand on my face, "are you alright? You're looking a little peaked," she said. I shook it off, "yeah, I'm fine," I said, "you said you haven't seen Jake since then right? Why do you think that is?" I was curious to know what she thought. "I don't know. He's probably afraid that I'm going to kill him. I'm not sure what I'd do if I ever saw him again," she said, laying on her back again.

I needed to ask one more thing, "do you think I could take him?" she smiled and sat up, "come here," she said leading the way to her office. She rummaged around in her desk and cabinets until she found what she was looking for. "Here," she said, "this is Jake." she handed me a folded in half tattered black and white photograph. He and I were roughly the same height and build. He looked to have light colored hair and blue eyes according to the photo. He was handsome, maybe even better looking than me, I thought, but she still hadn't answered my question. So I asked her again, "Do you think I could take him in a fight?" I asked her more assertively this time. She took the photograph and put it in the back of one of her cabinet drawers. "Let's hope we never have to find out," she said.

It almost made me mad that she wouldn't give me a straight answer, but I didn't want to ask her a third time. "Is that the only picture you have of him?" I asked. She nodded. "Why do you still have it? If all he ever did was hurt you, why keep it?" I said. She looked down at her feet. "Because if I get rid of it, it's like it never happened. If I forget what he did to me, I'll never be able to fully move on from my trauma." I could tell that bringing him up was causing some bad memories to resurface.

I took her hand and led her back to our room. I grabbed her phone off the nightstand and turned the camera feature on. "What are you doing?" she asked as I sat down in the chair. I pulled her on top of me so she was sitting in my lap now. I draped one arm over her shoulder holding the phone and put the other around her. "I'm taking a picture of us so you can remember this moment forever," I said, snapping the picture. I kissed her cheek and took another one. I didn't even know if she was smiling, I just kept taking photos. Around the fifth or sixth one she put her hand up to stop me.

I looked at her to see what the matter was, she was slightly smiling as she kissed my lips. I held up the phone to get one last picture. We looked over the photos and laughed. She wasn't smiling in the first few but as we went on her grin grew wider and wider. My favorite one was the last one though. You could feel our love radiating through the picture. She took her phone back from me and started doing something on it. "What are you doing?" I asked. She got up and walked across the hall then promptly returned. She was carrying a picture frame. She set it down on the nightstand next to where her phone sat at night. "There," she said, "much better." I moved in closer to get a better look. She had printed out the last picture and framed it. My heart started to swell seeing the two of us sitting there.

"Does it look alright?" she asked. "It's perfect," I replied. I pulled her in and began kissing her all over, I had grown accustomed to doing so now. She pulled at the draw strings of my pants until she got them undone. I held onto her as I drug her onto the bed. She lifted her arms and I took her tank top off in one fluid motion. I clawed at her back as she pulled my face in closer to her chest. I didn't just want her, I needed her. We lay there in position for a few moments while I tried to get my pants down. She kissed me tenderly all over my face. I was sitting with my back up to the headboard now. She started moving her hips and I lost it.

Suddenly, I had her laying on her back as I forced myself on her. I couldn't stop, I didn't want to stop. I kept going until my legs finally seized. I felt terrible, I hadn't even given her a chance to enjoy herself. "I'm sorry," I said out of breath on top of her still. She looked at me puzzled, "what do you have to be sorry for?" she asked. I started to blush, "well, I didn't even let you...you know..." she laughed at me and kissed me again. "Honey, as long as you're good, I'm good. Ok?" I placed my head on her shoulder trying to catch my breath. I nodded my head then kissed her neck. Next time, I thought, next time I'd try and take it easy for her.

I got off her and pulled up my pants. She walked over to her closet to pick out her outfit for the day, a denim skirt paired with my old high school sweatshirt. I liked seeing her make use of it. She combed her hair and put two french braids in her hair, pigtail style. She looked like she was a cheerleader ready to cheer at a high school sporting event. I walked past her and went to pick out my own clothes, black jeans and a gray t-shirt.

We went downstairs to see if anyone was there. Xander was sitting in the living room playing video games with William. "Where's Ben and the girls?" I asked, already knowing the answer. "Ben drove them today, I stayed here because Ben's been getting on my nerves," Xander said, "he's back on the same campaign about him becoming the new leader and how he'll run things one day," he scoffed and rolled his eyes. William made a finishing move in their game ending the match, "there's been a few new sightings around the area boss. You might want to take a look at them. I emailed you the documents," he said.

New sightings? I thought, rogue vampires perhaps or maybe some more werewolves. "What kind of sightings?" Isa asked. She opened up her email on her phone. "Weird ones," Will replied, "It's like someone is trying to get caught by leaving strange markings on the bodies." Strange markings, like how strange? I thought. "I'm gonna go do some research upstairs Adam. Why don't you just hang out down here and fix yourself something to eat?" she said. I didn't want her to go, even if it was only just upstairs. I nodded as she gave me a kiss on the cheek. "Eeewwww…" both Xander and William said about our public display of affection.

Isa went upstairs and I made my way to the kitchen. I made myself a sandwich then rejoined the other two in the living room. I sat in the chair eating my sandwich when Xander said, "you guys are so cute I could puke," he laughed after finishing his sentence. I smiled, "oh yeah? What about you and my sister?" I asked him. "Yeah, but we're not consummating like rabbits like you guys are." I choked on my sandwich. How does he know that? My face started turning red. He glanced at me and chuckled again.

"I didn't know everyone knew that," I said sheepishly. "We didn't, you just confirmed it," William said with a laugh. Oh great, way to go Adam, now everyone knows how horny you are. I tried to change the subject, "so, whatcha playing?" Xander looked over at me, "oh no, we're not done talking about the two of you yet. Has she told you about if Ben challenges you, what we're gonna do?" he asked "yeah, the two of you are going to step in if he goes too far that way Isa can still remain the alpha, right?" I said. "Yeah, we'll be right there if you need us, unless of course you win against him," Will said. "Do you really think I have a chance at beating him?" I said. Xander replied now, "It's hard to say, I wish I could have been there last night when he tried picking a fight with you. Man I bet he was sure surprised when you managed to rip his arm out of the socket."

I shuddered at the thought about yanking his arm out of place again. Maybe I did stand a chance. "Do you think you guys could help me get ready to fight him?" I asked. They both looked at each other, then turned the TV off. Xander stood up, "sure. Let's go outside and I'll show you how it's done," he said. William stood up too, and made his way out to the front yard. I followed behind them. We walked until we were between the house and the willow tree. "Here's good," William said. They took off their shirts and threw them on the ground. Was I supposed to do the same? I led by their example and took mine off too. We all stood in a triangle, waiting. "Now," William said, "the first thing you're gonna want to do is get low. You don't want to give him too much to work with. The lower to the ground you are, the harder you'll be to flip over". William demonstrated a low stance without getting down on all fours. "Second," he continued, "You're gonna need to use your body weight to try and knock him around. If that doesn't work you need to hold your ground until the last possible moment before you take him down." They both got into position, William down low and Xander towering over him.

They began to wrestle until William pinned Xander down and counted to three. "Lastly," he said, "if that doesn't work, you need to constantly keep moving in hopes you'll tire him out." They stood up again and proceeded to circle each other. Will was crouching low to the ground and swiftly moved out of the way every time Xander lunged at him. I was entranced watching them fight. Could it really be that easy? I thought. Will managed to pin Xander down again after flipping him over onto his back. Xander laid there momentarily catching his breath. I reached down to help him. He accepted my hand and stood up. "You're turn," he said to me, giving me a pat on my back. I was a little nervous about fighting either one of them. Xander was significantly larger than I was and William was extremely agile.

I crouched down to face off with Will. "Ready?" he said with a smirk. I nodded my head, "ready," I said. He lunged forward, getting his shoulder underneath my chest, sending me flying backwards. I lay there on the ground gasping for air. "You gotta plant your feet, otherwise he's going to do that again," Xander said, helping me up. I tried again, this time securing my footing before I said I was ready. "Go," I said. William pushed off hard from the ground and hooked his arm in mine. I struggled for a second until he spun me around and pinned me down. "That was better," he said, "now try Xander." I got up again, starting to get irritated with losing. I knew that if I managed to dodge him, he was still stronger and would easily beat me.

We readied ourselves. I dug my feet in and lowered my body, "ready?" I said to him. He chuckled, "go!" he said. I lowered myself and hit him head on. He wrapped his arms around me and flipped me over his back. I landed with a thud. I rolled over and growled in frustration. "Again!" I shouted. They continued taking turns wrestling me. I hadn't beaten either of them even once yet. My muscles were starting to ache from being thrown around, but I needed to push through. William looked at me laying on the ground again, "I think that's enough for one day Adam," he said. I shook my head, "no. One more" I got into position one last time. Xander didn't look too convinced as he came up to face me.

I made myself ready, this time I was going to try something different. We nodded our heads signifying the start of the match. Xander launched at me but instead of taking one to the chest I dropped down on the ground, letting him sail right over me. He landed on his stomach. I quickly hopped up again and waited for him to face me. He stood up slowly, looking at William. This time he didn't wait for us to say, 'go' and he dove at me again. I jumped back doing a flip. Finally, years of my gymnastics training was paying off.

He faced me again with a wild look in his eyes. He lunged forward one last time and I used his shoulders to hoist myself up over him. We landed on the ground with me sitting in his back. I did it, I thought. I was able to pin him down once. He pushed me off and stood hunched over now. He started to snarl at me then got down on all fours slowly growing fur. He was so mad he was changing, I thought. I started to back away, his large wolf body beginning to consume him. He took a step closer to me, his teeth bared. "What do I do?" I frantically asked William. He was now in wolf form too now, standing by my side.

I took another step back, never taking my eyes off of Xander. I saw a shadow flash across the sky and Isadora landed between us. She pushed me away with one hand, "No, Xander!" she shouted at him. His eyes focused on her then he relaxed, sitting on his haunches. "Are you alright?" She said frantically patting me down. "I'm fine," I said, grabbing her hands, "really I am." Her eyes darted around doing one more look at my body before looking me in the eyes. She sighed then turned to William and Xander. "What the hell were you thinking?" She said angrily. "He wanted to spar a little bit to try and get the feel of things. We didn't hurt him, Izzy. It was all in good fun," William said. "Good fun?" She said, "Then why was Xander about to attack him?" He looked over at Xander who was now in his human form again. "It was my fault," he said, "he bested me and I wanted to take him down." She looked back at me now. The look of shock in her eyes. "You beat Xander?" She asked me. I nodded my head looking back and forth between William and Xander. Was that such a big deal? I thought.

She started to smile then began laughing. It made me jump to hear her laugh like that. She pulled me in close and kissed me, it took my breath away. "If you can beat Xander then you'll definitely be able to take on Ben and win. There's no doubt in my mind," she said, hugging me tighter. I embraced her. She believed I could do it, and I wouldn't let her down. I could hear William snickering behind us. I turned to look at him, "what's so funny?" I asked. He put his shirt back on before he answered, "it's nothing," he said, "but since you just beat Xander technically you already out rank him and Ben." I was stunned. I didn't think we were actually fighting for positions in the pack yet. Xander put his shirt on too, "yeah well, we'll see about that once you're able to transition. Then we'll have a rematch when you can't get all fancy and flip yourself around anymore," he chuckled menacingly.

I honestly didn't care if I beat him or not, all I cared about was making sure Ben wouldn't get a chance to become the new alpha. "Here," Isa said, handing me my shirt, "we should all get ready to head to the club now. You guys driving separately from us?" She asked. They both nodded. "Good. We'll see you there then," she said as they walked towards the house. We stood there watching them walk away when she jumped on my back. I faltered for a second but caught her. I stood there holding her piggyback style. She nuzzled my ear and whispered, "I'm so proud of you."

The hairs on the back of my neck stood up from the touch of her lips on my ear. She wasn't mad at me? I thought. I began walking to the house whilst I carried her. "Thanks," I said, smiling like a hero. She kept her head next to mine, "you need to be a little less reckless though. Xander means well but you still could have been seriously injured," she said. I nodded, "I know. I didn't think I was actually going to win that last one but I did. Do you think he would have hurt me?" I asked. She held me tighter, "maybe, he wouldn't have done it intentionally though," she replied.

She was so worried about my safety and making sure everyone was taken care of, how could Ben possibly ever want to replace her? I thought. When we got up to the house Xander and William were just getting into the Camaro, "you kids have fun now," Xander said, giving me a wink and laughing. I knew what he was insinuating. I put her down once we entered the house. "Do you wanna take a shower?" she said to me, giving me a playful look. I tried to race her up the stairs but she was too fast for me. She was already waiting in the bathroom undressed by the time I got up to the bedroom. I followed her, taking off my clothes as quickly as possible.

After we finished showering, we got dressed and headed out to the car. She took the keys from me indicating she wanted to drive today, I didn't mind. She placed her hand on my leg as she drove. It made me a little excited knowing her hand was so close. I thought about my fighting lesson from William and Xander. She seemed so scared when she came in between Xander and I. "What are you afraid of?" I asked curiously. She glanced my way, "Afraid of?" She said, biting her lip. "Yeah, like I'm afraid of heights. What scares you?" I asked. It took her some time to answer me, "You," she finally said.

"Me? You're afraid of me?" I said baffled, "Why?" Her eyes remained on the road ahead. "I'm afraid of what will happen when you finally realize I'm not worth it in the end," she said. I couldn't believe her, how could she possibly think that? "When are you going to realize that I'm in it for the long haul?" I replied to her. She smiled, "I guess you'll just have to keep reassuring me forever I suppose." I held her hand now, stroking the top of it gently with my thumb. She sighed, "I was scared today because I knew you wouldn't be needing me for very much longer. If you can take on Xander and win, you won't need me to protect you from anything," she said.

I looked at her, I wanted to say that I would always need her and that I would never want to be without her. "He really messed you up that bad, didn't he, huh?" I asked. I felt her tighten her grip on my hand. She looked at me, "more than you'll ever know," she said quietly. We pulled up to the alley and parked the car. I didn't want to go in yet, I just wanted to sit with her and let her know how much I loved her. "Isa, I'm not him," I said. She looked down now, "I know," she said softly. "And I will never be like him," I said now. "I know Adam, it's just hard to move past old wounds, that's all. Just give me some time and I'll be fine," she said, giving me a slight smile.

She had already suffered for a couple hundred years, how much longer was it going to take to get over him, I thought. "Do you love me more than him?" Her head whipped around to face me, "Adam! That's not even a comparison I'm willing to make. Of course I love you more than I could ever love him. What we had was a love built on tragedy and distrust. I trust you with my life, Adam. You wouldn't be sitting here with me if I didn't truly love you." Her words seemed to make me feel better but there was still something bothering me, "would he ever try to win you back?" I said wearily. She took my hands in her own, "if he were to ever step foot back in my life, I would end him before he ever got the chance to ask."

Chapter

17

The next few weeks seemed to slowly pass by. I trained more with Xander and William on how to control my emotions and how to win a fight if I was challenged. I managed to remain calm at work knowing that if something were to happen with Isa she would take care of the problem herself. Even Sarah and Isa seemed to be hitting it off now, going to get their nails done and things like that. Ben had also toned it back a notch after he found out I was able to defeat Xander at practice. I was beginning to become stronger and faster. I could almost keep up with Isa when we went running through the woods now. She began using her strength to test my limits more too. Tonight was my first full moon and I was nervous but ecstatic about finally being an official member of the pack.

We had lucked out that the full moon landed on a day we didn't have to work. Everything was working in my favor. Isa woke me up bright and early that morning. She kissed me until I was awake enough to kiss her back. "Good morning sleepyhead," she said with a giggle. I pulled the covers over my head. "No, it's time to wake up," she said, lightly shaking me. I wanted to sleep more. We were going to be up all night after all so I figured a few extra hours of sleep wouldn't hurt me. She reached under the blanket to try to coax me out. I rolled over so she couldn't reach what she was grabbing for. She playfully spanked me and I laughed at her.

"Don't make me come in there?" she joked. I lifted the blanket slightly so I could peek out at her. She was sitting on her knees staring at me. I tucked the blanket back around me. She stood on the bed over me and ripped the blanket completely off of me. "Now I've gotcha!" she said, pouncing on me. I rolled over again with her sitting on top of me. I pulled her into me now holding her arms at her sides. She tried to kiss me again but I held her at bay. She pushed back harder until I let her go.

This time she kissed me uncontrollably all over my neck and face. What's got into her? I wondered. "Are you alright?" I asked, catching my breath. She moved her hands lower down my torso until she reached my waistband. She stopped briefly to answer, "It's the moon," she said, kissing me some more, "I get a little extra rambunctious when it's the full moon. Sorry," she said, pulling her hand back out of my pants. I caught her hand before she could fully remove it. "No, don't stop," I begged her. Her eyes lit up as she took her top off.

We fooled around for a while until we were both panting. She looked deep in my eyes, "I love you," she said. I smiled and kissed her again, "I love you too Isadora, for all eternity." We wrapped our arms around each other and lay there now. "Are you nervous about tonight?" she asked. I was but I didn't want to let it show. I kept my heart rate down now after much practice the last few weeks, "not really," I said. She shot me a look, she knew I was bluffing. "Ok, so I'm a little worried about how everything's going to go but it's gonna be fine. I've been preparing myself for weeks now and I think I'm going to do alright," I said quickly.

She nestled her head in the crook of my arm. "I'm not worried," she said nonchalantly. "You're not?" I asked. She shook her head, "no, I have complete faith in your abilities. You're gonna do great. Just remember not to challenge Ben, let him come to you." I nodded at her reminder. It was better to lose a fight as the opponent than it was the challenger. If Ben wanted a fight, he'd have to work for it. I was allowed to refuse a challenge by someone of a higher rank but I couldn't back down if I challenged them. I was still planning to fight him if he challenged me however. I hadn't told Isa that though.

She had enough to worry about without me letting her know my plans. William and Xander would still step in if I needed them to so that she could remain neutral. "What's the plan for the rest of the day?" I asked. She shrugged, "we could just do this until the moon rises I suppose. I'm in no hurry to watch you suffer later tonight," she said. I chuckled at her statement. I wasn't too excited about that part either. Hopefully I would be able to compose myself enough so that neither Sarah or Isa would have to see me in too much pain.

I twirled a piece of her hair in my fingers. I started thinking about asking her to marry me again. I was sure she would say yes but I didn't know how to ask. It was hard to talk about it to anyone else too, she had such sensitive hearing I didn't want to spoil the surprise. I looked over at my nightstand drawer. I had gotten her a small plain silver band with a solitary petite diamond in the middle. It wasn't much but it was all I could afford. I hoped she would like it. I had been hiding it around her room for about a week now hoping she hadn't caught on to me.

She placed her hand over my heart, "what's on your mind?" she asked. I panicked trying to think of something clever. "I'm just thinking about tonight," I said. She smiled, "your heart is telling me otherwise, Adam." I placed my hand on top of hers, feeling my chest move rapidly. Damn it, I thought, now she's gonna know something's up. "You don't have to tell me, that's alright. You're entitled to have your own personal thoughts," she said. I kissed her head. Thank you, I thought to her.

I wanted to go ask Will what his opinion was on asking her tonight. Maybe I'd ask him to go for a run later and then tell him deep in the woods, I thought. "What are you thinking about?" I asked her. She chuckled, "if I tell you, you might be disappointed," she said. What could she be thinking of? Did she find the ring? Did she not like it? I wondered. I was starting to get worried. "What is it?" I pried. She rolled over to face me, "I was just thinking about you actually fighting and losing against Ben. Not that I think you would lose but if you did, we could leave the pack and move somewhere else." I had to think about what she said. Did she want to leave? "Aren't you happy here?" I asked.

"It's not that I'm not happy. I just don't like to get stuck in one place for too long, you know with the whole not aging thing. After so many years, we have to move anyway before people start getting suspicious," she said. I stroked her face, "do you want to leave?" I said. "No," she replied, "it was just something that's been on my mind for a while. I told you you'd be disappointed," she said, kissing my nose. I wasn't disappointed, I just wasn't expecting it, I thought.

"Where would we go, hypothetically speaking?" I asked. She sat up now, her eyes twinkling with excitement. "We could go anywhere you'd like. The U.S., Asia, Europe. I haven't been to France in ages and would love to show you everywhere I've been in my lifetime," she said. I had never been outside the state, let alone an entire country before, I thought. "I've never thought about traveling the world before," I said to her, "Is Paris nice?" She was practically giddy as she got off the bed.

"Oh it's positively ghastly, but that makes it more fun. The food is exquisite but the people there are horrendous if you don't speak the language." She went on to talk about the architecture and the catacombs, even going so far as to talk about her history with the guillotine and where she was laid to rest a few times. I loved watching her talk about something so passionately. "Is there anywhere else you'd like to go?" I asked her. She paused to think carefully about her decision.

She came and sat on the bed again, "it doesn't matter where I go, as long as you're coming with me. I could live here with you for the next few years but we'd have to move eventually," she said softly. The thought of moving intimidated me. I had moved around so much as a child the thought of doing it all over again for the rest of my life seemed rather unsettling, never truly being able to belong somewhere. "What if I don't want to move around all the time?" I asked. She sighed, "That's just something we'll have to cross at a later date then." She leaned in to kiss me again, and I pulled her closer to me. "Just stay with me," I whispered, burying my face in her hair. "I'm not going anywhere, I can assure you of that," she replied.

We got dressed and headed down stairs. There was a thin layer of frost on the grass today. That would make for an even chillier night, I thought. Isa made lunch for everyone and we all sat down at the table to eat. "Everything ready for tonight?" William asked me. I nodded, taking a bite. How was I going to speak to him alone? I wondered. Sarah and Xander were talking about something I didn't quite hear, and Ben and Lexa were talking about what they were going to do after the moon rose. I couldn't pay attention to any of it. I was still caught up on Isa's desire to move.

"Are you OK, Adam?" I faintly heard Sarah say. I looked around the table, all eyes were on me. "I'm sorry what?" I asked, not knowing what she said. "I asked if you were alright. You're looking a bit out of it right now," she said. "I'm sure he's just got pre-moon jitters," Xander laughed, "he'll be fine." Everyone continued to eat. Isa had a questioning look on her face, not understanding what was going on in my head. I put my foot up to hers to soothe and let her know I was fine.

I resumed eating along with everyone else. "Hey, Will. Can we race after we're finished here? I wanna get one more in before tonight," I asked, trying to seem less conspicuous. "I'll go for a run with you," Isa said. "No!" I answered too quickly and she looked surprised, "I mean, no thank you. I'd really like to race William this time, if that's alright," I said. She nodded her head with a confused look on her face. I'm sorry Isa, I thought to myself. "Yeah, that's fine. I was going to ask you anyway if you wanted to go again," William said, giving me a suspicious look.

When we were all finished I ran upstairs to grab a sweatshirt before my run with Will. I snatched the ring box out of my nightstand and put it in my pants pocket. Isa was on her way up the stairs as I was coming down. She startled me and I clutched my pocket tightly. "Where are you going?" I questioned her. "I'm going up to my office, is that ok with you?" she asked sarcastically. "Ok, sorry," I said as she stepped past me, "I love you," I whispered to her as she continued up the stairs. "See you later," she said. I hoped I didn't make her mad by telling her she couldn't go with me.

I didn't have time to think about that right now, I needed to meet Will next to the willow tree. I jogged out to the tree where William was waiting for me. "What's up with you today? Sarah's right you seem a bit off," he said once I caught up to him. "Shhhhh..." I said raising my finger to my mouth, "I don't want Isa to hear us. How far away do you think we need to be for our conversation to be private?" He tilted his head to the side. He was trying to figure out what I wanted to talk about, I think. He nodded his head like he understood then got himself into position for our race. "On your mark, get set, go!" He said bounding out in front of me. I followed him through the trees past the lake and deep into the forest.

We ran past the tree Isa had carved our initials in. He took me way beyond where he'd ever taken me before. How far is he going to go? I thought. We came into a clearing near the water's edge and stopped. I stood there catching my breath. "Is this far enough?" I asked, leaning against a tree. Will nodded his head, "Yeah. We were good about ten minutes ago but I figured we needed to make it look like we were actually going for a longer run," he said sitting down by my feet. I slid down the tree and sat by him.

"What did you want to talk about that you didn't want Izzy to hear?" he asked, wiping the sweat from his face on the bottom of his shirt. I felt my pocket to make sure the box was still in it. It was. I took it out of my pocket to show Will. His eyes grew wide when I handed it to him. "Is this what I think it is?" he said. I nodded as he opened the box. "It's nothing fancy, but it was all I could afford. Do you think she'll like it?" I asked. He carefully took the ring from its box and looked at it in the sunlight. "I think she'll love it. She's not really into big shiny things anyway. When are you gonna do it?" he said. I sighed and shrugged my shoulders, "I'd thought about doing it tonight but I didn't know if it would be too much pressure with it being my first moon and all. What do you think?" I asked him. He put the ring in its box and handed it back to me.

"That's up to you, man. If you do it tonight you'll have to do it after the moon has gone away, otherwise she can't wear it while she's a wolf," he said. Why not before? I thought. "How come?" I said. He stood up again. "Because, her clothes don't stay on like ours do. She basically breaks out of everything she's wearing, and you don't want her to lose it the second she gets it right?" He had a point. I had forgotten about that. "Maybe I should just wait until tomorrow then," I said. Will placed his hand on my shoulder, "no Adam, if you wanna do it tonight, then I say go ahead and do it. I've never seen her this happy before in my life. She loves you wholeheartedly, and that's something I wasn't sure she could ever do. You changed her," he said.

I'd changed her? I thought. "Like in a good way, right?" I asked, concerned. He laughed, "Like in the best way. She used to be so cold and distant to everyone and everything, even to me and she practically raised me. Now she's actually participating in the group instead of just being our solitary leader." I liked hearing his input on how our relationship was going, it made me feel good to know he had noticed a difference in her. "Do you think she'll say yes?" I asked now. He smiled, "Yes, Adam. She'll say yes," he then went in for a hug with me. As he was slapping my back he said, "But if you ever do anything to hurt her, just know I'll rip you to shreds." I couldn't quite tell if he was joking or not so let out a slight chuckle. He released me, giving me a nod. He had meant it and that was fine, if I ever did anything to upset her in any way I would deserve it.

We made our way back home again slowly. We weren't in any particular rush, we still had a few hours until sundown before the moon would be out. When we came to the open field between the house and the willow tree we saw Sarah, Lexa, and Xander putting together a huge stack of wood. "What's this for" I asked. Sarah turned to me, "it's supposed to snow tonight and I don't want to be cold watching you transition so I asked Izzy if we could build a bonfire for tonight." That was a great idea, then she'd be able to see us better in the dark too. "Need any help?" I offered. Ben came out of the woods carrying a huge stack of logs, "no, we're fine. Why don't you run along and report back your findings like the little lap dog you are?"

I was instantly enraged. "Ben!" Lexa said as she hit him in the stomach for saying something so disrespectful. "What the hell's your problem with Adam, Ben? Has he done something to you that we don't know about? Or are you really just an asshole?" Sarah yelled at him. He let out a low growl and Xander stood in front of Sarah to block her from him. "I wasn't talking to you, I was talking to him," he pointed at me, "we've all seen how she treats you. You're nothing but a pet to her. She only keeps you around for a good lay every once in a while."

I lost my temper and tried to lunge at him but William pulled me back, shaking his head. I knew what Ben was trying to do and I still let him get to me. I felt so stupid at that moment. I shook off Williams' hold on me and walked around the wood pile they were stacking. I could hear Ben still heckling me as I walked in the house. I breathed a huge sigh of relief when I shut the door behind me so I couldn't hear him as clearly. Calm down, I thought walking towards the staircase.

I climbed the stairs but when I got to our room I found it empty. That's strange, I thought, maybe she was in her office. I went across the hall to check. She wasn't there either. My heart sank, had she followed us on our run? I quickly ran to the balcony and looked out the glass doors. I could see her standing with her wings out next to the bonfire pile. Shit, I thought. I took the box out of my pocket and shoved it back in my drawer. I heard her wings flap as she leapt off the ground heading for the balcony again. I sat on the bed and tried to act as naturally as I could. I heard the thud of her bare feet when she landed and opened the doors.

She was muttering to herself, "Of all the days, why did he have to choose today to pick a fight with everyone." She looked at me sitting on the bed. "Hi," she said, continuing her rant to herself. She paced back and forth across the room mumbling now. I watched her as she walked. I wanted to comfort her but didn't know how. I stood up and walked towards her. She flinched when I put my hands on her shoulders. She briefly looked at me then pushed me aside, "not now Adam," she said, continuing to pace. Boy, he must have really pissed her off, I thought.

I decided it was best just to let her work out whatever was going through her mind alone and took a shower. After I was done she was gone again. I got dressed and went looking for her. When I checked her office I saw her sitting at her office chair with her knees pulled tight to her chest. I walked inside and sat down on her couch. "Are you ok?" I asked knowing full well something was wrong. She shook her head but didn't say anything. "Is it something I did?" I said. She shook her head again. "Was it something Ben said?" She looked up at me. I could see the desperation in her eyes. "Adam, you can't fight him tonight. I know you're still planning on accepting his challenge when he offers it to you, but you can't."

How did she know? I hadn't even told William or Xander of my plans yet. "Why not?" I asked, "Was it because of what he was saying out there earlier?" She shook her head again, eyes wide, "you just can't. It's not that you won't win, it's that you shouldn't. If you happen to be losing the fight and then you can't control your emotions, I'm afraid Lexa will step in to try and save Ben," she said. Lexa? What did she have to do with any of this? "I thought you said significant others weren't allowed to fight back in retaliation against their spouse?" I said. "They're not, but that doesn't mean she wouldn't do whatever it took to keep him safe," she replied.

I was still confused, so I stood up and started walking around the room. "But you still haven't told me why, I shouldn't fight him other than Lexa maybe coming to his rescue. Why does that matter if she comes to his aid?" I said, getting frustrated. She put her legs down then rested her elbows on the desk folding her hands together like she was praying and sighed, "Because Adam, Lexas' pregnant," she whispered.

"What?" I said, my mouth hanging open. I wasn't sure if I'd heard her right. Lexa was pregnant? I thought. "Yes, Adam, you heard me right," she said resting her head in her hands now. I was dumbfounded. "But I thought you said Ben didn't want to have any children?" I questioned her. She nodded her head, "that's right, I did. But he also knows that if the fight is ending up poorly in his favor and Lexa steps in, that fighting you could possibly harm the baby giving him another reason to try and cut me out of the equation when I try to intervene." The sick manipulative son of a bitch, I thought, he did this on purpose knowing exactly how this would all play out.

"How could he do that?" I said, raising my voice, "how can you use your own girlfriend and child like that just so you can become the alpha?" she shrugged her shoulders, "I don't know. And Lexa has been waiting for this for so long, I can't allow you to fight him tonight." Knowing what he did made me want to challenge him that much more. Not to hurt Lexa or the baby but to let him know what an absolute piece of trash he really was. "Did she tell you she was pregnant?" I asked, not knowing if I was getting too personal. "No, I could hear the heartbeat out there and I knew it wasn't coming from Sarah. It's more obvious in regular people compared to werewolf bodies. She has to be about two maybe three weeks along now.

I laid down on the couch, now I completely understood why she was in such a mood after I got back from my run. "What a shit show," I said. She agreed, "Yeah, my hands are tied. I absolutely can not intervene tonight no matter what. You can not fight him, that is exactly what he wants." I sat up again, "I understand. I won't do it. There's too much at stake now. I still can't believe he planned this whole thing," I said. She came and sat down next to me, "neither can I. I knew he was a vindictive prick but I never thought he'd stoop so low to dangle Lexa like that as bait."

"Does anybody else know?" I asked, putting my arm around her. "I don't know. It's pretty rude to just walk up to someone and ask them if they know if they're pregnant or not," she said with a chuckle. She was right. I'll bet that if Xander knew he'd be on their side too if I did end up fighting them. "Do you think anyone else could hear what you did?" I was curious to see how good her hearing actually was. "No, my ears are attuned to the sound of beating hearts. You all have excellent hearing but mine is still ten times better."

She leaned her head against my chest, "this one's my favorite though," she said with a smile. My heart began to dance. I knew right then, I was going to ask her to marry me, tonight. I led her back into our bedroom and sat down on the bed. "Are you still feeling frisky?" I asked with a devilish grin. She laughed then came over to sit with me. "Yes and no," she said, "I want to but my head wouldn't be in the right place now after all that. Wouldn't you agree?" I thought about it and she was right. My head had been all over the place today and I didn't think I could perform to my best abilities either. "Let's just take a nap then," I said, tucking her into my body. She took her phone out of her back pocket and set an alarm for two hours then curled up with her head on my chest.

When the alarm went off I was feeling groggier than when I fell asleep. She kissed me then went to her closet to get changed. She came out wearing a long white cotton dress, I suppose it was easier to take off than pants and a t-shirt would be before she transformed. I looked outside to see that the sun had already set. My stomach was in knots anticipating what was about to happen to me. When we descended down the stairs, I could hear everyone gathered in the living room talking all at once. They were arguing about something.

What was everyone talking about? I wondered. I walked in the living room and everyone went silent. "What's going on?" I asked. "Sarah wants to take a group picture of us before and after your transition but half of us don't want to do it," Xander said. A picture, why? I thought. "Why don't you want your picture taken?" I said. "It's not me," he motioned with his eyes to Ben and Lexa. I looked at Isa now, "What do you think? It's fine with me," I said. Isa looked at the group, "Two pictures that's it, but it has to be with the polaroid camera so there isn't any trace left on a phone in case it gets stolen or lost," she said. Everyone agreed and she went to get the camera.

Sarah came up to me wearing a sweatshirt and a jacket, she was anticipating the cold. "Are you excited?" she asked, "I am." I smiled at her and nodded. Isadora returned with the camera and we all headed outside. "Get in position everyone," Sarah said, motioning for us to stand together. She turned the timer setting on and set the camera down on the deck railing then got in line with the rest of us. It went, Isadora, myself, William, Xander, Sarah, Ben, then Lexa. The camera flashed and spit out our picture. She hurried to catch it before it fell on the wet ground.

"That's a keeper," she said giddily. We all walked over to the massive pile of wood that had been stacked in a teepee formation. Isa snapped her fingers, producing a small ball of light then flicked it on the wood. Within moments, the whole thing was a blaze. I didn't know she could do that, I thought. We all stood in front of the fire in a semicircle. I could just barely make out the light of the moon peeking over the trees. Isa squeezed my hand, "It's time," she said before kissing me. She took off her dress and handed it to Sarah. She was just wearing her undergarments now.

It was lightly starting to snow as she walked out a few paces and faced the moon as it came up. I could see her rubbing her eyes and holding her body as she slowly knelt down in the snow. She let out a scream that turned into a howl. My heart was aching watching her in pain knowing my turn was soon to come. Her hair engulfed her and she began to transform. Suddenly there was a pure white wolf standing where Isadora once stood. It turned around and walked up to me. It may have not been the face I was accustomed to but her eyes remained the same, two beautiful deep green emeralds.

I slowly reached out to pet her ears, she let out a soft growl but let me continue. They were so soft, I thought. I turned to face the others but they were all standing in their wolf forms now too. Only Sarah and I remained. The moon crept higher in the sky revealing a ring around it. "Not much longer," I said to Sarah. Xander was sitting on his haunches between us now, probably just as a precaution in case I lost myself in the beginning of my transformation. I was glad he was there. The longer

I stood in the moonlight, the more uneasy I felt. I wasn't sure if it was just nerves or if something was actually happening to me.

The fire burned on and the moon got higher as the night went on. When it was directly above us Isadora walked over to me and licked my hand with the scare on it. I didn't know what she wanted me to do. I held out my hand for her. She let out a gust of air that sounded like a sneeze then looked to the sky. I still didn't know what she meant. "She wants you to raise your hand at the moon," Sarah said, demonstrating with her hand. I looked at Isa who seemed to nod at me. I did as I was told and held out my hand towards the sky. I waited there, holding it high in the air above my head, but nothing happened.

I turned to Isa, "Is something supposed to..." I felt a sharp pain starting with my hand traveling all the way through my body into my feet. I hunched over in pain, it felt like my insides were trying to explode. I cried out in anguish as my bones began to pull out of their sockets. "Adam!" Sarah shouted trying to come to my rescue. Xander stood in front of her blocking her path. "It's fine, stay there!" I yelled at her. I dropped to my knees frantically clawing at my own chest. It felt like I was suffocating in my own skin. I heard a cracking sound as my legs began to change shape. I wanted to scream out in pain so many times, but I didn't want to put Sarah through that again. My head was pounding and my jaw dislocated. Now I couldn't scream even if I wanted to. I lay down on the ground hoping death would steal me away from the insurmountable amount of discomfort I was feeling. Then at last I blacked out.

I awoke to the sounds of whimpering and something licking my face. I slowly opened my eyes. I was woozy and couldn't see straight yet. I blinked a few times to see Isa as a white wolf laying in front of me. I tried to stand up but found myself too weak to. She nudged me with her muzzle encouraging me to try again. I managed to make it on all four feet this time. I stood there shaky looking out at a whole new world. I could see everything now. Everything was so crisp and colorful. My ears twitched, I could hear Sarah sobbing behind me. Xander was back in his human form holding onto her. "Look, he's coming around now," he said to her.

She ran forward to embrace me. I stumbled trying to back up from her and yelped. Xander stopped her before she got close to me. "Don't rush him. He's like a real wild wolf right now. He can't control his actions and you might trigger his fight or flight response." I looked down at where my hands should have been, there attached to me were two large white and gray paws. I stood up again and tried to get a better look at myself. It seemed that I just looked like a regular light gray wolf.

Isa rubbed up against me under my neck. Her scent was so strong now that it almost hurt my nose. She pranced away towards Xander and Sarah then sat down. I timidly walked closer to them then sat next to her. "I think Izzy wants us to take that picture now while he's still calm," Xander said. The rest of the pack, including Xander, now sat around Isa and I. Sarah readied herself with the camera and took the shot. The flash scared me and I jumped up and began growling at her. The hairs on my neck and shoulders were standing on end. Sarah froze in place. Xander pushed me to the ground and pinned me there. I yielded to his dominance and he let me go.

Isa rubbed herself underneath my neck again this time flicking her tail in my face. Did she want me to follow her? I thought. I left the fireside and trotted after her. My lungs were full of the crisp fresh air around the lake. She stood in a playful stance and waited for me to join her. I leaned down too and we began to play. She would gently bite my neck and tackle me then I would do the same for her. Out of the corner of my eye I could see Bens' black silhouette slowly lurking around the fire. Was he about to ambush me? I turned around to face him but he was too fast. He came at me from behind. I dodged out of the way and waited for him to try again. He snarled at me, trying to make me back down. I wouldn't. Will came rushing in and pinned Ben down growling intensely in his face. Ben yielded and William let him back up.

I walked back over to Isa who was standing near the woods now. She took off running and I chased her. We ran for miles, never getting tired. Finally we stopped at our tree. She laid down and put her head down. I did the same. She nuzzled me again as she carefully inched her way closer to me. I kept my head down when she placed her head on top of my shoulder blades. We lay there for hours just waiting for the sun to come up. I didn't see anyone else the rest of the night. I fell asleep to the sounds of nature and the falling of snow.

The next day, I awoke to find myself still laying under the tree but with a blanket wrapped around me. My head was resting in Isa's lap and she was still only wearing her bra and underwear. "Did we spend the whole night out here?" I asked stretching my back. Everything hurt today. "Yeah, I figured you'd change back once you fell asleep so I stashed a blanket out here for you just in case." Why hasn't she gone back to the house to get some clothes on? I thought. "Damn it, my whole body aches," I said, wrapping the blanket around me as I sat up. "That'll happen, when your body literally has to restructure itself to suit the transformation," she said with a chuckle. She stood up then helped me stand up as well. My legs felt like Jell-O as I tried to walk. It was such a long way back to the house.

We started our journey slowly until my muscles finally warmed up after sleeping outside all night, then we were moving at a normal pace. "What did you think?" she asked, "was it what you expected it would be like?" I shook my head, "it was better and worse at the same time. It hurt so much to initially turn into a wolf but once I finally did, everything was great," I said as I wrapped the blanket around her. She accepted it and we continued on walking. "Does it hurt you too to transform?" I asked her. "Yes," she said, hopping over a fallen tree, "it's excruciating. I tried not to react so much last night because I didn't want you to worry." It looked like she was in pain when she transitioned though. The way she screamed before it happened still haunted me.

She bounded out in the field before me when we got to the edge of the woods. My legs were still aching and I didn't want to run yet. She took off the blanket and handed it to me again. She ran up to the willow tree and retrieved something. What's that she's holding? I thought. It was her dress from the night before. She put it on then returned to me. "Did Sarah leave that there for you?" I asked. "Yes. She and Xander went to bed after we ran off but before they did he told her to leave my dress by the tree in case I wanted it in the morning." She reached out to hold my hand. I obliged her and we continued walking towards the house. The field had a thin layer of snow on it. I could see our tracks all around the burnt pile of logs when we walked up to it. I remembered that Ben had tried to pick a fight with me, "did I do alright not fighting him last night?" I said. She nodded, "yes, you did very well by dodging out of his way and then waiting for William to pin him down. I was very impressed," she said with a smile. We were almost to the house now, "do you think he'll try to challenge me again any time soon?" I said. "Probably, it's hard to say. It would have been the perfect opportunity last night but we had everything worked out so well that he couldn't follow through with his plan," she replied. I didn't like the thought of having to constantly watch my back from now on until I was actually ready to fight him. "Do you want to go in the front door or just fly up to our room?" she asked, stopping outside the house. If I went through the house I could run into Ben and I didn't want to deal with him just yet. On the other hand, there was a specific little box waiting in my nightstand for me to pop the question. I didn't know what to choose.

"Let's just go through the house," I said, "I don't feel like flying up three stories right now." My heart started pounding thinking about going up to the bedroom. I needed a little bit more time to think about how I was going to ask her. She entered the house before me and stopped in the living room. "Everyone's still sleeping," she whispered, "Now's our chance." We quickly ran through the house and up the stairs. I didn't even need to catch my breath when I got to the top. It's like my lungs stayed at the same capacity from when I was a wolf. She noticed my surprise when we made it up the stairs, "breathing easier?" she asked. I nodded," yeah, it's like I'm still a wolf," I said. She chuckled, "you can see and hear better too now can't you?" She was right, everything was clearer than it had been the day before. I set the blanket down on the bed and laid down. I was still exhausted even if I could breathe easier. She made her way to the closet to change into something else. I quickly sat up when she disappeared and reached in my drawer. I grabbed it and put it in my pocket. Now was my chance. When she came back out I would ask her, I thought.

She came back out wearing black baggy sweatpants and my hoodie. She was braiding her hair as she walked over to me. "Are you alright? Your heart rate is a little erratic right now," she said concerned. I couldn't control my breathing. I had been caught. She sat down on the bed next to me and stroked my face. I leaned into her hand. "Isa," I said quietly, "I need to ask you something." I took her hands in mine, I was beginning to shake. She gave me her full attention, looking me in the eyes. Now's my chance, I thought. I reached in my pocket and pulled out the box. I slid off the bed onto one knee. Her eyes grew wide. "Isadora, will you marry me?" I said opening up the ring box. I could see her eyes beginning to tear up as she moved her left hand forward. I took the ring out of the box and slid it on her finger. She leaned forward to kiss me. I kissed her back waiting for her to reply. She pulled away from me and whispered, "Yes."

I smiled and kissed her again this time pulling her body close to mine. "Really?" I asked in disbelief. She nodded her head and kissed me some more. My heart was soaring now. I held her close, not wanting this moment to end. She pulled away and began looking at her hand. "I'm sorry it's not much, but I hope you still like it," I said. She held up her hand to get a better look at the diamond. "I love it," she said, "I wouldn't want it any other way. I think it's perfect." Her reassurance made me feel better about the situation. "When did you get this?" she asked, looking at me now. "I did it a couple weeks ago when you sent me to go get lunch. I've been hiding it in my nightstand ever since," I said.

She admired the ring some more before speaking again. "That's why your heart rate would elevate every time I got near it. I was wondering about that but I didn't know what was wrong. You were really starting to worry me," she said. I laid down on the bed, relieved that the whole thing was over now. She had said yes, I thought. I couldn't believe it. She laid her head on my shoulder and playfully drew circles across my chest.

"Did anyone help you plan this?" she asked. "No," I said, "I showed William yesterday when we went for our run and asked his opinion but other than that nobody knew." I felt a little guilty for not bringing Sarah into the loop, she would have loved to help me pick out the ring and help me figure out how I was going to propose. I wondered if I should go wake her up to tell her the news. "Do you want to tell everybody right away or wait?" she said, it was like she could read my mind. "What do you want to do?" I asked, interlocking my fingers into hers on my chest, "do you want to tell everyone?"

She smiled, "I'll leave the decision up to you whether you want to let everyone know or not. It doesn't matter to me. They're going to find out sooner or later when I'm wearing it all the time though." She smiled when she said that. It made me excited to think about her showing it off. "Let's tell everyone tonight before work," I said. She rolled over to kiss me again. I pulled her on top of me to give her better leverage. She started tugging on my shirt. I leaned forward and took it off. She did the same and took off her sweatpants too. She sat on top of me now, swaying back and forth. I loved her with every fiber of my being. I pulled her closer to me as I rolled her over onto her back. I undid my jeans and made myself ready. We rolled around, our bodies writhing together. She clawed at my back making me want to go faster. She made a sound as I pushed harder against her. I kissed her mouth pulling her tongue into mine. She obliged me. My heart was beating so fast now. I kissed her neck causing her to trill in my ear, giving me goose bumps. We continued to passionately lay together, until she wrapped her legs around me tightly causing me to stop moving.

I lay there panting on top of Isa, her legs quivering around me. She slowly released me and relaxed. "I love you so much right now," she said to me, petting my chest. Every time she said that my heart skipped a beat. I was the luckiest man alive, I thought. "I love you too, Isa," I said, kissing her again. She playfully bit my bottom lip before pulling me in. "Careful," I said to her, "You don't wanna make me bleed. I don't want you to get sick." She smiled at me, "I won't, I've learned my lesson," she said. I shifted my body weight off of her and onto the bed. She pulled my head to her chest.

We lie there for a few moments in silence, listening to each other breathe. "What do you think they're going to say about our engagement?" I asked her. She rubbed my back, "I'm sure Xander and Lexa will be excited. William already knows so he won't be surprised and Ben will be indifferent. What do you think Sarah will say?" she said inquisitively. I wondered that myself. Would she be upset with me for not talking with her first? "I don't know. I hope she isn't too mad about not asking her to help me. She seems to be coming around nicely to the two of us together but I'm not sure what her opinion is on marriage."

Marriage, I thought. It seemed to be such a scary thought only one day prior but now it was all I could think about. "When do you want to get married?" I asked, lifting my head off her. She smirked, "let's worry about breaking the news to everyone first before we pick a date, ok?" I understood, I was just so excited to call her my wife instead of my girlfriend. I wondered how this was going to affect the pack. Would I become her second once we were married? Would William resent me for taking away his rank?

My head started spinning with all sorts of questions. "Do you think William will be mad at me if I end up taking his position in the pack?" I asked. She shook her head, "that's not exactly how it works, I could just appoint you in as my second in command or we could still go by the challengers rule. That will be a tough decision for me to make in the future. Will has been with me the longest and has earned his rank but I would feel much better if you were the one constantly by my side."

I wanted to become her second but I didn't want her to just hand it to me. "I think you should just stick to the challengers rule," I said. She looked at me questionably, "really?" she asked, "why?" I sat up and put my shirt back on. "Because, if I'm going to spend the rest of my life with you, I don't want to start it off by stepping on anyone's toes. William was there first and I respect him, so the only way for me to become second is if I challenge him and win." She looked at me, surprised with my answer.

"Don't worry, you'll get there someday. I think William's become tired of being in charge of things for so long. He'd probably bow out to let you win even." I didn't want him to bow out, I wanted to actually fight for my right to become the alphas second. "But that's not what I want," I said, "I want to earn that right instead of just getting it handed to me. People respect him and I wanna be like that too." She nodded with understanding. "I get it," she said, sitting up now too. "We can discuss it later if you'd like, but for now, we should get ready for the day. I wanted to go in early today so I could dance before work." I nodded my head, "OK. I'll take a shower so we can go then."

I kissed her then headed for the bathroom. Isa remained on the bed. When I looked back to get a quick glance of her before shutting the door, I saw her staring at her hand again. She was grinning ear to ear.

She loves it, I thought, closing the door. After my shower my muscles seemed to feel better. Isa was still sitting on the bed waiting for me to return. "Feel better?" she said standing to greet me. "Yeah, much better. My chest still feels really heavy. Is that normal?" I asked. She traced her fingers around my pectoral muscles causing me to shudder. "Sometimes. It probably has to do with the cold air in your lungs last night. You may have gotten a touch of frostbite," she said. That made sense. "Sarah's awake, by the way if you wanted to talk to her," she continued with a smile. I suddenly became bashful. I wasn't sure if I wanted to tell my sister yet or not. "Will you come with me?" I asked her. "Of course I will. Always," she replied, taking my hand. We headed down stairs to the second floor where Sarah and Xander were sharing a room. I knocked on the door. My anxiety about my sister's approval instantly skyrocketed. What if she thought I was rushing into things?

"Yeah," Xander opened the door, "What's up?" he said standing in the doorway. I stood there not saying anything to him. He looked at Isa and then myself. Say something, I thought. Isa squeezed my hand. "Do you wanna talk to Sarah?" he asked. I nodded my head nervously. "She just left with Lexa and Ben. They got called into work at the hospital for a few hours. She'll be back tonight for work though. What did you need from her?" He asked. "Umm, I just wanted to talk with her for a little bit. It's fine. I'll just talk to her later," I said, turning around pulling Isa with me. We went back upstairs. I was shaking as I shut the door. "What happened?" She asked running her fingers through my hair trying to comfort me. "I panicked. I don't know what came over me. He opened the door, and I lost my head," I said frantically.

She stroked my face, "Calm down. We don't have to tell anyone yet if you're not ready." But I was ready. I wanted the world to know that I loved her and wanted to be with her forever. "No, I want to tell them. Maybe I'll just wait until we're all together tonight, I replied. She agreed. I wrapped my arms around her, holding her tightly. "I love you so much, Isa." She kissed my throat, "and I love you to Adam. Let's just head to the club and worry about this later," she said. I held onto her a few seconds longer then let go. "Ok," I said, turning to face the door again. As we got in the car I saw Will come out to the porch. I was his lips moving and listened, "Check your phone," I heard him say. I reached in my pocket and pulled out my phone. I had one new message. I opened the text and read it, 'did you do it yet? Let me know. I'm dying here man!' I stiffened as I read it. "What's wrong?" Isa said putting the car in drive. "Nothing. William just texted me, that's all," I replied. I wasn't technically lying to her, he really did text me, I just didn't reveal the contents of the message.

She sighed, "If you're going to lie, you need to do it better," she sounded a little irritated now. I sank back in my seat, "sorry. He just wanted to know if I proposed or not yet. I should have just told you," I said. She reached over and rubbed my thigh, "secrets are lies, if you have to keep something a secret it's the same thing as lying," she said softly. I had hurt her feelings by not telling her the truth. I wouldn't make that same mistake twice. I held her hand that she had on my leg as we drove towards the club. Arriving at the club I realized we hadn't eaten yet that day. "Are you hungry?" I asked, "I could go get us some stuff from Angelo's," I suggested. "Sure. I'll just be practicing when you get back." She leaned over to kiss me then got out. I watched her walk up to the back door before driving away.

When I got to the cafe, I ordered some burgers and fries to go and sat down at the counter to wait for our food to get done. The place was very busy for a Wednesday afternoon, almost every booth was filled. I got out my phone to text Will back. 'She said yes. Gonna tell everyone tonight,' I sent him. A few moments later he sent back a thumbs up emoji. 'You didn't tell anyone did you?' I sent him. 'I may have said something accidentally to Xan after you left. He said you were acting weird earlier,' he replied. I clapped my hand on my head. Of course he did, I thought. I quickly texted him back, 'Tell him not to say a word to Sarah. I want to be the one to tell her.' He replied again, 'I figured that out and told him not to say anything.' Thank god, I thought.

I got our food and brought it out to the car. There was a man standing next to the Corvette when I came out of the restaurant, he was looking in the windows for something. "Excuse me?" I said to him as I unlocked the doors. He turned around to face me. He was wearing a long black jacket with jeans and dark sunglasses over his eyes. "Oh, sorry there. Is this your car?" he said to me with a smile. Something about him was unsettling. "Uh…no," I said, opening the passenger door and putting the food on the floor, "it belongs to my fiancé." He looked surprised, "your fiancé?" he repeated. I nodded as I shut the door. "Have you known her long?" He asked. What was this guy's deal? I thought. "Yeah, I've known her for a while through work," I said, trying to walk around the front of the car. He stepped in front of me, blocking my path. I was starting to get frustrated. "Where do you work?" he asked now. "At the Moonlight Club on the west side of town," I replied, pushing past him. I opened the driver door and got in. He stood there staring into the car. I put the car in drive and backed out of the parking lot. "That was weird," I thought out loud.

I opened the back door and walked down the dark corridor. I noticed it didn't seem that dark anymore after my transition the night before. I could hear Isa playing her violin as I entered the building. I brought our food out to the table directly in front of the stage. I sat down and watched her dance. She was so graceful and delicate looking as she twirled herself around. She vigorously played the violin as she stepped to the music. Her braid whipped around her face as she moved. The song ended and she posed with her arm in the air, the last note of the violin still echoing throughout the building. She looked at me startled. "Sorry, I wasn't paying attention to you coming in. I got lost in the moment," she said, hopping off the stage. She sat down with me and began eating. "You looked beautiful up there," I said to her with a smile.

She took a fry from her container, "thank you. Was it really busy at Angelo's today? It seemed to take you a while to get back," she said. I nodded while taking a bite of my burger, "it was really packed in there today." We finished eating then cleaned up the table. She put her arms around my neck, "Do you wanna dance?" she said, pulling herself close to me. I blushed, I wasn't too fond of dancing. "I'm not a good dancer though. You go dance and I'll watch or I could play for you," I said trying to persuade her. She smirked and shook her head. "But I want to dance with you," she pleaded.

She gave me a sad, pouty look trying to convince me. She was too irresistible and I nodded, "ok." She giggled and led me up the stairs to the stage. "How are we going to dance with no music though?" I asked, hoping to deter her. She smiled walking over to the piano. She ran her fingers along the keys starting at the left side working her way all the way to the right. I could see her lips moving but I couldn't understand what she was saying. Something "Musica melodiam." Music melody? I thought, I think that's what it means in Latin. She lifted her hand off it and the piano started playing on its own. I jumped back as it began playing. "How did you do that?" I said amazed. She laughed as she wiggled her fingers at me, "magic," she said. The melody was soft and sweet as the keys played themselves.

She moved in close to me, putting my left hand on her waist. I lifted my other hand up so she could place her hand in mine. She rested her other hand on my shoulder. "I don't know what I'm doing," I whispered to her. She took a step closer to me, "don't think about it, just feel the music," she said as she slowly began to sway. I looked down at my feet, trying not to step on her toes. "Hey," she said softly, "Eyes on me." I looked up at her, looking her in the eyes. I locked my eyes on hers and kept moving back and forth. She began to smile. I was doing it, I thought. We danced together alone on the stage until I heard the doorknob turning for the back door. It was William and Xander. I tried to let go of her but she put her other arm around my neck now. "Not yet, the song's almost done," she said standing all the way up on her pointe shoes now.

She leaned away, lifting one of her legs. I held up my one hand and spun her around. She tucked her arms in as I lightly held her waist while she spun in a circle. The song ended and she stopped. She quickly grabbed my hand and placed it over her heart. I could feel it beating rapidly. I smiled and pulled her in for a kiss. She jumped so I would catch her. Once I was holding her we remained kissing as I spun her around again. I heard William and Xander enter the bar now. "Whoa sorry, didn't mean to catch you two getting busy on stage," Xander said jokingly. Isa shot him a look as I set her down again.

"Oh shut up Xander, leave them alone. Can't you see they were having a moment?" William said. Isa ran her fingers over the piano keys again stopping it from playing another song. I wonder how she was able to get it to play specific songs like that. We walked down to the bar where Will and Xander were standing waiting for us. William was practically bursting at the seams when we arrived. Not yet, I thought. Isa kept her left hand clasped in mine so Xander wouldn't see the ring, she knew I wanted to wait until Sarah got here.

We stood there talking about what had happened last night during the full moon, like Ben trying to pick a fight with me and Will coming to my rescue. There were a few things I was still curious about though. "So I can change into a wolf whenever I want to now, right? How do I do that exactly?" I asked them. "You have to focus on transforming before you do it. Now that your body has done it once it should go smoother the next time. It all depends on your emotions too. If you get too angry or frightened, or," Will paused, "excited, you could spontaneously shift over."

That didn't help me, I already knew that part. "But how am I able to transform without all the emotional stuff?" I asked. "It's just a feeling you get. Your body will let you know before you do most of the time. It's sort of an involuntary thing, like a hiccup." Xander said. A hiccup? I thought. Great, how was I supposed to function at work now if I have to worry about hiccupping the wrong way and turning into a wolf in front of everyone? Isa squeezed my hand. "I'm gonna go get changed. Everyone else should be here shortly," she told me then gave me a kiss.

After she walked away, Xander started taking down the chairs and William started jittering behind the counter. "Can we tell him yet?" he said in a hushed tone. I knew Isa could still hear him but I didn't know if Xander could. I shook my head. He whined for a second then joined Xander and I as we set up for the night. I went to my locker to grab my uniform. Should I go change in her dressing room? I thought. Not tonight, I'll just go get ready in the bathroom. I brought my clothes with me and changed quickly. I still haven't mastered tying my own bowtie yet.

"Will, can you help me with this thing?" I asked after I rejoined the guys at the bar. He laughed and came over to help me. My anxiety was raging again thinking about telling Sarah. I felt like I could use a strong drink. I looked over at the liquor bottles and chose one grabbing three shot glasses. "What are you doing? I thought you didn't drink." William said. I filled them full. "I don't usually, with the exception of special occasions." I passed them out and took my shot. The liquid burned my throat as I swallowed it. I needed another. "What's the occasion then?" Xander asked, taking his shot. I poured each of us another one and slammed mine.

246

"You'd better slow down Adam," William said with a stern look on his face. I was starting to feel pretty good after my second shot but I figured one more wouldn't hurt. I filled my glass one last time. Before tipping it back I said, "I asked Isadora to marry me," I paused, "and she said yes." Xander immediately started choking on his drink as I swallowed mine. I felt much better saying it out loud to them now. "You what?" Xander coughed, "you asked her to marry you?" I couldn't tell if he was happy or otherwise.

"Yeah, this morning after we got back from the woods," I replied. The look on his face was priceless. It was a mixture of terrified and excited both at the same time. "I am so happy for you guys!" he finally said, that's why you two came looking for Sarah this morning. Why didn't you just say that in the first place?" I shrugged my shoulders, "I don't know. I guess I was still too nervous to tell anyone yet." Xander looked over at Will who was just quietly smiling next to us. "And you knew about this?" he asked. William burst out laughing, "I only knew about it yesterday when we went for our run. I wasn't harboring the secret for long," he said.

They both pulled me in for a hug, slapping my back and congratulating me. I could feel the buzz kicking in from my shots now. I hoped it would give me enough courage to tell my sister next. Moments later Sarah, Lexa, and Ben all emerged from the curtain leading to the back hallway. "What's going on?" Sarah asked after she gave Xander a kiss. Both William and Xander looked at me with huge smiles on their faces. "Well, are you going to tell her?" Xander asked. She looked concerned seeing a bottle of alcohol sitting in front of me. "Tell me what?" she said.

I took a deep breath before I spoke, "I asked Isa to marry me, and she said yes." Sarah gasped when I finally said it, then started to cry. "Are you being serious Adam, because if you're just playing a trick on me I swear to God I will kick your ass," she said. I laughed at her, "No, it's no joke. I gave her the ring this morning." She rushed over to me and gave me a big hug. I was relieved that she wasn't upset with me, or at least that she didn't show it.

Everyone else joined in except Ben for a group hug. He stood by the stage with a sneer on his lips. Sarah looked around, "Where's Izzy? I wanna see the ring," she said. "She's getting dressed, she'll be out in a little bit. It's nothing much to look at, Sarah. It's not even a half karat, but she seems to like it," I said. She shook her head, "I'll be the judge of that. I can't believe you didn't take me with you to pick out the ring," she said disappointed. I looked at her apologetically "I'm sorry. I just thought it would be easier to keep it a secret if you didn't know." She seemed to be offended by my statement. "I'll have you know I am an excellent secret keeper," she said and I laughed at her.

Isa poked her head through the curtain, trying to get my attention. She was wearing her white button up shirt with the black pleated skirt now and her hair was down, all wavy from her braid. I walked over to her and took her hand. Everyone cheered when we did this. I passionately kissed her in front of our friends. "I love you," I said to her, holding out her hand for Sarah to see. She squealed with excitement when she looked at it. "It's so dainty and delicate. Nice choice," she said to me.

After a few more minutes of congratulating us, Isa let go of my hand and walked to the stage. "Ok everyone. I know we're all a bit excited right now," Ben scoffed and rolled his eyes, "But we've gotta open in less than fifteen minutes so we all better get ready." Sarah and Lexa quickly went to their lockers to get their uniforms to change into and Ben just stayed standing in front of the stage.

I got behind the bar and cleared away the dirty shot glasses. That was enough alcohol for me for one night, I thought. I placed the bottle back on the shelf. Everyone was ready in their positions now. Xander and Ben at the doors, Lexa and Sarah on the floor, and Will and I behind the bar. She nodded her head at Xander and he unlocked the doors. There was an abundance of people here tonight.

They all adjourned to the tables out on the floor. Isa came down from the stage and began handing out drinks. "When do you want me up there?" I said to her when she came up asking for another drink. "Wait another hour or at least until the crowd seems to slow down," she said. She touched me as she grabbed the glasses out of my hands. She winked at me and I smiled. "I love you," she mouthed before turning around again. My heart began racing, I was overjoyed. Tonight was going to be a great night, I thought.

I kept myself busy for another hour. William turned to me, "You could probably go up there now. I got this." I washed my hands and made my way toward the stage. I sat down and began playing. As my fingers hit the keys, I felt lighter than air. Isa had accepted my proposal and was proudly wearing my ring, everything was perfect. I entertained the audience for a few hours until I noticed Isa standing near the stairs. Did she want something? Was I supposed to come over to her? She waited until I was finished before making her way up the stage. "Wanna do a duet?" she asked with a twinkle in her eye. I smiled excitedly, "with you? Always," I said. She walked around the piano and picked up her violin that she had left there. "What did you have in mind?" I asked. She shyly looked at the ground, "Do you know *Iris* by *The Goo Goo Dolls*? That song reminds me of us." I smiled, wanting to go over and kiss her. "Yeah, I know it. Are you gonna sing too?" I said. "No. This'll be the last song of the night. Let's just play together," she said, placing her violin under her chin.

She counted off, "one, two, three…" and we began playing. A hush fell over the crowd as she slid the bow across the strings. I wonder if she'll get lost in the moment and start dancing? I thought. I hoped she would. The lyrics flashed through my head as we played, "and I'd give up forever to touch you, cause I know that you'd feel me somehow." She said this song reminded her of us, I thought. Would she really give up forever just to be with me? "You're the closest to heaven that I'll ever be, and I don't wanna go home right now." I thought about the lyrics more, she was letting me know how much she cared about me by playing this song. She pulled the bow across the strings with such passion. She closed her eyes and allowed herself to start dancing.

I smiled as I watched her. Everyone in the audience was watching us now too. I looked out to see a strangely familiar figure lurking in the back of the bar past the doors. Who is that? I thought. We continued to play until the song reached its finale. Isa stopped dancing as the last note slid off her strings. She opened her eyes now with a smile as the crowd enthusiastically started cheering for her. They were all mesmerized by her as well. I walked over to her and took her hand. She held on tightly as we bowed once. She froze when we stood up again, her eyes fixed at the back of the club. "What's wrong?" I whispered. She didn't say anything. I searched the crowd to see what she was looking at. I tried to pull her off the stage but she didn't move. I looked over at Will, confused. He was staring in the same direction she was. What were they looking at?

I heard Isa snap her fingers and saw a flash of light land on the back curtain. I turned to see what it was as I saw the whole thing start to engulf itself in flames. "Fire!" I shouted, releasing her hand. I quickly got off the stage and rushed over to the fire extinguisher next to the bar. "Leave it!" William growled. "What?!" I said frantically. Was he insane? "We need to get these people out of here, now!" he said. Confused, I nodded. "Everybody out!" I yelled, instructing people to head for the exit. I looked back to see Isa still standing on the stage. "What is she doing?" I muttered to myself.

Everyone started pushing and shoving trying to make it to the doors, Sarah and Lexa got lost in the crowd. Xander managed to swim his way through and found Sarah, leading her towards the bar. "What happened?" She said watching the fire grow higher on the stage. "I don't know. I think Isa may have started it," I said. Everyone managed to get out safely leaving us seven behind. I hurried up on stage trying to get Isa to move. "Isadora, we have to leave!" I shouted at her. The back of her shirt ripped as she opened up her wings. They weren't her soft gray feathers I had grown accustomed to, they were her giant scaly dragon wings. She flapped her wings twice, lifting her off the stage and extinguishing the fire. She absorbed them and continued to stare off in the distance.

The smoke created a layer of haze throughout the building and I began coughing. "What's wrong Isa? Why did you start a fire?" I said. She still didn't reply. I grabbed her shoulders and shook her violently trying to get her to snap out of it. She blinked then looked at me. "What happened?" I said again. She turned to look out towards the back of the club. I followed her eyes. That mysterious figure was still standing there. Who is that? I thought. The smoke began to clear. He stepped forward, revealing himself. He was wearing the same long black jacket and sunglasses I had seen him wearing earlier that day. This was the guy who was looking at the car when I was getting food from the cafe. "Who is he, Isa?" I asked her. She took my hands off her shoulders and held them firmly in hers. She spoke barely above a whisper, "Jake..."

My body stiffened. Jake? I thought. As in her ex Jake that left her all those years ago? I turned to face him. He took off his sunglasses to reveal a pair of piercing blue eyes. "Hello sweetheart," he said with a smile. I let out a low growl. I could feel my body wanting to transform but I stayed on the stage holding her hands. He walked forward slowly, taking off his jacket and placing it on a barstool. Xander stood in front of Sarah in a defensive manner. "Don't worry big fella, I'm not going to hurt your girl. I just want to talk with Isadora," he said, raising his hands. Isa pulled me behind her. "What do you want?" she hissed. Jake slowly made his way past Xander and Sarah towards the stage. He was standing in the middle of the club now when he stopped.

"A little birdie told me you were getting married." My heart sank, I was the one who told him that. I had no idea who he was at the time though. He looked over at Ben and Lexa now who were standing next to where the band usually played. "And another told me that he was a werewolf not fit to be a member of the pack." He continued walking again. William jumped over the bartop in his wolf form standing between Jake and the stage. He let out a deep growl. Jake smirked, "you think i'm intimidated by you? I've been alive longer than you've had a tail."

He walked closer in Ben's direction. Has Ben been in contact with him? Why else would he be walking over there? I thought. Isa turned her body, still pushing me behind her. "You're not welcome here, Jake," she said. Lexa shifted into a wolf and was standing between Jake and Ben now. Jake looked at her unamused. "This yours?" he said to Ben.

Ben backed away from her. "Yeah, but I don't know for how much longer," he said. Lexa let out a whine and backed away from Jake. The three of them stood in a triangle formation now.

"Lex, what are you doing?" Xander said worried. He tried to take a step closer. "Don't move Xander. She's made her choice," Isa said slightly crouching down. Xander stayed with Sarah. "What is it you want Jake?" she said with a ferocious look in her eyes. He smiled again, "you took something away from me long ago, now I'm going to do the same to you." He looked in my direction. I felt his icy eyes burn into my soul. I put my hand on Isa's shoulder, trying to get around her. "No, that's just what he wants. Stay with me," she pleaded. "He's rather brave, thinking he could challenge me and win. I admire that," he said sitting on one of the tables.

William snarled at him revealing his large teeth. "And this one, didn't she mangle you in the first place? Now you're protecting her and that other pup? You should join us. Start a new pack with someone who really has the group's best interest at heart," he motioned to Ben. Rage was flowing out of every pore on my body. I stepped back from her as I felt my body trying to transition. It wasn't as painful this time around but that could have maybe been due to the situation we were in. I will kill you, I thought as I took another step closer on the stage. Isa placed a hand on my back, signaling me to stop.

"It's me you want, why not leave them alone and fight me instead?" She leapt off the stage and landed in front of Will. She was standing three feet away from Jake now. I couldn't move, she must have done something with her alpha abilities so I wouldn't follow her. He smiled at her, reaching out to touch her face, "you look so beautiful Isa," he said, stroking her cheek. I tried to fight whatever was holding me back but I couldn't. He looked at me, "someone doesn't like having his toys played with."

She swatted his hand away, "forget about him. It's me you want. Let's go." she started walking towards the door. No! You can't leave with him! I thought. I began viciously snarling. I looked at William who was doing the same thing. He began to follow her. I let out a howl and she looked back at me, tears in her eyes. I had to push though, I had to fight for her. I looked over at Lexa who was slowly beginning to creep

252

forward. She lunged at his back, biting his shoulder. He pulled her off, wrapping his arms around her neck. There was a loud crunching sound and he released her. She slumped over a table and fell to the floor. "No!" Xander wailed, hurling himself at her lifeless body.

It was too late, she was already dead. Ben rushed forward and got in Jakes' face, "that wasn't part of the plan!" he shouted. Jake pushed him away, "plans change. Maybe she was more loyal to the pack than you thought." Xander held onto Lexas' body as she turned back into her human form. He sobbed while he did it. Jake turned to Isa again and grabbed her elbow, "come on," and began pulling her toward the door. She ripped her arm out of his grasp and flung him to the ground. "I'm not going anywhere with you!" She snapped her fingers rapidly, flinging balls of fire all over the club.

The whole place quickly caught on fire. Her concentration was broken now and I could join her on the floor. I jumped forward, landing next to William. Xander still hunched over on Lexa, let out a growl and transformed, getting in line with us. Jake stood up and turned to look at us. He started backing away. Ben placed himself between Jake and the rest of us baring his teeth. I couldn't believe it, his girlfriend was just murdered and he was still defending this guy.

I paced forward, taking the lead position. Ben crouched down then attacked me. The whole place was burning as we fought, causing chairs and tables to flip over. I saw Isa dart over to Sarah who was cowering next to the bar. She picked her up and carried her out the back door. I could hear sirens in the distance now. It wouldn't be long before the fire department got there. I bit down on Ben's neck hard causing him to whine in pain. I could taste the blood as I ripped him over a table.

I felt a hand grab the scruff of my neck. "Adam we have to go!" William shouted at me. I turned to look back at Ben but he was gone. Pieces of the rafters were starting to fall all around us. I tried to transition back but couldn't. Xander picked up Lexa and carried her body out with William following behind. I looked around for Isa but didn't see her. Suddenly something hit me in the face. Jake had picked up a chair and threw it at me. I sat up, now in my normal body. I must have blacked out for a second. There was blood dripping down my forehead.

Jake walked through the fire stepping closer to me. I started pulling myself up when he shoved me hard to the ground again. "You think you deserve her? You'll never be good enough for her!" he yelled, pulling me up by my shirt. He hoisted me into the air so my feet were dangling off the ground. I struggled to get free. He placed his hand around my throat and began squeezing. I could feel him begin to crush my windpipe, making it difficult to breathe. Isa struck him from behind causing him to release me. I lay crumpled up on the floor gasping for air. He turned around to face her.

"You think this mutt could ever replace me?" he said angrily. She pushed past him to get to me. "Come on, Adam," she whispered to me, helping me to my feet. She stood with my arm around her shoulder as she held onto my chest. "Why now, Jake, after all this time?" she said. He stepped closer, "because, I want you to be alone forever just like you cursed me to be." He had a wild look in his eyes as a wooden beam fell behind him. My lungs were burning from breathing in all the smoke. "Just leave her alone," I said. He looked at me now.

"Never, I will never stop searching now that I've found her. I've been killing people for years trying to get your attention, Isa." She tensed up. "It was you. You were the rogue vampire that was leaving marks on bodies to make it seem more noticeable," she said. "Ding, ding, ding. We have a winner," he laughed. "But why?" I said confused. Why would he want to kill people and make it look like a vampire killed them on purpose? "Why? Because I knew she would be watching for vamps like that, not wanting to have an overpopulation of vampires just killing for sport."

She pulled me close to her, not letting me get away. He inched closer to us. Our backs were against the stage now. "I still want to be with you Isa, if you'll have me. We can forget about this whole thing if you just let me kill him and come with me now. I'll even let the rest of them live if you come quietly." he held out his hand for her. I gripped her arm, letting her know I wasn't going to let her go. "Never!" she screamed, opening her wings again. She held onto me as we flew up towards the ceiling. I braced for impact as we crashed through it.

Pieces of debris landed all around him as we soared through the air. I held onto her with all my might. She slid down the side of the building near the cars. Xander and Sarah had already left, leaving William standing next to the Camaro. "Izzy!" he exclaimed. She set me down and fell to her knees. She had a large piece of metal sticking out of her abdomen. "Just leave it for now," she said, standing up again. The fire trucks were here now trying to put out the blazing inferno.

"Let's go," she said walking to the car. "What about that?" I said, referring to the club. She looked back at it. "There's nothing we can do. We need to get home. Now, before he gets a chance to follow us. I can put up the barrier once we're through the gates." She winced at the pain she was feeling. Barrier? I thought. Will got in his car and sped away. "I'll drive," I said before Isa could get in the driver's side. She nodded. I hit the gas and tore off after William. With every bump in the road, I could tell she groaned softly.

She tugged on the metal, trying to pull it out. "Don't do that, you'll bleed out!" I said. She chuckled as she pulled it out and tossed it in the back. "Trust me, that's the last thing that'll happen." She leaned back her seat and began putting pressure on the wound. I drove as fast as I could, blowing through stop lights and everything. "Slow down a little bit, you don't want to get in an accident." Was she serious? The whole club was burning to the ground and Lexa was dead, getting in a little fender bender was the least of my concern.

"What were you saying about a barrier?" I asked, trying to distract myself. She groaned as we hit another bump, "it's the fence around the whole property. It can keep out unwanted creatures and hunters. I need to get home to activate it before Jake gets there." Her eyes were getting heavier now. "Hey, stay with me! We're almost there," I said. Her eyes fluttered open and she sat her seat upright again. We reached the dirt road and I stepped on the gas.

"I'm going to need blood," she said weakly. I held out my arm for her. "Here, take it," I said. She shook her head. "Can't. I did the spell on your blood remember. I'll just make things worse." Her head rolled to the side. Shit, I forgot about that. "Do you have any at the house?" I asked. She shook her head again, "no, it hasn't been long enough since the last time I fed so I haven't stock piled anymore yet." I was losing her. I grabbed her hand. "Please, don't die," I whispered. We got to the gate where William was waiting for us.

He had pulled his car to the side and was standing waiting for us to pull up. I rolled down the window, "She's not doing good. She said she needs blood but there isn't any at the house!" I yelled at him. His eyes grew wide with panic. "Get up to the house and see if Sarah is willing to give her some," he said. She groaned, "No, I promised her I wouldn't do that," she sank in the seat, going unconscious. I needed to get her to Sarah, fast. "I'll make sure the gate is closed then I'll do a once over of the perimeter. You get her home!" He ordered me. I nodded and hit the gas again.

The car screeched to a halt when I pulled up to the house. Sarah came running out to meet us by the car. I got out and opened Isa's door, lifting her out of the car. I set her on the ground next to the tires. "What happened? Is she going to be alright?" she asked. I looked at Sarah, "she needs blood. Can you give her some of yours, please?" I begged. She held her hand to her throat, shocked at my request. "But, doesn't she have any in the house? I'll go look," she turned to run back towards the door. "No!" I shouted, "There isn't time. She needs it now!"

She was scared now looking at us. "I won't let her take too much, I promise Sarah. I need you to do this for me." I looked deep in her eyes so she knew how much I needed her. She nodded her head then got down on her knees. "How do we do this?" she said, rolling up her sleeves. I took her hand and placed it in front of Isadora's mouth. She didn't move. "Come on," I said. I looked around for something sharp. I reached in the back seat and held out the bloodied sharp hunk of metal. Sarah flinched, pulling her arm away.

I hesitated for a moment, "If I cut you with this, that means you'll turn into a werewolf too next full moon. There's too much of her blood on here for you not to." She looked at Isa laying on the ground. Would she really take the risk just to save her? She sighed, "Go ahead. I was planning on talking to her about becoming one anyway after today." She held out her arm again. I carefully made a small cut on her wrist, allowing the blood to flow down her arm. She held her hand over Isa's mouth again, dripping drops of blood on her lips.

Isa's eyes slightly opened and she reached out for Sarah's arm. She stifled a scream when Isa bit her. I sat there watching carefully to make sure Sarah was doing alright. "Adam, I'm starting to feel lightheaded," she said. I brushed the hair away from Isa's face and knelt down to whisper in her ear, "that's enough. You can let go now." Another minute passed before she let go. Sarah held her wrist trying to stop the bleeding. Xander came out of the house and saw us sitting in front of the car. "What have you done?" he said to us. Sarah stood up and ran to him.

"She needed my blood. I didn't give her a lot, just enough to wake her up again." she said. Xander stood there furious. "Lexa's dead because of her, you should have just let her die too." he said. He couldn't have meant that. He was just grieving the loss of his sister. "Xander, we need her. She didn't mean for any of this to happen." Sarah placed her hands on his face trying to calm him down. He stared at her and began breathing normally again. "Did she bite you or did you have to cut yourself?" he asked, looking at the bloody piece of metal.

"I had to cut her. It's the metal that caused her to bleed out," I said, worried what he might do next. He looked at Sarah again, "so now you've been inoculated too?" she nodded her head. He reached down and buried his face in her neck, picking her up by her waist. At least he wasn't mad about that, I thought. I looked at Isa still laying on the ground. Her eyes were fully opened now. "Do you need help sitting up?" I asked. She slowly pulled herself up, holding her abdomen. "No. I need to close the barrier."

She stood up using the car to steady herself. I held out my hands for her. "Where do you need to do it?" I asked. She pointed towards the willow tree. I picked her up and began jogging over to the tree. I set her down slowly once we got there. She pushed on the tree, drawing symbols in the bark. The ground began to rumble underneath my feet. What was happening? I thought. She turned to face the driveway watching for something.

I could see a thin layer of sky flowing out above the trees. Was this supposed to be some sort of force field? It grew larger in the sky until it was covering the whole valley. It left a purplish haze over everything. "There," she said, sitting on the ground, catching her breath. I knelt down next to her, "are you alright? Do you need me to carry you to the house again?" I asked, trying to help her. She nodded her head, "that would be nice." She wrapped her arms around my neck as I picked her up again.

I walked slowly so that I didn't jostle her around. "What's gonna happen now?" I asked her. She rested her head on my shoulder. "I'm not sure," she said quietly. We arrived at the house and I set her on her feet. I walked in first to make sure she was alright. Xander and Sarah were in the living room looking at Lexa's body. Xander was in front of the couch where she lay crying. "Why would he do this?" he asked, looking up at Isa. "Why would Ben align himself with someone like that?" She shook her head, "he was obviously desperate to get rid of me. I am so sorry for your loss Xander, both of them." He looked at her funny. "Both?" he said, "what do you mean?"

She walked over and placed her hand on his shoulder. "Xander, Lexa was pregnant." His jaw dropped when she told him the news. He was inconsolable now. Sarah was crying harder now too. "How could she keep this from us?" she said. "Ben knew that if I fought against him that she would defend him and if something were to happen to her and the baby that it would cause chaos within the pack. That was his plan from the very beginning," I said.

Xander grit his teeth now, "If I ever see Ben again, I'm going to kill him for what he's done." Isa reached over and smoothed Lexa's hair. "We need to cremate her Xander, before that can happen." Nodded, "I'll go get wood for the pyre," he said. "I'll help you," Sarah said, reaching for her jacket. They left us standing in the living room alone with her. She looked like she was peacefully sleeping on the couch.

Isa started making her easy toward the stairs. "Where are you going?" I asked. "I need a shower and to change out of these wrecked clothes. Come help me?" she said, giving me a little smile. We made our way up the steps, each one slower than the last. She must really be in pain, I thought. I lifted her up and finished carrying her the rest of the way. "Thanks," she said when we made it to the top.

I undid the buttons on her shirt helping to pull it away from her wound. She winced when it got caught on her skin. "Did I hurt you?" I asked frantically. "No, the blood is dried and you just tugged on it, that's all." she took her shirt off the rest of the way. She had a large gash on the left side of her body. It hurt me to see her like that. "You can wait out here if you'd like, I don't want to put you out." How could she even think that? I stood closer to her.

We went to the bathroom and I turned the water on. She stepped inside letting the water wash over her. The water in the bottom of the shower was a murky reddish brown color from all the blood. She carefully washed the area with her hands. I watched her whimper when she touched it. I needed to look away but I wanted to be there for her. I got her a towel for when she was finished. She took it, patting herself dry.

She wrapped the towel around her body now as she stepped out of the shower. She didn't seem to be bleeding anymore which was good. I helped her put a bra on then her pants. "Can you go into my office and grab me the little black case sitting on one of the shelves?" she asked. I quickly bounded across the hall to retrieve it. I returned victorious, "Here you go," I said. She opened it up, it was a sewing kit with needles and thread. My stomach dropped, "What are you gonna do with that?" I asked her, worried what she was going to say.

"I'm going to close it up so I can heal myself," she said, threading a needle. I couldn't watch. I turned my back to her and waited for her to finish. I could hear her making noises as she sewed her skin together. I hope she's not going to pass out from the pain, I thought. I slowly turned my head to look at her. She had just stuck the needle in again and was pulling the thread tight. I looked away again, closing my eyes. "I'm done now," she said. I could breathe easier again. There was a jagged line of black thread along her stomach now.

I handed her the shirt she had gotten out before her shower. She put it on then laid back on the bed. I sat on the bed next to her. What a night? I thought. "We need to go down stairs. There's no telling where Ben might be. I need to make sure he didn't slip in the barrier before it closed. I need to find William." She sat upright. "You need to take it easy," I said, trying to make her lay back down. "No! He's already killed Lexa, I'm not going to lose anyone else tonight." I couldn't hold her down, she was too upset.

"Please, just for a little while," I begged her. She looked at me with sympathetic eyes. "Fifteen minutes," she sighed. I scooted closer, wrapping my arms around her. I kissed her forehead as she lay her head on my chest. "Why do you think Jake came back after all this time?" I asked her. "I don't really know. It seems to me he was in cahoots with

Ben about getting rid of you and then taking over as leader of the pack. But why would Jake care about that? Something seemed odd about him, like he wasn't himself," she said.

What did she mean? "He seemed like an asshole to me," I said. She chuckled, "yes, but besides that. He seemed rather desperate for me to come with him. I wonder why," she pondered out loud. I didn't have an answer, all I know is that he wanted her and I wasn't going to go down without a fight. I held her tighter and she drifted off to sleep while I was holding her. She needed a little rest so I didn't wake her up right away. I thought about what she said, if it had been so long, why now was he desperately trying to be with her?

A few moments later she awoke with a gasp. She looked towards the french doors and ran to the balcony. "Shit!" she yelled jumping over the railing. I rushed over to see what she was looking at. The willow tree was on fire now. Ben had taken one of the logs from Lexa's funeral pyre and torched the tree, breaking the barrier protecting the valley. I ran down the stairs to be with her. She was already standing in front of the tree now as I came running across the field.

Xander and Ben were fighting next to the pyre in their wolf forms. "Adam!" Sarah screamed. A gust of wind came up from behind me knocking me to the ground. It was Jake. Can he fly too? I thought. I stood up to face him. William came limping out of the treeline towards Isa. Ben must have attacked him so he couldn't warn us. I looked around for Jake. He was walking closer to the burning willow tree now. William snarled and lunged at him. Jake easily hit him away, knocking him out.

I began running towards Isa in hopes to reach her before Jake did. I pushed past him and stood in front of Isadora in my wolf form, protecting her. I showed my teeth trying to make myself more intimidating. He laughed, "Seriously, Isa, this guy? Come on, let's go," he said, taking another step closer. I leapt for him, he hit me hard between the shoulder blades. I felt one of them break as he did. I tried to stand up normally, but the pain was too much. He took another step for her.

I gathered my strength and tried to get him again, this time biting the back of his calf. His leg buckled and he was on one knee now. He tried to grab my head but I was too quick. I bit his arm and began shaking him. I could feel his arm crunch in my teeth. He managed to get up and kick me in the ribs, sending me flying back towards Isa. I lay there on the ground gasping for air, he must have broken something, I thought. I struggled to stand now. Xander ran from the pyre and landed on Jake's back, flipping him over. William got up and charged at him as well. I looked over to see Ben laying motionless in the snow, as a human. Xander must have killed him, I thought.

I stood my ground in front of Isadora. Will and Xander joined me now. We had him beat, he wasn't getting any closer. I growled and we all attacked him. He was punching and kicking as we piled on top of him. He threw Xander towards Ben's body and kicked William towards the trees. Only I remained now. He grabbed my throat and began crushing it again. I could feel the life draining from my body and I transformed back into a human. He slammed me into the ground.

I lay there gasping for air as he took another step towards Isa. "You can't have her!" I managed to say, "She doesn't love you!" I was kneeling on all fours coughing up blood now. He turned to look at me, "she doesn't have to love me. She just needs to leave here with me," he said, winding up to kick me again. I braced for impact, closing my eyes. The blow never came. I opened my eyes to see Isadora crouching down in front of me, her arms draped around my neck. She was protecting me.

"If you ever loved me, you'll go and never come back. Otherwise I will spend the rest of my eternity making sure your life is the most miserable existence!" she screamed. He put his foot down. "You already made sure my life was miserable," he said quietly. She turned to look at him. "What?" Her face showed confusion. "Haven't I been punished enough, to live forever as you do?" He paused for a moment. "But to take away my choice to fall in love with someone, you're the cruel one. Not me."

She slowly stood up, keeping one hand on my shoulder. "Do you love someone Jake? I ended that curse on you years ago. You should be able to fall in love now," she said calmly. He seemed to look angrier now, "I know you did. That's why I'm here." I used her arm to pull myself up and stand beside her now. "You're not making any sense. If you found someone to love, why are you trying to take Isa away?" I asked. He looked at me now, "Because, Isadora is the only one who can help me get her back," he said. I looked at her, "From who?" I asked. He furrowed his brow at me, "From Sarrora," he said.

"Sarrora? But I thought she died when her mirror was shattered?" I asked. Jake looked at me surprised, "you told him about her?" he asked Isa. She turned around to face him, still positioning her body in front of mine. "I told him everything, Jake. He deserved to know what he was getting himself into." She held her hand out for me, I took it. He rolled his eyes, "So are you going to help me or not?" he demanded. Isa shook her head, "I'm not sure what you're even asking me to do. I killed Sarrora, remember?" He put his hands in his pants pockets, "yeah you did, I was there. But over the years I have slowly been putting the pieces back together." She gasped, "But I burned the pieces?" He shook his head, "but did you though? Or did you just burn the pieces of a mirror I brought you?" Isa was livid now, I could feel her start shaking through her hand.

"When?" she said, "when did you finish putting it back together?" She was starting to hurt my hand so I loosened her grip. "About a hundred years ago. She didn't start manifesting herself until recently though. That's when she came through the mirror in Hope's room." She put her hands up, "hold up, who's Hope?" she said. He smiled smugly, "My girlfriend." Isa looked concerned. "Is she still human?" she asked him. He laughed, "of course she still is, you know I can't turn anyone into a vampire. You made sure of that." She shook her head, "does she know you can't die?" He looked down, "no. She's the first person I had feelings for after I left you. I didn't want to scare her off." She sighed, "You're playing a very dangerous game, Jake. How long have you known her?" she asked.

Xander and William had changed back now and began getting closer to us. Jake's eyes darted towards them. "We're just having a conversation, aren't you going to call off your dogs?" he joked. She wasn't impressed, "those dogs just lost two members of their family because of you. I think they're allowed to get closer to make sure you won't try anything again." He took a step farther away from us, ready to flee. "Xander, William, take Sarah and Adam back to the house. I need to talk with Jake alone," she said, releasing my hand. "No," I protested, "I'm not leaving your side."

She turned to me, "Adam, your shoulder is dislocated and may have punctured a lung from your cracked ribs. I need you to go in the house with them." She was stern when she was talking to me. I looked at Jake, I didn't like the smile he was giving me but I had no choice. She was right about my injuries and I needed Sarah to take a look at me. "Fine, but you only get one hour," I said. I turned to face Jake, "don't try anything." He made a face, mocking me. William limped over to me and put my arm around his shoulder. "Wait," Isa said, coming over and kissing me passionately, "now you can go." She smiled when my heart began racing.

They led me to the house after Xander threw Bens' body on the pyre with Lexas'. I set a timer on my phone so I knew when I could go back out to her. Sarah pulled off my shirt to survey the damages. "Yep, definitely broken," she said as she delicately ran her fingers across my ribs. Xander stood looking out the living room window watching Jake and Isa's interaction. They just seemed to be talking out there by the fire. I cried out when Sarah touched my back, "ouch! Be careful Sarah," I said to her. "Sorry, I think the only way to fix you is to pull it back into place then tape it up so you can't use it."

William came back from the other room carrying a large medical duffle bag. "Don't bother taping him up. We heal fast and if he shifts forms again it won't matter anyway, anatomically speaking," Will said, "you can tape his ribs though, that shouldn't matter too much." She nodded then began working. "So that's Jake, huh?" I said to Will. "Yep, that's him. Do you believe what he's saying about Sarrora?" he asked. I tried to shrug, "I don't know. Isa said he seemed a bit off earlier when we got back from the club so, maybe?" Will shook his head, "I'm not buying it, there's gotta be some sort of ulterior motive."

He pulled on my arm until we heard it pop back into place. I let out a yowl as he did it. Sarah then began wrapping my ribs in tape. "They're headed toward the house," Xander said. "Hurry up," I said to Sarah in a rush, "I need to be ready when they get here." Sarah stopped what she was doing, "if I go any faster, it's going to hurt you more," she said. I leaned closer to her, "then just do it!" I demanded. She frowned and began taping me quicker. She was right, this did hurt more. She finished and handed me my shirt, "here. That's all I can do for you right now." I put it on and walked to the front door.

When they arrived, Jake stopped by the cars while Isa kept walking. "How do I know you'll keep your word?" he called after her. She stopped to face him, "because unlike you, I keep my word. Have I ever lied to you before?" What were they talking about? She continued walking towards me. I looked back behind her to see Jake but he was already gone. "Where did he go?" I said I panicked. "Wallachia, where Sarrora's mirror is located," she said. "Where?" I asked. "I mean Romania, we'll meet him there in a couple of days," she said, walking in the house and shutting the door.

"I'm confused, we're going to meet him in Europe in a couple of days. Why?" She put her hands on my waist and rested her head on my chest. "Adam, I will tell you everything, I promise, but right now I just need to rest for a few minutes. OK?" She was shaking. I put my arms around her, "ok, I'm sorry," I said softly, holding onto her. We stood there in the doorway for a few minutes until she stopped shaking. "Better?" I asked. She looked up at me, "better."

We walked hand in hand to the living room where William, Xander and Sarah were. "Listen up everyone. I know it's been a rough night but we're not done yet," she sighed. "In the next few days I will be heading to Europe to help Jake get his girlfriend back from my sister, Sarrora." We all protested at the idea of her helping him out. She held her hand up to stop us. "Please, let me finish." We all quieted down. "I have to go help him because she is my responsibility. I'm the one who brought her through the mirror in the first place now I need to be the one to make sure she stays there. Are there any questions?" My hand shot up.

"How do you know this isn't a trap?" William and Xander agreed with me. "I don't know if it's a trap or not. Either way I still need to see this through," she said.

William spoke now, "who's coming with you then to make sure you're safe?" That was going to be my next question. She shook her head, "no one. I'm going alone." I was enraged. I got up off the couch and stormed up the stairs. I could hear everyone squabbling as I walked away. I couldn't just sit there and listen to her say she didn't want anyone to come with her. How did she expect me to react? I slammed the door when I got to our room. I was pissed. I kicked off my shoes and lay down on my stomach on the bed. I wanted to break things, I was so mad. I thrashed on the bed like a toddler having a tantrum. My ribs and my back hurt but I didn't care. I transformed into a wolf, still laying on the bed. My ears twitched as I heard the sound of the doorknob turning. I sat upright, it was Isadora.

I laid back down after I saw her. She came into the room, shutting the door behind her. "Adam," she said to me. I softly growled at her. "Adam, we decided that you should come with me when I go." My head whipped around. Was she serious? I tried to change back but couldn't. I walked around on the bed and laid my head on her lap. I'm sorry, I thought, I hope she could understand what I was doing. She pet my head. "Adam, I'm not abandoning you, that wasn't my intention for leaving you behind. I just wanted to keep you safe. I don't trust Jake not to try something with you there." She kissed my muzzle. "Please change back if you can so I can kiss you properly," she said with a smile. My heart began racing. I sat up to lick her face. I leaned into her, my snout shifted away and I was human again.

I kissed her lips. She held onto my face as I kissed her. She pushed me onto my back and sat on me. "Ow!" I shouted. She got off quickly. "I'm sorry, are you ok?" she said, worried. "It's fine, it's just my ribs," I said, trying to pull her back on me. She wouldn't budge though. "Come here, please?" I begged her. "I don't want to hurt you though," she said, touching my ribs. Her cold hand felt good against my skin. I whimpered as she walked around the bed to get changed. She glanced back at me with a smile. She took her shirt off then came back to me. I gently traced the new scar she was going to have on her abdomen. I kissed the skin where she had sewn herself back together, it made her giggle. "I'm sorry you got hurt tonight," I said to her.

She ruffled my hair, "it wasn't your fault. I didn't tuck myself in enough when I broke through the ceiling of the club. I'm just glad you didn't get hurt when I did too." Her eyes looked sad now. "Why did he have to come back though?" She whispered looking down. I put my finger on her chin, lifting it up. "What happened tonight is not your fault. It was all Ben's doing and he's gone now and what happened to Lexa was an accident. Everyone else is safe. We may have a few cuts and bruises but we're all still alive and that's what matters."

I pulled her on top of me again. This time she was more observant of where she placed herself. "Is this alright?" she said putting her knees on either side of my hips. I nodded at her. She didn't lay completely on me, she just sort of hovered. I pulled her the rest of the way down so she could be close to me. I didn't care about the pain, all I cared about was being with her. Just her laying with me made everything that happened tonight worth it. I kissed her vigorously until she rolled me on top of her. She pulled on my jeans signaling that she was ready for me. I obliged her and began.

She lay there after we finished with her head on my chest, my heart was racing. "Promise me something," she said without lifting her head. "Anything," I replied. "Promise me that if something happens to me in the next few days you won't wait for me." She sat up, looking at me. Her face was somber but serious. I looked at her confused. "What do you mean?" I asked. She wrapped her fingers in mine. "If I were to die in the next few days, I don't want you to spend your whole life waiting for me to return. I might not come back." Was she serious? How could she even ask me that?

I sat up, "no! No, I will not agree to that!" I said, raising my voice. "Why would you even say that? Of course you're going to come back if something were to happen to you, not that anything will." I was completely floored by her request. If she died there's a good possibility that I would die too trying to protect her. I stood up and began pacing the room. "Because it could happen. If something were to go wrong with Sarrora who's to say I'd survive. Obviously I didn't kill her the first time so now she'll be out for blood." she said. I couldn't believe we were discussing this. "What if I die, Adam, because it's the only way to kill her too?" I didn't understand.

"What are you saying?" I asked, trying to calm down. She stood up next to me. "What I'm saying is, what if I have to die too in order to finish her off? She was born from a mirror. Mirrors have two sides, hers, and mine. What if that's the only way to stop her?" She placed her hands on my hips holding me still. "Maybe you would come back. You've done it before, why would this time be any different?" I said putting my hands on her arms. She shook her head, "I don't know. That's why I want you to promise me that you won't wait for me." I held her tightly against my body. "I'll think about it, but I'm not promising anything right now."

We sat back down on the bed. "Why do you have to help Jake anyway?" I asked. She sighed, "Because he has to live forever because of me, the least I can do is make sure he's not alone like me too," she said. Boy, was she being the bigger person. "Why not just kill him too along with Sarrora?" She looked at me with sad eyes. "If I have to, I will, but it'll be hard. Apparently he's been trying to kill himself for years now but my curse has prevented him from ending his own life." I thought about it for a minute. "Is that why he saved all the pieces of her mirror, in hopes that she would be able to kill him?" I asked curiously.

She smirked at my observation, "yeah, I'm pretty sure that's why he did it. He's spent the last couple hundred years being a playboy traveling the world surrounded by beautiful people, but just because you have people around you doesn't make you any less lonely. It wasn't until this last year when he met this girl named Hope, that he realized the curse about not loving anyone wore off." I felt sorry for him, I mean I hated the guy but I felt sorry for his situation.

"Does she love you back?" I asked. She shrugged her shoulders, "it's hard to say. She's only nineteen and knows nothing about this stuff. I'm sure she's scared out of her mind right now though. Jake said Sarrora came to her at night and stole her through her mirror." I was intrigued, "How does he know she took her through the mirror?" I said. "He keeps a shard of glass from the mirror with him at all times so he can keep an eye on her. When he woke up the next morning to find Hope gone, her mirror was smashed in."

I looked over at her vanity mirror, "so, could she potentially climb though that mirror then?" I said pointing at it. She laughed, "No. This house wards off anything like that. She wants me to come to her, then she'll try and pull me inside so she can replace me," she said. "Why does she want to do that? Wouldn't she rather just be her own person?" I asked. She bit her bottom lip thinking about her answer. "I think it's because she isn't the original. If you get rid of the original you're free to take their place. We both can't exist I suppose, everything needs to be balanced."

She played with my fingers as we sat on the bed. "Why do you think she chose to come back to life again?" I needed to know what her thoughts were. She laid down on the bed, "because she could sense a change in me, I suppose. Either that or she's been listening though the shard of glass Jake carries around and saw an opportunity. That's the more likely scenario". I thought about everything she'd just said. "How would you kill Jake if he can't die either?" I finally asked. "Well, he's basically an immortal human. He doesn't crave blood like I do so the only way to kill him would be to turn him human again," she paused waiting to hear my response. "Can you really do that?" I asked. She stretched her back and sat up again. "I think so. I've never tried before so I'm not sure. Otherwise, I'll put that bracelet on him so he can't be at his full strength and so he'll be as close to human as I can get him." She played with the leather bracelet wrapped around my wrist.

A thought occluded to me, "so, if I wasn't wearing this tonight, could I have potentially been strong enough to beat him?" I said holding up my wrist. She took my hand and began unwrapping the leather. "Probably. Since you just had your first full moon, you're stronger than the rest of the pack. I'm not sure if you could have prevented everything that happened but it would have been a fairer fight." She finished unraveling the bracelet and placed it on the bed beside her. I twisted my wrist to stretch it out. "I still don't think it's a good idea to go there and trust that everything he's saying is true," I said. She nodded, "I know. I don't trust him either but if what he said is true, I need to stop Sarrora before she hurts anyone else." I took her hands in mine, "can you promise me something, now?" I asked, "Can you promise me that you'll do everything you can before you try to kill the two of you? I don't want to lose you, Isadora." She gave me a slight smile. "I promise. I will do everything in my power to make sure it doesn't come to that," she whispered.

I leaned forward to kiss her and she wrapped her arms around my neck, up the back of my head. "I love you," I said, "and I will never stop loving you till the day I die." Her eyes seemed to light up. "Do you wanna go get married tomorrow?" She asked with a smile. I was shocked, I hadn't expected her to say that. "Um…where?" I said. "Right here. William can perform the ceremony and Sarah and Xander could be our witnesses." She was serious. She actually wanted us to get married tomorrow. "But don't you like, wanna get a dress or something?" I asked. My heart rate was elevated. She shook her head, "I could get married naked in the snow if it meant I got to marry you. I could run into town and get one though if you'd like?" I smiled, "no. I'm sure you have something you could wear." She kissed me again and got off the bed. "Where are you going?" I said as she headed for the door. "To tell the others so they're not overwhelmed tomorrow," she said leaving the room. I laid down on the bed. "I'm getting married tomorrow," I said to myself.

She returned shortly with a huge smile on her face. "What?" I asked, starting to smile too. "They're all for it. We can do it tomorrow afternoon," she jumped on the bed to lay next to me. I rolled over on my side so I could touch her. "We're getting married tomorrow," I repeated. She curled up next to me so she could lay her head on my chest. "Yes we are," she replied. I pet her head as we lie there. She was going to be my wife, I thought. "Will you take my last name or keep your own?" I asked. She chuckled, "which would you prefer? Keep in mind a vampire with the last name Christenson is rather ironic." Why was it ironic? I thought. "Can you not go to a church or be around crosses?" I asked. She chuckled again, "no, nothing like that. It's just that clearly God must have a sick sense of humor by giving me the life I've lived. It's like he knew I needed you so he sent you to me. After all, Adam was the first man." I'd never thought about it that way. "How about you hyphenate your last name? Christenson-Dragoss?" I asked. She thought about it for a second, "Yeah I suppose I could do that," she said. "Isadora Christenson, I love you," I said to her. "Adam, my wonderfully warm sweet Adam, I love you too." She was dozing off as she said it. I pulled on the blanket and covered us up. She let out a soft cooing sound letting me know she was asleep. I kissed her head and closed my eyes.

It was late morning when I awoke the next day. Isa was still softly snoring in my arms. She'd had a long day yesterday so I just lay there awake letting her sleep more. I heard my phone buzz on the nightstand. I carefully reached out to grab it. Sarah had messaged me. 'Good morning! Send Izzy my way when she's awake. Xander and Will want to talk to you too.' What's that about? I thought. I typed back, 'ok. Why?' and waited for her reply. My phone buzzed again, 'I want to help her pick out an outfit then do her hair and makeup.' That seemed innocent enough. 'What about Xander and Will?' I said. 'I don't know. They just told me to text you to meet them by the tree.' This worried me a bit. I slid Isa off my chest and onto the bed. I kneeled next to her face from the floor. "Good morning," I whispered to her. She smiled then opened her eyes. "Good morning," she said back, kissing my nose. She rolled over and stretched. Her shirt pulled up and I could see her makeshift sutures. She caught me staring at them. "Don't worry. I plan on taking it out after I shower. I should be healed enough now." She pulled down her shirt and sat up.

"Where are you going?" she asked. I gave her my phone to read the messages. She smiled, "that's sweet of her. Tell her I'll be right down." She got up and walked towards the bathroom. "What about Xander and Will?" I quickly said before she could make it all the way there. She turned back, "I don't know. Guess you'll have to go see what they want." She shut the door behind her and left me alone in our room. I went to the closet and put some clean clothes on. My ribs and back didn't hurt as much today. Man, we must really heal fast, I thought. I made my way downstairs after I was finished. Sarah met me on the second story landing. "Is she up?" she asked excitedly. I smiled at her, "she's just showering now. Give her a few minutes before you head up there." I continued walking down the stairs. What could they want? I kept thinking. I left the house and headed for what used to be the willow tree. Xander and William were standing on either side of the pile of ashes talking.

"I think it should go here," one said. "No, it should be closer to the tree line," said the other. "What should go there?" I asked once I was closer to them. They turned around. "Hey, we were just trying to figure out where to put the archway for the ceremony," William said. I looked behind them. There was a crudely constructed arch built out of birch and willow branches. "When did you make that?" I said. "This morning. There were a few remaining branches from the tree that didn't burn last night, so we decided to use them," Xander said. It looked sort of pretty the way they had wrapped the vines along the birch wood. "I think it should be closer to the water, don't you think?" I said. They looked at the lake then back at their arch. "Works for me," Xander said, standing it up and walking it over to the water's edge.

"Is that all you needed?" I asked Will. "No. We wanted to talk to you about Jake too," he said. My eyes narrowed thinking about him. "We know you want to go with her but we don't think it's a good idea. You haven't lived as long as we have so we know more about fighting vampires," Will said, as I folded my arms. He continued, "what if you get there and Jake has a whole fleet of vampires waiting for you? You can't possibly fight them all off yourself. It would be better if Izzy went alone or if I went with her." I let out a low growl, "are you serious? There's no way I'd let her go by herself, I don't care how much knowledge you have on the subject. She already said I could go and I intend to!" I was severely frustrated and could feel myself about to change. "Calm down Adam, it was just a suggestion. No need to bite our heads off," Xander said, rejoining us. "You guys are acting like it's a suicide mission, going with her!" I shouted. Neither of them said anything. I stopped, "you guys think it's a suicide mission, don't you?" I waited impatiently for their response. "We just don't wanna see you end up hurt. She told us her plans about ending her life if she has to and we don't want you to follow her lead." What was he saying? William spoke now, "we're worried that if she dies, you'll try and kill yourself too." I was shocked at his accusation. I hadn't thought about that option. What if she did die? Would I really want to live in a world without her?

"Your silence is very reassuring," he said sarcastically. I shook my head, "I'm not going to do that because she's going to be fine. We're gonna go there, take out her sister and then we're coming home again. That's it!" I yelled at them. Xander put his hand on my shoulder, "I know you believe that, but there's no telling how things will go. You need to

271

be prepared for the worst. I don't want her to die either, Adam." His words were kind as he tried to make me understand the gravity of the situation. I relaxed my shoulders and remained in my human form. "Do you really think she would do that?" I said to myself, walking over to the arch, "would she break her promise? Will walked over to me, "let's just get through the day and worry about it tomorrow." I nodded my head.

"Do you own a suit?" Xander asked. "No, I was just planning on wearing my jeans and a nice shirt. Why?" He smiled now looking at William. "Then you'll have to borrow one of mine," William said, slapping my back. They led me back toward the house. I was feeling a little melancholy about our conversation but I wanted to push through. We went to Will's room and he began sifting through his closet. "Any idea what color she'll be wearing? White? Red perhaps?" he asked. I had no clue what she was planning on wearing, let alone what I should be wearing too.

He pulled out some options for me to try on. I didn't like the way the dark blue one fit me and the brown one just didn't look right. "You sure have a lot of these," I said. He smiled putting a shirt back on the hanger, "I do have a life outside of this house and the club you know." I laughed at him. Xander pulled out a dark gray jacket, "How bout this one?" he said. I tried it on. I looked at myself in the mirror, something was missing. "Red or black?" William said, holding up some ties for me to choose from. "Black," I said, pointing to the one on the left. He tied it in a bow around my neck, "one of these days I gotta teach you how to do this yourself," he laughed.

I stepped back again to get the full view of myself in the mirror. This was it, this was what I wanted to get married in. I started to imagine her walking down the aisle to me. "Dude, you're gonna make me cry," Xander said, rubbing his eyes. I chuckled. "What time is it?" I asked. William took his phone out of his pocket. "Isa said she's almost ready. I'd say we have another twenty minutes or so before it's time to head outside." I nodded at him. "I'm gonna go check on her," I said. "No!" they both said. I looked at them surprised. "Why?" I said. "You can't see the bride before the wedding!" William said.

I laughed again, "OK, you're right. I'll just go wait downstairs then." I made my way down to the living room and sat in the chair. The house seemed so quiet now. I closed my eyes and leaned back trying to picture what she was going to look like. After a while I heard someone walking down the stairs in heels. I opened my eyes to see Sarah wearing a knee length black dress. Her hair was done up and was styled in a braided bun. I stood up when she made it to the couch. "You look great Sarah. How is she?" I asked, beginning to get nervous. She gave me a hug, "she's beautiful, Adam. I'm so happy for you." She released me and stood back to check me out. "You clean up pretty good too," she giggled. "Thanks," I said, fluffing my jacket. William and Xander joined us wearing black suits. "Are we ready?" William asked. I exhaled then nodded.

Chapter

21

We all walked out to the arch down by the water. Xander had given his jacket to Sarah because she was cold and was just wearing his white dress shirt and black pants now. I stood on the right side of the archway waiting for Isa to arrive. Will was standing in the middle of the arch next to me with Xander on my other side. Sarah stood on the opposite side waiting for Isa to stand in front of her. I could hear the french doors open from her balcony. I looked over in their direction. I could faintly see her as she spread her feathered wings to take off. She flew through the air and landed twenty-five yards from us. When she landed, the wind created from her wings sent a thin layer of snow blowing through air, causing it to fall on us now.

She stood there in front of us wearing a pearlescent white dress with the capped sleeves draped off her shoulders. I saw she was also wearing the sunflower pendant I had got her resting above her cleavage. She was breathtaking. She slowly walked forward making her hair blow in the wind. I reached my hand out for her when she got to me. She took it gently and turned to face me. "You look incredible," I whispered. She smiled and used her other hand to wipe my eyes. I hadn't even noticed I was crying. I could hear Sarah sniffle when we faced William.

"We're gathered here today to join these two in the sacred bonds of marriage," William started. "From this day forward, you two will be tethered together, in sickness and in health, so long as you both shall live." I stroked her hand with my thumb. "With these rings, as a symbol of your love and commitment, I pronounce thee, wed." Rings? I thought. Isa turned to Sarah and took something from her. "What's that?" I said. She held out my hand and started sliding the ring up my finger. "I made this for you. I've had this piece of silver since the crusades and I wanted you to have it." She made it for me? I thought. I took her hands in mine. "I love it," I said.

William continued, "Do you profess your love, Adam?" I looked into her wonderfully green eyes. "I do." She smiled. "And do you profess your love, Isadora?" She squeezes my hands, "I do." Sarah let out a tiny squeal. "Then by the powers that be, I present you to each other. You may now seal your everlasting life together," he finished. Isa and I stood there looking deep into one another's eyes. Xander leaned forward, "kiss her already," he said. We all laughed. I ran my fingers up her neck and through her hair, pulling her face closer to mine. Everyone cheered when our lips met. She pulled me in so I would be closer to her.

I slightly pulled away from her face, "I love you, forever," I said, as I dipped her back. She giggled, kissing me once more. I lifted her up again. "I love you too," she said. We stood there holding each other as everyone crowded around to congratulate us. William reached around Isa to give her a hug and Sarah came up and did the same for me. "I can't believe it, you're married!" she exclaimed. I was married, I thought, to the most incredible person in the entire universe, and she picked me.

We all walked to the house with Isa and I trailing behind everyone. "You look super handsome," she said, pulling on my jacket. "Thanks, William lent it to me. And you, you look stunning. Did you already have this dress?" I asked. She smiled, "yeah. It's vintage from the 1400's. It used to be longer but I had to cut the burned portion off of the bottom." She cut her dress. "Why was it burned?" I said. "They tried to burn me at the stake but that's when my wings grew out and rescued me," she said. "And you kept it for all these years?" I asked. She nodded, "Rarely do I ever throw anything away that I could need. For example, the material used to make your ring. I've had that just as long as this dress."

She picked up the hem and swayed with it. When we got to the porch I stopped. "What's wrong?" she said. I scooped her up, "nothing. I just wanted to carry you across the threshold." Her eyes lit up when we made it through the door and I set her back down. "So what's the plan for the rest of the day?" I asked. "Well, Will wanted to go access the damage at the club to see if anything's salvageable, Sarah wanted to go out with Xander after the wedding, and we should really consummate the marriage." She said that last part with a sly look on her face. I wasn't about to argue with her either.

"We're heading out," Sarah chimed, when we got closer to the living room. "Me too, I'll be back later. I wanna check out the club," Will said. "I wanna check it out too before we do anything else, if that's ok with you, Sarah," Xander replied. She nodded and grabbed her coat. "You kids have fun now," Xander said as he exited the house. Sarah got after him for his comment as she followed him. "I'll bring home Thai later whenever I get back, sound good?" William asked. "That would be great," Isa replied. He smiled at us then followed Sarah and Ben out the door.

We were completely alone again for the first time in a month. She pulled me closer to her body and began kissing me. "Let's go upstairs," I said, breathing heavily. I grabbed her hand and led her to our room. Once inside I buried my face in her cleavage. I tried to undo the corset on the back of her dress but I couldn't get it. "Just rip it," she said, taking off my jacket. I did as she told me. I found a small insert for my fingers and tore the back of her dress off, then I picked her up and carried her to the bed.

She pulled at my pants as she undid the zipper. She seemed to be in an even bigger hurry than I was. I ran my hand up her thigh until it was under her dress. She grabbed the bottom part of it and ripped it clear up to her stomach. She pulled me in as I kneeled on the bed on top of her. She was still sitting up when she grabbed my head and whispered in my ear, "don't hold back." She was giving me permission to lose myself and unleash my inner demon.

Our bodies became entangled with one another, she wasn't holding back either. She was so strong that at one point I thought she cracked another one of my ribs. I pinned her down as hard as I could, putting my full body weight into each motion. The tatters of her dress made it difficult to stay on her so I finished tearing it apart the rest of the way, throwing the pieces to the side. She moaned louder with each thrust I gave her. I bit her neck while I was kissing it, she seemed to like that a lot. I wouldn't let her get close to mine though, for fear she might draw blood and make herself sick.

This went on for hours. We'd end then lay together for a while then start back up again. By the start of the third hour I was spent. She tried to get me to sit up for her but I couldn't. Out of breath I said, "We have to stop. I'm exhausted." She curled herself around my body laying her head on my chest. "Pretty amazing, isn't it?" she said. Confused, I answered, "What is?" She laughed, "It's amazing to not be restricted by that bracelet anymore, isn't it?" Was that what had stopped me before? The second she took it off me I felt stronger and the most in control that I'd ever been.

"Is that why you told me to not hold back, because you knew I could handle it now?" I asked. She yawned, "yes, but I didn't know you could hold out for so long. That kind of threw me off guard. I'm exhausted too after all that." She placed her left hand on my stomach gently. "Sorry if I hurt you at all," she said. I shook my head, "no worries, although I think you may have cracked another one of my ribs." She laughed at that. "I didn't, but I'm sorry anyways. I got a little carried away before you held me down and started kissing my neck." She began drawing circles on my chest. "Are you sure I didn't hurt you either?" I asked. She snorted, "No, I can take it. That was a wise choice to keep your heck away from me though. There were a couple times I really wanted to bite you, not to drink your blood, but if I had broken skin and got a taste, that would have been bad."

We lay there in each other's company for a few minutes before I spoke again. "So, when do we leave?" I asked. She sighed, "if it was just me I would leave tonight but since you're not really a big fan of my flying, we'll leave tomorrow. I asked Will to get you a passport today while he was out." She was gonna fly all the way there herself? I thought. "I've never flown in a plane before either. Is it scary?" I said. She shook her head, "No, the takeoff and landing are a bit unnerving but once we're in the air you'll be fine," she reassured me. "Can all vampires fly or at least, can Jake?" I was curious about that from last night when he seemed to show up in a gust of wind, knocking me down. "Not all, but yes, like a fool, I gave him wings. They're stronger than my feathers but not as tough as my dragon scales. He never really liked flying either, but I gifted them to him when Sarrora was still alive," she replied. "How did you gift them to him?" I asked. She sat up and began opening her wings, revealing a small empty patch in her left wing. "I plucked out some feathers and bonded them to his flesh. After a while, they grew into wings." I wondered.... "Could you do that to me?" I said. She laughed out loud, "I could, but you'd look rather silly as a wolf with wings. They don't grow back if I forcibly take them out either."

She absorbed them again and laid back down. I stroked her hair, "everything's going to be ok," I told her. She sighed, "I know." She sat up again, "they're back. We should go down to eat something. I'm sure you're famished after all that." I smiled and sat up too. "I don't know, maybe I could go one more time," I playfully joked. She shook her head, "let's put a pin in that and we'll see how you feel later." We stood up to get dressed. My legs were weak from our vigorous encounter. I looked over to see the pile of white fabric on the floor. "Sorry about the dress," she shrugged. "I wouldn't have told you to rip it off if I was trying to save it."

We went to the closet to find new clothes to wear. She chose a pair of short shorts and an oversized light pink sweater. I, on the other hand, found a pair of jeans and a black t-shirt. We made our way down the stairs to the kitchen. William was getting out plates for everyone when we arrived. "Everything smells so good," Sarah said. She reached for the container of soup. "Don't do it Sar, it'll be too spicy for you. Just let Isa have it," I said to her. She left it alone and opened a container of rice and poured some on her plate. "How did the club look?" Isa asked. Xander looked up from his plate, "It's gone, Izzy. Nothing left but a pile of bricks and part of the piano." My heart sank, I had only been playing again for a couple of weeks and now it was gone. I didn't know if I'd ever get to play for Isa again and watch her dance.

"That sucks," I said, putting some noodles and vegetables on my plate. "What will we do now?" I asked. Isadora put down her soup before she spoke, "I have some properties scattered around town, small businesses, apartment complexes and so forth. The club was more of a hobby for us anyway. We can open another one in a year or so." She had other properties? I thought. "Which apartments do you own?" I asked. William chuckled to himself. Isa turned to look at me, "oh, just a building formerly owned by a greedy Russian man that was giving some people a hard time." Russian man? Mr. Petrov? I thought. Had she bought the building when we were going to be evicted? She smiled at me. I knew I was right.

"But why would you buy our building? It wasn't even in good shape." I said. She smirked, "it's only money, this way I knew you'd have a place to live. I plan on remodeling the whole thing anyway and have you be the new building manager." She continued to eat her food. I was stunned, she had gone to great lengths to not only make sure I had a place to live, but to also ensure I had someplace to work. "Why would you do that?" I asked. "Well I can't be everywhere at once. I'm gonna need some help maintaining the building and overseeing the renovations," Will said. That made sense I guess, I thought. If William needed my help, I would.

"I got your passport too," he said, slurping up a noodle. He reached in his pocket and pulled out an envelope. I opened it somewhat confused, "but I thought it took a couple weeks for you to get a passport? How could you possibly get it today?" I asked. They all looked at each other. "It wouldn't be the first time we needed to disappear rather quickly. There are ways of expediting the process, especially when you own your own plane," Xander said. I looked at Isadora, "you have your own plane?" Will interrupted her before she could speak, "of course she does. What, did you think she was going to fly herself all the way there in broad daylight where everyone could see her?" I felt stupid for ever thinking that. "No," I said sheepishly. William and Xander started laughing at me.

Isa touched my hand, "yes, I have a plane and no I'm not going to use my wings to fly all the way there. It's too great a distance for me to cross over oceans and land like that. Someone might see me," she explained gently. "When do we leave then?" I said. She took her bowl and headed for the sink. "We need to be at the hanger by midnight. I already packed our bags this morning," she replied. She washed her bowl then turned to face me again. "I'd tell you to get some rest but you can sleep during the flight," she continued, "is everything else ready, Will?" What else was there?" I thought. He glanced at me quick. "Yeah, everything's set," he said. What was set? I thought.

"Good, then I'll leave you to it then." She walked away without saying another word. Where was she going? I got up to follow her. Sarah put her hand across the table to stop me, "just hang out with us for a little bit. She'll be fine." I looked back in the direction Isa left. Was something the matter? Should I go to her? "Is she ok?" I asked them. "She hasn't been back since Jake left her there. I'm sure she's just dealing with the trauma of having to go back to face him again," Will said. I didn't like the thought of her being upset by having to see Jake again but her mind was already made up. We were leaving in a few hours and if she needed some space, I'd give it to her. I sat back down. "Do you have any advice on how to fight him if I need to?" I asked Will and Xander. "Don't. That's the best advice I can think of," Xander said, "he's too strong for you to beat by yourself without the pack. I think only Izzy could take him out fully but I don't know if she ever would." I frowned. "Why not?" I asked. William sighed, "because of their history. I know you don't want to hear this but he was her first." My stomach was in knots. "Her first, what?" I said, starting to get irritated.

"Everything," he said. "He was her first everything. First love, first and only person she's ever made into a vampire. He was with her through some of the most difficult times in her existence. You don't just quit caring for someone after all that even if he did leave her." I didn't want to listen to this. I stood up, knocking my chair over. Sarah jumped causing Xander to put his arm on the table in front of her. "Just because she has a history with him, doesn't mean she wants him around in her future. I'm not going to let him hurt her any longer!" I was furious. "Adam, he's not saying that. Of course she doesn't want him around. We're just saying that it might be difficult for her to kill him is all. Please just leave her alone for now," Sarah begged.

I tried to control my breathing as I was standing in the kitchen. Finally, I relaxed enough that I could pick up my chair and sit on it again. "If I die in the next few days, will you guys promise to look out for her?" Sarah gasped at my question. "Adam, no. You can't think that way!" she argued. My mind was made up. I shook my head, "there's no guarantee I'll come out of this unscathed, Sarah. I don't plan on killing myself but if I happened to die, I need you to promise me you won't let her blame myself for my death. She's suffered enough to have to beat herself up about me. I'm the one who wanted to go with her, and I plan to be by her side, till death do us part."

Xander nodded his head and held out his hand, "I accept your terms, although I hope I never have to keep my promise." We shook on it. I looked over at William now. He wasn't too sure about it. I held my hand out for him, "Will, can I trust you to look out for her like you always have in the past?" He eyed my hand. He slowly reached out and shook it. "I'm not gonna lie, she may kill us just for agreeing to this," he said. Xander and I chuckled. I turned to Sarah now. "Sarah, if something happens to me, can I trust that you will forgive her?" Tears had started streaming down her face. She got up and ran around the table to embrace me. "I'll try. I can't say I wouldn't be upset with you too if something were to happen. Please just come home safe," she said.

I hugged her back but not as tight as usual, I didn't want to hurt her. "So it's settled then, you're not dying, and if you do, we're not allowed to let Izzy be sad," Xander said. We all agreed that this was the plan. I was going to stay by her side until the very end even if it killed me. We joked around and talked for the next few hours until Isa made her way back to us. "Time to go," she said somberly. She was carrying two large backpacks, one for each of us. William went over to give her a hug goodbye. "See you soon," he said, giving her a kiss on the cheek. She stroked his face along his scar line then ruffled his hair. Xander got up and picked her up in a big bear hug, "give 'em hell, Izzy," he said, letting her feet touch the ground now. Sarah gave her a quick squeeze, "please come back, for all our sakes."

Isa smiled at everyone. "I'll have him back in no time, then everything can go back to the way it was," she said. I picked up our bags and headed to the car. They followed us out of the house and stood on the porch. I waved at everyone as I got in the passenger side. I didn't want to leave them, they were my family, all of them. Isa put the car in drive and sped off into the night. "How far is the hanger?" I asked as we went through the gates. "It's about twenty minutes from here," she said, keeping her eyes focused on the road.

I reached out for her hand but she didn't accept me. Was she upset by what I said to them back there, about promising to take care of her if I died? I'm sure she was. She didn't say anything the whole ride to the airport. When we arrived she parked the car inside the hanger and got out. There was a gentleman waiting for us once we parked the car. "Ms. Dragoss?" he said to her. "Mrs. Christenson-Dragoss," she corrected him. He smiled, "yes of course, this is your honeymoon isn't it. Congratulations. Please step into the aircraft. We'll be departing shortly." He walked away in a hurry towards the plane's boarding stairs. I grabbed our bags out of the back and followed her.

I have to admit, it gave me a sense of pride hearing her use my last name as her own. We boarded the plane and took our seats. She sat there silently staring out the window. I wanted her to talk to me. "This is our honeymoon, huh?" I said. She nodded, "as far as he knows it is." She continued staring out the window. The man joined us on the plane and made his way to the cockpit. "Fasten your seatbelt please as we prepare for take-off. I buckled myself in then looked over at Isa. She hadn't moved. I unbuckled and quickly went over to her side to buckle her in. She flinched when I touched her. She was looking me in the eyes now, "thank you," she said quietly. I went back to my seat and buckled myself in again.

I was really nervous about the take-off. I could feel the plane rumble as we pulled out of the hanger and onto the airstrip. I gripped my seat and started hyperventilating. You need to relax, Adam. You're more likely to die in a car accident than a plane crash, I kept thinking. I was being pulled back in my seat by the force from the plane taking off. I looked over at Isadora to see she was holding her hand out for me now. I grabbed it and held it tight. She pet my finger with her thumb during the entire take off trying to reassure me everything was going to be alright.

Once in the air, the captain turned off the seatbelt sign letting us know it was safe to walk about the cabin. She unbuckled then stood up. She was still holding my hand and tried to pull me with her towards the sofa that was sitting behind us. I was too scared to move. She came to me and undid my seatbelt. I was still clutching the seat with one hand when she reached out for it and pulled me to my feet. She put her arms underneath mine and held me. I wrapped my arms around her as tight as I could. "Just breathe. I'm right here," she whispered. I slowly began to relax my shoulders until my breathing was no longer irregular.

She stood on her tiptoes and found my lips with hers. "Better?" she asked. I let out a sigh of relief, "better. I let her walk me to the sofa where she had flipped out into a bed. She opened the overhead compartments and pulled out two pillows and a blanket. "Here, you need to get some rest. It's a twenty-four hour flight from here to the Carpathian Mountains. I can put you in a trance to help you sleep if you'd like." I wanted to talk with her though. "No, that's alright. I'll just stay awake for a while." She laid down on the bed facing away from me. She must really be upset, I thought.

I laid down behind her and scooted myself closer. "What's wrong? You've been acting differently since you went upstairs." I said. She didn't say anything. "If it's about what I said to William, Xander, and Sarah, I'm not apologizing for that. I meant every word, till death do us part." She stiffened when I said that. "It isn't what you said, I'm just tired." she replied. "If you're tired I can roll over so you can get some sleep," I said. She scrunched herself in a ball, "I'm not sleepy, I'm just tired of the way things are. Somebody is always in constant danger around me, and there's nothing I can do to save them."

I placed my hand on her waist, "what do you mean?" I asked. "Like Jake, none of this would be happening if I'd just stayed in my room or let him die that night. But instead, I thought I needed to save him. I should have just stayed the monster they made me out to be." I wasn't going to allow her to bring herself down like that. I rolled her over so she would face me. "If you hadn't left your room and saved him that night, we may never have met. And you are not a monster, you are beautiful, smart, funny, and you care deeply about those around you. I will never stop loving you and I thank God every day that your past has brought you into my future."

She gave me a little smile, "you really are my sunflower. Even on the darkest days, you stand tall and find the sunlight." She caressed my face with her hand. I leaned forward to kiss her as she ran her fingers through my hair. I lay there holding her as we kissed. Would this be the last time we'd ever be together like this? Who knew what tomorrow would bring. She rested her forehead on my chin. I kissed the top of her head. "Now sleep, please," she whispered again. I laid down the rest of the way so she could put her head on my chest. She did, then started humming. It sounded like 'Brahms Lullaby.' My eyes grew heavier and it became harder to keep them open. Was she putting me to sleep? I thought. I couldn't take it any longer, I closed my eyes and drifted off to sleep.

I heard a bell 'ding.' The captain had turned on the seatbelt sign again. I sat up to find Isa already sitting in her seat. The plane was shaking as it made it decent. I quickly fastened myself in and held out my hand for her. She took it and rubbed my fingers with her thumb. "It's alright, we're just landing," she said. I looked out my window to see cloud covered mountains all around us. I clenched my eyes shut for the rest of the landing. When the pilot landed the plane and drove us across the air strip, I started feeling nauseous. Had I just slept for a full twenty-four hours straight? She must have made me sleep the whole time we were in the air and now I was so hungry I felt like throwing up. "I don't feel so good," I said, gripping my stomach. "Just a little bit longer, we'll get something to eat after we get off," she reassured me.

The plane coasted to a stop and the captain made his appearance once again, "thank you for flying with us today. Do you know when you'll be returning?" he asked us. Isa let go of me and started digging through her backpack. She pulled out an envelope and handed it to the captain, "here's you per diem for while we're gone. It should only take us a few days to get there and back." He took the envelope and smiled as he opened it. "Thank you. Enjoy your trip," he said exiting the plane. She started undressing and putting on new clothes she had pulled from her pack. "Get dressed. It's going to be chilly where we're going." I opened my bag and took out a pair of thermal lined jeans and a new pair of hiking boots. "Are we going to be doing a lot of walking?" I asked. She nodded, pulling a tight black long sleeve shirt over her head. "It's

284

a day's hike up the mountains from here. We should be there by day break tomorrow."

I put on my new pants and laced up the boots. "How long would it take us if you just flew us up there?" I said. She pondered the question, "I think it would take me by myself only a few hours but carrying you, I'd have to stop often to make sure you weren't getting too cold from the wind. I'd say it would cut our journey in half through. Maybe six hours?" Six hours? That sounded better than hiking in snow covered mountains for a whole day. "I think we should try that. The sooner we get there, the sooner we can leave." She looked at me, not convinced. "Are you sure? I'll have to fly pretty high in the cloud cover so no one sees us then." I shuddered at the thought of being that high, but I didn't want to show that I was scared. "Yes, let's do it," I replied.

We finished getting ready then left the plane. We made our way through the terminal out to a car that was waiting for us. "We can drive part of the way but we'll have to leave the car in the village if you want to fly," she said. She drove us an hour north until we made it to a small town. "Here," she said, handing me some foreign currency, "go get something to eat and meet me at the far edge of town. I'll be waiting there for you." I was confused, "aren't you getting anything?" I asked. She shook her head, "no, the more out of sight I stay, the better. This is the old country and they still very much believe in vampires. They probably still tell stories about me," she said. "But that was hundreds of years ago. How could they still be looking for you?" I asked. She shrugged, "people can hold grudges for centuries and what I've done here in the past isn't something you just forget about." We stepped out of the car and she put up her hood. "One hour, then come meet me," she whispered. She disappeared in a gust of wind.

I wandered around the town trying to make sense of the signs labeled above the buildings. I finally found one that looked promising. I went inside. There were a plethora of people talking in another language. "Hello?" I said shyly. A lady walked up to me, "American?" she said with a thick accent. I nodded. She led me to the counter where I sat down. "You want the special? Is good," she said. I didn't know what the special was but I figured it was safer than trying to order something else. I nodded then placed my hands on the counter. An older woman was sitting next to me and noticed my ring. She touched my finger and began speaking to me. I didn't understand what she was saying though. "I'm sorry. I don't know what you're saying." She beckoned for the waitress to come back. "She says, someone loves you very strong. Deep magic in this ring. Keep you safe." The old woman smiled at me then spit on the ground as she let go of my hand. "Why'd she do that?" I asked. "She ward of evil spirits. Added protection." She turned and brought me my food. They were cabbage rolls. I sighed when she placed it in front of me. At least I knew what this was. I ate my food then thanked her for the meal. I didn't know how much to pay so I gave her everything Isa had given me.

I left the establishment and made my way in the direction Isadora had pointed me. I could see her standing with her back to me facing the mountains. She turned as she heard me walking up. "Feel better?" she asked with a smile. I grinned back at her, "Yes." I took her hand and we began hiking away from the town. "There was a woman in there that liked my ring," I said. "Oh yeah?" She replied, giving my hand a squeeze. "Yeah. She said something about a strong love and deep magic." Isa stopped walking. "You met a Gypsy then. Did she say anything else?" Her eyes, questioning me. "No," I shook my head. "She just spit in front of me after that." She sighed and we continued walking. "It's a good thing I didn't go with you. Gypsies are very perceptive to the supernatural and she probably would have caused a scene. She would have known what I was right away," she said. "What about me? Aren't I supernatural now that I'm a werewolf?" I asked. She laughed, "Yes, but you're still new. If Will or Xander had been with you it would have been different. The longer you live the more of an aura engulfs you causing sensitive people to pick up on your energy," she said. I was fascinated.

"How come I can't see anything?" I asked. She looked at me, "because some of us are just better at hiding it. Sometimes we let off a sort of glow, others it's just a weird feeling you get." I thought back on when I first met Jake, not knowing who he was yet. I got a strange sense of familiarity that I couldn't pinpoint before. Perhaps that's what she was talking about. We walked along a goat path leading into the mountains for about an hour until we could no longer see the town. Isa stopped walking, "this is where we fly if you're still willing," she said.

I gave her a nod. She took off her backpack and set it on the ground. "Give me your phone," she said. I gave her my phone, confused. She did something on it then gave it back. "There. Now you have this place marked on your maps for when it's time to head back." I took off my pack and set them behind a boulder next to hers.

"How's this going to work?" I asked. She stepped closer to me, "Probably the easiest way would be to wrap our legs together facing each other. I'll hold on to you and you'll hold onto me around my stomach." She looked around then released her wings. She hovered in the air in front of me as she wrapped herself around my body. She put her arms around my head and pulled me close to her chest. I did as she said, holding my wrist firmly behind her back. "Hold tight now," she said, taking flight. We soars through the sky, the cold air piercing my face. I turned my cheek so it wasn't in the wind. Each flap carried us higher and higher until I could no longer see the ground through the clouds and fog. I clenched my eyes shut, gripping her tighter, she chuckled.

"I told you, you weren't going to like it. Just let me know if you need me to stop, OK?" She said. I nodded. We flew for what seemed like forever, my hands were raw from the cold and from holding onto her so tightly. I opened my eyes again to get a glimpse of the scenery as we passed over it. My eyes began to water. "I need a break," I said loudly. "Are you sure? It's just a little bit further," she said in my ear. I nodded vigorously. I felt her dive down towards the ground. My hands began slipping as she made her decent. I felt her grip my shirt with her hand. We softly landed on a gravel road near a large pine tree. I pried my hands away from her and began rubbing them together. "I should have brought gloves," I said. She held my hands in hers then leaned forward and blew in them. Instantly they began warming up. "How'd you do that?" I asked her, amazed. She smiled, "I may feel cold all the time but fire is my main element of choice. I don't have to just snap my fingers to produce a flame, I can also breathe fire if I wanted to." She blew on my hands again, creating steam.

"Can you shift completely over into the body of a dragon too?" I asked inquisitively. She shrugged, "don't know. I've never tried to, so maybe." Her feathered wings changed into her blacked scaled ones. She raised them up above us and made us a little shelter from the wind then cupped her hands around her mouth. She blew into them creating a ball of flames. She pulled her wings closer to me making me crouch down on the ground. We sat there warming up as she held her fireball, "how much further is it?" I asked. "It's just up those cliffs. Another hour or so if we push hard." I warmed my hands over hers, "are you nervous to see your sister again?" I said. She looked at me with distress in her eyes, "I'm terrified," she answered.

We sat there for a while until I was able to feel all my appendages again. "I'm ready if you are," I said. She closed her hands together making the fire go out. We stood up as she absorbed her wings once more. It had started to lightly snow and you could see an outline of where she had been hunkered down. I took her hand and kissed it. "And you call me a sunflower. You're the one that literally just warmed up to me to my core." She blushed and pulled me closer to her, "Adam, will you please kiss me? I don't know what's going to happen up there and I just want to hold on to this moment a little longer." I brushed her cheek with my hand as I leaned in to kiss her. I wanted to give her the longest kiss I could. She wrapped her arms around me. I held her there until I she slightly pulled away. "I love you," she whispered. My heart started beating erratically. I wiped a snowflake from her cheek. "I'll love you forever." She kissed me again but this time it was different, like she was trying to tell me something.

The path was treacherous up ahead, loose rocks and fallen trees littered the road. She led the way up until we reached the edge of the cliff. I looked back to see a river flowing down below. We're so high up, I thought. Not paying attention I missed a step and started falling. Isa reached for me grabbing the front of my shirt. She pulled me back on the trail. "Careful Adam! One wrong step and you'd tumble all the way down." She was right, I needed to pay better attention to where I was walking. From the edge I could look up and see crumbling ruins. "Are we there?" I asked. She looked ahead of us, "yes, this was my home. It used to be so beautiful, until I burned it down." She walked a few paces in front of me. "Didn't you say Jake was going to meet us here?" As soon as I said it I felt the hairs on the back of my neck stand up. I looked around to see what was causing me such alarm.

"Sure took your sweet time getting here," he shouted our way. I looked up to see Jake standing on the trail in front of Isa. I rush up to get in front of her. She put her hand against my chest to stop me. "But I'm here, Jake. Just like I promised," she said. I didn't like the way he was looking at her. "Why'd you bring your little pet? Not kennel trained yet?" He laughed at his own joke. I tried to push past Isa but she wouldn't let me budge. "For your information, this pet is now her husband!" I shouted. Jake's smile faded. "Is he serious Isa?" he asked. She took my hand, "does it matter?" she said. He put his hands in his pockets. "No. I just never thought you'd ever pull the trigger. That's all." I let out a low growl. Isa squeezed my hand signaling me to calm down.

"Where is she, Jake?" she said. He pointed with his head, "back there. Where else would she be?" he said. Isa was getting annoyed, "does she know I'm coming?" she asked. He shook his head, "no, I'm not stupid. If I wanted to kill Hope, don't you think I would have already done that?" he jeered at us. Isa walked forward with her eyes narrowed, "what are you going to do with Hope once I release her?" He seemed to flinch at her tone of voice. "I'm going to take her home again," he answered. "And what if she won't go willingly with you? After all, she knows nothing about who you really are." He relaxed his shoulders and sighed, "Then I would ask you politely to wipe her memories of me." I was shocked, could she do that? I turned to her, "can you really wipe people's memories?" I asked. She kept her eyes on Jake, "yes. But he knows that if I did that, he could never see her again no matter how much he wanted to." I frowned, "why not?" I asked. Jake answered my question, "Because, if the person who's been erased from someone's memories sees that person, all their memories will come flooding back at once and it can kill them with an overload of emotions." He walked over to us, "sometimes you can get lucky and just cause the person to have a nervous breakdown that can be adjusted over time, but usually it means death." I looked at Isa, "you never wanted to do that to me did you?" I asked. She laughed, "No, although I have done it to other people in the past. Mostly people I've let live after I fed on them so they wouldn't remember who I was."

I was learning so many new things about her, it's like Jake brought out this whole other side to her. It made me jealous that he already knew absolutely everything about her. "Let's go," Isa said. Jake held his hands up, "wait, can I talk to you first, alone," he glanced at me. I felt a snarl form on my lips. I wasn't going to let him anywhere near her alone. "It's fine, Adam. I'll be right back. You just wait here a moment." She kissed my cheek then went to him. He placed his hand on the small of her back, leading her forward. He smiled a devilish grin when he did it, knowing it would upset me. I tried not to let him see if phase me. They walked up the hill out of sight and began talking. The wind was blowing the wrong direction so I couldn't hear anything they were saying.

They talked for a while as the sun was setting. It'll be dark soon, then how are we going to be able to see what we were doing? I thought. They returned to me promptly and waited for me to walk to them. We all walked up the path until we came to a crumbled stone wall with an opening. I thought about transforming so I would have better night vision as a wolf but then I wouldn't be able to hold her hand and make sure she was safe. We walked through a narrow passageway until we reached a stairwell. We walked down the stairs in a single file line. "I can't see anything," I whispered. Isa snapped her fingers and threw a ball of light in front of us. The stairs went deep underground. We got to the bottom where there were three different choices of hallways. "Which way?" I asked. "Left," Jake and Isa said at the same time. I followed close behind them. We came to a metal door with bars across it. The hinges were bent and the door was hanging to one side. Isa held tight to my hand, "that's it," she whispered. I could see her eyes were wide in the firelight. Where were we? I thought. "Do you want me to go first?" Jake asked her reaching out to her. I pulled her away from him with a growl. "Jeez, relax. I was just going to help her through the door," Jake said.

"Do you hear that, Jake?" She said. We all listened. "No," he said confused, "I don't hear anything." She looked at him, "neither do I." I tried to listen again, "shouldn't we be able to hear his girlfriends' heartbeat or at least her breathing from in there?" I asked. Jake's face dropped, when the realization kicked in. He flung the door open and dashed inside. "Nooo...!" We heard him wail. Isa rushed in after him leaving me alone in the hall. I could hear three voices now, Jake's, Isadora, and another person's. I slowly crept inside to survey the scene. Years of neglect lay beneath my feet. There were broken pieces of furniture strewn about the place and scorch marks on the walls. I saw a thin brunette girl laying on the ground with her eyes open. Is she dead? I thought. I made my way over to her. To check her pulse. She was cold as ice. "Do something! Anything! Turn her into a vampire!" Jake demanded.

"She isn't dead, Jakey dear. I merely took her essence of life and brought in here with me." Who said that? It sounded like Isa but I didn't see her lips move. "And who is this? A new toy perhaps?" the voice spoke again. I looked around to see where it was coming from. "Adam, you need to come here. Now!" Isadora's voice was sharp when she spoke to me. I did as she said. When I got behind her I looked to see a giant floor length mirror standing across from the girls' body next to where I was just standing. The mirror had ornate designs around the outside edges but the glass seemed to have been shattered then put back together.

The reflection did not mirror the dark and dingy space we were standing in. It was beautiful with lush reds and purples throughout the room. There was a thin girl sitting on the floor, holding her knees to her chest in the exact spot her body lay on our side. And in the background I saw four people standing. Jake, myself, Isa and someone who looked identical to her. What's going on? I thought. Isa held her arm out to try and tuck me behind her but I stood my ground. I looked over Isa's shoulder to check if I could see her doppelgänger beside her. It was just the three of us standing here though. "Is that...?" They cut me off, "Sarrora," they both said in lowered voices.

She smiled when they said her name, "have you missed me, sister?" she asked. I saw her walk closer to me in the mirror and place her hand on my chest, I could feel a warm hand press against me. I jumped, looking down at myself. There was nothing touching me. "Boy, he's sure got a strong heart. How'd you ever manage to find someone like him to love you? Not even Jake cared this deeply," she said to Isa with a smirk. "He's none of your concern. I'm the one you want," Isadora replied. She took her hand off my chest in the mirror, releasing the pressure I was feeling. Jake took a step closer to the girl's body, "give her back Rory, she's innocent in all this," he said. She chuckled at his remark, "innocent? No one is innocent. She was playing with fire the second you laid eyes on her, and now that she's been burned you want her back? Where were you when they burned Isa at the stake, huh?" He looked away from the mirror towards Isa.

"I wasn't ready," he said, taking another small step closer. "Ready? Ready for what? You had already spent three hundred years with us, and then all of a sudden you weren't ready to make a commitment?" she said. I was frozen with fear as they talked. "It's not like that. I did love her, but I couldn't stay trapped inside these four walls forever. I needed a break," he said. A break, after all that time? Why not just stick it out? I thought. Sarrora walked over to his reflection and put her hand around his throat. "You needed a break? I should break your neck for what you did to us. If you had just stuck to the plan like I asked in the first place, none of this would have had to happen." What was she talking about? I could hear his neck starting to crack under her fingers. "Rory, stop it!" Isa said, "What do you mean, if he had stuck to the plan?" Sarrora let go of Jake and walked closer to the mirror with a twisted smile. "He didn't tell you?" she said with glee. "He had a change of heart about getting rid of you. He wanted me to replace you so he could be free to roam wherever he pleased but instead, he chose to make you believe we were conspiring to raise an army of vampires. He never intended to hurt you, he just wanted you safely out of the picture." Isa looked stunned, over at him, "Jake? Is that true?" He looked away for a second then back at her, "I've never stopped loving you. I just wanted you to trade places with Rory for a while so I could have some time to myself. It was never my intention to leave you alone like this for so long." He still loved her, I thought. The hair on the back of my neck began bristling.

Isa placed a hand on his arm, "but why? Why did you stay away so long if you still you still had feelings for me?" she said in a hurt tone. He turned to completely face her now. "I figured you'd be mad and never want to see me again anyway so I left you alone. It wasn't until years later that I discovered you had cursed me," he replied. She shook her head, "that was fifty years later though, I only did that after I was resurrected, and the only reason I did it was because I thought you wanted to create vampires of your own and wreak havoc." I tried to pull her back to me but she wouldn't move. Did she actually still harbor feelings for him too?

"You see, what's that thing you like to say Isa, secrets are lies? He's been lying to you for centuries now, and if he hadn't lied, you never would have forced me back in here and shattered me." Sarrora pointed forward at the broken glass. Isadora turned to face the mirror again, "yes I would have. You were causing too many problems and you wanted too much from this world. You needed to go back and stay where you came from otherwise you were just going to end up hurting more people." Sarrora folded her arms, "I'm not the one who used to nurse innocent people just for the hell of it, Izzy. You're not innocent here either," she said. "I've never said I was innocent and I served my punishment of each life took through my own deaths. This isn't about me though, it's about the girl. You need to give her soul back so she can return home."

Sarrora walked up to the girl sitting on the floor and placed her hand on her shoulder. She flinched away at her touch. "I don't think so. It's been rather lonely in here and now that I have a companion, I'm not giving her up. Say hello dear," she flashed a wicked smile at the girl. "Hello, Jake? Help! Get me out of here!" she screamed. She stood up and ran for the mirror, appearing bigger the closer she got. She began banging her fist on it making the broken glass clink with each blow. Jake ran forward to the mirror placing his hands on it, "Hope! Don't worry, I'll get you out of there. Just hang on a little longer." She looked up at him, "I feel so cold Jake. Like I may never be warm again," she said starting to cry.

"What's happening to her?" I asked. "She's been out of her body for too long. If she remains in the mirror her body will start to decompose without her soul," Isa said walking forward. "What do I have to do for you to release her?" She said. Sarrora chuckled, "You know what you need to do. I want out, and the only way that'll happen is if every piece on the mirror is put back in its place." Jake reached in his pocket and pulled out a shard of glass, making her eyes light up. "And you even remembered to bring it with you, I'm impressed. I was sure she would have taken it from you already." She pointed towards the bottom right of the mirror. "Now just put it there, and I'll give her back. Plain and simple." Isa lunged forward, grabbing the piece out of Jake's hand. "Let her go Rory, she doesn't have time for you to play games. She needs to get back in her body," Isa said.

"I don't think you're grasping the situation, I hold all the cards. If you let her die Jake's going to be a complete mess and probably go after, what was his name again? Adam? But if you let me go, I'll make sure no harm befalls him." I transformed and stood beside Isadora, snarling in the mirrors direction. I wasn't going to let her use me as a pon. Sarrora looked surprised, "oh, seems like you've been a busy girl. I didn't even notice he was a werewolf until just now. Doesn't matter, Jake could still take him. What do you say? Tradesies?" She pointed to the bottom of her mirror. "Please, Isa," Jake begged, "She's going to die if we don't get her out of there." The look on his face was wrought with anguish. He really cared about this girl and was willing to do anything to bring her back, I could respect him for that. I felt the same way about Isa.

Isa looked at me and lightly touched my head, "if this goes south, I need you to run Adam. Please," she whispered to me. I let out a whimper as I looked up at her. She stroked my ear then began walking forward. "OK, but I'm warning you. If you try anything, I will make sure it hurts as I drag you there to hell myself." Sarrora scoffed at that remark. Isa placed the piece of glass in on designated spot. The mirror began to crackle as the glass seemed to bond and heal itself together. It looked like it had never been broken now. Hope fell through the glass where she was resting her hands and collapsed on the floor. She was see through now. Isa quickly helped her up, "here, lie down," she said. Jake and Isa both helped her lay back onto the body on the floor. Her soul joined her body with ease. I watched Sarrora to see what she would do.

She placed her hand out through the mirror into the room. She slowly crept all the way through until she was standing behind Isa. Hope caught her breath with a loud gasp as began breathing rapidly. The color quickly returned to her cheeks and the rest of her face. "Jake?" she said barely above a whisper, "Where am I?" She asked. Jake sat her up, "You're sitting in a dungeon in the far north eastern part of Romania. I came to rescue you." His eyes lit up when he touched her. Was that how I was with Isa? I thought. I could tell he really cared for her.

I looked away from Sarrora for just a moment, suddenly she grabbed a broken piece of furniture and smashed the glass in. Shards fell all around them. "No!" Isa shouted. She stood over Hope and Jake trying to shield them from the broken glass. "Get her out of here!" she yelled at

Jake. He picked her up and fled out the door. Sarrora picked up a large piece of glass and held it firm in her hands. "Finally, I'm free," she said. Isa was standing beside me now. She turned to me, "I can't put her back in without all the pieces, but I may have figured out a way I can kill her." She pulled out a small dagger with a black handle. An athame? I thought, what was she going to sacrifice with that? She took the knife and drug it across her wrist. Sarrora let out a shriek of pain as her wrist began bleeding. "What are you doing?" she screamed.

Chapter

23

I whimpered as the blood dripped down her arm. She took the knife again and cut her other wrist. Sarrora began screaming again as her wounds matched Isadora's. I stood there helpless, not knowing what to do. "You were born of my reflection, now you'll have to die with me," Isa said. Sarrora hurled herself forward, trying to grab the knife. She managed to knock it out of her hands, as it clattered to the ground. I leapt into action and tackled the two of them. Isa managed to slip out and head for the knife. Sarrora took the shard of glass she'd been holding and pressed it to my throat. "Stop! If you take one more step I swear to you, I will kill him." I tried to wriggle myself free but she was too strong.

Isa stopped reaching for the knife then stood up. "OK, just let him go Rory. It's me you want, not him." She slowly made her way back to us, carefully choosing each step. I transformed back in hopes of getting away from Sarrora. She grabbed me by my hair and held me there on my knees. The glass was digging into my neck, I was trapped. "Don't do it Isa, just kill her!" I shouted, trying to pull away. "Shut up!" Sarrora screamed, gripping my hair tighter. Isa stopped. "There, now let him go," Isa demanded.

Sarrora brought her face close to mine, "I don't know, he seems like too much of a liability for me to keep around." She pulled the glass across my throat. I waited to feel the blood start rushing down my neck as I was about to die. Nothing happened. "What the?" She tried doing it again. Was the glass too dull? It shouldn't be, I could feel the sharp edge of it against my skin. "What's wrong with him?" Sarrora shouted.

Isa smiled and relaxed her shoulders. "You see that ring on his hand, I made that out of a piece of silver I enchanted to keep him alive. There's nothing you can do to him. He can't die."

Sarrora looked down at my hand. I had no idea she had done that. She knew I would have gladly sacrificed my own life for hers. Sarrora pulled me up and began trying to pull my wedding band off. It wouldn't budge. Was it just stuck? Isa started walking back over towards the athame laying on the floor. "You see, the only person who can take it off, is the one who put it on, and I will never take it off him. I promised his sister I wouldn't let anything happen to him and I intend to keep my promise."

She picked up the knife once more then turned back to face us. "Isa, what are you doing?" I asked frantically. I knew what she was planning. Jake reappeared in the doorway. "Jake, I need you to get Adam out of here at all cost," she said. Sarrora let me go and started backing up. Isa took one step closer and the ground began rumbling. I stood up and ran to her. "Isa no, let's just go and forget about her," I pleaded with her. "I can't Adam, this has to end. I won't let her hurt anyone else." She placed her hand on my cheek. "I really do love you, Adam, but you need to go now." She pushed me at Jake as a stone from the ceiling fell near us.

"No! I won't let you do this!" I said as I turned into a wolf again. Jake grabbed me by the scruff and started dragging me out of the room. I tried with all my might to break free from his grasp. I snarled and growled, twisting my body. "Knock it off, I'm trying to save you," Jake hissed. I could hear screaming coming from the room as he pulled me up the stairs. The ground beneath us was shaking causing more stones and bricks to come tumbling down all around us. He pulled me until we made it out of the hole in the wall outside. I tried to push past him to go back but he blocked the entrance. "Stop! It has to be this way, she had no choice." I reared my head and charged him.

He flung me on my back, knocking the wind out of me. "Quit it! I promised her I wasn't going to hurt you," he said. She made him promise not to hurt me? The passageway crumbled behind him now, completely sealing up the only way to reach her. I changed back and began trying to clear the debris. "Help me!" I yelled. He just stood there watching me trying to sort through the rubble. "She's gone, Adam, she had to do it. This was the only way to save both you and Hope." I turned to look at him. "The hell with Hope, where is she anyway? I'm surprised you didn't just leave her there to die like you did Isa." I was furious.

He looked toward the east, "she's safe now and she won't remember a thing. Isa made sure of that." I stood up to face him. "What do you mean, Isa made sure of that?" I asked. He folded his arms, "she whispered the spell to her as she put her soul back in her body. It's better this way," he said looking down. I turned back to the rubble, "well you can give up on your girl but I'm not giving up on mine. She needs me," I said.

Jake stood there watching me trying to unearth her. I dug for hours in the dark until my fingers were bloodied and the sun came up. I was exhausted but I couldn't stop, I knew that if I stopped, it would be like admitting defeat. "Adam…" I turned my head towards him, "she's not coming back." I clawed at the earth harder. I could feel a lump forming in my throat and my vision became blurry. "She can't be gone. She promised to spend the rest of her life with me." He walked up behind me, "I know, and she did. She made sure the last few hours she had with you were special. She told me so."

I hated him for talking about her that way, he had no right. "What do you wanna do? I told her I'd make sure you got home safe. Staying here isn't going to bring her back," he said. I wiped the tears from my face then stood up. "She can't sleep without me. I don't want to leave her alone. Isn't there some other way to get down there?" I asked. He shook his head, "only one way in and one way out. The Count didn't want her to sneak out when he was alive." I looked at him, "what about the other hallways, where did they lead?" I said. "They just branched off into other parts of the dungeon. There's no other entrance than this one," he replied.

I wanted to tear him to shreds for letting her go through with her plan. He looked at me apologetically as he spoke, "I really am sorry for your loss, she was really special wasn't she?" I let out a low growl, "Stop talking about her in the past tense! She's going to be fine, you'll see! Give her time and she'll be back again," I yelled at him, getting in his face. He sighed and backed away, "If you say so. She used a black athame dagger though. Those are specifically used for sacrifices. She knew what she was doing when she used it."

A sacrificial dagger? She never intended on living through this. With the ring and talking to Jake beforehand, she knew what she was going to do. She made the ring before the wedding ceremony after spending the day with Sarah. I'm sure she was in on it too, she said she promised her to keep me safe. What about William and Xander? Did they know too and were trying to prepare me before the wedding about everything? I'll bet they did. I stared at Jake, "what else did she say to you?" I asked. He leaned against a stump. "She told me she forgave me," he said, "I know I don't deserve it though, for leaving her the way that I did. I still loved her with every fiber of my being. She made me what I am today, not just immortal, but a better person. I used to secretly resent her for years after she changed me, but she was just so full of light in the darkness that I couldn't stay mad at her."

I felt the same way, she could light up the room with her very presence. And now her light was gone from the world. How was I going to survive without her? "What else did she say?" I said. He smiled at me, "she said you were her reason for living. She really did love you. I envy you for that. She never looked at me the way she looked at you. Even after hearing all about her past you stuck by her. How come?" He asked. I didn't really know how to answer him, "I can't describe it. I never felt unsafe with her. She only wanted to make sure I was taken care of," I sat down on a stone, "she pushed me to be a better version of myself too. She didn't want me to end up alone or fall behind." I sniffled thinking about her. What I wouldn't give for just one more embrace, just one more kiss, one more smile from her.

I twirled the ring on my left hand finger. "Even the Gypsy woman knew about it before I did. She told me about a strong love and a deep magic but I didn't listen. What do you know about this?" I said, raising my hand. His eyes grew wide, "She made that didn't she? I can see her signature in the silver." I looked at it closer, I hadn't noticed it before. In tiny letters it read, 'Isadora' with a little heart at the end, I smiled at it. "Yeah, she did. She said something about it preventing me from getting hurt or dying. I guess she knew my plan was to fight till the end if I had to. I would have much rather taken her place." Jake stood up and walked over to me, "not only that, but it bonds you to her."

I frowned at him, "Of course it does, it's a wedding band. It symbolizes our love and life together." He shook his head, "no, I mean it bonds the two of you together in a way that if one of you were to die, the other person's life force keeps them alive. Can you take it off?" he said. I tried pulling it off, but it didn't budge. "It's stuck," I said. He started laughing, I didn't understand what was so funny. "That sneaky minx. If you can't remove it, that means she's still alive in some way, shape, or form. You just have to wait for her." I looked at the divot filled with stones, could she really be alive still? I thought. I started digging again. "No, I'm afraid after that you'll have to wait longer than an hour for her to come back. It may take her a few years." I stopped digging again. He was right.

"What should I do then?" I asked. He placed his hand on my shoulder, "live. Go out and live your life until she comes back to you I suppose. She wouldn't want you to wait for her here. There's no science to how long this could take." I slowly started walking away from where I had been digging. "I love you, Isa. I'll be waiting for you at home, whenever you're ready," I whispered. I followed Jake back down the cliff towards the river.

"We're not going to fly all the way back, are we?" I asked him. He chuckled, "not on your life. We'll walk down to the nearest village then take a car. Where did you guys land?" I had no idea what the name of the town was. Then I remembered my phone, Isa had marked on my maps where she left our backpacks. I took it out and showed him. "That was smart. Did Isa do that for you?" he asked. I nodded, "yeah, it makes sense now given the circumstances. She knew I wouldn't be able to get back by myself so she marked it on my phone." We walked together down the side of the mountain until we came to a road. Jake stopped walking and turned to me.

"You have to go into town yourself, I can't run the risk of seeing Hope there." Was this where he brought her after her soul was restored? "How will I get a ride from someone back to that other town?" I asked. "Don't you have any money?" he said. I felt around my pockets and pulled out my wallet. I opened it to see a new credit card that hadn't been there before. Isa must have put it in there. It said my name on it and had a tiny piece of paper stuck to it. 'The pin is your birthday,' it read. "I guess I have this, I have no idea how much money is on it though," I said, showing him the card.

"When you get into town, call the number on the back and see how much there is. I'll be waiting for you where you showed me on your phone," he said, making his wings come out. They were not as pretty or well-manicured as Isa's but they were the same gray color. He jumped in the air and took off. I wandered down the road, following it all the way to the town. I did as he said and called the number on my card. The automated voice instructed me to put in my card number and pin. Once finished, she said, "Your balance is ten thousand dollars and zero cents." My jaw dropped when I heard her say the full amount. Ten thousand dollars? Was she insane? Why had she given me so much money?

I walked around the village looking for someplace to purchase a ride. I saw a man standing next to a cab, "Excuse me? Do you accept credit cards?" I asked. He nodded. I pulled out my phone, "Can you take me here, money's no object?" I said. He leaned forward and nodded his head gladly. "You'll pay for fuel, too," he said. I agreed and got in the car. I didn't feel right about leaving Isadora but there was nothing I could do. We drove off heading west. I looked back up towards the mountain, hoping I would see her standing in the distance.

The car ride was long and tiresome. I slept for most of it and only woke up when the driver tapped on the door, indicating he needed me to pay for gas. It took us two days to get back to the place we had left our packs. He stopped at the edge of the village and asked for my card. I gave it to him as he rang up my bill, "need receipt?" he asked. I rubbed the sleep from my eyes and nodded. I got out of the car after getting my card and the receipt. He smiled and waved at me as he drove off. "That guy probably over charged me for the ride," I said out loud. I didn't care. I made my way up the hill following the GPS on my phone.

When I got up to where we had stopped, I looked around for our packs. It has snowed more in the last few days and I had to dust them off. I heard a rustling around me and looked around. Jake made himself known by slowly walking up to me. "Took you long enough. I thought maybe you decided to stay there. I was just about to head back to check on you," he laughed. I knelt down to open our bags. "The driver sure took his sweet time didn't he. I think he got paid by the hour instead of the mile," I replied. I opened my bag and pulled out a new sweatshirt. I took the old one off and put it in the pack. I heard the sound of paper crinkling when I put it on.

"What's this?" I said taking an envelope out of the pocked. It said my name on it. "Looks like she knew you'd make it back here just fine," Jake said. I wanted to open the letter but couldn't bring myself to do it. I put it back in my pocket. "Aren't you even going to read it?" he asked. I shook my head, "I'm not ready yet. I'll do it later." I picked up our bags and headed back into town. The car was still sitting where we left it. Jake brushed the snow off with his arm. "Do you want me to drive?" he said. I gave him the keys.

I sighed heavily as we drove toward the airport. Everything was beautifully blanketed in snow. I wondered if we'd even be able to take off in this weather or not. "How are you doing?" he asked. I shrugged, I didn't have anything to say to him. "It's OK to be angry at her. She shouldn't have lied to you about what she was doing." My head whipped around, "I'm not mad at her! I'm just a little distracted by the fact that she died protecting everyone from something that could have been prevented!" He looked at me stunned.

"What, you think I planned this? I was perfectly fine never seeing her again until Rory crawled through Hope's mirror," he said. "What about the broken mirror? Why did you put it back together in the first place, huh?" Jake stared at the road ahead of us. "You had to have known that Isa would be the one to set things right again, right?" He ignored me again. "You're the one who came to us, remember? We didn't ask for you to show up and kill Lexa either." He slammed on the brakes, "enough! Yes, I did it! I put the mirror back together in hopes of getting Isa back years ago but when Rory didn't show herself I moved on. And yes, you didn't ask me to show up in your lives and kill that poor girl but Ben said he could get me close to her, so I took a chance, alright? I'm just as broken up about her dying too, you're not the only one who's allowed to mourn her!"

I was livid, "how dare you even say that. You lost that right the second you walked out on her. She was my responsibility not yours and I didn't see you trying to do anything to save her back there!" He gripped the steering wheel tight in his hands, "you think it was easy seeing her with you?" he said, "All she wanted me to do was get you out of there when the time came. She didn't want me to fight for her, she wanted me to protect you." I was silent. She told him not to fight? I couldn't believe that. "Yeah right, you just wanted to get Hope out of there as quickly as possible so you could make your escape," I said.

He put the car in drive again, "think what you will, but just remember, I loved Isa first, not you." I clenched my fists trying to compose myself. He was just looking for a fight now. We were grieving, both of us. I took some deep breaths and calmed down. "What will you do after you drop me off at the plane?" I asked. He snorted, "Oh I'm coming with you. I promised Isa I would get you home safe and I intend on keeping that promise." What was I, a child in need of a babysitter? "Why?" I said. "Isa didn't know if she was going to come out of this alive or not and wanted me to make sure you didn't try to follow her to the grave, even with the ring. You can't necessarily die but you can still hurt yourself."

I folded my arms, she really thought long and hard about all this even before we left. We sat in silence the rest of the way there. We arrived at the airport parking lot and got out. The captain was sitting in the cockpit of the plane when we boarded it. He came out to see who walked inside. "Ah yes, Mr. Christenson and Mr. Rylan I presume?" We nodded. "The misses told me she would be staying behind and that you'd have a new companion. Can I get you anything before the flight?" he asked. "No, thank you. I'm just a little tired. When will we be departing?" I asked. He looked at his watch, "we'll be airborne in thirty minutes." He dipped his hat at us and went back to the front of the plane.

'The misses,' I thought, she should be here with me. I sat down in my seat and reclined it. I could faintly smell her scent of vanilla in the plane and breathed it in. Would I ever be able to breathe in her fragrance in person again? A half hour passed and the captain turned on the seatbelt sign. I was already buckled but saw Jake scrambling to put his on. He seemed nervous. "You ok?" I asked, puzzled. His face was pale, "I try not to fly if I can avoid it. I don't even like doing it myself."

He gripped the armrests as the plane began moving. I was nervous too without Isa, but there was nothing I could do about that. I watched out the window as we took off, passing over the mountain range we once were. "Goodbye," I whispered, knowing I may never see her again.

Once in the air, I started to hum. Jake leaned forward to talk to me, "did she sing you to sleep too?" he asked. I closed my eyes, not wanting to look at him, "only once. She usually fell asleep first on my chest. It was the only way she could sleep without having her night terrors," I said. "Night terrors?" he replied. Did she not have them when they were together? "Yeah, she would relive every time she died when she tried to sleep normally. The sound of my heartbeat soothed her though," I said. I continued humming as we flew. "That's surprising, she never used to sleep at all when I lived with her. She was constantly awake, twenty-four, seven. I wonder what caused her to be able to sleep?" he said. "Maybe she didn't trust you enough to sleep in front of you." He chuckled at me. "Yeah, maybe. I was an awful boyfriend to her, but she still kept me around for some reason."

I didn't want to think about the two of them together. He left her then she ended up choosing me. That's all I needed to know. "Did she ever mention me?" he continued. I sighed, "Yes, but only when I asked about you," I said, "she never brought you up willingly because I think it was too painful for her." He thought about my response, "It wasn't always bad, you know. We had our moments. Like when she discovered she could go out in the sun. We would watch the sunrises together. The way the sun hit her face was magnificent. It really made her green eyes sparkle too." I thought about the time the sun shone through the stained glass windows in the club. The way the fragments of light danced all around her really was spectacular.

"I'm sorry," he said. I wasn't paying attention to him. "What?" I said. He repeated himself, "I said I'm sorry, what I had was centuries and you, only weeks." I looked at him, "it's not the time passed, it's how you spent it. I spent every minute I could with her and I would have happily dedicated the rest of my life to being by her side." He shook his head, "you see, that's where we're different, you and me. I took for granted all the time we spent together and resented her for making me like this. That's why she never made anyone else into a vampire. She saw what it did to me and didn't want to make the same mistake." He looked sad as he spoke.

"She didn't think you were a mistake, Jake." He looked at me surprised. "She didn't?" he asked. "No. She needed you in her life. She told me so. If it wasn't for you, she probably never would have left that place. By leaving her, it brought her out into the world. She may have fallen off the wagon and went off the deep end for a couple of decades but still, if that hadn't happened, she never would have founded a family of werewolves that cared and looked out for her. You gave her a purpose, Jake. Without you, I never would have met her."

I hated to admit it, but it was true. Isa never would have been in my life if it wasn't for him. He smirked at me, "Are we gonna be friends now?" he asked. I laughed, "I don't know about that. I still can't stand to be around you right now and just because Isa forgave you doesn't mean I have to." He laughed, "yeah, I don't think your friends are gonna like me much either when we get there." He put his arms over his head. "My friends? Don't tell me you're coming home with me too?" I didn't know how Xander would react to his sister's killer being on the property and I don't think William would appreciate me bringing home Isadora's ex. He looked at me again, "I promised her I'd get you home safe, all the way home. I may stick around and poke my head in from time to time to see if Isa has returned too." I groaned, "I hope they rip you to shreds when we get there," I said. He chuckled, "oh I'm sure they'll try their damnedest.

After our conversation I tried to take a nap. We flew for hours, I thought we'd never get there. The flight went so much faster after Isa had made me fall asleep on our way there but the flight back seemed to be taking forever. Occasionally I'd get up to walk around or go lay on the couch. I held tight to the pillow she used, imagining it was her in my arms. Jake was just as restless. With every bump of minor turbulence he'd clutch the armrests tighter.

We finally made our descent late in the evening. It was almost eleven o'clock at night. I thanked the pilot and exited the plane. Jake rushed past me so he could be the first one on the ground. He breathed a sigh of relief once he was standing on the tarmac. "Thank God that's over. Next time, I'm going by boat," he said. I chuckled and made my way to the Corvette. It was still parked where we had left it, inside the hanger. I checked Isa's backpack for the keys. They were in the outermost pocket in the front. I unlocked the doors and climbed in. I turned on the car's GPS to get us home then turned my phone on to see if I had any new messages. I was hopeful that maybe Isa had already resurrected and maybe tried to get a hold of me, but she hadn't. I had multiple messages from Sarah, William, and Xander trying to check up on us. I couldn't call them. They needed to hear what happened in person, they deserved that much. Jake hopped in the car and we drove away, out of the hangar.

"Aren't you going to call them to let everyone know you're coming home?" he asked. I shook my head, "I need to figure out what I'm going to say to them before we get there. I have time." I set the cruise and drove on down the road. What was I going to say, had she told them everything already before we left? Or did she only tell them what they needed to hear in order to make sure I was safe? I couldn't be sure until we got there. I passed the brownstones with the white picket fences and turned down our long gravel road. There was a pain building in the pit of my stomach, the dread of coming home empty handed. Would they be disappointed in me for not bringing her back? William would be for sure, she was his surrogate mother.

I got to the big iron gates and clicked the button. "No turning back now. You can leave if you want to," I told him. "No, I need to see this through, for Isa." The gates opened wide and I hesitated before driving in. I can't do this, I thought. Not alone, not without her. My heart began racing and I started hyperventilating. "Hey," Jake said, "If it helps, I'll do all the talking. I owe you that much." I thanked him with my eyes and continued slowly down the driveway. I could see the lights of the house as we rounded the lake. I was still breathing rapidly when we pulled into the front yard. The porch light was on, waiting for us to come home. I parked the car and turned off the engine. This was it, I thought.

Chapter

24

Sarah was the first to exit the house. She came running outside in her pajamas and her jacket. She looked into the car to see me sitting in the driver side. She fell to her knees sobbing. I got out of the car and went to her. Xander and William soon joined us. I knelt down to hug her. She pulled me in and held on tight. "I'm sorry," I whispered to her. I looked up at William and Xander now too, "I'm so sorry, I couldn't save her." I could feel the lump in my throat growing again. I rested my head on Sarah's shoulder softly crying into it as she held me. I heard a low growl from Xander then he stood in front of us. I looked up to see Jake standing beside the car, leaning on the passenger door.

"No, it's fine. He brought me home," I said. They all looked at me confused. "But he killed Lexa?" Xander said, crouching in his stance, ready to pounce. I stood up and ran in front of him, "wait, he isn't as bad as we think. He didn't mean to kill her, that was just an accident. He told me so." I raised my hands up to try and block Xander. "It's alright, Adam. If he needs to fight me to get it out of his system, let him," Jake said walking up behind me. "Will, help me out here!" I shouted. William just stood there looking at us, not moving. His eyes were wide. "She's gone, isn't she?" he said. Xander turned to look at him and relaxed his shoulders, the realization hadn't quite set into him yet.

"What? Izzy's gone?" he said looking back at us. I nodded my head slowly, "yes." Xander growled again, this time more ferociously, "then we should just kill him and get it over with. There's three of us and only one of him!" Sarah stood up and got in front of Xander, "What would that solve? Izzy and Lexa are dead, he can't hurt them anymore." She placed her hand on his chest trying to calm him down. William stepped forward now, "what exactly happened, Adam?" he asked. I looked down at my ring finger, then held it out.

"Isa made this ring so that nothing could happen to me. When we got there, Sarrora had taken Hope's soul out of her body and was holding it captive until we put her mirror back together. Once we got Hope back, Isa took out an athame and began cutting herself, trying to hurt her sister. It worked but the only way to ensure Sarrora wasn't going to come back, Isadora had to sacrifice herself. The ground caved in as she was cutting herself and the dungeon was demolished. I only made it out because before we went down there, Isa made Jake promise he'd get me out. I owe my life to them."

William looked at Jake, "is this true?" he asked. Jake nodded, "more or less, yes. He tried to dig her out but couldn't move the rubble," he hung his head, "but you see, the ring is still stuck on his finger. If she were truly dead it would just slip off, show them," he said to me. I held up my hand and tugged on the ring. It slid effortlessly off my finger. "No..." I said breathlessly. "No, this can't be! It was still stuck on my hand just an hour ago!" I looked at Jake with wide eyes. He stared at the ring that was no longer on my finger. I put it back on and tried to pull it off again. It came off with ease.

I dropped to my knees. She wasn't coming back, I thought. She would never be back. Sarah tried to reach down to touch me but I snarled at her. I put my ring back on and ran for the woods. "Adam, wait!" she shouted after me. I couldn't stop. I needed to run away. I transformed and ran as fast as my legs would carry me. I ran past the burnt willow and along the lake until I came to our tree. I stopped and looked at it. I let out a loud howl that burned my throat. I slashed at the tree with my claws tearing the bark around our initials. What have I done? I thought. I changed back and tried to put the pieces back together. They fell off the tree again.

I yelled out at the void. My voice echoed throughout the forest. I stood there panting, resting my head where our initials once were. "You idiot!" I said to myself. The one thing she left for me, gone now. I slid down the tree and sat with my head between my knees. I heard the paper crumple in my pocket. I reached in my pocket and pulled out the envelope. I opened it and pulled out the letter that was inside.

Dear Adam,

If you're reading this, please try to understand that I didn't do this to hurt you. I knew you wouldn't let me go willingly so I let you come with me to Romania, knowing I would not be coming home with you. My decision about enchanting your ring was a hard one, I knew you wouldn't accept it if you were aware that you could not die while wearing it. I wanted it to be one last gift, a symbol of my undying love for you. Please keep it and think of me often. If it falls off, don't worry, know that I will be forever grateful for the time we spent together, no matter how brief it was. You brought light into my life again and a warmth that I hadn't felt in centuries. Watch over William for me and let him know how sorry I am about leaving him. Keep Xander's head level and make sure you take care of Sarah, she loves you so much. Please thank Jake for getting you home safely and for keeping his promise to me. Lastly, live your life to the fullest, because each day is a blessing. I loved you until my last breath and I hope you can forgive me someday.

With love to you, my Helianthus eternal,
Isadora.

I opened the envelope to find the picture of us from our room in it. I began sobbing uncontrollably. How could she do this to me? My heart was broken. I didn't know if I would ever be able to recover from this. I clung to our photograph and the letter she left me. I wanted to die. If we couldn't be together I didn't want to live anymore. I stood up and began walking toward the lake. I made it to the water's edge and carefully put the letter and picture back in the envelope, then I took my shoes and sweatshirt off.

The water had a thin layer of ice on it. The cold water was nothing compared to the pain I was feeling right now though. I waded in the water up to my chest then swam out into the middle of the lake. My lungs hurt as I tread water. I took a deep breath in and dove down. I swam under the surface, pulling myself further and further down. I slowly let out my breath and let the water come into my mouth. I had to fight my instincts to swim towards the surface to remain under water. I started gasping for air and my body started convulsing. Everything was going dark, I would soon be with her.

My body stopped moving and I could feel my heartbeat slowing. I was sinking lower in the water when I felt something grab my arm and rip me up to the surface. My body hit the ground with a hard thud. The water started slowly running out of my lungs as I rolled on my side. "Breathe damn it!" I felt something hit me hard on my back and I began choking and coughing up water. I was incoherent as someone kept rubbing my back trying to make me cough up more water. "What the hell, Adam? I didn't save you just so you could come home to kill yourself! Would Isa want you to do this?"

It was Jake, he had dove into the water and pulled me to safety. "What...what are you doing?" I mustered to say. He looked at me angrily, "are you stupid? I know things seem rough right now but you can't just give up that easily! Isa worked her ass off to make sure you'd be set for the rest of your life. Don't you go wasting this!" I looked around to see William, Xander, and Sarah standing around me. They were all distraught staring at me. I slowly got to my knees. "I don't want to be here without her. She took everything with her when she died."

Sarah walked up and slapped me across the face. I sat there stunned. "You're not the only one who lost something, Adam. Xander lost a sister, I lost a best friend, William lost a mother, and you lost your wife. Even Jake lost someone. We're all grieving Adam, you can't just run away from your pain, it's not going to go away." She knelt down in front of me, "We can overcome this together. Now please, just come back home."

I carefully stood up and nodded. She walked with her arm around me the whole way back to the house. Once inside, William walked me upstairs while Sarah went to get a dry pair of clothes for Jake. I opened the door to our room and saw how empty it was inside without her. He went into the closet and grabbed a clean pair of clothes and laid them on the bed. "Here, you'll catch pneumonia if you don't change out of those."

I nodded then took them with me into the bathroom. After I changed, I emerged and sat on the bed. William handed me the envelope, "I found this on the bank. I thought you'd like to have it back." I looked up at him, "Did you read it?" I asked.

He shook his head, "no, I figured it was for your eyes only so I didn't bother." I took the envelope and then placed the picture back in its frame. "You don't have to stay up here if you don't want to. Your old room is still open downstairs." I shook my head at him, "No, Sarah's right. The pain isn't gonna go away if I run from it. I need to stay here," I said. He nodded then headed towards the door, "if you need anything, just let us know." I didn't say anything when he left the room. There wasn't anything to say. She was gone and I was alone again.

I wrapped the blanket around me to keep warm, breathing in her scent. I stared at our picture on the nightstand. I didn't want to sleep, I just wanted to lay awake and talk with her once again. Have her lay her head on my chest and draw circles on it. I wanted her to run her fingers through my hair as she kissed me. I needed to hear her sweet melodic voice as we sang together while I was practicing for the night. Lyrics from the song *Iris* played through my mind and I quietly sang, *I'd give up forever to touch you, 'cause I know that you'd feel me somehow. You're the closest to heaven that I'll ever be and I don't wanna go home right now…*

A tear trickled down my face remembering her playing the violin with me. She had such passion in her and a fiery personality, but the softest touch and the kindest smile. I looked at my ring again, and took it off. I looked at her signature on it with the tiny heart. She made this for me. How long are you supposed to wear your wedding band if your spouse dies? I thought. I put it back on. I wanted to wear it as long as I could.

I laid on my back trying to sleep then I rolled over onto my stomach trying to get comfortable. Nothing seemed to be working. I started at our picture again. I could almost hear her laughter. I squeezed my eyes shut and tried not to think of her. After a half hour of not sleeping, I decided to take a walk downstairs. I tiptoed down the steps trying not to wake anyone. I made it to the kitchen and looked in the fridge. I wasn't the slightest bit hungry but shuffled things around anyway looking for something to eat. I found a bag of apples and took one.

I bit into the apple, the taste was crisp and sweet. I walked into the living room to sit by the fire, only to find there was none. Strange, there'd always been a fire roaring since the first time I visited the house. I knelt down to start the fire. "It won't light," William said. I jumped around so fast I almost dropped my apple out of my mouth. "Why not?" I said. "It only burns if she's nearby, otherwise it's just a stone fireplace," he said. Yet another thing that was taken from us, her warmth, I thought. I sat down on the couch in front of the empty fireplace, William joined me. "You couldn't sleep either?" I asked. "No, it just doesn't seem real to me yet. She always comes home again, but not this time," he said. I sighed in agreement.

"Where do you think she is?" I said. He looked at me strangely. "I mean, did she believe in heaven and hell, or what happens when someone like her finally dies?" I asked. Jake rounded the corner by the bathroom, "she believed but I don't know what happens when people like her die. As far as she was aware, she was the only one of her kind." That didn't put my mind at ease. "I'd like to think she did enough good to outweigh her sins to help her get into heaven. Otherwise, what's the point? She always said she had a balance to uphold but I never quite knew what she meant," William stated, "if she is in heaven, I hope someone's giving her all the answers she needs to have a peaceful eternity." We all nodded our heads in agreement.

"How long are you planning on staying here, Jake?" I asked. He looked at me with a smirk on his face, "I don't know yet, are you planning on jumping in the lake again anytime soon?" I gave him a weak smile, "no, I'm done trying to hurt myself." His smile grew, "Then I'll probably just stay here for a week or so, until you seem to be doing better. If that's alright with you of course," he said. We both looked at Will. "Don't look at me, the house, the land, everything is in your name now Adam. She wanted you to take over when she was gone and I believe you should be our new alpha, when you're ready."

Me, become the alpha? Could I really fill her shoes? Jake looked at me now. "So you're the new king of the castle then? She must have really seen something special in you," he said. I was frazzled, "but shouldn't you be the alpha now? You were her second after all," I stammered. Will nodded, "Yes I was her second but that all changed once you two were married. Her rank is now your rank." There was still so much I had to learn about being a werewolf. "Would you be my second then and show me how things are done?" I asked him. He gave me a little chuckle, "I'd be honored to," he said.

We talked about Isadora long into the night until the sun started peeking over the treetops. By now the jet lag had finally set in and I was having trouble staying awake. "I need to get some sleep, I can barely keep my eyes open," I said to them. They both stood up and waited for me to head upstairs. I got up and started the long climb up the three flights of stairs. William left me alone on his floor but Jake kept walking with me. "Are you following me?" I said groggily. He nodded and caught me when I missed a step.

"I'm just curious about something," he said. "What?" I asked as he led me up the stairs. "Did she ever have any pictures taken of herself? I know there's the portrait downstairs but did she ever have any physical photographs taken?" I thought about his question before answering. She had printed off the one of us that was sitting on my nightstand but I didn't think there were any others. When we got to the top I pulled my phone out of my pocket and went to my messages. I still had the two saved pictures she had sent me before we started dating.

I went over to her office door and went in. Jake followed me close behind. I turned on her printer and connected my phone to it. The printer hummed as it began printing my pictures. When the printer spit them out I held them out for him. "Which one do you want?" I asked. He studied them both and chose the one where she was laying on her bed with her hair all around her. "This one. It looks like she had a specific reason why she sent you the one with her tongue out," he laughed. She did, she had been flirting with me and I didn't know how to react at the time.

"Can I keep this?" he asked. I nodded, "You should have something physical to remember her by too, I shouldn't be the only one." He smiled at me. "She was right, you know, about you being like a ray of sunshine. I can see it glowing off you right now." I was bewildered. "What are you talking about?" I asked. He looked surprised, "She must not have told you. Some people give off auras or colors that only certain people can see." I thought back to our conversation about the Gypsy I met.

"Go on," I said. He continued, "She told me you have a light that shines out to people and makes them feel good. I can see it right now." I looked around at myself, trying to see this mystical light. "How come I can't see it?" I asked. "Probably because you can't see your own light, just what it does to others. Isa called you her own personal sunflower," he said. "Helianthus," I muttered under my breath. He laughed, "Yeah, see she did tell you about it then."

"She told me, I brought light in her life and a warmth she hadn't felt in centuries, in her letter. She also told me to tell you how grateful she was for getting me home safely and keeping your promise." His smile faded. "She always trusted me, even when I didn't deserve it," he said sitting down on the office couch. "How did we ever get so lucky to have known and been loved by her?" he looked up at me with tears welling in his eyes. I shrugged. "Maybe you have a light about you too that you and I can't see. She wouldn't have saved either of us if we weren't worth saving I suppose.

He laughed again, wiping his eyes, "Yeah, maybe." He stood up again. "You'd better get some rest. Tomorrow's going to be another long day." Jake was really starting to grow on me. He had so many stories and interesting theories about Isadora. "You can stay, by the way," I said walking out the office door. He quickly followed me out, "How long?' he asked. I turned to look at him, "As long as you like, so long as you pull your own weight and don't cause trouble." He snickered, "Me? Cause trouble? Never." I laughed and opened my door.

He walked away and I shut the bedroom door. Alone again, I thought. I crawled into bed and pulled the covers all around me. I looked at our picture once more before closing my eyes to sleep. "Goodnight, Isa. In the spring I'll plant sunflowers for you so you will always see my light, wherever you are.

Chapter

25

It had been a year and a half since that fateful November night when I lost Isadora. It was summer again and the fields surrounding the lodge were covered in sunflowers. Sarah had become a full werewolf now and had graduated with honors and became a registered nurse. William, Xander, Jake and I all foresaw different properties throughout the town, just like Isa had planned for us. Everything was going great. I sat in the office spinning my ring, when there was a knock on the door. "Come in," I said, putting my hands on the desk. "You need to eat something," Sarah said carrying in a plate of food. I rolled my eyes at her.

"I just ate a few hours ago, I think I'll be fine," I said as she set the plate down in front of me. "I know but I just want to come in and check on you. You know it's our birthday today right?" she asked. I looked at her surprised, I had completely forgotten what day it was. I stood up to give her a hug, "Happy twenty-fifth birthday Sarah!" I said, trying to make it seem like I had remembered. She raised one eyebrow at me then smirked, "You totally forgot didn't you?" I laughed and nodded my head.

"You have to come out with us tonight and celebrate," she said. I didn't go out anymore. I went and checked over the properties I was responsible for then I came home to do paperwork. "Not tonight, Sarah. Maybe some other time." She looked disappointed. "Fine, then we'll all just stay in then. If you're not coming with, then I won't go either." She folded her arms and sat down on the couch. "Sarah, you and I both know I don't do crowded places anymore, especially bars," I said sternly.

She stood up again, "OK, then let's just all go to dinner somewhere, anything to get you out of this house." I started twisting my ring again and she caught me. "Adam, it's been almost two years, don't you think it's time you took it off and moved on?" Her eyes were sympathetic when she spoke. I sighed, "I'm just not ready yet Sarah. I've tried but I just can't bring myself to do it." She reached out her hand, "Then I'll do it," she said waiting for me to hold out my hand for her.

I hesitated then slowly reached out to her. She tried to pull it off but it got stuck at my knuckle. "Ow!" I said pulling my hand back. "My fingers must be swollen from working on renovations yesterday. I was wearing gloves while swinging a sledgehammer all day." I flexed my fingers in and out to feel how tight they were. "Fine then, we can try again another day. Will you at least say you'll think about coming out with us tonight?" she asked, batting her eyelashes. I chuckled, "I'll think about it."

She left the office and headed down the stairs. I know I told her I'd think about it but my mind was already made up, I wasn't going. I opened my bottom right drawer and pulled out a photo. It was the one where Isadora was winking and sticking out her tongue. I traced her face along the picture. Everyday, I felt just a little bit less lonely and the slightest bit less heartbroken. I would heal, but with more time. I had stopped listening to music entirely after the night Jake and I got back. There was no sound as sweet as her voice.

I hadn't even tried change forms since that night either. I put the picture back in its drawer and stood up from my desk. I needed to go for a walk. I made my way down the stairs out to the front porch. The flowers shone bright in the sunshine and reflected across the lake. "Where are you going?" Jake asked, bounding up behind me. I turned to look at him, "I just need to go for a walk, that's all. I'll be back in about an hour." He let me leave but watched where I headed. He knew exactly where I was going.

I stopped along the tree line and picked the nicest sunflower I could find. I carried it with me all the way through the forest until I got to our tree. The letters on the tree had mostly been scratched out from my rage that night. Only the heart shape remained around them. I placed the new flower next to all the other ones then sat on the ground in front of the tree.

"Hi Isa, it's me," I spoke. "It's my birthday today. We're the same age now, can you believe it?" I chuckled. "Sarah wants me to go out with her to celebrate but I don't think I can. She thinks I need to just let you go and move on but it's hard." My voice cracked, "I'm still in love with you and I don't think I could ever stop." The wind blew through my hair. "Jake is doing great with us here and has become a really valued member of the family, you'd be so proud of him. Xander and Sarah have been talking about moving out and starting a family but I think I'm holding them back.

I felt a tear hit my cheek. "Remember that one time we talked about having kids and what their names would be? I don't even remember what my name suggestions were but I remember that you wanted to call them Elizabeth and AJ and that they would have been so beautiful just like you." I wiped the tip of my nose on my sleeve. "I just wish you were here with us, Isa. I've tried to stay positive through everything but it's just so hard living here without you." I looked at my sleeve where I wiped my nose then pulled it down to cover up the big scar on my wrist.

"I'm sorry it took me so long to come visit you again, they try to constantly have someone checking up on me to make sure I won't try to hurt myself again, and I don't want to talk to you with them around. I think Jake is the only one who really understands what I'm going through." I chuckled again. "Isn't that sad, the ex and the widower are best friends now. Do you see all your sunflowers? They grow taller and brighter each day. I like to think you have something to do with that." I listened to the birds fluttering through the trees and felt the warm summer breeze on my face.

I heard a twig snap somewhere behind me, "I guess I should go. Someone came to check on me now." I stood up and placed my hand upon the heart on the tree. "I love you Isa," I whispered, "see you soon." I started walking away with my hands in my jeans. I made it to the water's edge and stopped. "You can come out now," I said. A reddish brown wolf trotted up to me, it was William. He changed forms and was now standing on the bank beside me. "Hey," he said. I nodded. I didn't like having to be babysat but I understood why they did it. After my last episode six months ago, I would watch me like a hawk too.

"What is it?" I finally said. He jumped at my tone. "Just wanted to see how you were doing, Jake said you were taking a walk so I followed you," he said. I was annoyed, "Did you listen in on our conversation?" I asked. He leaned down and picked up a handful of pebbles, "no. I kept my distance and just watched you from afar." He threw a rock in the water trying to skip it. "Do you think I've gone crazy, Will?" I asked him. He threw another rock, "No, but I do think you're severely depressed. Have you been sleeping alright or are you still plagued by nightmares?" he asked.

"Not nightmares, just one in particular where I hear her screaming but I can't get to her in time before the ceiling caves in, then I wake up, so no, I guess you could say I'm not sleeping well," I answered. He threw the rest of his rocks at the water, causing ripples at the surface. He turned to look at me, "why not come out with us tonight? It'll be fun, and if you get too overwhelmed I'll bring you right home." I know it would make Sarah happy to see me out and about but I just wasn't sure. "OK," I said, "I'll come but only because you said you'd take me home if it was too much."

He smiled at me, "awesome! I'll run ahead and tell the others," he turned to head towards the house then stopped, "You should really shave, that scruff makes you look like you're pushing forty, not twenty-five," he said before darting away. I leaned forward to look at my reflection in the water. I looked horrendous, my hair was getting long and my beard was taking over my face. I decided I would give myself a trim when I got back to the house.

I turned to follow Will out of the woods, I'm sure he was already at the house before I left the spot I was standing in. I walked through the sunflower fields back up to the house. Sarah was chittering with excitement when I walked through the door. "Will just told us you're coming out with us tonight! How exciting!" She squealed. I smiled at her, "Yeah. I just need to take a shower and get cleaned up first. When did you wanna go?" I asked. I looked at the clock on the wall, it was almost five in the afternoon. "We can go whenever you're ready," Xander said, joining us in the living room. I nodded, then continued on my way towards my room. After I was inside, I shut the door and breathed a sigh of relief. It's going to be alright, I thought, you're just going out with your friends to celebrate yours and Sarah's birthday. What could possibly go wrong?

I rummaged around in the closet looking for something presentable to wear. It had to have long sleeves to cover the scars on my wrists. I found a thin gray shirt with three buttons down the chest. "That'll work," I said, pulling it off the hanger. I placed it on the bathroom counter along with a clean pair of jeans. I opened the drawer and grabbed the pair of scissors then began cutting my hair. It wasn't a professional job but it would do. I got out my razor and started shaving my face. It had been months since I'd seen my bare face again. I turned the shower on, letting the bathroom steam up. I stood there letting the water trickle over me. Little bits of hair slid off my neck and onto the bottom of the shower. I washed myself then got out. I looked at myself in the mirror again as I got dressed. I saw the scissors sitting on the counter. I was surprised Sarah had let me keep them in my possession along with my razor. She had taken away everything else that was sharp. I lifted my sleeves to look at my wrists. The scars went vertical up my arms. I traced the one on my left.

I remembered taking a box cutter out of the office and locking myself in the bathroom. Sitting on the shower floor I cut my wrists hoping I would die before anyone found me. Jake had burst in the door and picked my limp body up off the floor and wrapped towels around my arms. He brought me downstairs so Sarah could dress my wounds. After that, she took away anything that I could use to harm myself. I pulled my sleeve down again, that was six months ago when the anniversary of Isa's death came around. She would be so ashamed of me for trying to kill myself again. I sat on the bed and laid down. "I don't want to do this," I said to myself. I looked over at the nightstand. The picture hurt my heart every time I looked at it but I couldn't stop myself. I brought my hand up to my face and tried to pull the ring off again. My fingers were still swollen and I couldn't get it off. "Looks like you're trying to tell me something," I said to the picture.

I sat up again then stood beside the bed, reaching for my phone on the nightstand. "I'll see you later, my love," I said walking towards the door. I met them all down in the kitchen. Sarah was wearing a new yellow sundress and she'd curled her hair. "Don't you look nice," she said to me with a smile. "Thanks, so do you," I said. I sat down at the island waiting to hear what the plan was for this evening. "First we're going out to eat at my favorite restaurant then we're going to that new bar downtown. How does that sound, Adam?" Is nodded at her then looked at Will, "If I say I'm done, I'm done. Got it?" He smiled, "Got it. Anything else?" he asked. I shook my head, "No. That should be it. I just want Sarah to have a good time for her birthday tonight." She pushed my shoulder, "our birthday, Adam. It's your day too." I smirked at her. I suppose she was right, I still didn't feel like celebrating though.

We walked out to the cars. Xander and Sarah got in the blue mustang while Jake, Will, and I piled in the silver Camaro. I sat in the back while William drove and Jake was the passenger. We took off driving down the driveway, following Xander. I played with my ring, nervous about how this evening would unfold. Jake turned his head back to look at me, "really glad you decided to tag along, otherwise I was just going to stay home with you," he said. I gave him a nod, "You wouldn't have to do that. You could have gone out with them. I would have been fine." Jake looked at Will, "no, I'd rather stay home with you and go over the plans for the rebuilding of the club. We've been putting it off long enough now." My heart sank. I was putting it off because I didn't want to go back there. There was nothing left of Isa, just painful memories we shared together. "I suppose we could have done that. I've been getting notices about the area being unsafe recently, so we need to start construction soon, I guess." I stared out the window, watching the trees pass by.

The car sped along on our way to the restaurant. We pulled up and parked close to the doors. I opened my door and stepped out of the car. Sarah and Xander were already standing out front waiting for us. "Ready?" she asked me. I smiled. We all entered the building. Sarah led the way, following the server. I sat down next to Jake and William with my back to the rest of the people sitting around us. We ordered our drinks and waited for our food to arrive. They all talked about their day and what their plans were for the weekend. William was meeting someone tonight at the bar we were planning to attend and Sarah and Xander were planning on going away for the weekend.

Jake hadn't been super outgoing the whole time he'd lived with us. Most of the time, it was just the two of us left at the house. He was good at keeping me company and distracting me throughout the day though. I appreciated that about him. Sometimes we would just sit around and talk about Isa. He had thousands of stories to tell me about when they were living together, I envied him for that. I didn't have many stories to share, not that I wanted to bring them up anyway. I was content just listening to Jake talk about her and everything she'd done in her life.

We had grown pretty close in the last eighteen months. He was usually the first one up and would meet me in my office while I worked. He didn't always speak to me, he just sort of came in and laid down on the couch. I think he was lonely too. I wonder if the reason he'd stayed all this time was because of the promise he made Isadora about keeping me safe. He wouldn't admit it, even if that were the case.

Our food arrived and everyone began eating. I still wasn't all that hungry but forced myself to eat a couple of fries. When we were finished I saw Sarah's eyes light up at something coming towards the table. I turned my head around to see four servers gathering around behind us carrying two desserts for Sarah and I. I frowned and ducked my head. Xander put his arm around her smiling proudly. "Sorry, I didn't know," Sarah mouthed to me. I gave her a nod. The servers sang to us then gave us our desserts. I pushed mine out in front of me, I didn't want it. Xander and Sarah shared hers and William took mine and started picking at it.

"Sorry, Adam. I know you don't like the attention but it's only fair for both of you to get sang to, ya know?" Xander said. "I know, it's alright. I'll get over it," I replied. I paid for everyone then headed back out to the car, they followed close behind. "Where's this new bar at, exactly?" I asked Will as he unlocked the doors. "Um, I think it's past the city center, near some other bars downtown," he said, pulling it up on the car's GPS. "Yep, it's called The Tavern. We should be there in like fifteen minutes."

The sun had already set and the city was alive with cars bustling around us. William followed the GPS until we found a place to park a block away from the bar. We walked along the sidewalk until we came to a neon sign that read, The Tavern. I opened the door and held it for everyone. Once inside, I found a dark booth in the back where I could watch people coming and going. "What'll ya have?" Jake asked me, standing in front of the table. My mind went blank, I didn't know what I wanted. "Surprise me," I said, "and get me a water too please." He walked away with a smile to go get us drinks. William was at the bar talking to his date and Sarah and Xander were dancing to the music.

It was overwhelming being in a place like this again. The place was pretty packed for a Friday night and I wasn't sure if it was a good idea for me to be here. Jake came back to the table carrying six shots of whiskey and water for me. "Are these all for me?" I asked, surprised. He laughed, "no, three for each of us. Let's go!" He slammed down the first one and waited for me. I followed his lead and drank my shot. It burned going down my throat and I coughed. "Again!" he said, drinking the next one. I did as he said and drank mine too.

I sat there holding my empty glass when he took it from me and replaced it with a full one. We clinked our glasses and finished them off. I was starting to feel really warm and fuzzy from the alcohol. Maybe I should start drinking again to try to numb the pain. I'd keep that thought in the back of my mind just in case. We sat there staring at the hoards of people crowding around the bar. Part of me missed making the drinks and meeting all sorts of interesting people but the other part of me just wanted everyone to disappear.

"Are you feeling alright?" Jake asked me. I took a sip of my water, "yeah, I'm fine for now. You can go mingle if you'd like." He shook his head, "no one's really caught my eye though. Although I see a little brunette that's been staring at you from across the bar that's making her way here now." I looked in the direction he was staring. A short brown haired girl wearing too much makeup was headed right for us. Her top was too tight and it looked like her cleavage was going to fall out. I tried to turn to the side to avoid her.

"Hi there," she said, being friendly. I ignored her. "Mind if I sit down?" she asked. I looked at Jake with pleading eyes. "Sure, I was just about to go back up to the bar anyway," he said, picking up our empty shot glasses. *Thanks a lot*, I thought. She took his chair and faced me. Her smile was bright but it didn't hold a candle to Isadora's. She placed her hands on the table then leaned forward trying to show off her chest to me. "I've never seen you here before," she said politely. "First time," I said, taking another sip of my water. Her eyes darted to my hand and touched it.

"So where's the misses then? She didn't wanna come out tonight or are you two taking a break?" She started playing with my fingers. I pulled my hand away from her. "No," I said sharply, "Neither, she died," She put her hand over her mouth, "I'm so sorry to hear that. When did she pass?" she asked sympathetically. I looked at her again, "almost two years ago now," I answered. She put her hand under the table and touched my knee. "Oh sweetie, if it's been that long, don't you think it's time you moved on?"

I took her hand off my leg. "No, alright. And I would appreciate it if people would stop saying that!" I raised my voice and stood up. I left her sitting at the table and made my way to the bathroom. No one was in there so I locked the door behind me. I stood in front of the sink breathing heavily. "You need to relax," I told myself, "She doesn't know anything about you and she was just being friendly." I splashed some water on my face then dried it off. I began hearing cheering from outside the bathroom. *What's that?* I thought. I unlocked the door and stepped out.

There was a crowd of people hovering around the dance floor. I could see Sarah standing in the center with her hands on her face. What happened? I thought. I started to make my way for her but Jake cut me off. "I think we should go outside for a little bit, don't you?" he said, blocking my path. I tried to push past him, "what's up with Sarah?" I said taking one step further. "Nothing, I just think we need to go outside," he stammered. What was he hiding? I made my way past him and walked towards Sarah.

Someone moved so I could get a better look. I saw Xander down on one knee in front of Sarah holding out a ring. My heart stopped, he was proposing to her. She looked in my direction. I was staring at them, not able to move. Jake pulled on my arm and brought me back to life. "We need to go, Adam. Here, Will gave me the keys in case you needed to go home. I think now is a good time to leave." I nodded and took the keys. We briskly made our way out of the bar and down the block. I made it to the car and just stood there, staring. "Are you driving or am

I?" Jake said. I tossed the keys back at him. I stared at my reflection in the passenger window. I pulled back and shattered the glass. Tiny pieces landed all over inside the car and along the ground. Jake didn't say anything. I opened the door and sat on the broken glass.

My knuckles were bleeding from the impact, I flexed my hand, opening and closing it. Jake put the car in drive and headed around the block. I felt my phone ringing in my pocket, it was Sarah. I handed Jake the phone, he answered it, "Hello? Yes, we're heading home now." He listened now as she talked, "I know that, I just think he was a little surprised by it." My eyes glazed over staring out the front window. "He'll be fine, I'll get him home then I'll come back for Will. You two enjoy your night. OK? Bye." He handed me back my phone. "She wanted me to tell you that she had no idea he was going to do that and that she's sorry if it upset you," he said to me now.

I had no real reason to be upset with them. They had been together now for almost two years. I was mad at myself for not being happy for her. She deserved happiness too, even if I didn't. I didn't say anything to him the whole ride home. The wind howled through the broken window as he drove. I felt like I was going to throw up from the way my chest hurt so much. My heart was breaking all over again. Jake slowed down when we got to the gravel road so the car wouldn't get filled with dust. It was making me angry driving this slow. "Can you just drop me off at the gate? I'll just walk home the rest of the way." He looked at me, "are you sure? I can just drive you up to the house instead. I'm not in a rush to get back for William, if that's what you're thinking."

I nodded my head calmly, "I'm sure. I need to walk around for a while before I can go home. I don't wanna talk to anyone right now," I said. He thought about it then agreed. We came up to the iron gates and stopped. He pressed the button and they opened. I got out of the car causing shards of glass to fall on the road. I wasn't going to worry about that right now, I'd have either Will or Jake take it to a shop on Monday to get the window replaced.

He leaned over to talk to me, "If I come home and you're dead, Sarah's going to kill me. Please just go home," he begged. I didn't want to lie to him, I was thinking about it. "I won't be dead, I promise," I said. He waited for me to start walking before he turned around and headed back down the road away from me. I very slowly walked down the driveway. He proposed, today of all days. The one day I decided to actually be a member of the pack again. He had to be insane, was he trying to make me lose my mind again?

The crescent moon hung low in the sky tonight. The crickets were chirping and the frogs were croaking as I walked along the driveway. I played with my ring like I did every other time something upset me. I spun it around in a circle over and over again. "He proposed to her," I said quietly like someone was listening. No one answered. I rounded the curve in the road and looked up at the house in the distance. Only the porch light was on but something was different. I could see light colored smoke leaving out the chimney where the living room fireplace was. "Is the house on fire?" I said.

I ran through the house and burst in the door. Everything was fine, nothing was burning except the fire in the fireplace. "That's weird. I don't remember that being lit before we left." There was a strange sense of electricity in the house as I walked through it, like someone was here with me. I went to the bathroom and cleaned up my hand. I bandaged myself up and began walking throughout the house. "Hello?" I called out. No one replied. I brushed it off that I was just imagining things. I went upstairs to change clothes.

My pants legs still had glass stuck to them down by my feet from where the pieces landed in my shoes. I took them off and shook them over the trash can. I found myself a pair of black sweatpants then put them on. I breathed deeply as I went to sit down on the bed. I was overreacting, Xander didn't mean any harm by proposing tonight. He probably just wanted me to be there too when he did it. I needed to go tell Isa, she would be so happy for them.

I put my shoes back on and went downstairs. Something still didn't feel right to me. I grabbed a flashlight out of the drawer in the kitchen and made my way outside. I walked to where the willow tree once stood. Will had planted a sapling there and it was growing quite nicely. I got to the edge of the trees and I became uneasy. What was this feeling? I pulled a few flowers and entered the woods. I shined my light as I silently made my way to the tree. I heard a deer run away from me when I got close to it.

The forest seemed dark and ominous this evening. I flashed my light at the tree when I walked up to it. The hairs on the back of my neck stood up, I felt like I was being watched. "Hello," I hollered into the abyss. It echoed through the trees. I turned off my light when I got to our tree. I pressed my back to it and sat down, placing the flowers next to me.

"Hello again. Did you miss me?" I laughed. "I suppose not. Xander proposed to Sarah tonight. I don't know if she said yes though, I left before she could answer. Some girl came up and was flirting with me at the bar too, she saw my ring and told me I should just move on already." I rested my head against the bark. "I had fun tonight. It probably didn't seem like it to them but it was ok up until that girl asked me about you. I wish you could have been there." I rubbed my ring, moving it back and forth.

I stood up and placed my hand over the heart for a few seconds before leaving. I walked down to the water and watched the waves ripple up on the bank. Something caught the corner of my eye, something white far off in the water's reflection. Was someone out here? I took off running through the trees until I made it to the open field near the willow tree. I could see someone walking through the sunflowers in the dark. I became enraged and started walking towards them.

"What are you doing here?" I yelled. They kept walking away from me. "Hey! This is private property! You need to get out of here!" They ignored me still and bent down to look at a flower. I was almost to them now. "If you don't vacate the premises, I'm going to have to use force!" They kept their face down. I grabbed their shoulder and turned them around, "Hey!" I yelled, then I stopped. She smiled at me with her lovely green eyes, "Did you plant these for me?" she asked.

I collapsed to the ground. Was I seeing a ghost? I don't think you can feel a ghost though. "Isa…" I said breathlessly. Her hair was cut short at her shoulders now and she was wearing a white strapless dress. Was she really standing there in front of me? She leaned down and reached out her hand. I flinched and began backpedaling on the ground. She stood up again and just smiled at me. It had to be her, either that or I was finally dead. "Adam, did you plant all these sunflowers for me?" she asked again.

Hearing her say my name confirmed it, it really was her, but how? I slowly stood up, keeping my distance from her. "Am I dead?" I asked. She chuckled, "No," and took a step closer to me. "Are you dead?" I said. She shook her head. We walked along in a circle, never getting close to one another. "How?" I whispered. She tucked the hair behind one of her ears, "After it happened, I did die, but something kept pulling me back. There was a light shining through that was calling me. It told me I needed to fight, so I did. I dug myself out of the earth and found my way home again."

I was stunned by her words. She took another step closer. "What about Sarrora?" I asked. Her smile faded, "she's gone for good this time." I wanted to reach out to touch her but couldn't bring myself to do it. "What about the ring?" I said holding it up to show her. She took my hand and easily pulled off the ring, "I told you, as long as I'm living, only I could take it off." I didn't understand. "But I took it off when we got home." She placed it back on my finger. "I've only been awake for a few days now. I was crushed under the weight of the stones and my hair kept getting stuck, so I had to cut it off." She laced her fingers into mine. I felt my heart start racing.

She had died and came back to me. I rested my other hand on her cheek touching her hair. "Is it really you?" I said. She took the last remaining step between us, now we were only six inches apart. "Yes Adam, it's me, Isa." I pulled her in close and kissed her passionately. She ran her fingers through my hair, pulling it gently. I could feel my hot tears streaming down my face onto hers. "Please don't cry. You were right, I was able to come back to you." She placed her arms around my neck and I picked her up. "It's been so hard living without you Isa. I've been lost without you. I even tried..." I stopped myself before I could tell her. She looked at me confused as I set her down.

"What did you try to do?" she asked. I pulled up my sleeves to reveal the marks from my last suicide attempt. She gasped then carefully kissed each scar. "You promised you weren't going to wait for me and move on with your life. Why would you do this?" she asked. I was so ashamed, "Because I needed you. Life hasn't been the same since I left you there and if we couldn't be together I wanted to join you." She wiped the tears off my face. "Adam, I am never going to leave you ever again." She stood on her tiptoes and kissed me again. I wrapped my arms around her. I was never going to let her go either.

I heard the sounds of cars and the gates opening wide. She pulled away slightly, "is that everyone else?" she whispered. I nodded but kept embracing her. It would be another few minutes until they made it to the house and saw us standing in the sunflowers. "Do you want to just stay here until they find us?" she asked. I kissed her again. "Yes, just stay here forever in my arms. I never want to go through that ever again." She smiled at me.

"Adam, you're glowing. I think it was your light guiding me back when I died." I started to smile, "No, my light only shines when I'm next to you. You are my sunshine, my helianthus eternal, and I will always love you Isadora." Our lips met once more as the cars pulled into the driveway, shining their lights on us. "I love you too, Adam. Forever…"